CERVANTES

SIX EXEMPLARY NOVELS

SIX
EXEMPLARY NOVELS

MIGUEL DE CERVANTES

The Dialogue of the Dogs
Master Glass
The Gipsy Maid
Rinconete and Cortadillo
The Jealous Hidalgo
The Illustrious Kitchen Maid

INTRODUCTION AND TRANSLATION

BY HARRIET DE ONÍS

BARRON'S EDUCATIONAL SERIES, INC.

WOODBURY, NEW YORK

Library of Congress Catalog Card Number: 61-8942

INTRODUCTION

If Miguel de Cervantes had not written *Don Quixote* his literary reputation would rest, for the most part, upon his *Exemplary Novels* and his short plays, or *Interludes,* which, despite the difference of form, closely resemble the *Novels.* And his name would still rank among the greatest in Spanish literature. (It should be pointed out that the term "novel" as used here is a translation of the Italian "novella," meaning short story or tale, not "novel" in the modern acceptance.) But the fame of *Don Quixote* has so overshadowed Cervantes's other writings that there is a tendency to dismiss the *Exemplary Novels* too lightly. They are as original in their field as was *Don Quixote* in that of the novel, of which Cervantes is universally recognized as the creator. And far from "warbling his native woodnotes wild"—a pretty phrase, but as untrue of him as it was of Shakespeare—Cervantes was an artist who was fully conscious of what he was about. In his preface to the *Exemplary Novels,* twelve in number, first published in 1613, he wrote: "I am the first to essay novels in the Castilian tongue, for the many which go about in print in Spanish are all translated from foreign languages, while these are my own, neither imitated nor stolen. My genius begat them, and my pen gave them birth." This, which at first glance might seem literary arrogance, is the simple truth. As the distinguished Hispanic scholar, James Fitzmaurice-Kelly, has pointed out, when Tirso de Molina referred to Cervantes as "our Spanish Boccacio . . . the phrase sufficiently indicates Cervantes's position among Spanish writers at the same time that it suggests his literary ancestry. Yet it would be a mistake to imagine that Cervantes is in any way substantially indebted to his Italian predecessor; the qualities common to both are a happy simplicity in narrating, direct and original observation of life, and a general fidelity to nature. Unquestionably he knew other Italian *novellieri,* but he gained nothing from them . . . we may rightfully hold Cervantes to be, as he claimed to be, 'the first to essay novels in the Castilian tongue.' "

i

Aside from their intrinsic value, the *Exemplary Novels,* the majority of which were written at the same time that Cervantes was at work on *Don Quixote,* have the added interest of being intimations, foreshadowings of themes and methods which were to reach their full flowering in *Don Quixote.* They are as important for students of literature as Michelangelo's or Leonardo da Vinci's sketches to students of art.

To understand and appreciate these *Novels* fully, one must know something of the life and career of their author. In the field of literary creation there is none greater, and his peers can be counted on the fingers of one hand. Yet in attempting to evaluate him we must discard the idea that his genius consisted in his being different from other men. Of course he was, for genius is always a thing apart, a divine gift. What Matthew Arnold wrote of Shakespeare is equally true of Cervantes:

> Others abide our questions, thou art still,
> We ask and ask, thou smilest and art still,
> Out-topping knowledge.

But outwardly, perhaps more than any other of the world's great writers, with the exception of Shakespeare, Cervantes was during his lifetime what we could call a commonplace—if not a common—man, whose memory the dust of time would have effaced if it had not been for his immortal creations. Inasmuch as scholars have traced in minute detail every available fact of his life, we are enabled to explain (insofar as this is possible) the relation between his vital experience and his creative processes, while at the same time being given an insight into the life of the "average" man in the Spain of his day. If that of Cervantes was a compound of actions and incidents which today seem to us extraordinary, this is due less to his own personality than to the fact that he shared the grandeur and heroism, as well as the misfortunes, of the moment and background against which he had his being. Just as Shakespeare reflected the ideals and the temper of Elizabethan England, so Cervantes in himself and his writings represents the Spain of Philip II, the Golden Age.

He was born in Alcalá de Henares in New Castile in 1547. Although the precise date of his birth is not known, he was baptized on October 9th of that year, the fourth of the seven children of Rodrigo de Cervantes and Leonor de Cortinas. The name "Cervantes" is of Galician origin; the family was one of the myriad which moved southward with the gradual reconquest of the Iberian peninsula from the Moors. In 1480 his great-grandparents were already established in Seville and Cordoba in Andalusia. His father was a not-too-successful doctor, the son of a lawyer who had held civil posts in various provincial cities, and he was hard put to earn a living for his numerous family. They belonged to the minor gentry of Spain —the hidalgos—which, broadly speaking, constituted the middle class of that day. The family moved from Alcalá to Valladolid, then to Madrid, to Seville, and back to Madrid, in what were undoubtedly efforts on the part of the father to improve his position, though they met with little success. Cervantes's education was perforce irregular and interrupted with so many changes. Possibly while in Seville he attended one of the Jesuit schools there which he praises in *The Dialogue of the Dogs*. The only definite facts we have in connection with his studies are that in 1568 the distinguished humanist, Juan López de Hoyos, director of a recently founded college in Madrid, refers to Miguel de Cervantes as "my beloved pupil," and that he wrote an elegy, in the name of the school, to Queen Isabel de Valois, which, together with three other poems by Cervantes, was published in a memorial volume prepared by López de Hoyos in honor of the deceased queen. Although he never went on to complete a university career, these facts would indicate that Cervantes was a gifted student who gave early evidence of his literary vocation.

Toward the end of 1569 Cervantes entered the service of Cardinal Acquaviva, then papal delgate in Spain, accompanying him on his return to Rome. This experience, shared by so many other Spaniards of his day, of contact with the life and culture of Italy, which he so frequently recalls throughout his work, had a profound influence on his intellectual development.

In 1570 he enlisted as a soldier, taking part that same year in the battle of Lepanto in which the Christian forces under the command of Don Juan of Austria, Philip II's half-brother, won a resounding victory over the Turkish fleet. Although Cervantes was ill at the moment, and his officers and friends advised him to remain below deck, he answered them, saying: "Gentlemen, in every engagement at which I have been present until now in the wars against His Majesty, I have fought like a good soldier, and I shall not do less now that I am ill; it is better to fight in the service of God and His Majesty and die for them than to go below deck." And requesting a post of danger, he fought bravely, receiving a wound in the breast and another in the left hand which maimed it for the rest of his days. He continued as a soldier until 1575, and we know that he must have distinguished himself, for when in September of that year he set out for Spain to seek recognition of his services, he carried letters of recommendation from Don Juan of Austria and the Duke of Sesa, viceroy of Sicily. But the galley on which he was sailing was captured by pirates of the Barbary Coast, and Cervantes was taken prisoner. The episode foreshadowed the ironies of fate which were to plague him relentlessly. The glowing letters he carried led the pirates to believe him a highly important personage, and they set his ransom high. Again and again he attempted to escape, and when each time the plans failed, he took all the blame and punishment on himself, refusing to involve his companions. His family finally managed to scrape together the necessary ransom fee, and in 1580 he was returned to Spain.

With this the heroic period of his existence came to an end, unless we believe that facing the slings and arrows of outrageous fortune, suffering the vexations, frustrations, and indignities that comprised the fabric of his subsequent years, without becoming embittered, distilling from them the humor, the compassion, the poetry, the understanding which inform all his work, require heroism of a higher order than "seeking the bubble reputation even in the cannon's mouth." Hemingway's definition of courage as "grace under pressure" describes him perfectly. There now set in for him a new life which was characterized by its drabness and futility in contrast to the rollicking gaiety of his years in Italy (recalled in *Master Glass*) and his stirring experiences as a soldier, including the dramatic period of his captivity. He applied for and was given various temporary minor administrative posts, and somehow, between 1583 and 1587, he managed to write a number of works, including his pastoral novel, *La Galatea*, which was published in 1585, and some twenty or thirty plays, most of which have been lost, achieving a certain reputation as a playwright. (*The Dialogue of the Dogs* reveals his intimate acquaintance with the world of the theater.) In 1584 he married Catalina de Salazar Palacios, of the town of Esquivias near Toledo, who was nineteen years his junior. She brought him a modest dowry, but gave him neither children nor the companionship he needed. From Esquivias, where he lived for a time, he travelled frequently to Madrid and Seville on matters having to do with his writings and his attempts to find a secure livelihood. But he was unsuccessful, and in 1587 there began for him a long period of a migratory existence, holding one petty post after another, and having to sacrifice his literary ambitions to the dour necessity of earning a living. As he himself said, referring to this phase of his life: "I had to occupy myself with other things; I laid aside pen and plays." Although he never wholly gave up his writing nor broke off his literary connections and friendships, from 1587 until 1604, when he completed the first part of *Don Quixote*, which was published the following year, that is to say, between the age of forty and fifty-seven, his energies were almost completely absorbed in his efforts to support himself and his household which consisted of his two sisters, his natural daughter, and a niece.

In 1587 he went to Seville, having been appointed a collector of supplies for the provisioning of the fleet, the Invincible Armada, which Philip II was outfitting for an attack on England. The contrast in his fortunes is highlighted by the role he played in the two great naval battles of his century: that of victorious Lepanto, in which he participated directly and heroically, and that of the Armada, which ended in disaster, and in which his off-stage action could hardly have been more obscure and insignificant. Tax collecting was a hateful, poorly remunerated task, and although he carried it out honestly and faithfully, he was constantly under fire. On the one hand, he had to contend with people's reluctance to pay the tax, and, on the other, with the inevitable official red tape. He was excommunicated for having seized wheat which the Church claimed belonged to it, and was imprisoned on several occasions because of apparent irregularities in his accounts. In 1590 he applied for a post in America, which was refused him. Little is known of his life between 1597, when he was imprisoned in Seville, and 1604, when he was living in Valladolid, in poverty and near squalor, with his household of women. Ironically enough, our knowledge of him in Valladolid is due to the fact that, as the result of the mysterious killing of a young nobleman in front of his tenement dwelling, Cervantes and his family were arrested, though finally cleared of any participation in the affair, which was never solved. (A somewhat similar episode occurs in *The Gipsy Maid.*)

The measure of Cervantes's genius and nobility of soul is revealed by his capacity to rise above the mire of his existence to the most sublime spiritual heights. For the fruit of those years of complete obscurity was several of the *Exemplary Novels* and the first part of *Don Quixote*. No greater alchemist ever lived. Old, poor, a worldly failure, he was able to transmute the dross of life into the purest gold. In the words of Don Quixote: "The wicked enchanters may deprive me of fortune, but nobody can take from me my spirit and my courage." To be able to laugh in the face of adversity is to recruit armies against despair. All his experiences are transfigured in his writings, not only the heroism and bright morning of his early years, with their hopes, dreams, ambitions, but the mean, drab defeats of his later years. "The twenty years he employed in his wanderings about Spain," writes Federico de Onís, "gave him that intimate knowledge of his country which is reflected in his works and makes them a mirror of the society of his day. The life he was obliged to lead brought him into contact with people of every class and every walk of life in cities like Seville and Madrid, and in the villages of Castile and Andalusia. In prison he made the acquaintance of rogues and criminals; in his travels, that of mule-drivers, inn-keepers, and all the restless souls in which Spain abounded at the time. And the result of these experiences was that familiarity with the language and customs of the infinitely varied gamut of personages who so magically live in his works, and his profound penetration of the human heart."

With the publication of the first part of *Don Quixote* in 1605 there begins a new and final phase of Cervantes's life. As he had nothing else to do, he devoted himself entirely to his writing. In the short span of years from 1605 to 1616, when he died on April 23, his major works appeared in rapid succession. Poverty harassed him to the end, but his reputation had become world-wide. It is told that on one occasion a Spaniard, being asked about Cervantes by some French gentlemen, was obliged to answer "that he was old, a soldier, an hidalgo, and poor." "If it was poverty that obliged him to write," one answered, "God grant that he may never know abundance, so that his works, though he be poor, may enrich the whole world."

The reason that *Don Quixote* has overshadowed Cervantes's other writings is because it includes them all, presenting in their entirety what in the others exists partially. The themes and qualities of *Don Quixote* are to be found throughout his work; in it they come together to form a magnificent symphony.

The *Exemplary Novels*, most of which were written contemporaneously with *Don Quixote*, reveal its same newness of method, its same artistic quality. They have often been divided into two groups, the realistic and the idealistic; but the so-called realistic ones, such as *Rinconete and Cortadillo, The Jealous Hidalgo, Master Glass,* and *The Dialogue of the Dogs,* vary greatly in form and treatment. Others, such as *The Gipsy Maid* and *The Illustrious Kitchen Maid* belong as rightfully in one category as the other. In *The Dialogue of the Dogs* Cervantes says: "The charm of certain stories is contained and held within themselves; of others, in the way in which they are told." It is the six foregoing stories which make up the present collection; interesting as the others are, these are the best known and most highly regarded. A characteristic common to all of them is the youthful spirit that infuses them. Even the sadder ones, such as

The Jealous Hidalgo and _Master Glass_, bubble over with gaiety, sunlight, and mischief. But this is not surprising, for few writers have understood and loved young people as did Cervantes. Perhaps his major artistic achievement was to imbue his humdrum, middle-aged village gentleman, Alonso Quijano, whose main activity had been the reading of the romances of chivalry which unhinged his wits, with all the ardor, recklessness, and optimism of youth when he gives him new birth as Don Quixote of the Mancha. And it is only when these qualities have become dimmed through failure, disappointment, and even triumph in the repeated encounters between the ideal world of his disordered imagination and the world of reality, when he comes to realize, as he pathetically says, that "in the nests of yesterday there are no birds today," that age overtakes him (for the true essence of youth is the seeking, not the achieving), he regains his senses, and dies.

The telling of tales is one of the earliest forms of human pastime, and its origins are lost in the mists of antiquity. From the primitive form of the fable, or _example_, as it was sometimes called, designed to teach some principle, it grew and took on a multitude of expressions which reflected the taste of successive epochs. Before Cervantes's day there existed all the derivations of the epic, the novels of extraordinary adventures, the romances of chivalry, the pastoral novels, the earliest of the Moorish and picaresque novels, these latter both of Spanish invention. But the novel as we know it today came into being with _Don Quixote_. All these preceding forms meet and fuse in it in a new and glorious synthesis. Cervantes was so in advance of his day that, despite the instant popularity of _Don Quixote_, it had no immediate successors; and it was not until the nineteenth century, when the novel came to be the prevailing literary mode, that his invention was fully understood and utilized. The realistic novel, what Thackeray called "the novel without a hero," dealing with ordinary people seen against their commonplace background, had its origins in Cervantes. And its finest cultivators, forerunners like Fielding, Sterne, Smollett in the eighteenth century, Flaubert, Dickens, Dostoievsky, Pérez Galdós, our own Mark Twain, who was never without a copy of *Don Quixote* in his pocket, William Faulkner, who is quoted as saying that he has two passions, his daughter and *Don Quixote*—in short, all novelists deserving of the name have acquired the basic canons of their art directly or indirectly from Cervantes.

In the case of the *novella* or short story, prior to Cervantes the procedure had been for a person, or several persons, as in *The Arabian Nights,* the *Decameron,* and *The Canterbury Tales,* to narrate a series of stories linked together by a common thread. Each of the *Exemplary Novels* is complete in itself, diverse in theme and form, completely independent of the others. Cervantes does not choose famous legendary or historical figures as his protagonists; they are, for the most part, ordinary beings such as he had seen and observed during his errant years. When he does introduce idealized figures, as in the case of Preciosa in *The Gipsy Maid* or Costanza in *The Illustrious Kitchen Maid,* the background against which they are set is so realistic that the contrast between the worlds of truth and poetry engenders an artistic tension of the highest order. In Seville he undoubtedly knew at first hand the endless variety of rogues he portrays with such grace in *Rinconete and Cortadillo.* But to assume that it is a picaresque novel would be an error. The novels of roguery were autobiographical, and their object was not to portray the life of the rogue, but the society in which he moved, of which he was the product and victim, and their vision was bitter and cynical. In the eyes of the rogue, mankind was a bad lot. Menéndez y Pelayo, speaking of Mateo Alemán, the author of *Guzmán de Alfarache,* the archetypal picaresque novel written about the same time as *Don Quixote,* which engendered the flood of similar works that followed in every language, says that not only does he not seem a contemporary of Cervantes, he hardly seems his fellow being. Drawing on the observations of his incomparable vision, Cervantes gives us in *Rinconete and Cortadillo* an amusing, impudent, joyous picture of the life of these bullies, thieves, artful dodgers, and their ladies of light virtue, which is a marvel of narrative and character. In a way *The Dialogue of the Dogs* more closely approaches the picaresque form.

The dogs describe the masters they have had, as the rogues did, the life they have led, and pass judgment on society. But its source is rather the dialogues which were so popular in the Renaissance, such as those of Erasmus, the brothers Valdés in Spain, and, more remotely, Lucian of Samosata. The criticism is of ideas rather than persons, and the dogs' witty arraignment of human vices and follies is a veritable moral tract. *Master Glass* is a foreshadowing of *Don Quixote*, but whereas the Don's madness is a dynamic force, setting everything with which it comes in contact into motion, acting as a catalytic agent, Master Glass's mania or hallucination induces a kind of paralysis of the will and his action is negative, limited to a criticism of mankind. "He has not," Fitzmaurice-Kelly observes, "Don Quixote's stateliness and charm, nor does he stay long enough with us to win affection . . . Yet how brilliant his retorts, how biting his wit, how pregnant his criticism of our elaborate hypocrisies!"

In the prologue to the *Exemplary Novels* Cervantes assures the reader that of the twelve tales there is not one "from which thou couldst not derive a profitable example." In this there is perhaps a touch of the dissimulation typical of the period, when it was important to render virtue at least lip-service. Cervantes was too great an artist to have edification as his main objective. What he was depicting was human nature, the infinite workings of the human heart, which may often be less than exemplary but always interesting. With his glorious humor he laughed humanity's foibles, weaknesses, even vices, not to scorn but to love. The judgment the great critic Samuel Taylor Coleridge passed on *Don Quixote* applies equally to the *Exemplary Novels*: ". . . he blends with the terseness of Swift an exquisite flow and music of style, and, above all, contrasts with the latter by the sweet temper of a superior mind, which saw the follies of mankind, and was even at the moment suffering severely under hard mistreatment, and yet seems everywhere to have but one thought as the undersong—'Brethren! With all your faults I love you still!' "

Harriet de Onís

THE DIALOGUE OF THE DOGS

The Story of a Conversation Between
Cipión and Berganza, Two Dogs of
the Hospital of the Resurrection in
the City of Valladolid Beyond the
Campo Gate, Generally Known as
the Dogs of Mahudes

CIPIÓN: Friend Berganza, tonight let's leave the Hospital to take care of itself, and withdraw to this quiet spot where upon these mats we can enjoy unbeknown to anyone this boon which Heaven has conferred upon the two of us at the same time.

BERGANZA: Brother Cipión, I hear you talk, and know that I am speaking to you, and yet I cannot believe it, for it seems to me that for us to be talking oversteps the bounds of nature.

CIPIÓN: How true, Berganza; and the miracle is all the greater in that not only do we talk, but we discourse with reason, when in fact we are devoid of it; for the difference between animals and man is that man is a rational creature and animals are irrational ones.

BERGANZA: I understand all you are saying, Cipión, and the fact that you are saying it, and I understanding it, produces in me further amazement and wonder. To be sure, in the course of my life I have heard talk of our great qualities, to the point where there are those who affirm that we have a natural instinct so quick, so keen-witted in many things, that it gives evidence and proof that little is lacking to indicate that we have a certain amount of understanding which is capable of reasoning.

CIPIÓN: What I have heard praised and extolled is our great memory, our gratitude, and fidelity, so much so that we are made the symbol of friendship. You must have seen (if you have taken notice) that on alabaster tombs, which, as a rule, bear the statues of those buried beneath them, in the case of a husband and wife they put between the two of them at their feet the likeness of a dog as a token of the inviolate friendship they bore each other during their lifetime.

BERGANZA: I know indeed that there have been such devoted dogs that they have thrown themselves into the grave with their deceased masters. Others have lain beside the grave where their master was buried, without moving from it, refusing food until death came to them. I know, too, that after the elephant, the dog comes first in seeming to have reason; after the dog, the horse; and last of all, the monkey.

CIPIÓN: So it is; but you will have to admit that you have never seen or heard it said that any elephant, dog, horse, or monkey ever talked, which leads me to think that this business of our suddenly having the gift of speech falls under the heading of what are called portents, whose manifestation and occurrence, experience has shown, presage some great public disaster.

BERGANZA: In that case, I won't be going too far afield if I take as a portentous sign something I heard a student say the other day as I was going through Alcalá de Henares.

CIPIÓN: What did you hear him say?

BERGANZA: That of the five thousand students enrolled at the University that year, two thousand of them were studying medicine.

CIPIÓN: And what do you infer from that?

BERGANZA: What I infer is that either those two thousand doctors will have patients to cure (which would be a great calamity and misfortune), or they themselves will die of hunger.

CIPIÓN: Be that as it may, let us talk, portent or no, for whatever Heaven has ordained no human effort or wisdom can prevent. So there is no reason for us to begin discussing how or why we talk. Instead, let us take advantage of this good day, or good night, and since we are so comfortable here on our mats, and we do not know how long this luck of ours is going to last, let us make the most of it and talk all night, without letting sleep deprive us of this pleasure which I have so long desired.

BERGANZA: Me, too. Ever since I was big enough to gnaw a bone I have wanted to talk and say things I had stored up in my memory which, growing old or dim there, either rusted away or I forgot them. But now that, so unexpectedly, I find myself endowed with this divine gift of speech, I intend to enjoy it and profit by it to the fullest, making haste to say all that I can remember, even though it comes out all higgledy-piggledy, for I do not know when I shall have to surrender this boon which I look upon as loaned.

CIPIÓN: Then let's do it this way, friend Berganza: tonight you tell me the story of your life and the steps by which you have reached the point where you now find yourself, and if tomorrow night we still have the power of speech, I shall tell you mine, for it is better to spend the time telling our own lives than prying into those of others.

BERGANZA: Cipión, I have always looked upon you as wise and a good friend, and now more than ever; for as a friend you wish to tell me your experiences and to know of mine, and dividing the time for the telling shows your intelligence. But first let's make sure nobody can hear us.

CIPIÓN: Nobody, I think, even though there is a soldier nearby having a few nightcaps, but by this time he must feel more like going to sleep than listening to anybody.

BERGANZA: Well then, if I can talk with this assurance, listen. If what I have to say bores you, either pull me up or tell me to keep quiet.

CIPIÓN: Talk until morning, or until we know that we are being overheard, for I shall listen with great pleasure without interrupting you unless I see that it is necessary.

BERGANZA: It seems to me that I first saw the sun in Seville, in its slaughter-house, which lies outside the Carne Gate, and this would lead me to believe (except for something I shall tell you later on) that my parents must have been mastiffs of the sort raised by the ministers of that confusion, who are known as butchers. The first master I knew was a certain Nicolas the Flat-Nosed, a strong fellow, heavy-set and hot-livered, as are all those who follow the butcher's trade. This Nicolas taught me and other pups, in the company of the old mastiffs, to charge the bulls and take them by the ears. I quickly showed myself a master at the game.

CIPIÓN: I am not surprised, Berganze, for as evil-doing is inborn, it is easy to learn.

BERGANZA: What shall I tell you, brother Cipión, about what I saw in that slaughter-house, and the unbelievable things that happen there? First off, you may assume that all who work there, from the lowest to the highest, are persons of elastic conscience, cruel, fearing neither man nor devil; most of them are married without benefit of clergy; they are birds of prey, and they and their doxies live on what they steal. Every meat-eating day, before daylight, there is a crowd of wenches and urchins at the slaughter-house, each carrying a bag which when they come is empty and when they leave is full of chunks of meat, and servant girls who take testicles and almost whole tenderloins. Not an animal is slaughtered of which these people do not carry off the tithes and first fruits, the tastiest and the best. And as there is no meat inspector in Seville, each one can bring in the animal he likes, and the first killed is either the best or the cheapest, and by this arrangement there is always an abundance. The owners trust to these good people, not that they will not steal (for that is impossible) but that they will show moderation in their filching and swindling of the slaughtered animals, for they pollard and prune them as though they were willows or vines. But nothing surprised me so much, or seemed worse to me, than to see how those butchers kill a man as readily as a cow. Over the least difference, before you know it, they bury a bone-handled knife in a person's belly as though they were pole-axing a bull. Rarely does a day go by without fights and wounds, and at times, deaths. They all pride themselves on being tough and having a touch of the ruffian; and there's not one of them who doesn't have his guardian angel in the law courts, bribed liberally with tenderloins and tongues. In short, I once heard a wise man say that the king still had three strongholds to win in

Seville: the Street of the Grass, the Costanilla and the Slaughter-
houses.

credit: I read Bergamín, I even are going to take as long to describe the quality... the masses as you had and the shortcomings
of their ... have with this one, we'd better pray that
Heaven will ... part of speech for at least a year, and I
am still all ... are going on won't get more than
half-way there ... want to make out one thing to
you, which ... you in your business, and it is
that the ... maintain ... hold within themselves ... What I mean to
say is ... without preambles and
fine ... decked out with
words with ... changes of tone, thus
making some ... and interest to
what would other ... then I forget this
work of advice, and ... re candidate ...
remanera. So I will ... will overcome the great
temptation I feel to talk ... afraid I am going to have trouble
holding myself in ch ...

... there's nothing in this life that is
more ...

... basket-maker happened to carry a basket
in ... against anyone who tried to take it
from ... way to his lady's house, and thus
her ... coming to the slaughter-house because ... what he had stolen at night. One
mo ... his big dog ... way to take her her
sha ... standing at the window, I raised my
eyes ... familiarity, and confused. I stopped
and ... hurrying off. The again, I went over to
her, as ... coming, and it was to take what
I was ca ... which she put an old shoe in place

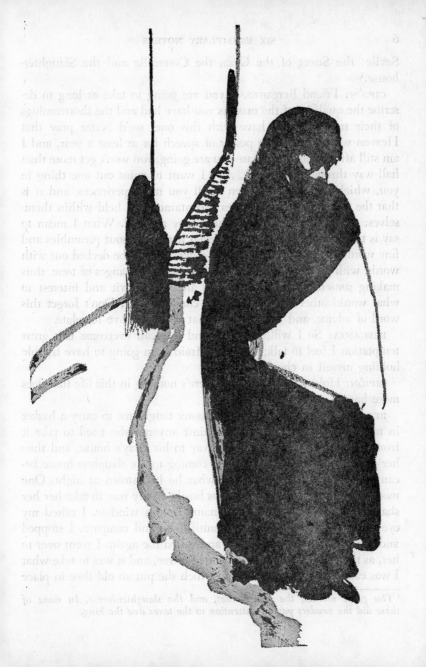

Sevile: the Street of the Caza, the Costanilla and the Slaughter-house.[1]

CIPIÓN: Friend Berganza, if you are going to take as long to describe the qualities of the masters you have had and the shortcomings of their trades as you have with this one, we'd better pray that Heaven will grant us the power of speech for at least a year, and I am still afraid that, at the rate you are going, you won't get more than half-way through your story. And I want to point out one thing to you, which you will see when I tell you my experiences, and it is that the charm of certain stories is contained and held within themselves; others, in the way in which they are told. What I mean to say is that there are some which, even if told without preambles and fine words, are entertaining, while others have to be decked out with words, with gestures of hands and face or with changes of tone, thus making something out of nothing, and giving wit and interest to what would otherwise be dull and commonplace. Don't forget this word of advice, and utilize it in what you still have to relate.

BERGANZA: So I will, if I can, and if I can overcome this great temptation I feel to talk; but I am afraid I am going to have trouble holding myself in check.

CIPIÓN: Hold your tongue, for there's nothing in this life that does more harm.

BERGANZA: Well, to go on, my master taught me to carry a basket in my mouth and to defend it against anyone who tried to take it from me. He also taught me the way to his doxy's house, and thus her servant did not have to bother coming to the slaughter-house because every morning I took her what he had stolen at night. One morning, just at daybreak, as I was busily on my way to take her her share, I heard someone call my name from a window. I raised my eyes and saw a girl who was beautiful beyond compare. I stopped and she came to the street door and called me again. I went over to her, as though to see what she wanted of me, and it was to take what I was carrying in the basket, into which she put an old shoe in place

---

[1] *The game market, the fish market, and the slaughter-house. In none of these did the venders pay any attention to the taxes due the king.*

of its contents. I said to myself: Flesh to flesh. And when the girl had taken the meat from me she said: 'Go along, Gavilán, or whatever your name is, and tell Flat-Nosed Nicolas, your master, not to put his trust in animals: of the wolf, trust but a single hair, and that when he's dead.' Of course, I could have recovered what she took from me, but I did not want to soil those clean white hands with my dirty slaughter-house mouth.

CIPIÓN: You did right, for beauty has its prerogatives, which must always be respected.

BERGANZA: Which I did, and so I returned to my master without the basket's contents and with the old shoe. It seemed to him that I was back too soon; and when he saw the shoe and gathered what had happened, he pulled out one of his knives and made a lunge at me, and if I had not got out of its way you would never have heard this story nor the many others I intend to tell you. I took to my heels, running for dear life, cutting behind San Bernardo and through the fields, wherever fortune might lead me. That night I slept in the open, and the next day it was my good luck to come upon a flock of sheep and rams. As soon as I saw them I decided that my troubles were over, for it seemed to me the natural and fitting office of a dog to guard the flock, which is as worthy a task as defending against the mighty and overbearing those who are meek and defenseless. No sooner had one of the three shepherds watching the flock laid eyes on me than he began to call: "Come here, boy, come here, boy." And as that was just what I wanted, I came over to him, head hanging and wagging my tail. He ran his hand over my back, opened my mouth, spit into it, looked at my teeth to tell my age, and said to the other shepherds that I had all the earmarks of a thoroughbred. Just then the owner of the flock came up on a gray mare, riding with short stirrups and carrying a lance and buckler. He looked more like one of the coast guard cavalry than a sheep owner. He said to the shepherd: 'Where did that dog come from? He looks like a good one.' 'So he is,' answered the shepherd; 'I have examined him carefully and he has every sign of becoming a fine dog. He just came here, and I don't know whose he is, though I do know that he doesn't belong to any of the flocks around here.' 'In that case,' answered the owner, 'put the collar of Leoncillo, the dog that died, on him, and give him the same rations as the others, and pet him so he will take a liking to the fold and stay here.' With this he left, and the shepherd put a steel-pointed collar around my neck, but first he gave me a big wooden bowl of bread and milk. And he gave me a name, too, calling me Barcino. So there I was, well-fed and happy with my second master and my new job. I guarded the flock carefully and diligently, never leaving it except at the siesta hour, when I went off under the shade of a tree or some rock, or beside a bush growing along one of the many brooks that run through that region. And during those hours of rest I was not idle, for I employed my memory recalling many things, especially my life in the slaughter-house, and that of my master, and the others like him who have to humor the impertinent whims of their lady-loves. Oh, the things I could tell you that I learned in the school of that lady of my butcher master! But I shall keep them to myself lest you judge me long-winded and a gossip.

CIPIÓN: Inasmuch as I have heard that a great poet of antiquity once said that it was a difficult thing not to write satire, I shall permit you to gossip a little, giving light but not drawing blood, that is to say, merely pointing out without wounding or ridiculing anyone in any particular thing. For gossip is not a good thing if it kills one person, even though it makes many laugh. And if you can please without it, I shall consider you very wise.

BERGANZA: I shall take your advice, and shall eagerly await the hour when you tell me your experiences. For from one who can so well recognize and point out the defects I reveal in telling mine, one may expect that he will relate his own in such a way that they enlighten and entertain at the same time. But to go back to my interrupted story, I was saying that in that silence and solitude of my siestas, among other things I thought that what I had heard told of shepherds' lives must not be true, or at any rate, those my master's lady read about in books when I went to her house. All of them dealt with shepherds and shepherdesses, saying that they spent their days singing and playing bagpipes, flutes, rebecs, tabors, and other rare instruments. I would stop to listen to her read, and she read how the shepherd Anfriso sang like an angel, praising the peerless Belisarda, and there was not a tree in all the mountains of Arcady beneath whose boughs he had not sat to sing, from the time the sun arose from the arms of Aurora until it sank to rest in those of Thetis. And even after the dark night had spread its black wings over the face of the earth he did not cease his well-sung and better-wept laments. Nor did she forget the shepherd Elicio, more enamored than valiant, of whom it was said that, neglecting his loves and his flocks, he took upon himself cares that were not his. She also told about the great shepherd of Filida, the only one who painted a portrait, and how he had been more trusting than happy. About Sireno's swoons and Diana's repentance she said she gave thanks to God and to the wise woman Felicia who with her magic water confounded that web of confusion and lighted up that labyrinth of difficulties. I recalled many other books of this same sort that I had heard her read, but they were not worth bearing in mind.[2]

CIPIÓN: You are profiting by my advice, Berganza; gossip, touch lightly, and pass on, and let your intention be pure, even if your tongue seems not.

BERGANZA: On such topics the tongue never errs except by intention. But just in case through carelessness or malice I should gossip, I will answer whoever rebukes me in the words of Mauleon, a silly, stilted, satirical poet of the Academy of Imitators, who when someone asked him what he meant by *Deum de Deo,* answered that it meant *de donde diere.*[3]

CIPIÓN: That was the answer of a fool; but you, if you are wise or hope to be, should never say anything for which you have to apologize. Say on.

BERGANZA: I would say that all the thoughts I have mentioned,

---

[2] *The reference is to various of the pastoral novels, so popular in their day, whose idealized shepherds and shepherdesses were in striking contrast to the real ones Berganza knew.*

[3] *Deum de Deo . . . de donde diere. An untranslatable play on words.*

and many others, came to me from seeing the difference between the behavior and occupation of my shepherds (and all the others along that coast) and all that I had heard about shepherds in books. For when mine sang, it was not modulated and well-composed songs, but

Look, Juanica, there comes the wolf

and others of the same sort. And not to the accompaniment of tabors, rebecs, or bagpipes, but of one staff beaten against the other, or clappers held between the fingers. Nor in a delicate, sonorous, moving voice, but raucously; and whether they sang alone or in chorus it was more like shouting or grunting than singing. They spent most of the day picking fleas off themselves, or mending their leather sandals; and not one of them ever mentioned Amaryllis, Phyllis, Galatea, or Diana, nor were there any Lisardos, Lausos, Jacintos, or Riselos, but Antonios, Domingos, Pablos, or Llorentes. All of which convinced me of what all should realize: that those books are thought up and designed for the entertainment of idlers, and there's not a word of truth in them. If there were, among my shepherds there would have been some vestige of that delightful life, those pleasant meads, spreading woods, sacred hills, beautiful gardens, clear brooks and crystalline fountains, and of those amorous declarations, as pure as they were well-worded, and that swooning of a shepherd here, a shepherdess there, and the sounding of one shepherd's flute or another's reed pipe.

CIPIÓN: That will do, Berganza; back to your story.

BERGANZA: Thank you, friend Cipión. If you hadn't pulled me up, my mouth was getting so hot that I wouldn't have stopped before I had set forth in its entirety one of those books that had led me astray. But the day will come when I shall tell you the whole thing, with better reason and discourse than at present.

CIPIÓN: Do like the peacock, Berganza: look at your feet and you will furl your tail. What I mean to say is that you should bear in mind that you are an animal devoid of reason, and if at the moment you seem to have some, we have already agreed that it is something supernatural and unheard of.

BERGANZA: That would be the case if I were still as ignorant as at first. But now that I have recalled what I should have told you at the beginning of our conversation, I am not only not amazed that I talk, but astounded at what I am not saying.

CIPIÓN: And can't you tell now what you have recalled?

BERGANZA: It is something that happened to me with a famous witch, a pupil of Camacha de Montilla.

CIPIÓN: Then let's hear it before you go on with the story of your life.

BERGANZA: No indeed, not until the time comes. Be patient and listen to my experiences in their proper order, and that will give you more satisfaction than hearing the middle before the beginning.

CIPIÓN: Well then, be brief, and tell what you like and the way you like.

BERGANZA: Well, as I was saying, I was content with my job of guarding the sheep, for it seemed to me that I was earning my bread by the sweat of my brow, and that idleness, the root and mother of all vice, played no part in my life; for if it is true that my days were leisurely, by night I did not sleep, often having to attack and drive off the wolves. No sooner did I hear 'Get him, Barcino' than I rushed off, ahead of the other dogs, to where they pointed out the wolf: I charged through the hollows, searched the hills, followed the path through the woods, leaped chasms, crossed roads, and in the morning I returned without having found a wolf or the trace of one, panting, tired, half-dead, my paws slashed by thorns, to find in the fold a dead sheep or a lamb with its throat torn out and half devoured by the wolf. It enraged me to see how little my great care and diligence helped. The owner of the flock arrived; the shepherds went out to meet him with the skin of the dead animal; he upbraided them for their negligence and ordered the dogs punished for their laziness. We were cudgeled and they were berated. One day I was punished without cause, and when I saw that my zeal, agility, and courage were of no help in catching the wolf, I decided to change my tactics; instead of setting out to find it as I had been doing, away from the flock, I would stay close by, and then if the wolf came, it would be easier to catch. Every week an alarm was sounded, and one pitch-black night I lay in wait for the wolves against which it was impossible to guard the flock. I crouched down behind a bush, the other dogs, my companions, rushed ahead, and from where I was I kept watch, and I saw two of the shepherds take hold of one of the best rams of the flock and kill it in such a way that it really seemed as though it had been slaughtered by the wolf. I was amazed and confounded when I saw that the shepherds were the wolves, and that the very ones who were supposed to watch over the flock were destroying it. They immediately notified the owner of the wolf's depredation, they gave him the hide and part of the meat while they ate most of it, or the best part. The owner scolded them again, and again the dogs were punished. There were no wolves; the flock was diminishing; I wanted to reveal everything, and there I was unable to talk. All this filled me with wonder and distress. 'God help us,' I said to myself, 'and who can remedy this evil? Who has the power to make it known that the defenders are the offenders, that the sentinels sleep, that the trusted steal and those who should protect kill?'

CIPIÓN: You speak rightly indeed, Berganza. There is no greater or slyer thief than the servant of the house, and many more die at the hands of those they trust than those they distrust. But the trouble is that it is impossible to live at ease in this world without trust and confidence. But enough of this, for I do not want us to sound like preachers. Go on.

BERGANZA: I will. I thereupon decided to leave that calling, even though it seemed such a good one, and find another in which for doing my duty, if I were not rewarded, at least I would not be punished. So I returned to Seville and entered the service of a rich merchant.

CIPIÓN: How did you manage to find a master? For, as things are, it is difficult today to find a decent man to serve. The lords of the earth are very different from Him of heaven. The former, before they hire a servant, first investigate his origin, test his ability, take note of his appearance, and even want to know what clothes he owns. But to enter the service of God, the poorest is the richest, the lowliest, of highest lineage; if only he has a clean heart and the wish to serve Him, he is at once entered on the pay-roll, and his wages are so good that in abundance and amount they almost exceed his desire.

BERGANZA: You are preaching again, friend Cipión.

CIPIÓN: You are right, and so I shall hold my tongue.

BERGANZA: As to your question about how I managed to find a master, as you already know, humility is the foundation and corner-stone of all the virtues, and without it none of the others exist. It surmounts obstacles, conquers difficulties, and is a path that always leads us to glorious ends. It makes friends of enemies; turns aside wrath, abates the arrogance of the proud; it is the mother of modesty and the sister of temperance. In short, over it vice can win no lasting triumph, for against its gentleness and meekness the arrows of sin fall blunted and deflected. So I employed this when I wanted to enter service in a house, after first weighing and considering care-fully whether it was a house that could maintain and make use of a big dog. The next step was to station myself at the door and when a stranger, as I judged, went in, I barked at him, and when the master came, lowering my head and wagging my tail, I went toward him and licked his shoes. If they drove me away with blows, I suffered them, and with the same meekness fawned upon the one who beat me, who never repeated the punishment seeing my determi-nation and my noble behavior. In this way, after several tries, I entered the house. I performed my duties well, they became fond of me, and nobody ever cast me out. It was I who dismissed myself, or rather left; and I finally found a master in whose house I might still be if adverse fortune had not pursued me.

CIPIÓN: In the same way you have related I took up with the masters I had. It is as though we read each other's thoughts.

BERGANZA: As our experiences in such matters have been similar, I shall relate them to you when the time comes, as I have promised. But now listen to what happened to me after I left the flocks in the power of those scoundrels. I went back to Seville, as I have said, which is the asylum of the poor and the refuge of outcasts, for amidst its grandeur there is not only room for the lowly, but even the mighty are lost sight of. I stationed myself at the door of the fine house of a merchant, went through my usual performance, and before long I remained there. They kept me tied behind the door during the day, and let me loose at night. I served them with great care and zeal; I barked at strangers and growled at those who were not well-known to me. I did not sleep at night, making the rounds of the stables, going up to the roof, acting as a universal sentinel of my own and the neighboring houses. My master was so pleased by my good services that he ordered me treated well, assigning me a ration of bread and the bones that were left or thrown from his table, along with the scraps from the kitchen, for which I showed my gratitude, leaping and bounding whenever I saw him, especially if he had been away from the house. My display of joy was so great, and I strained so hard at my leash to approach him, that he ordered me loosed both day and night. As soon as I was unfastened, I would run up to him and circle around him, but never once putting my paws on him, for I remembered the fable of Aesop about the ass who was such an ass that he tried to behave toward his master in the same way as his lap dog, for which he was soundly thrashed. It seemed to me that this fable is to teach us that what pleases and delights in one person is not fitting in another. Let the buffoon jest, the actor do tricks, the rogue bray or imitate the song of birds, and the lout who is so inclined imitate the gestures and acts of animals and men; but this is not becoming in a man of standing on whom none of these skills reflect honor or credit.

CIPIÓN: That will do. Proceed, Berganza, for you have made yourself clear.

BERGANZA: Would that those for whom it is meant understood it as well as you do! I don't know what kind of decent streak I have that makes me hate to see a gentleman tell coarse jokes and pride himself on his skill at dicing, at sleight-of-hand tricks, and because nobody can dance the chaconne as he does. I know a gentleman who boasted that at the request of a sacristan, he had cut thirty-two flowers out of paper to put on a monument against black draperies, and he cut a great stock of similar designs which he brought his friends to see as though he were taking them to view the trophies and spoils of enemies displayed on the tomb of his forbears. Now this merchant I am talking about had two sons, one twelve and the other around fourteen years old, who were studying grammar in a Jesuit school. They travelled with great display, accompanied by a tutor and pages to carry their books and school bag. To see them go with so much ceremony, in sedan chairs if it was sunny, in a coach if it rained, made me consider and notice how simply their father went to the Exchange to carry on his business, with only a Negro servant, and at times he even rode there on a mule that was not even well-saddled.

CIPIÓN: You should know, Berganza, that it is the custom and manner of the merchants of Seville, and even of other cities, to display their status and station, not in themselves but in their children, for the merchants are greater in the shadow they cast than in themselves. And as they rarely concern themselves with anything but their sales and contracts, they do not put on airs. But as ambition and wealth yearn to display themselves, they pour them out on their children, and treat them and bring them up as though they were the children of a prince. Some of them secure titles for them so they can wear on their breast the insignia that distinguish the person of rank from the commoner.

BERGANZA: Ambition it is, but a generous ambition, that which attempts to better itself without doing harm to others.

CIPIÓN: Rarely or never can ambition be satisfied without harm to others.

BERGANZA: We agreed that we were not going to gossip.

CIPIÓN: But I am not gossiping about anybody.

BERGANZA: Now I see the truth of what I have often heard. Some evil-tongued gossip has just slandered ten noble families and calumniated twenty good persons, and if someone reprehends him for what he has said, he answers that he has not said anything; and if he did, it was not with evil intent; and if he had thought it would offend anybody, he would not have said it. Truly, Cipión, the person who wants to carry on a conversation of two hours without falling into gossip must know a lot and be very much on his guard. For I see from myself, animal that I am, that after saying four thoughts, words come to my tongue like flies to wine, and all of them malicious and slanderous. And so I repeat what I told you before, that doing and speaking evil comes to us from our forbears, and we drink it in with our mother's milk. It can be plainly seen in the child who is no sooner out of his swaddling clothes than he raises his hand with the intention of avenging himself on whoever has crossed him, and almost the first word he utters is to call his nurse or mother a whore.

CIPIÓN: That is true; I confess my error, and beg you to overlook it as I have overlooked so many in you. Let's forgive and forget, as children say, and no more gossiping from now on. You get on with your story which you broke off when you were telling me about the pomp with which the merchant's children went to the school of the Company of Jesus.

BERGANZA: To Him I commend myself at every turn; and although I am afraid that giving up gossip will be hard, I plan to use a remedy I heard about that a man much given to swearing used to employ. Ashamed of his bad habit, each time he swore after he had repented of it, he pinched his arm or kissed the ground as punishment for his fault. But for all that he kept on swearing. So every time I go against the injunction you have laid upon me not to gossip, I will bite the tip of my tongue till it hurts, and that way I will remember my transgression and not repeat it.

CIPIÓN: If you really use that remedy, I am afraid you will bite yourself so many times that you will have no tongue left, and in that way you won't be able to gossip.

BERGANZA: Well, anyway, I'll do all I can, and may Heaven do the rest. As I was saying, one day my master's children left their school bag in the courtyard where I happened to be. And as I had been taught to carry the basket of my master the butcher, I took the bag in my mouth and went after them, determined not to let go of it until I reached the school. Everything turned out as I hoped. When my young masters saw me coming with the bag in my mouth, carefully held by the straps, they sent a page to take it from me. But

I would not let him, nor did I let go of it until I went into the class room with it, which caused great laughter among the students. Going over to the older of my masters, I delivered it into his hands with what seemed to me great delicacy, and went and sat down at the door of the room, my eyes fixed on the teacher who was reading the lesson. I don't know what there is about virtue that, understanding it as little as I do, or not at all, I was much pleased to see the love, the kindliness, the concern and the devotion those blessed fathers and teachers brought to the teaching of those boys, inclining the tender twigs of their youth so they would not be bent and turned away from the path of virtue, a subject taught them along with their letters. I observed how they reproved them with gentleness, punished them with mercy, encouraged them by example, stimulated them with rewards, and handled them wisely; and, above all, how they painted the ugliness and horrors of vice and held before them the beauty of virtue so that, loathing the former and loving the latter, they might achieve the purpose for which they had been born.

CIPIÓN: Well spoken, Berganza, for I have heard it said of those good men that as statesmen of this world there are none so prudent as they, and as guides and captains on the road to Heaven, few can equal them. They are mirrors which reflect chastity, Catholic doctrine, great prudence, and above all, deep humility, the foundation on which the whole structure of well-being rests.

BERGANZA: You have put it very well. Now, to go on with my story, my young masters liked to have me bring them their school bag every day, which I gladly did. In this way I led the life of a king, and even better, for it was very pleasant. The pupils liked to play with me, and I was so gentle with them that I let them put their hand in my mouth, and the smaller ones climbed on my back. They would throw their caps or hats, and I would retrieve and fetch them without soiling them, enjoying the game. They would give me of their food as much as they could spare, and they loved to see me take walnuts or filberts and crack them like a monkey, leaving the shell and eating the meat. One of them, to see what I would do, brought me in a handkerchief a big mess of salad, and I ate it as though I were a human being. It was winter time, when Seville abounds in buttered muffins which I liked so much that more than one Latin grammar was pawned or sold so I could have them. In a word, I spent my student days free from hunger or the itch, which is a way of saying how good it was. For if the itch and hunger were not so much a part of student life, there would be no other more pleasant and delightful, for in it virtue and pleasure go hand in hand, and the days of youth are spent in learning and playing. From this glory and peaceful state I was removed for what I believe is known as "reasons of state," in whose name many other reasons are overridden. What happened was that those teachers came to the conclusion that during the half hour between classes, the students, instead of reviewing their lessons, spent their time playing with me, and so they told my masters not to let me come to school any more. They did as they were bidden, and I had to go back to my former occupation of watching the house door; and as my master forgot the boon he had given me of letting me run loose day and night, I had to submit my neck to the collar once more and my body to a mat behind the door. Oh, friend Cipión, if you only knew how trying it is to pass from a state of happiness to one of infelicity! Listen: when misery and misfortunes are of long and continuous duration, or come to a quick end through death, or their persistence develops the habit and custom of suffering them, however bad, one can endure them. But when from a distressful and calamitous state, without thinking or expecting it, one passes to another of well-being, contentment, and happiness, and then, after a little while, returns to that first state and the earlier trials and misadventures, the suffering is so keen that if it does not put an end to life it makes the torment of living worse than death. In short, I went back to my canine rations, and the bones that a slave of the house tossed me, and I even had to dispute these with two spotted cats who, as they ran lose and were quick as lightning, could easily rob me of everything that did not fall within the radius of my chain. Brother Cipión, may Heaven grant you everything your heart desires if you will just let me philosophize a little without taking it amiss; for if I omit saying the things that happened then which just this moment came to my mind, it seems to me that my story would be incomplete and of little profit.

CIPIÓN: Make sure, Berganza, that this desire to philosophize that has come over you is not a snare of the devil. For gossip has no better veil to attenuate and conceal its viciousness than when the gossiper implies that all he is saying are philosophical maxims, and that speaking ill is reprehending, and revealing the shortcomings of others is done with good intent. And mark well that there is no gossiper whose life, if examined and looked into, will not be found full of vices and insolence. And now that you know this, go ahead and philosophize as much as you like.

BERGANZA: You may be sure, Cipión, that I will not gossip any more, for I have so made up my mind. Well, then, as I spent my days doing nothing, and idleness is the mother of thought, I went over in my memory some of the Latin I remembered of the much that I heard when I was going to school with my young masters; and as it seemed to me I found my understanding improved thereby, I decided, as though I knew how to talk, to make use of it whenever the opportunity arose, but in a different way than many of the ignorant often do. There are those who, when speaking their own tongue, in the course of conversation throw in from time to time some brief, pithy Latin phrase, implying to those who do not know them that they are great Latin scholars, when they can hardly decline a noun or conjugate a verb.

CIPIÓN: I consider this less harmful than what those who really know Latin usually do; some of them are so lacking in taste that when they talk with a shoemaker or a tailor they spout Latin like water.

BERGANZA: By the same token we might say that those who talk Latin in front of those who do not know it are as guilty as those who use it without knowing it.

CIPIÓN: You might also take note of something else, and that is that there are those who, although they know Latin, are still asses.

BERGANZA: Who doubts that? The reason for this is apparent. When in the times of the Romans everybody talked Latin as their native tongue, there must have been numskulls among them whose knowing Latin did not keep them from being fools.

CIPIÓN: To keep quiet in one's own tongue and to talk in Latin takes a lot of sense, brother Berganza.

BERGANZA: How right you are. It is as easy to talk nonsense in Latin as in one's native tongue; and I have seen educated fools, and tiresome grammarians, and those with a smattering of learning who quickly exhaust the patience of everybody, not once, but time and time again.

CIPIÓN: That's enough of that; now let's hear your philosophy.

BERGANZA: You've heard it; it's what I was just saying.

CIPIÓN: Which?

BERGANZA: That about Latin and the vernacular, which I began and you finished.

CIPIÓN: And you call gossiping philosophizing? That's a nice state of affairs! Go on, Berganza, go on sanctifying this foul plague of gossip, and call it by whatever name you like. It will give us the name of Cynics, which means gossiping dogs. For Heaven's sake, keep still and go on with your story.

BERGANZA: How can I go on with it if I am to keep still?

CIPIÓN: What I mean is for you to stick to it and not make it seem like an octopus with all the tails you keep adding to it.

BERGANZA: Speak with decorum; one does not refer to the tails of an octopus.

CIPIÓN: That's the error the man fell into who said it was not coarseness or lewdness to call things by their right names, as though it were not better, if you must allude to them, to do so with circumlocutions and indirect expressions to mitigate the disgust occasioned by hearing them called by their rightful name. Decent words are an earnest of the decency of the one who speaks or writes them.

BERGANZA: I will accept that. What I was saying was that fortune, not content with having deprived me of my studies and the happy and tranquil life that went with them, and keeping me tied up behind a door, and exchanging the liberality of the students for the niggardliness of the Negro slave girl, disposed that the peace and quiet I enjoyed should be turned to alarm. Cipión, you may take it for true and proven, as I do, that misfortune will pursue the unfortunate and hem him in, though he hide himself in the remotest corner of the earth. And I say this because the Negro girl of the house was in love with a Negro, who was also a slave there, who slept in the hallway between the outer and the inner door behind which I was tied, and they could only meet at night, and to do this they had stolen the key or had a copy made. Nearly every night the girl came down, and stopping my mouth with a piece of meat or cheese, opened the door to the Negro, and they had a fine time together, thanks to my silence and at the expense of the many things the slave girl filched. There were days when the girl's gifts played the devil with my conscience, for it seemed to me that if I were deprived of them my sides would shrink and I would be transformed from a mastiff into a greyhound. Nevertheless, being decent by nature, I wanted to fulfill my duties to my master, for I took his wages and ate his bread; and this is the proper behavior not only for self-respecting dogs, who are known for their gratitude, but for all those who serve.

CIPIÓN: Now that, Berganza, deserves the name of philosophy, for its arguments are based on truth and understanding. But go on, and don't make a rope (since you don't want me to say tail) out of your story.

BERGANZA: But first I would like you to tell me, if you know, what philosophy means. For even though I have heard the word, I don't know what it is. All I can gather is that it is a good thing.

CIPIÓN: I shall explain it briefly. The term is made up of two Greek words, *filos* and *sofia*, *filos* meaning love and *sofia* knowledge. So what philosophy means is love of knowledge, and philosopher, lover of knowledge.

BERGANZA: What a lot you know, Cipión! Who the devil taught you Greek words?

CIPIÓN: Really, Berganza, you are a fool to be impressed by that.

Those are things any schoolboy knows, and there are also those who pretend to know Greek without knowing it just as in the case of Latin.

BERGANZA: That's just what I say, and I wish they'd take them and put them in a press and turn the screw until they got out the juice of what they know so they would not go around fooling the world with tinsel on their tattered breeches and their pretended Latin, as the Portuguese do to the Negroes of Guinea.

CIPIÓN: Now, Berganza, you can really bite your tongue and I can chew mine, for all we're saying now is gossip.

BERGANZA: Yes, but I don't have to do what I have heard told of a certain Corondas of Tyre,[4] who passed a law that nobody could enter the town hall of his city bearing arms, under penalty of death. He forgot about it, and one day he came into the council room wearing his sword. When this was pointed out to him, recalling the penalty he had fixed for it, he unsheathed his sword and ran himself through the breast, thus being the first to pass and break a law and pay the penalty. What I said was not passing a law but promising that I would bite my tongue whenever I gossiped. But things are no longer done in the manner and with the severity of olden times. Today a law is passed, tomorrow it is broken, and perhaps it is better so. At one moment a person promises to correct his vices, and the next he falls into other worse ones. It is one thing to praise discipline, and another to carry it out, and it's a long way from the word to the deed. Let the devil bite himself, for I'm not going to, nor hide my light under a bushel where nobody can see me and praise my upright behavior.

CIPIÓN: According to what you are saying, Berganza, if you were a person, you would be a hypocrite, and everything you did would be feigned and false, for appearance's sake, covered with a veneer of virtue, seeking only praise, as all hypocrites do.

BERGANZA: I don't know what I would do then. I only know what I want to do now, and that is not to bite my tongue with so many things still to be said, and I don't know when or how I can

---

[4] *Error for Charondas of Thurii.*

utter them all, especially fearing as I do that with the rising of the sun we will be left in darkness, our powers of speech gone.

CIPIÓN: Heaven will look after us. Go on with your story, and don't keep straying from the main road with idle digressions. In that way, however long it is, you'll soon finish it.

BERGANZA: Well, as I was saying, after seeing the effrontery, thieving and immorality of the Negroes, I made up my mind, like a good servant, to prevent this as best I could; and I did so well that I achieved my purpose. The slave girl came down to regale herself with the Negro, trusting to hush my mouth with the pieces of meat, bread or cheese she tossed me. Gifts are very powerful.

CIPIÓN: Very. Don't lose your place. Go on.

BERGANZA: I remember that when I was a student I heard one of the teachers repeat a Latin proverb called an adage, which says: 'Habet bovem in lingua.'

CIPIÓN: Oh, how inopportunely you have thrown in your Latin! Have you so quickly forgot what we said a little while ago about those who lard their talk with Latin?

BERGANZA: But this Latin is a perfect fit here, for you must know that the Athenians used, among others, a coin stamped with the figure of an ox, and when some judge failed to say or do what was right and just because he had been bribed, they would say: 'That one has an ox on his tongue.'

CIPIÓN: I don't see how it applies here.

BERGANZA: Isn't it perfectly clear that the Negro girl's gifts silenced me for many days and I neither wanted to nor dared bark when she came down to meet her lover? I repeat that gifts are very powerful.

CIPIÓN: I have already told you that they are, and if it were not to avoid a long digression I would prove with a thousand examples what they can do. Maybe I will, if Heaven grants me the time, opportunity, and powers of speech to tell you the story of my life.

BERGANZA: May God grant your wish. Now listen. Finally my good resolution triumphed over the Negro girl's designing gifts, and one dark night when she was coming to her usual pastime, I rushed at her without barking so as not to arouse the house, and in a second I had ripped her shift to shreds, and torn out a piece of her thigh. It was enough to keep her in bed for more than a week, pretending to her masters that she was sick of I don't know what. She got well, came down another night, and I had another fight with the bitch, and without biting her, I scratched her whole body until she looked as though she had been carded like a blanket. Our encounters were noiseless, and I always came off the victor and the Negro girl got the worst of it. But her anger was reflected in my coat and my health. She took away my rations and the bones, and gradually you could count mine. Nevertheless, even though they took away my food they couldn't take away my bark. The girl, to get rid of me once and for all, brought me a sponge fried in lard; I recognized her evil intent, I knew that it was worse than powdered glass, for it swells up in the stomach and there's no way of getting rid of it except it carries off life itself. And as it seemed to me that it would be impossible to avoid the snares of such sworn enemies, I decided to put distance between us, removing myself from the sight of their eyes. Finding myself unchained one day, without taking leave of anyone in the house, I went out in the street, and before I had gone a hundred paces I was fortunate enough to meet the constable I mentioned at the beginning of my story who was a great friend of my master Flat-Nosed Nicolas. He recognized me as soon as he laid eyes on me, and called me by my name; I, too, recognized him and went up to him with my usual display and caresses. He took me by the collar and said to two of his assistants: 'This is that famous watch dog that belonged to a friend of mine; let's take him home.' The assistants were delighted and said that if I was a watch dog I would be of use to all of them. They wanted to take hold of me to lead me away, but my master said this was not necessary, for I would go along because I knew him. I forgot to tell you that the spiked collar I was wearing when I detached and freed myself from the flock was taken from me by a gipsy in a tavern, and in Seville I was not wearing any. But the constable put one on me, all embossed with Moorish tin. Give thought, Cipión, to the turning wheel of my fortune: Yesterday a student and today a constable.

CIPIÓN: That's the way the world goes, and there is no call for you to start yammering now about the inconstancies of fortune. Besides, I don't see much difference between being the servant of a butcher or a constable. I can't stand listening to complaints about their bad luck from certain men whose greatest luck was the anticipation and expectation of becoming squires. How they curse it! What insults they heap upon it! And for no other reason than that the person hearing them shall think they have fallen from a high, prosperous, goodly estate to the low and miserable one in which he sees them.

BERGANZA: You are right. Now I must tell you that this constable was the friend of a notary with whom he associated. The two of them had taken up with two wenches, not the in-between, half-good, half-bad kind, but the all bad. To be sure, they were fairly good-looking, but as brazen and tricky as whores. These women served them as net and hook for fishing on dry land in the following manner. They dressed themselves in such a way that by their appearance you could see a mile off that they were women of easy virtue. They always had an eye out for foreigners, and at fair time in Cadiz and Seville they reaped a harvest, for there was not a Breton they did not mark down for their prey. And when one of those greasy fellows fell into their clutches, they passed the word to the constable and notary of where and to what inn they were going, and once they were there, these worthies entered and arrested them as fornicators. But they never put them in jail because the foreigners always bailed themselves out with money.

It so happened that Colindres, as the constable's girl was called, got hold of a Breton who was dirtier than a pig. She arranged to dine and spend the night at his inn. She slipped the word to the constable, and the two had no more than undressed when he, the notary, the two assistants and I showed up. The lovers were confounded; the constable magnified the crime and ordered them to put on their clothes immediately for he was taking them to jail. The Breton bemoaned his fate; the notary, moved by pity, intervened, and after much pleading got the penalty reduced to a hundred *reales*. The Breton asked for his leather breeches which he had left on a chair at the foot of the bed, where he had money to pay for his freedom, but the breeches did not appear, nor could they. For as soon as I came into the room I caught a whiff of bacon which pleased me greatly. Following the scent, I found its origin in a pocket of the breeches, that is to say, I found there a piece of splendid ham, and in order to enjoy it and get at it without making a noise, I dragged the breeches into the street, and there I gave myself completely over to the ham. When I returned to the room the Breton was shouting and saying in his broken, confused language, which nevertheless was intelligible, that he wanted his breeches back for he had fifty gold florins in them. The notary came to the conclusion that Colindres or the constable's assistants had stolen them and the constable was of the same opinion. He called them aside, nobody would admit it, and all were beside themselves. When I saw what was taking place, I went out to the street where I had left the breeches to bring them back, for the money was of no use to me, but I could not find them as some lucky soul who chanced to pass by had taken them. When the constable saw that the Breton had no money to buy him off, he fell into a rage, and decided to get from the mistress of the inn what the Breton did not have. He sent for her and she appeared half-dressed. When she heard the shouts and imprecations of the Breton, saw Colindres naked and weeping, the constable in a fury, the notary annoyed, and the constable's assistants taking everything in the room that they could lay their hands on, she was not at all pleased. The constable told her to get dressed and to come to jail with him for allowing her house to be used for immoral purposes. And then the lid blew off. Then the voices really rose and the confusion mounted. 'Mr. Constable and Mr. Notary,' said the hostess, 'those tricks don't work with me; I know which way the wind blows; I am not taken in by threats and bombast; hold your tongues and be on your way; otherwise, by my faith, I shall stop at nothing and proclaim to the four winds all that's behind this. I know the lady Colindres very the whore — calls her.

well, and I know that for a long time now the constable has been her protector. And don't make me say any more, but give this man back his money, and let's settle all this amicably, for I am a respectable woman, and my husband has his patent of nobility, with its *ad perpetuam rei memoriam,* and its lead seals, God be praised, and I run this place decently and without harming anyone. My license is hung up where everybody can see it, and don't come to me with mare's nests, for I know how to handle them. Just catch me letting women come in with the lodgers with my connivance! But they have the key to their rooms, and I am not a lynx who can see through seven walls.'

My masters were confounded by the hostess's diatribe and at seeing how well she knew what they were up to. But as they had nobody to fleece except her, they insisted on taking her off to jail. She complained to high heaven at the abuse and injustice of which she was the victim, with her husband away, and him the high-born hidalgo he was. The Breton was screaming about his fifty florins. The constable's assistants swore that they had not seen the breeches, as God was their witness. The notary, by signs, urged the constable to search Colindres, for he suspected that she must have the fifty florins, as she was in the habit of examining the purses and secret places of those who got entangled with her. She said that the Breton was drunk and must be lying about the money. In short, all was confusion, screams, oaths, and there seemed to be no way of restoring order, nor would there have been if at that moment the Lieutenant Governor, who was on his way to visit the inn, had not heard the goings-on and come into the room. He asked the reason for that hubbub, and the hostess informed him in full detail. She told who the nymph Colindres was (by this time she was dressed), informed him of her notorious friendship with the constable; brought to light their tricks and methods of robbing; she defended herself against the charge that any woman of ill repute ever entered her house with her consent; she made herself out a saint and her husband one of the blessed, and called to a servant to go and get her husband's patent of nobility out of the chest so the Lieutenant

Governor could see it, saying that he would see by it that the wife of so honorable a husband could do nothing evil, and if she kept that lodging house it was because there was nothing else she could do. And God only knew how much she deplored it, and how, if she only had enough for her daily sustenance, she would prefer it to that. The Lieutenant Governor, annoyed by so much talk and flaunting of the letters patent, said to her: 'Sister bed-renter, I am willing to believe that your husband has a letter patent, provided you admit he is an hidalgo inn-keeper.' 'And proud of it,' answered the hostess. 'And what lineage is there, pray tell, however high, that does not show an occasional blot?' 'What I can tell you, sister, is to get yourself dressed, for you're coming to jail.' This news hit her like a sledge-hammer. She tore her hair, her screams mounted, but for all this, the overzealous Lieutenant Governor took them all off to jail, that is to say, the Breton, Colindres, and the hostess. Later on I learned that the Breton lost, in addition to his fifty florins, ten more which he had to pay as costs, the hostess an equal sum, while Colindres got off scot-free. And the very day they let her go she picked up a sailor, who made up for the Breton by falling for the same old trick. And so you see, Cipión, the many and dire consequences that came from that tidbit of mine.

CIPIÓN: Rather you should say from the roguery of your master.

BERGANZA: You just listen, for that is not the end of it, even though I dislike speaking ill of constables and notaries.

CIPIÓN: Yes, but to speak ill of one is not to include all of them; as you know, there are many, even plenty of notaries, who are good, honest, law-abiding, and who like to amuse themselves without doing harm to others; not all of them drag out law-suits, or give information to the other litigant, or charge more than their just fees, nor do all of them go prying into other people's lives to criticize them, nor are all of them in connivance with the judge with a 'you scratch my back and I'll scratch yours' understanding. Neither do all constables associate with vagabonds and scoundrels, nor do all have the kind of lady-loves your master had to help them in their frauds. Many, plenty of them, are gentlemen by nature and well-born by instinct; there are many who are not bold, insolent, ill-bred, sneak thieves, like those you find in the inns, measuring foreigners' swords, and if they find them a hairsbreadth longer than they should be, they pillory the owner. No, not all of them release as quickly as they arrest, acting as judge and attorney when they feel like it.

BERGANZA: My master had higher ambitions; he trod a different path. He prided himself on his bravery and his record of arrests. He upheld his courage without running any danger to himself, but at the cost of his purse. One day at the Jerez Gate he seized single-handed six well-known rogues without my being able to help him in any way because I had a rope muzzle on my mouth, which he kept on me by day and took off at night. I was amazed at his courage, his spirit, his daring; he darted in and out among the six swords of the ruffians as though they were willow wands. It was a wondrous thing to see how agilely he charged them, the thrusts, the parrying, the timing, his eye ever alert that they should not take him from the rear. In a word, to me and to all who saw or heard about the fight he was looked upon as a new Rodomonte,[5] for he drove his enemies from the Jerez Gate to the statues of the College of Master Rodrigo, a distance of over a hundred paces. He left them locked up, and returned to collect the trophies of battle, which were three sword sheaths; these he took at once to the Lieutenant Governor who at the time, if I remember correctly, was the Licentiate Sarmiento de Valladares, renowned for his destruction of La Sauceda. As my master walked through the streets he was the center of all eyes, and they pointed to him as though saying: 'There goes the brave man who alone and unaided challenged the flower of the ruffians of Andalusia.' He spent the rest of the day strolling about the streets to exhibit himself, and night found us in Triana, in a street close to the Powder Mill. And my master, after scanning the horizon (as the old ballad goes) to see if anyone was looking, went into a house, with me following, and there in the courtyard were all the ruffians who had taken part in the fight, without cape or swords, taking their ease. One who must have been the host was

[5] *The boastful leader of the Saracens in Ariosto's* Orlando Innamorato.

holding a big jug of wine in one hand, and in the other a tall glass of the sort used in taverns, which he filled up with the foaming heady wine and drank the health of all. No sooner had they laid eyes on my master than they all rushed toward him with open arms, and toasted him, and he accepted the invitations of all, and would have done so with as many more if it had suited his convenience, for he was of an affable nature and not given to annoying anyone over trifles. If I were to try to tell you now what was talked over there, the dinner they ate, the fights they recounted, the thefts to which they alluded, the ladies whose conduct they praised or disparaged, the praises they lavished on one another, the absent ruffians whose names they mentioned, the analysis of the fine points of swordplay, getting up in the middle of the dinner to demonstrate the feints in question, using their hands as foils, the exquisite language they employed, and last but not least, the person of mine host, whom all honored as their master and father, it would be like entering a labyrinth from which there is no easy exit. In a word, I gathered beyond a doubt that the master of the house was a certain Monipodio, who was the accomplice of thieves and the cloak of ruffians, and that the great fight of my master's had been arranged with them beforehand on condition that they would retire leaving behind their sheaths, for which my master paid there in cash, as well as what Monipodio said was the cost of the dinner, which went on almost until daybreak, to everyone's delight. And with the dessert a report was brought to my master of an out-of-town ruffian who, all fresh and untarnished, had come to the city; he must have been braver than the others, and out of envy they informed on him. My master arrested him the next night lying naked in his bed. I could see from his build that if he had been dressed he would not have let himself be taken so easily. With this arrest, which followed the fight, the fame of my craven grew, for my master was more cowardly than a hare and upheld his reputation for bravery through free meals and drinks, and everything he earned at his job and by his schemes disappeared and was drained away in supporting his claims to valor.

But be patient and listen now to an incident in which he was involved. I shall not add or subtract one iota of the truth. Two thieves stole a very good horse in Antequera. They brought it to Seville, and in order to sell it without getting into trouble they employed a trick which seems to me shrewd and cunning. They went to lodge at different inns, and one of them went to court and filed a complaint stating that Pedro de Losada owed him four hundred *reales* which he had borrowed, as vouched for by a signed receipt which the complainant presented. The judge ordered inquiries made of Losada as to whether he acknowledged the receipt, and if he did, his property was to be attached for the amount in question, or he would have to go to jail. This commission was entrusted to my master and his friend the notary. The thief led him to the lodging of his accomplice who at once acknowledged his signature, admitted the debt, and gave the horse as security for it. When my master saw it he fell in love with it, and marked it for his own if it came up for sale. The thief let the legal limit for payment of the debt elapse, and the horse was put up for sale and auctioned off to an intermediary acting for my master. The horse was worth as much again as was paid for it; but as it was to the seller's interest to dispose of it as quickly as he could, he let it go to the first bidder. The thief collected the debt not due him, the other the receipt for payment which was superfluous, and my master kept the horse, which turned out to be worse for him than that of Sejanus[6] for its owners. The thieves skipped out immediately, and two days later, after my master had mended the horse's fittings and refurbished them, he rode forth on it to San Francisco Square, prouder and more puffed up than a peasant in his holiday clothes. He was showered with congratulations on his fine bargain, and told that if it was worth a cent, it was worth a hundred and fifty ducats. Putting the animal through its paces, he played out his tragedy in the theater of the aforementioned square. As he was going through all this prancing and curvetting, two men of goodly appearance,

---

[6] *Sejanus, a Roman who owned a horse that brought misfortune to him and all its subsequent owners.*

finely attired, came up and one of them said: 'By the living God, that is my horse, Ironfoot, which was stolen from me a few days ago in Antequera!' The four servants with him said this was true, that the horse was Ironfoot which had been stolen. My master was dumfounded, the owner lodged a complaint, brought forward proofs which were so convincing that the case was decided in his favor and my master had to return the horse. The shrewd trick of the thieves, which was to sell their stolen goods under cover and with the help of the law itself, came to light, and nearly everyone rejoiced that my master's avarice had defeated its own ends.

And that was not the end of his misfortunes. That night the Lieutenant Governor himself went out on patrol, for it had come to his ears that there were thieves prowling about the San Julian quarter; and as he came to a street intersection, a man was seen running, and the Lieutenant Governor cried out, taking me by the collar and urging me on: 'Get the thief, Gavilán! Get him, boy, get him.' By this time I was tired of my master's wicked ways, and carrying out my orders to the letter, I rushed on my own master whom, unable to defend himself, I threw to the ground, and if they hadn't pulled me off him, I would have settled a number of accounts then and there. The assistants wanted to punish me, and even beat me to death, as they would have done if the Lieutenant Governor had not said: 'Nobody is to touch him. The dog did what I ordered him to do.' The malice of his words was clear, and I, without taking my leave of anyone, slipped through a hole in the wall into the fields, and before dawn I was in Mairena, a village that lies some four leagues from Seville. I had the good luck to find a company of soldiers there on their way to take ship in Cartagena, as I heard. Among them were four ruffian friends of my master, and the drummer was one who had been a constable, and was a great joker, as most drummers are. They all recognized me, they all spoke to me and inquired about my master as though I could answer them. But the one who took the greatest fancy to me was the drummer, and I decided to throw in my lot with him, if he was agreeable, and make the journey with him, even if it took me to Italy or Flanders.

For it seems to me, and I would think to you, too, that in spite of the proverb, 'A fool in his home town is a fool anywhere,' knowing other lands and dealing with a variety of people makes a man wise.

CIPIÓN: That is so true that I can recall hearing one of my masters, who I always thought had a fine wit, say that the famous Greek called Ulysses was held to be wise only because he had travelled through many lands and had known diverse peoples and nations. So I find your idea of going wherever they took you commendable.

BERGANZA: It so happened that the drummer, to add to his stock of jokes, began to teach me to dance to the sound of the drum, and other monkey tricks which would have been impossible for any other dog to have learned, as you will hear when I tell you about them. As we were outside the prescribed district, we moved slowly; there was no commissioner to keep us in bounds; the captain was young, though a fine gentleman and a great Christian; the lieutenant had only recently left the court and the pages' dining table; the sergeant was tricky and shrewd, and a great leader of levies from the recruiting center right to the port of embarkation. The company was full of marauding ruffians who committed abuses in the villages through which we passed, thus giving a bad name to those who did not deserve it. It is unfortunate that a good king should be blamed by some of his subjects for the faults of others of his subjects, for certain of them are the scourge of others without the ruler being to blame; for even though he wishes and tries, he cannot prevent this mischief, inasmuch as all or most things having to do with war are accompanied by harshness, severity and annoyances. In short, in less than fifteen days, with my keen wits and the persistence on the part of the master I had chosen, I knew how to jump at the name of the King of France and not at that of the mean tavern mistress. He taught me to curvet like a Neapolitan horse, and to walk in a circle like a mill mule, along with other things which if I had not been wise enough not to learn too quickly would have made people wonder if it was not some devil in the shape of a dog who was performing them. I became known as the wise dog, and no sooner had we reached our billet than the drummer, beating his drum, went through the town crying that anyone who wanted to see the wonderful tricks and skill of a wise dog should come to such and such a house or hospital where they could be seen for the price of eight (or four) *maravedís,* depending on whether the town was large or small. With all this fanfare, there was not a person in the place who did not turn out to see me, nor one who did not leave amazed and happy at having seen me. My master was in clover with all he took in, and supported six comrades in kingly fashion. Greed and envy aroused in the ruffians the idea of stealing me, and they waited for an opportunity, for this business of earning one's living without turning a hand has many addicts and admirers. That is why there are so many jugglers in Spain, so many puppeteers, so many sellers of pins and ballads whose entire stock, even if they sold it all, would not keep them for a week. Yet notwithstanding, they all spend their days in wineshops and taverns the year round, which makes me think that the money for their drinking comes from some other source than their profession. All these people are lazy, worthless, wastrels, wine sponges and bread weevils.

CIPIÓN: That will do, Berganza; let's not fall into past errors. Go on; night is slipping away, and I would not like it if with the coming of the sun we were left in the darkness of silence.

BERGANZA: Be quiet and listen. As it is easy to improve on what has already been invented, when my master saw how well I could imitate the Neapolitan horses, he made me a harness of embossed leather and a little saddle which he fastened on my back, and in it he set a light figure of a man with a little lance for tilting at the ring, and taught me to run straight at a ring which he hung between two poles. On the day I was to perform, he went about crying that the wise dog was going to tilt at the ring that day, and perform other new tricks never before seen, which I thought up out of my own head, not to make a liar of my master. On our march we finally came to Montilla, the city of the renowned and most Christian Marquess of Priego, head of the house of Aguilar and Montilla. My master managed to get himself billeted in a hospital.

He at once made his customary proclamation, and as fame had already carried the news of the skills and tricks of the wise dog, in less than an hour the courtyard was full of people. My master was delighted to see that the harvest was going to be abundant, and that day he played the buffoon for all it was worth. The first act of the show was my jumping through a paper hoop that looked like that of a barrel; he asked me all the usual questions, and when he lowered a quince switch he held in his hand, it was the sign for me to jump, and when he held it high, I remained still. The first order of that day (which stands out among all those of my life) was: 'Come, Gavilán boy, jump for that old lecher you know who dyes his whiskers; or if you don't want to, for the airs and presumption of Doña Pimpinela of Plafagonia, who was a companion of the Galician maid who served in Valdeastillas. You don't feel like it? Well, then, jump for Bachelor Pasillas, who signed himself Master without having any degree. Oh, you're feeling lazy? Why don't you jump? But I understand your sly ways; all right, then jump for the wine of Esquivias, equal in fame to that of Ciudad Real, San Martín, and Rivadavia.' He lowered the switch and I jumped, well aware of his malice and meanness. Then he turned to the audience and said in a loud voice: 'Do not think, oh noble public, that what this dog knows is a matter for jest. I have taught him twenty-four tricks, any one of which would baffle a falcon. What I mean is that it is worth walking thirty leagues to see the least of them. He knows how to dance the sarabande and chaconne better than their inventor himself; he quaffs off a beaker of wine without leaving a drop; he can carry a tune as well as a sacristan. All these things, and many others which I have omitted to tell, Your Excellencies will see during the time the company is billeted here. And now, my smart fellow, give one more jump and we'll go on to the main feature.' With this the entire audience, which he had called the senate, was hanging on his words, eager to see all that I could do. My master turned to me and said: 'Come, Gavilán boy, now neatly and featly give the same jumps you have given backward, in memory of the famous witch they say used to live here.' He had no more than uttered these words than the hospital matron, an old woman who looked to be over seventy, broke out: 'Scoundrel, mountebank, charlatan and whoreson, there are no witches here. If you have Camacha in mind, she has paid for her sins, and is wherever God decreed; and if it's me you're referring to, buffoon, I am not and never have been a witch; and if I've come by that reputation, because of false witnesses and guilt by association and the ignorance of an insolent judge, everybody knows the life I lead to atone, not for witchcraft, which I did not perform, but for the many other sins which, as the sinner I am, I have committed. So, sly drummer, get out of this hospital, or by my faith I'll chase you out in short order.' And with this she began to scream so loud, and to heap such vituperation on my master that she confounded and alarmed him; in short, she forbade the performance to continue. My master was not too sorry about the hubbub, for he kept the admission money and postponed for the next day and at another hospital the rest of the show. The audience left cursing the old woman and calling her a witch as well as a worker of spells, and not only old, but bewhiskered. In spite of all this we spent that night at the hospital, and when the old woman came upon me in the barnyard alone, she said to me: 'Is it you, Montiel, son? Is it by chance you, son?' I raised my head and looked at her fixedly, and when she observed this, she came over to me with tears in her eyes, threw her arms around my neck, and if I had let her, she would have kissed me on the mouth, but this revolted me and I did not let her.

CIPIÓN: You did right, for it is no treat but torture to kiss or be kissed by an old woman.

BERGANZA: This that I am about to tell you, I should have told you at the beginning of the story, and in that way we would not have been so amazed at seeing ourselves with the gift of speech. Because you must know that the old woman said to me: 'Montiel, son, follow me and you'll see where my room is, and try to come there alone tonight; I will leave the door ajar. For I have many things to tell you about yourself that will be of benefit to you.' I lowered my head in sign of obedience, whereby she was convinced that I was the dog Montiel she was seeking, as I afterwards learned. I was surprised and perplexed, waiting for night to come to see what would be the upshot of that mystery or marvel the old woman had alluded to. As I had heard her called a witch, I expected great things from seeing and hearing her. The moment finally came when I was with her in her room, which was dark, narrow, and low, and illuminated only by the wan light of a candle in a clay holder. The old woman trimmed it, and seating herself on a little chest, and drawing me to her, without saying a word she embraced me again, and I took care not to let her kiss me. The first thing she said was:

'I put my trust in Heaven that before these eyes of mine closed in their last sleep, I would see you again, my son, and now that I have, let death come and bear me away from this weary life. You must know, son, that there lived in this town the most famous sorceress in the whole world, Camacha de Montilla, as she was called. She was so unique in her profession that the Erichthos, the Circes, the Medeas of whom I have heard that books are full, did not come up to her. She could congeal the clouds whenever she wanted to, covering the face of the sun with them, and when she liked she could turn the stormiest sky serene; in the twinkling of an eye she could transport men from distant lands; she could repair as by a miracle maidens who had been a little careless with their chastity; with her help widows, feigning to be virtuous, could lead a loose life; she unwed wives, and married off those she wanted to. In December she had roses blooming in her garden, and in January she planted wheat. Growing water cress in a bread bowl was the least she did, or making visible in a mirror, or a baby's nail, the living or the dead she was asked to reveal. It was said she could turn men into animals, and that she had actually used a sacristan for six years as a mule, though I have never understood how it was done. For what they tell about ancient sorceresses, who turned men into beasts, those who know best say it was nothing, but that by their beauty and flattery they attracted men to themselves in such a way, and so dominated them, using them as they pleased, that they seemed beasts. But in you, my son, experience has shown me the contrary, for I know that you are a rational being, and I see you in the form of a dog, unless this is done through the magic art known as Tropelia, which makes one thing seem another. Be that as it may, what I most regret is that neither I nor your mother, who were pupils of great Camacha, ever came to know as much as she did. And it was not for lack of wits, or skill, or courage, of which we had more than enough, but because of her abounding malice, for she never would teach us the most important things, keeping these only for herself.

'Your mother, son, was called Montiela and, after Camacha, she was the most famous; my name was Cañizares, and if I was not as wise as the two of them, at least my desires were as good. The truth is that the courage of your mother in drawing and stepping inside a circle, and remaining there with a legion of devils, was not surpassed by Camacha herself. I was always a little timid; calling up half a legion was enough for me. But it may be fairly said of both of us that in the matter of preparing the ointments with which we witches anoint ourselves, neither could outdo the other, nor could any of those who today follow and observe our rules. Let me tell you, son, that I, who have seen and do now see how swiftly life, which flies on the light wings of time, comes to an end, have decided to give up all the vices of sorcery in which I was engaged for so many years, and the only thing that has remained with me is the taste for being a witch, which is a difficult vice to relinquish. Your mother did the same; she renounced many vices; she did many good works during her lifetime; but in the end she died a witch, and she did not die of any sickness but of grief at seeing the envy that Camacha, her mentor, bore her because she was coming to know as much as she did, or because of some rift due to jealousy. When your mother was about to give birth she came to be with her and received in her own hands the fruit of your mother's womb, and showed her that she had brought forth two puppies. As soon as she beheld them, she said to your mother: 'There has been mischief at work here; there is crookedness in this! But, Sister Montiela, I am your friend. I will cover up this miscarriage, and you think only of getting well, and rest assured that this calamity will be buried in silence. Don't take the matter to heart, for you know that I know that, except for Rodríguez, that worthless friend of yours, you have had no dealings with anyone else for a long time, so this doggish birth has some other origin and holds some mystery.' Your mother and I (who was present at this strange affair) were amazed. Camacha left, taking the pups with her. I stayed to look after your mother, and she could not grasp what had happened. Camacha's last day came, and in the final hour of her life she sent for your mother and told her that she had changed her babies into dogs because of a grudge she bore her, but that she was not to feel badly, for they would recover their shape when least expected, but not before they had seen with their own eyes the following come to pass:

> They will recover their true shape
> When they with quick diligence see
> The fall of the high and mighty,
> The rise of the lowly downtrodden,
> By the power of a mighty hand.

These were the words Camacha said to your mother when she was dying. Your mother took them down in writing and learned them by heart, and I took careful note of them in my mind in case the moment ever came when I could tell them to one of you. And in order to recognize you, whenever I see a dog your color, I call it by the name of your mother, not because I think the dog will know the name, but to see if it answers when called by a name so different from that of other dogs. And this afternoon, when I saw you do so many things, and that they called you a wise dog, and also by the way you raised your head and looked at me when I called you there in the barnyard, I came to the conclusion that you were the son of Montiela, and with the greatest pleasure I am informing you of what happened to you and how to recover your pristine form. I only wish it were as easy as the way Apuleius tells in *The Golden Ass*,[7] which was simply by eating a rose. But in your case, it depends on the acts of others, not on your efforts. What you must do, son, is commend yourself to God in the depths of your heart, and hope that these which I do not want to call prophecies, but rather riddles, will come to pass quickly and favorably. Without a doubt, as they came from the mouth of Camacha, they will occur, and you and your brother, if he is still alive, will see yourselves as you hope.

'What I regret is that with my end so near I won't have a chance to see it. Time and again I have wanted to ask my buck-goat how your affair was going to turn out; but I have never ventured to do so, for never does he give a straight answer to what we ask, but devious ones, capable of many interpretations. For that reason it is no good to ask this lord and master of ours anything, for he laces the truth with a thousand lies, and I have reached the conclusion that he has no certain knowledge of the future, but only conjectures. Nevertheless, he has those of us who are witches so under his spell that even though he plays us a thousand tricks we cannot give him up. We go to meet him far from here, in a great field, where a great group of us, wizards and witches, assemble, and there they give us foul-tasting food, and other things happen which out of respect for God and my soul I am ashamed to tell, so revolting are they, and I do not want to offend your chaste ears. Some think that we attend these gatherings only in our imagination, and that the devil calls up before our mind's eye the image of all those things which we afterwards relate as though they had happened. Others disagree, and say that we really go in body and in soul. For my part I believe that both these opinions are true, even though we do not know when we go in one form or the other, because everything that happens to us in our fancy is so intense that there is no difference between it and what really and actually occurs. The members of the Inquisition

---

[7] The Golden Ass *by the North African Lucius Apuleius (b. 125 A.D.) was a famous narrative widely read during the Renaissance in which the hero is turned into an ass until finally restored to human shape by the intervention of the Goddess Isis.*

have made certain tests of this with some of us who have been
arrested, and I think they have found what I say to be true.

'Son, I long to give up this sin, and I have made a thousand
attempts to do so. I have taken this post in the hospital, where I tend
the poor; some of them die and give me life with what they leave
me and what is to be found among their rags, which I go through
very carefully. I pray little and in public; I am a great gossip, but in
secret. It goes better with me to be a hypocrite than to be an open
sinner: the sight of my present good works is effacing in the memory
of those who know me my past evil deeds. In a word, feigned sanctity
does nobody any harm except the one who employs it. See here, son
Montiel, let me give you this piece of advice: be good in all that
you can; and if you're going to be bad, try as much as you can not to
seem so. I am a witch, I don't deny it. A witch and sorceress was
your mother, who cannot deny it either; but the goodly appearance
of both of us saved our reputation with everybody. Three days before
she died the two of us had been in a valley of the Pyrenees on a
great excursion, and yet when she died her passing was so quiet and
peaceful that if it had not been for a few grimaces she made a
quarter of an hour before she gave up her soul, it would have seemed
that she was lying in that bed as on a couch of flowers. What pierced
her heart like a sword was the thought of her two sons, and she
refused, even at the hour of death, to forgive Camacha, so firm and
steadfast was she in everything. I closed her eyes, and followed her
to the grave. There I left her to see her no more, although I have
not lost hope of seeing her before I die, because it is said about the
town that certain persons have seen her prowling near the cemeteries
and crossroads in various guises, and perhaps some day I shall encounter her, and I shall ask her if she wants anything done for the
relief of her conscience.'

Each of these things the old woman was telling me in praise
of my presumed mother was like a lance thrust through the heart,
and I would have liked to rush at her and tear her to pieces with my
teeth; and if I did not, it was so death would not take her with that
load of sin on her. Finally she told me that that very night she

planned to anoint herself to go to one of her accustomed gatherings, and when she was there she would inquire of her master what the future held for me. I would have liked to ask her what ointments these were that she spoke of, and it was as though she divined my wish, for she answered as if I had asked her:

'This ointment we witches anoint ourselves with is made of the juice of herbs that have the property of great cold and is not, as the populace says, made of the blood of children whom we strangle. At this point you might ask me, too, what pleasure or profit the devil derives from making us kill tender infants, for he well knows that once baptized, as they are innocent and free from sin, they go straight to heaven, and he suffers greatly over every Christian soul that eludes him. To this the only answer I can give you is what the proverb says: There are those who would pluck out their two eyes provided their enemy loses one; so it must be for the suffering he causes the parents by killing the children, which is the greatest that can be imagined; what matters to him most is that we should commit cruel and perverse sins at every turn. And God permits all this because of our sins, for I have seen from my own experience that without His permission the devil cannot offend even an ant. This is so true that once when I begged him to destroy the vineyard of an enemy of mine, he answered that he could not touch even a leaf of it, for God was unwilling. From this you may come to understand when you are a man that all the misfortunes that befall people, kingdoms, cities, and nations, sudden death, shipwrecks, falls from greatness, in a word, all the ills known as calamities, come from the hand of the Almighty and with His acquiescing will; and the evils and disasters of culpability arise and come from ourselves. God is without sin, from which it may be inferred that we are the authors of sin, forming it in our thoughts, words, and acts, God so permitting because of our sins, as I have said. You will be wondering, son, if by chance you understand me, how I came to be a theologian, and perhaps you will even say to yourself: "Listen to the old whore! Why doesn't she give up being a witch, since she knows so much, and return to God, Who she knows is more ready to forgive sins than to allow them?" To this I would reply, if you were to ask me, that the habit of vice forms a second nature, and this business of being a witch becomes flesh and blood; and in the midst of its ardor, which is very great, it puts such a chill in the soul that it benumbs and congeals even its faith; this makes it forget, and it does not even recall the punishments with which God menaces it, nor the glories to which He invites it. And as it is a sin of the flesh and the appetites, it is inevitable that it dull all the senses, and beguile and entrance them, preventing them from employing their abilities as they should. As a result the soul is left helpless, weak, and dispirited, unable even to harbor a good thought, and thus sunk in the abyss of its miserable state, refuses to raise its hand to that of God stretched out to it in His mercy to lift it up. Mine is a soul such as I have described to you; I see and understand everything, but as sinful indulgence has shackled my will, I have always been and shall be bad.

'But let us leave this and return to the matter of the ointments. As I was saying, they are so chill that they deprive us of all our senses when we anoint ourselves with them, and we remain sprawled and naked on the floor; and it is then they say we experience in our imagination all that which it seems to us really takes place. At other times when we have anointed ourselves it seems to us that we change our shape, and, transformed into roosters, owls or crows, go to the place where our master awaits us, and there we take on our pristine shape, and enjoy all the pleasures I refrain from telling you, for they are such that the memory is shocked to recall them and the tongue falters at repeating them. Yet with all this, I am a witch, and hide my many faults under the cloak of hypocrisy. It is true that although there are some who respect me and call me good, there is no lack of those who, not two fingers from my ear, call me by my right name, which is what aroused the fury of the hot-tempered judge before whom your mother and I were brought long ago, and who, delegating his anger into the hands of an executioner whose palm had not been greased, vented his full strength and severity on our backs. But that is over, and all this past; memories end, lives return not, the tongue grows weary, and new happenings bring forgetfulness of the old. I am the matron of a hospital, I give a good example by my conduct; my ointments bring me solace; I am not so old I cannot live another year, even though I am seventy-five. And as I cannot fast, because of my age, nor pray, because I get dizzy, nor go on pilgrimages because of the shakiness of my legs, nor give alms because I am poor, nor think good thoughts because I like to gossip, and since to do a thing, one must first think it, my thoughts will always be bad. Yet withal I know that God is kind and merciful, and that He knows what is to become of me, and that suffices. Now let us bring this conversation to an end for it truly saddens me. Come, son, and you shall see me anoint myself; for all sorrow is bearable with bread; and bring the good day into the house, for while we laugh we're not crying; what I mean is that even though the pleasures the devil gives us are lying and false, still to us they seem pleasures; and the greatest delights are those which we imagine rather than experience, though the opposite must be true of real pleasures.'

She got to her feet after this long harangue, and taking the lamp, went into another even smaller room. I followed her, torn by a thousand thoughts and amazed at what I had heard and what I hoped to see. She hung the lamp on the wall, and quickly stripped herself to her shift. Then taking a glazed pot from a corner, she put her hand in it, and muttering to herself, anointed herself from her feet to her head, from which she had removed her coif. Before she finished, she told me that whether her body remained in that room senseless, or whether she disappeared from it, I was not to be frightened, nor should I fail to wait there until morning, when I would receive news of what was still to happen to me before I became a man. I told her by lowering my head that I would do so, and with this she finished her anointing, and stretched out on the floor as though dead. I brought my mouth alongside hers, and saw that she was not breathing, either much or little. I will tell you the truth, Cipión, my friend: I was terrified at finding myself shut up in that narrow room with that figure before me which I shall describe to you as best I can. She was over seven feet long, a bag of bones covered with black, hairy, leathery skin; her belly, which was like cowhide, covered her private parts and even hung half way down her thighs; her dugs were like two dry shrivelled cow bladders, her lips discolored, her teeth clenched, her nose hooked and sharp, her eyes mismatched, her hair tangled, her cheeks hollow, her throat scrawny and her breast sunken, all gaunt and hideous. I began to look her over slowly, and suddenly a fright came upon me as I thought of the deplorable state of her body and the worse occupation of her soul. I wanted to bite her to see if she would recover her senses, but I could not find any spot on her that did not fill me with disgust. Finally I grabbed her by the heel and dragged her into the courtyard, but for all this she gave no sign of consciousness. There, under the sky and in the open, my fear disappeared; at least it was tempered so that I had the courage to wait and see what would be the outcome of the going and coming of that evil woman and what she would tell me of my future. At this point I asked myself: 'Who made this wicked old woman so wise and so bad? How does she come to know which are evils of calamity and which of culpability? How can she understand and talk so much about God, and equally of the devil? How does she sin so knowingly, without even ignorance as an excuse?'

With these reflections I spent the night, and day found the two of us in the middle of the courtyard, she still senseless, and I sitting beside her, alert, taking in her horrible, ugly appearance. The inmates of the hospital came out, and observing that scene, some of them remarked: 'Good old Cañizares is dead at last; look how gaunt and disfigured her penitence has left her.' Others, more thoughtful, felt her pulse, and finding that it was still beating, and that she was not dead, assumed that she was in an ecstasy and trance because of her religious fervor. There were those who said: 'That old whore must surely be a witch, and she must be anointed, for saints never fall into such shameful trances, and among those of us who know her, she has more of a reputation as a witch than a saint.' Some stuck pins into her flesh, burying them up to the head, but not even with this did the sleeper waken, nor did she come to herself until seven o'clock. When she became conscious of all the pin pricks, and the bites on her heels, and the bruises she had suffered when she was dragged from her room, and that she was lying there in sight of all those eyes, she thought, and rightly so, that I was the cause of her dishonor. So rushing at me, and taking me by the throat with both her hands, she tried to choke me, saying: 'Oh, ungrateful wretch, ignorant and malicious! So this is the payment I get for all my good works to your mother, and those I intended to do for you.' Seeing myself in danger of my life at the claws of that savage harpy, I shook myself free, and grabbing the flaccid folds of her belly I shook her and dragged her all around the patio, while she screamed begging the onlookers to save her from the fangs of that evil spirit.

On hearing the outcry of that evil old woman the others believed that I must be one of those devils who have sworn eternal enmity against good Christians, and some of them sprinkled holy water on me, others were afraid to come near me, others said I should be exorcised; the old woman groaned; I gnashed my teeth. The confusion mounted, and my master, who had come out at the sound of the uproar, was in despair at hearing them say that I was a devil. Still others, who knew nothing about exorcising, came over with three or four cudgels and began to tan my hide. This was a game I did not like, so I let go of the old woman, and in three bounds gained the street and in a few more I left the town behind me, with a swarm of urchins at my heels screaming: 'Take care, the wise dog has gone mad!' Others cried: 'He's not mad; it's the devil in the shape of a dog!' With this beating I left the town as though the bells had sounded an alarm, followed by many who without doubt believed that I was the devil, both because of the things they had seen me do as well as because of what the old woman had said when she awoke from her cursed sleep. I fled with such haste to get out of their sight that they thought I had vanished as though I were the devil. In six hours I had covered twelve leagues, and came to a gipsy encampment which was in a field near Granada. There I restored myself somewhat, for certain of the gipsies recognized me as the wise dog, and joyfully welcomed me and hid me in a cave so I would not be discovered if anyone came looking for me. Their idea, as I understood later, was to profit by me as my master the drummer had done. I spent twenty days with them, during which I observed their life and habits, and as they are most unusual, I must tell you about them.

CIPIÓN: Before you go on, Berganza, it would be well for us to give thought to what the witch told you, and find out whether the great lie you believe could be true. Look, Berganza, it is arrant nonsense to believe that Camacha could turn men into animals, and that the sacristan served all those years in the shape of an ass. All such things, and others of the same sort, are frauds, lies, or the devil's work. And if it seems to us now that we have a certain understanding or capacity for reason because we are talking although we are really dogs, or at least have their shape, we have already agreed that this is a miraculous, unheard-of occurrence; and even though we see it, we cannot believe it until its outcome reveals to us what we should believe. Shall I put it more clearly? Stop and think about what silly things and foolish items Camacha said our restoration depended upon. What seem to you prophecies are nothing but fairy stories or old wives' tales, like those about the headless horse and the magic wand, with which people while away the long winter nights beside the hearth. Otherwise, they would already have come to pass, unless the words are to be taken in a sense that I have heard called allegorical, which is not what they actually say but something which, although different, resembles them. Thus, to say

> They will recover their true shape
> When they with quick diligence see
> The fall of the high and mighty,
> The rise of the lowly downtrodden,
> By the power of a mighty hand,

taking it in the sense that I have said, seems to me to mean that we will resume our shape when we see that those who yesterday were at the summit of Fortune's wheel today lie trampled and spurned at the feet of misfortune, misprized by those who once most esteemed them. And, by the same token, when we see those who two hours ago had no part in this world but to swell the number of its inhabitants are now riding so high that we cannot see them, then if they were invisible before because they were lowly and downtrodden, now they vanish from our sight because they are so high and mighty. If our restoration to our true shape depended upon just this, we have already seen it and see it at every step, which makes me believe that it is not in an allegorical, but in a literal sense that Camacha's verses should be taken. Nor can our remedy consist of this, for we have seen what they foretell many times, and are still as much dogs as ever. Therefore Camacha was a false sorceress, and Cañizares a liar, and Montiela foolish, lying, and wicked—excusing the expression, just in case she is the mother of the two of us, or yours, for I don't want her for a mother. So I would say that the true meaning is that of a game of ninepins, in which those which are standing are quickly knocked down and those which have fallen are set up again, and this by the hand of the one empowered to do it. Just think how many times in the course of our lives we have seen ninepins played, and tell me whether on that account we have become men again, assuming that we are.

BERGANZA: I must admit that you are right, brother Cipión, and you are wiser than I had thought. From what you have said I conclude and believe that everything that has happened to us so far, and what is happening now, is a dream, and that we are dogs. But not on that account are we going to deprive ourselves of the pleasure of this gift of speech we possess, and the excellent faculty of human discourse as long as it is ours. So give me leave to tell you what happened to me with the gipsies who hid me away in the cave.

CIPIÓN: I will gladly listen to you, thus putting you under the obligation of listening to me when I tell you, God so willing, the story of my life.

BERGANZA: I spent the time that I was with the gipsies observing their great slyness, their trickery, their lies, their skill at thieving, women and men alike, from the time, you might say, that they are out of their swaddling clothes and can walk. Have you observed the multitude of them throughout Spain? Well, they all know and are in touch with one another, and they transfer and deposit the product of the thefts of some to the others, and vice versa. They give obedience less to their king than to one they call Count, who, together with all who succeed him, are surnamed Maldonado. This is not because they descend from this noble house, but because the page of a knight by this name fell in love with a gipsy who would not give him her love unless he became a gipsy and wed her. The page did this, and the rest of the gipsies became so fond of him that they made him their lord and rendered him obedience, and in sign of fealty they bring him a part of all they steal that is of value. To cover up their idleness, they ply the trade of ironmongers, making articles to help them in their thieving, and you will always see the men peddling tongs, drills, and hammers through the streets, and the women, trivets and fire shovels. All the women are midwives, and better than ours, because without trouble or fuss they deliver their patients, and bathe the new-born infant in cold water. From the time they are born until they die they are accustomed to suffer the inclemencies and severity of the weather, and you can see that they are all healthy, agile, and great runners and dancers. They always marry among themselves so their evil ways will not be known to others; the women keep faith with their husbands, and rarely does one of them offend him with men of another race. When they beg alms they get more through their witty sallies and lies than by their devotion, and as nobody trusts them, they do not work, and fall into laziness. To the best of my memory, I have rarely if ever seen a gipsy at the altar taking communion, even though I have often visited churches. Their one thought is how they can deceive and where they can steal; they talk over their thefts, and how they accomplished them. One day a gipsy was telling the others in front of me the trick he had used to rob a peasant. The gipsy had a docked ass, and to its hairless stump he attached a hairy piece which looked as though it was his natural tail. He took him to the market, a peasant bought him for ten ducats, and after he had sold it to him and received his money, the gipsy asked him if he wanted to buy another, brother to the first, as good as the one he had purchased, which he would let him have at a better price. The peasant told him to go and fetch it, and he would buy it, and while he went for it he would take the one he had bought to his inn. The peasant set off, the gipsy followed him, and somehow or other managed to steal from the peasant the ass he had sold him. In the twinkling of an eye he removed the false tail, leaving the animal with its own bare stump. He changed the saddle and headstall, and then had the audacity to go and look for the peasant to sell it to him. He found him before he had missed the first ass, and in no time had sold him the second. When the peasant went to the inn to get the money to pay for it, and found the animal gone, though he was himself a stupid animal, he suspected that the gipsy had stolen it, and refused to pay him. The gipsy went to get witnesses, and brought the officials who had collected the tax on the sale of the first animal, and they swore that the gipsy had sold the peasant an ass with a long tail, completely different from the second one. A constable was there who had witnessed all this and he backed up the gipsy so convincingly that the peasant had to pay for the same ass twice. They told of many other thefts, all, or most of them, of animals, in which they are experts and do most of their dealings. In a word, they are a bad lot, and although many and very wise judges have come out against them, not on that account do they mend their ways.

After twenty days they wanted to take me to Murcia. We passed through Granada where the captain, whose drummer was my master, had arrived; as the gipsies knew of this they shut me up in a room at the inn where they lived. I heard them tell why. I didn't like the idea of the trip they were planning, so I made up my mind to get loose. I did so, and leaving Granada, I came to the fruit farm of a descendant of the Moors, who took me in with right good will; I accepted with even better will, for it seemed to me that all he wanted me for was to guard the orchard, a job less onerous, so I thought, than guarding sheep. And as there was no discussion about wages, it was a simple matter for the Morisco to acquire a servant to command, and I a master to serve. I was with him for over a month, not because my life was so pleasant, but for the sake of learning about that of my master, and through it, that of all the Moriscos in Spain. The things I could tell you, Cipión, my friend, of this Moorish rabble if it were not that I am afraid I would not finish in two weeks! And if I were to go into details, I would not get through in two months. Nevertheless, I am going to tell you a little, and this will give you a general idea of what I saw and observed in these people. Only by exception does one find among so many of them one who truly believes in the holy Christian faith. Their one ambition is to come by and hoard minted money, and to acquire it they work and do not eat. Once a coin whose value is more than a farthing falls into their hands, they condemn it to life imprisonment and eternal darkness, and in this way, always hoarding and never spending, they come to accumulate the greatest amount of money to be found in Spain. They are its strong-box, its vault, its guardians, its custodians; they gather it all in, they hide it, they swallow it up. Just think how many of them there are—and every day they earn and put by a little or much, and remember that a slow fever can finish one off as well as a stroke. And as they multiply, the hoarders steadily increase and will go on increasing to infinity, as experience has shown. They don't know the meaning of chastity, nor do they ever take religious vows, either the men or the women. They all marry, and they all multiply, because frugality increases the powers of generation. They are not destroyed by war nor occupations that wear them out; they rob us without risk, and with the fruits of our patrimony, which they sell back to us, they wax rich. They have no servants, for they are their own; they spend nothing on the education of their children, because their only science is how to rob us. Of the twelve sons of Jacob who I have heard said went into Egypt, when Moses brought them out of that captivity they numbered six hundred thousand men, not counting the children and women. From this it can be inferred how the women of these will multiply, who are incomparably more.

CIPIÓN: A remedy is being sought for all the evils you have mentioned and touched upon. I know very well that those you have not listed exceed those you have set forth, and as yet the necessary solution has not been found. But our republic has wise guardians who, knowing that Spain breeds and has in its bosom as many vipers as there are Moriscos, will, with the help of God, find sure, swift and certain relief from so much harm. Go on.

BERGANZA: As my master was stingy, as are all of his race, he fed me on corn bread and left-over porridge, which was his usual diet. But Heaven helped me to endure this miserliness in the strange manner you shall now hear. Every morning at break of day there would appear seated at the foot of a pomegranate, of which there were many in the garden, a youth having the air of a student, wearing a baize suit, not so black and fuzzy that it did not seem gray and sheared. At times he would be writing in a notebook, and every once in a while he would slap his forehead, bite his nails, and look up at the sky. At other times he would be so lost in thought that he did not move hand or foot, nor even his eyelashes, so bemused was he. Once I approached him without his seeing me; I heard him mumbling to himself, and after a long while he gave a loud cry, saying: 'By the life of Our Lord, this is the best eight-line stanza I have written in my whole life!' And scribbling as fast as he could in the notebook, he gave evidence of great satisfaction. All this made me realize that the poor devil was a poet. I made my customary display of affection to assure him of my gentleness; I lay down at his feet, and he, with this guarantee, went on with his cavilings, scratched his head again, renewed his ecstasies, and again set down what he had thought up. While this was going on, another youth entered the garden, handsome and finely attired, with some papers in his hand, which he read from time to time. He came over to where the first one was and said to him: 'Have you finished the first act?' 'I have just ended it,' replied the poet, 'in the most elegant manner you can imagine.' 'How?' asked the other. 'Like this,' he answered: 'His Holiness the Pope comes out in pontifical robes with twelve cardinals, all dressed in purple, because the episode my play deals with took place at the time of the *mutatio caparum,* when the cardinals did not wear scarlet but purple, and so it is most desirable, for the sake of propriety, that these cardinals of mine should be wearing purple. This is a point which has a great bearing on the play, and without doubt others would err in it and commit all sorts of errors and absurdities. I cannot be mistaken in this matter, for I have read the Roman Catholic ceremonial from start to finish just to be sure about the attire.' 'And where do you think,' asked the other, 'that my manager is going to get hold of purple vestments for twelve cardinals?' 'Well, if he leaves out one of them,' replied the poet, 'I will no more give him my play than I will take wings and fly. God in Heaven, is such a magnificent display to be lost? Just try and imagine what it will look like on the stage to see a pontiff with twelve solemn cardinals, and the other accompanying ministers whom they must of necessity bring along. By my faith, it will be one of the finest and most stirring spectacles that has ever been seen in any play, including *The Nosegay of Doraja.*' At this point I realized that the one was a poet and the other an actor. The actor advised the poet to prune away some of the cardinals if he did not want to make it impossible for the manager to stage the play. To which the poet replied that they could give thanks that he had not included the entire conclave assembled for the memorable episode which he had endeavored to bring to the memory of the audience in his felicitous comedy. The actor laughed, left him to his occupation, and went off to his, which was to study a part in a new play. The poet, after setting down some more stanzas of his magnificent play, with great dignity unhurriedly brought out of his pocket some crusts of bread and about twenty raisins, which it seemed to me he counted, and I am not even sure there were that many, for they were mixed with crumbs of bread which made them seem more. He blew away the crumbs and ate the raisins one by one, stem and all, for I did not see him throw any away, and helped them down with the crusts which, from the fuzz of his pocket, looked moldy and were so stale that even though he tried to soften them by moving them from side to side in his mouth over and over again, their resistance was too much for him, which redounded to my benefit, for he threw them to me saying: 'Here, boy, here. Take this and I hope you enjoy it.' 'Hm,' I said to myself, 'look at the nectar and ambrosia this poet is giving me on which they say the gods and their Apollo feed in heaven.' In short, the poverty of poets is generally very great, but mine was greater for I was obliged to eat what he threw away. All the time he was working on his play he never failed to come to the garden, nor did I lack for crusts, for he shared them with me generously, and then we went to the well where, I lapping, and he drinking out of a bucket, we quenched our thirst like kings. But the poet departed and my hunger remained, and was so great that I decided to leave the Morisco and go to the city to better myself, which is the hope of those who make a change. As I entered the city I saw my poet coming out of the famous monastery of San Jerónimo. As soon as he laid eyes on me he came toward me with arms wide, and I ran to him with renewed display of affection at having encountered him. Immediately he began to pull out pieces of bread which were not so hard as those he used to bring to the garden, and gave them to me without first trying them out with his own teeth, which heightened my gratitude. The fresher crusts and the sight of my poet emerging from the aforesaid monastery made me suspect that his muses were poor but proud, as are those of many others. He walked into the city and I followed him, determined to take him for my master, if he was willing, thinking that the leavings of his castle would provide for my camp. There is no better or deeper purse than that of charity, whose generous hands are never empty, and for that reason I do not agree with the proverb that says: 'The hard-hearted give more than the naked,' as though the hard-hearted and miserly ever gave anything, whereas the generous naked at least give their good wishes if they can give nothing more. After much turning and twisting we came to the house of a theater manager who, if I remember rightly, was called Angulo the Bad to distinguish him from the other Angulo, not a manager but an actor, the most entertaining the theater then had and still has. The whole company had gathered there to hear the play of my master—for I now so looked upon him—and in the middle of the first act, one by one and two by two, they all left with the exception of the manager and myself, who acted as audience. The play was so bad that, even though I am a complete ass when it comes to poetry, it seemed to me that it had come from the pen of Satan himself, to the total ruin and confusion of the poet, who by this time was swallowing hard at seeing the solitude in which the audience had left him. And it would not be surprising if his prophetic soul had foretold the misfortune that was about to descend upon him, which was that the actors, more than twelve in number, returned and without saying a word, seized my poet; and if it had not been for the intervention of the manager, entreating and shouting, they would undoubtedly have tossed him in a blanket. I was speechless at what had taken place; the manager, disgusted, the actors, merry, and the poet crestfallen. With an air of resignation and great patience, though with a somewhat wry expression, he picked up his play and stuffing it in his bosom, said, half to himself: 'It is not good to cast pearls before swine.' And saying this he departed with great dignity. I was so mortified that I could not and would not follow him; and I did well, for the manager began to make so much of me that I had to stay with him, and in less than a month I was a great comedian and player of dumb roles. They put a braided bit on me, and taught me to attack whomever they wanted me to on the stage; and as most of the interludes conclude with slap-stick, in my master's company they all ended with me knocking down and overturning all the players, which made the ignorant laugh uproariously and earned my master much money. Oh, Cipión, if only I could tell you all I saw in this and two other companies I joined up with! But as it is impossible to encompass it in a brief, succinct narration, I'll have to leave it for another day, supposing that there will be another day in which we can converse. You see how long my tale has been? You see the many and diverse incidents? Do you realize how many roads I have travelled, how many masters I have had? Well, what you have heard is as nothing compared with what I could tell you of all that I observed, learned and saw among these people, their behavior, the life they led, their habits, their pastimes, their work, their laziness, their ignorance, their sharp-wittedness, and an infinite number of other things, some to be whispered in the ear, others to be bruited aloud, and all to be engraved on the memory to disabuse the many who worship feigned shapes and beauties of artifice and illusion.

CIPIÓN: I can see clearly, Berganza, the vast horizon that stretches before you to prolong your narration, and it is my opinion that you should leave it to be told on another occasion with more leisure.

BERGANZA: Be it as you say, but listen. With one company I came to this city of Valladolid where in a comic playlet I received a wound which almost proved the end of me; I could not avenge myself because I was muzzled at the time, and later I didn't want to do it in cold blood, for planned vengeance indicates cruelty and cowardice. I grew weary of that calling, not because it was hard work, but because I saw in it things that called for both correction and punishment. And as I deplored them without being able to correct them, I decided to avoid the sight of them, so I took sanctuary, as do those who give up their vices when they can no longer indulge them, though, to be sure, better late than never. So one night when I saw you carrying the lantern with that good Christian Mahudes, I thought how happily and justly and uprightly you were occupied; and full of praiseworthy envy, I decided to follow in your footsteps, and with this laudable intention I presented myself before Mahudes who at once chose me as your comrade and brought me to this hospital. What has happened to me here is not so devoid of interest that it would not warrant the telling, especially what I overheard from four patients whom misfortune and need had brought to this hospital, where the four of them were together in four adjoining beds. Allow me to tell it, for the tale is short and offers no opportunity for longwindedness, and it fits here like a glove.

CIPIÓN: Very good. Finish up, for it seems to me that day cannot be far off.

BERGANZA: What I was saying was that there were four beds at the end of this infirmary, and in one there was an alchemist, in another a poet, in another a mathematician, and in another one of those self-appointed political advisers.

CIPIÓN: I recall having seen those good folk.

BERGANZA: Well, one afternoon last summer, when the shutters were closed and I was taking the air under the bed of one of them, the poet began to lament his fate bitterly. And when the mathematician asked him what he was complaining about, he answered that he complained about his ill fate. 'And have I not reason to complain?' he went on, 'when I have observed all the rules that Horace laid down in his *Poetica,* that a work should not appear until ten years after its composition, and I have one on which I have spent twenty years writing and twelve of interneship, elevated in theme, admirable and new in invention, grave in meter, its incidents pleasing, its division marvelous, for the beginning is consonant with the middle and the end, so that all together they make up a lofty, sonorous, heroic, pleasing and solid poem. Yet in spite of all this I cannot find a grandee to whom to dedicate it. I mean a grandee who is intelligent, generous, and magnanimous. A miserable age and a depraved century this in which we live!'

'What does the book deal with?' asked the alchemist.

'It deals,' answered the poet, 'with what the Archbishop Turpin left unsaid about King Arthur of England, with a continuation of the Quest of the Holy Grail, all in heroic verse, part octaves, part free verse, but all dactylar, that is to say, in dactylic proper names, without a single verb.'

'I,' answered the alchemist, 'understand little about poetry, and for that reason I cannot rightly judge the misfortune of which you complain, although even if it were still greater, it does not equal mine, which is that for lack of equipment, or a patron to support me and provide me with the requisites the science of alchemy calls for, I am not at this moment running over with gold and richer than Midas, or Crassus, or Croesus.'

'Has Your Excellency ever attempted,' asked the mathematician at this point, 'to extract silver from other metals?'

'Up to now,' replied the alchemist, 'I have not done so; but I know truly that it can be done, and I need less than two months to complete the philosopher's stone by means of which silver and gold can be made from the very rocks.'

'How you gentlemen have exaggerated your misfortunes,' spoke up the mathematician at this point, 'for when all is said and done, one of you has a book to dedicate and the other is on the point of discovering the philosopher's stone. But what about mine, which is simply that I have nothing on which to rest? Two and twenty years I have been trying to find the fixed point, and here I leave it and there I take it, and when it seems to me that I have at last found it and that it cannot possibly elude me, before I know it I find myself so far from it that I am amazed. The same thing happens to me with the squaring of the circle: I have been so on the verge of achieving it that it is as though I had it in my pocket. Thus my suffering is similar to that of Tantalus, who was so near the fruit and dying of hunger, close to the water and perishing of thirst. At times it seems to me that I am at the very heart of the truth, and in an instant I am so far from it that I must again climb the mountain I have just descended with the stone of my work on my back, a new Sisyphus.'

Up to this point the political adviser had observed silence, which he now broke to say: 'Four complainers that you would think were inveighing against the Grand Turk have been brought together by their poverty in this hospice, and my curse upon callings and labors which neither amuse nor feed their masters! I, gentlemen, am a political adviser, and on different occasions I have given His Majesty many and various opinions, all redounding to his interest and without hurt to the kingdom. Now I have drawn up a petition beseeching him to assign me someone to whom to communicate a new recommendation I have which will bring about the complete achievement of all his aims. But judging from what has happened to my other proposals, I realize that this one, too, will wind up in the wastebasket. But so that you gentlemen will not look upon me as a dolt, and even though my proposal will thus become public, I am going to tell you what it is. The Cortes should decree that all His Majesty's vassals, between the age of fourteen and sixty, must fast one day a month, taking only bread and water, and this on a determined and appointed day, and all that would otherwise be spent on fruit, meat and fish, wine, eggs, and vegetables on that day, be turned into money and given to His Majesty, without cheating him of one penny, under oath. In this way, in twenty years he would be free of all difficulties and out of debt. Because if you add it up, as I have done, there are easily more than three million people in Spain within that age group, excluding the ailing and those who are outside the age limit. There is not one who does not spend at least a *real* and a half a day, and I would limit the contribution to one *real*, less than which they cannot spend even if they eat millet. Now, does it seem to you gentlemen that it would be as nothing to have every month three million *reales,* clean winnowed? And this would be beneficial rather than harmful to those who fasted because in this way they would please Heaven and help their king, and it would also be conducive to the good health of some. This is a simple, straightforward measure, and it could be carried out by parishes, without having to pay tax agents, who ruin the republic.' They all laughed at the adviser and his plan, and he himself laughed at his own nonsense, and I was full of amazement at seeing how the majority of those so constituted end their days in the hospitals.

CIPIÓN: You are right, Berganza. Now see if there is anything else you want to say.

BERGANZA: Only two things, and with this I will conclude my remarks, for day seems to be coming. One night when my master was going to solicit alms in the house of the mayor of this city, who is a fine gentleman and a most devout Christian, as we were alone it seemed well to me to take advantage of that solitude to inform him of certain observations I had overheard from an old patient of this hospital to remedy the scandalous ruination of so many idle young girls who, unwilling to work, fall into evil ways—so evil that every summer they fill the hospitals with those profligates who consort with them, an intolerable plague that calls for prompt and effective remedy. As I say, wanting to tell him, I raised my voice, thinking that I could talk, and instead of bringing forth coherent phrases, I barked so loud and so fast that it annoyed the mayor, who ordered his servants to drive me out of the room with a stick. One of his lackeys came at the sound of his master's voice, and it had been better that on that occasion he had been deaf. Grabbing up a copper water jug, which was the first thing he could lay his hands on, he gave me such a thwack in the ribs with it that I still bear the memory of the blow.

CIPIÓN: And are you complaining about that, Berganza?

BERGANZA: Of course I am complaining! Why shouldn't I, when, as I told you, it still hurts and I do not think my good intention deserved such punishment.

CIPIÓN: See here, Berganza, nobody should meddle in things that are not his business, nor interfere in matters that are not incumbent on him. And you should also bear in mind that the advice of the poor, however good it may be, is never taken into account, nor should the humble have the presumption to advise the mighty and those who think they know everything. The wisdom of the poor is beshadowed, for need and poverty are the dark and the clouds that shadow it, and if perchance it reveals itself, it is regarded as nonsense and treated with contempt.

BERGANZA: You are right, and having experienced this in my own person, from now on I shall follow your advice. Another night I went into the house of a lady of rank who was holding one of those lapdogs in her arms. It was so tiny it could have been hidden in her bosom. When this dog saw me, it leaped out of its mistress's arms and rushed at me barking furiously and did not stop until it had nipped me in the leg. I looked at it with concern and anger, saying to myself: 'If I were to meet you in the street, you wretched little beast, either I would pay no attention to you, or I would tear you to pieces.' I realized then that even cowards and the mean-spirited become bold and insolent when they find themselves in favor, and have no scruples about offending those who are worth more than they.

CIPIÓN: Proof and example of this truth which you have stated is to be seen in those petty men who in the shadow of their masters give rein to their insolence. But if death or some other accident of fortune lays low the tree that protects them, their worthlessness becomes instantly apparent, for their qualities have no other value than those their masters and protectors lend them. Virtue and good sense are always one and the same, naked or clothed, alone or accompanied. To be sure, they may suffer in the opinion of the world, but not in the true reality of what they are worth and deserve. And with this let us make an end to our conversation, for the light coming through these cracks shows that day is here, and tonight, if this great boon of speech has not deserted us, it will be my turn to tell you my life.

BERGANZA: So be it, and be sure to come to this same spot.

MASTER GLASS

Two gentlemen students were strolling along the banks of the Tormes River when they came upon a lad of about eleven, dressed like a peasant, asleep under a tree. They ordered a servant to awaken him, and then asked him where he was from and what he was doing sleeping there in that lonely spot. The boy answered that he had forgotten the name of the place he came from, and that he was on his way to the city of Salamanca to seek a master to serve in return for allowing him to study. They asked him if he knew how to read; he answered that he did, and write, too.

"If that is the case," said one of the gentlemen, "it is not for want of memory that you have forgotten the name of your home."

"Be that as it may," replied the boy, "nobody shall know it, or that of my parents, until I can be an honor to it and to them."

"And in what fashion do you hope to bring honor to them?" asked the other gentleman.

"Through my studies," answered the boy, "achieving fame by means of them; for I have heard it said that bishops are made of men."

This answer moved the two gentlemen to take him along with them and make arrangements for him to pursue his studies in the manner customary at that university for servants. The boy said his name was Tomás Rodaja, from which his masters inferred, by reason of the name and his attire, that he was the son of some poor farmer. In a few days they had outfitted him in black, and in a few weeks Tomás gave proof of exceptional ability. He served his masters with such loyalty, zeal, and attention that, while never neglecting his studies, it seemed that he had no thought but to please them. And as good service wins the heart of the master, Tomás Rodaja was soon not the servant, but the companion of his masters. In short, during the eight years he spent with them, he became so renowned at the University, thanks to his fine mind and exceptional gifts, that people of every walk of life esteemed and loved him. His principal study was law; but the field in which he outshone himself was the humanities. His felicitous memory was a marvel, and going, as it did, hand in hand with his keen wits, he was as famous for the one as for the other.

The day came when his masters had completed their studies, and were returning to their home city, which was one of the fairest in Andalusia. They took Tomás with them, and he stayed for a few days; but as he was so eager to return to his studies and to Salamanca (which casts a spell upon the will of all who have savored the graciousness of its life), he asked leave of his masters to depart. Courteous and generous gentlemen that they were, they granted it, and provided for him so well that he could support himself for three years on what they gave him.

He bade them farewell in words that proclaimed his gratitude, and set out from Malaga, which was where the gentlemen lived. As he was descending the Zambra hill, on the road to Antequera, he encountered a gentleman on horseback, splendidly attired for the road, and accompanied by two servants, also mounted. He joined them, learned that their route was the same, and they became travelling companions. They spoke of a number of things, and Tomás soon gave proof of his rare intelligence, and the gentleman of his gallantry and breeding. He told Tomás that he was a captain of infantry in His Majesty's service, and that his ensign was raising a company in the region of Salamanca. He praised the military life, and drew a vivid picture of the beauty of Naples, the gaiety of Palermo, the abundance of Milan, the banquets of Lombardy, the succulent meals served in the inns. He explained, affably and accurately, the meaning of such phrases as *aconcha, Patron; pasa aca, manigoldo, venga la macatela, li polastri, e li maccarroni.*[1] He

---

[1] *Garbled Italian as spoken by the Spanish soldiers, meaning: "Landlord, prepare us a meal, come here, you scoundrel, bring on the* maccatella, *the chicken and the macaroni."*

lauded to the skies the carefree life of the soldier, and the freedom of
Italy; but not a word did he say of the chill of sentry duty, of the
perils of attacks, of the horror of battle, of the hunger of siege, of
the havoc of mines, and other similar matters, which some look upon
as chance episodes in the soldier's profession, when they constitute
the warp and woof of it. In short, he talked so long and so persua-
sively that the good judgment of our Tomás Rodaja began to waver,
and his will began to incline toward that life which is so close to
death.

The captain, who was called Don Diego de Valdivia, was so
pleased at the goodly appearance, intelligence, and self-possession of
Tomás, that he invited him to accompany him to Italy, if only out of
curiosity to see it. He offered him his table and even, if he so desired,
his standard, for his ensign would soon be giving it up. It did not
take much persuasion for Tomás to accept, quickly convincing himself that it would be a fine thing to see Italy and Flanders, and other
different lands and nations, for travel makes a man wise, and this,
at most, would employ only three or four years which, in view of his
youth, were not so many as to prevent his returning to his studies.
And as though everything were to fall out exactly as he wanted it, he
told the captain that he would be glad to go with him to Italy, but
that it would have to be on condition that he would not enlist under
any flag, nor be entered on the rolls as a soldier, so he would not be
obliged to follow his standard. And even though the captain told him
that being entered on the rolls would not matter, since he could get
leave whenever he wanted to, and it had the advantage that he
would receive the same pay and benefits as the other members of
the company, Tomás answered:

"That would go against my principles and against yours, Sir Captain. I prefer to go without any constraint."

"Such a scrupulous conscience," said Don Diego, "better befits
a monk than a soldier. But be it as you please; we are now comrades."

They reached Antequera that night, and in a few days, by
travelling hard, they caught up with the recently recruited com-

pany, which was set for the march to Cartagena. It and four others were billeted in the villages through which they passed on the way. Tomás could thus observe the despotic attitude of the commissioned, the resentment of certain of the captains, the activity of the quartermasters, the paymasters' work and accounts, the complaints of the villagers over billeting, the laundering of the recruits, the quarrels, the impossible demands for more money than was needed ....

Tomás an old ......
those so-going ...... time one is ...
mened by bodbags, ... ked by the sailors;
assaulted by the nid ...... ollows. The heavy seas
and the storm; frighte ...... die too they ran into
the Gulf of Lyons, on ...... un aground on Corsica; ...
the other drove them ...... in France.

Finally, extenuated ...... and weary from lack of sleep,
they reached the south ...... mitial city of Genoa, where they
disembarked in its shel ...... in-made harbor. After a visit to a
church, the captain and ...... comrades made their way to a tavern,
where past amours were forgotten in drinking rejoicings.

There they made the acquaintance of the Tierno and wine's sweetness. About Tierno's full taste, Aspatino's hardness, and the richness of two Greek vintages, Candia and Soma. They came to know the magnificence of the Five Vineyards' produce, the sweetness and delicacy of Lady Guarnacha, the transcending flavor of Chentola. In whose lofty rank stood the lowly Roman wines never venturing to make an appearance. After mine host had recited the pany, which was set for the march to Cartagena. It and four others were billeted in the villages through which they passed on the way. Tomás could thus observe the despotic attitude of the commissioners, the resentment of certain of the captains, the activity of the quarter-masters, the paymasters' work and accounts, the complaints of the villagers, the trading of lodgings, the impudence of the recruits, the quarrels with the hosts, the demands for more luggage than was needed, and finally, the inevitability of doing nearly everything he saw done, deploring it though he did.

Tomás had outfitted himself in gay garb, after the showy fashion of soldiers, laying aside his student attire. Of his many books he kept only two, an *Hours of Our Lady,* and the poems of Garcilaso, unannotated, which he carried in his pockets. They reached Cartagena more quickly than they would have wished, for life in billets is endlessly diverse, and each day offered a new and pleasant experience. There they took ship in four Neapolitan galleys, and this gave Tomás an opportunity to familiarize himself with the curious life of those sea-going houses, where the better part of the time one is tormented by bedbugs, robbed by the galley slaves, irked by the sailors, assaulted by the mice and sickened by the billows. The heavy seas and the storms frightened him, especially the two they ran into in the Gulf of Lyons, one of which sent them aground on Corsica, and the other drove them back to Toulon in France.

Finally, exhausted, wet, gaunt, and weary from lack of sleep, they reached the opulent and beautiful city of Genoa, where they disembarked in its sheltered, man-made harbor. After a visit to a church, the captain and all his comrades made their way to a tavern, where past storms were forgotten in present rejoicing.

There they made the acquaintance of the Treviano wine's smoothness, Monte Frascon's full body, Asperino's headiness, and the richness of two Greek vintages, Candia and Soma. They came to know the magnificence of the Five Vineyards product, the sweetness and delicacy of Lady Guarnacha, the unassuming flavor of Chentola, in whose lofty company the lowly Roman wines never ventured to make an appearance. After mine host had recited the list of so many and such varied wines, he offered to produce for them, not merely as names on a map, but really and truly, such other varieties as Madrigal, Coca, Alaejos, Ciudad Real—more fittingly Imperial than Royal—wherein the god of laughter resides. He gave them their choice of Esquivias, Alanis, Cazalla, Guadalcanal, and Membrilla, without omitting Ribadavia and Descargamaria. In a word, the host named and served them more wines than Bacchus himself could have had in his cellars.

Our good Tomás was impressed by the golden hair of the ladies of Genoa and the courteous and gallant disposition of the men, as well as by the remarkable beauty of the city, whose houses seem set in the cliffs on which it is built like diamonds set in gold.

The next day all the companies bound for the Piedmont disembarked. Tomás, however, did not want to make this journey, but wished to travel overland to Rome and Naples, which he did; he planned to return by way of Venice the Great, and Loretto, to Milan and thence to the Piedmont where Don Diego de Valdivia said he would be, provided they had not been dispatched to Flanders, as was rumored. Two days later Tomás bade his captain farewell, and in five days reached Florence, having first seen Lucca, a small but very well-built city, in which, more than in other parts of Italy, Spaniards are favorably regarded and well-treated. Florence pleased him mightily, by reason of its pleasant location, its cleanliness, its magnificent buildings, its cool-flowing river and its unhurried streets. He spent four days there, and then left for Rome, the queen of cities and mistress of the world. He visited its temples, worshipped its relics, and was moved by its grandeur. Just as by a lion's claws one may judge the size and ferocity of the animal, so he deduced the grandeur of Rome from its shattered marbles, its whole or mutilated statues, its ruined arches and baths, its magnificent porticoes and huge amphitheaters, its famous and sacred river whose banks are always brimful of water and beatified by the countless relics from the bodies of the martyrs buried in them, its bridges which seem to contemplate one another, and its streets, whose very names give them supremacy over all those of other cities: the Via Appia, the Via Flaminia, the

Via Julia, and so many others. Nor was he less impressed by the
division of the hills within the city: the Caelian, the Quirinal, the
Vatican, and the other four, whose names reflect the grandeur and
majesty that was Rome. He remarked the authority of the College of
Cardinals, the majesty of His Holiness, the presence and diversity
of peoples of all nations who have come together there. He con-
templated, reflected on, and put everything in its rightful place. And
after making the stations of the seven churches, confessing himself
with a penitencer, and kissing the Pontiff's foot, he decided to leave
for Naples, loaded down with holy medals and beads. But as it was
the dog days, a bad and dangerous season for all entering or leaving
Rome if they travel by land, he took ship for Naples. To the admiration the sight of Rome had awakened in him, there was now added
that which Naples aroused, a city which, in his opinion and that of
all who have seen it, is the finest in Europe, and even in the whole
world.

From Naples he proceeded to Sicily, where he saw Palermo,
and afterwards Messina. The former impressed him favorably by
reason of its situation and beauty, and in Messina, the harbor and
the island as a whole by its opulence, for it is rightfully called
the granary of Italy. He returned to Naples, thence to Rome, and
from there to Our Lady of Loretto, in whose holy shrine neither
walls nor partitions were visible, for they were covered with crutches,
shrouds, chains, shackles, manacles, locks of hair, wax effigies, paintings, and altarpieces, which bore witness to the innumerable favors
many had received from the hand of God through the intercession
of His divine Mother, whose blessed image He had chosen to honor
and exalt through the performance of a multitude of miracles, in
return for the devotion of those who adorned the walls of her house
with those canopies of offerings. He saw the very room and chamber
wherein was communicated the mightiest and most important em-
bassy ever beheld and not understood by all the heavens, all the
angels, and all those who dwell in the eternal mansions.[2]

---

[2] *The reference is to the miracle-working shrine of the Virgin of Loretto, said
to have been transported by the angels from Nazareth.*

He then took ship in Ancona for Venice, a city which, if Columbus had never come into this world, would have no equal in it. But thanks to Heaven and valiant Hernando Cortés, who conquered mighty Mexico, great Venice was given a rival, so to speak. These two famous cities resemble one another in that their streets are all of water. That of Europe is the cynosure of the Old World; that of America, the wonder of the New. It seemed to him that its wealth was boundless, its government prudent, its location impregnable, its luxury vast, its surroundings pleasant; in a word, that the whole and all its parts deserved the fame it enjoyed throughout the world, which was further augmented by the activity of its famous shipyard, where its galleys and countless other vessels are built.

The delights and pastimes our young adventurer discovered in Venice were almost like those Calypso[3] offered, for they put him in danger of forgetting his original purpose. But after spending a month there, he returned by way of Ferrara, Parma, and Piacenza to Milan, Vulcan's smithy and the envy of France, a city which has the reputation of backing up its words with deeds. Its fame rests upon its own grandeur and that of its cathedral, and the incredible abundance of everything needed for human sustenance.

From there he proceeded to Asti, and arrived the very day before the regiment was to depart for Flanders. He was warmly welcomed by his friend the captain, and in his company and friendship travelled to Flanders, arriving in Antwerp, a city no less wondrous than those he had seen in Italy. He visited Ghent and Brussels, and observed that the whole country was preparing to take up arms and launch a campaign the following summer.

Having now satisfied the desire which led him to see what he had seen, he made up his mind to return to Spain and Salamanca to conclude his studies. As soon as he had so decided, he put the thought into effect, to the deep regret of his comrade-in-arms, who besought him, as they took leave of one another, to send him word of his health, safe arrival, and good fortune. Tomás promised to do all

---

[3] *Calypso. In Greek mythology a nymph who entertained Ulysses for seven years on his homeward voyage from Troy.*

this, and returned to Spain by way of France, without being able to visit Paris which was up in arms at the time. In due course he reached Salamanca, where he was warmly received by his friends, and with the help they had given him, he went on with his studies until he received his Master's degree in Law.

It so happened that at this time a lady arrived in that city, a woman versed in wiles and intrigue. All the birds of the city flocked to her call and snare, and not a student but visited her. Having been told that the lady claimed she had been in Italy and Flanders, Tomás, to see if he knew her, also called upon her, and as a result of the visit and interview, the lady fell in love with him. But he, who did not reciprocate her feeling, was reluctant to go to her house except when the others obliged him to. Finally she opened her heart to him, and offered him her fortune; but as he was more interested in his books than in other diversions, in no wise did he respond to her desires. When the lady saw herself scorned and, as it seemed to her, despised, realizing that by ordinary means she would not be able to level the fortress of Tomás's resolution, she made up her mind to employ other methods which she believed would be more effective and conducive to the fulfillment of her desires. And so, having sought the advice of a Moorish woman, she gave Tomás a so-called love potion in a Toledan quince, thinking thus to bend his will to love her, as though there were in the world herbs, enchantments, or spells that can sway a person's free will. Those who administer such love potions are rightly called envenomers, for what they do is to administer poison to their victims, as experience has repeatedly shown.

The unfortunate Tomás had no more than eaten the quince than he began to shiver from head to foot as though taken with an epileptic seizure. He did not regain his senses for hours, and when he did, he was as though stupefied; with a thickened, stammering tongue he managed to say that a quince he had eaten had been the death of him, and he told who it was that had given it to him. The authorities, when they heard of it, went to look for the malefactress, but she, seeing the turn things had taken, had gone to ground and was never seen again.

Tomás lay in bed for six months, during which time he withered away until he was, as the saying goes, nothing but skin and bones, and his wits seemed deranged. Although everything possible was done for him, he recovered only his bodily health, but not that of his mind. He became physically well, but afflicted with the strangest madness ever seen until then. The poor wretch was under the delusion that he was made of glass, and consequently when anyone approached him, he would begin screaming and begging and imploring them with seemingly sensible words and explanations not to come near him, for they would break him, as he was not like other men but all of glass, from his head to his feet.

To disabuse him of this strange notion, many, heedless of his shouts and pleas, rushed up to him and embraced him, pointing out to him that he had not been shattered. But all they got for their pains was that the poor wretch threw himself to the floor, screaming wildly, after which he fell into a swoon from which he did not recover for hours, and when he did it was to renew his prayers and supplications not to touch him again. He begged them to talk to him from a distance, and to ask him whatever they liked, for he would answer them with even clearer understanding, as he was now a man of glass and not of flesh, for glass, being a thin and delicate substance, permits the spirit to operate through it more quickly and efficiently than through the sluggish, earthbound body.

Some wished to test whether what he said was true, and so they put many and difficult questions to him, to which he replied at once with proof of the keenest mind. The most learned members of the University and the professors of Medicine and Philosophy were astonished that an individual possessed of such a rare madness as to believe that he was made of glass, should be endowed with such great intelligence as to be able to answer every question correctly and with insight.

Tomás asked them to give him some kind of covering with which to protect the brittle vessel of his body, lest in donning a tight garment he might break it. They provided him with a brown suit and a loose shirt, which he put on with great care, fastening it with a cotton rope. He refused shoes of any kind. And as for his food, he told them that, without coming near him, they should hang on the end of a stick a little straw basket and put into it such fruits as were in season. He refused all meat or fish, and drank only from a spring or stream, taking up the water in his hands. When he walked about the streets he kept to the middle of them, looking up at the roofs, fearful that some tile might fall on him and shatter him. In the summertime he slept in the open fields, and in winter he took lodgings at some inn where he buried himself up to the neck in the hay-mow, saying that was the most fitting and safest bed for glass men. When it thundered he shook like a leaf, and went out in the fields and did not return to town until the storm was over.

His friends kept him confined for a long time; but observing that he was getting worse, they decided to fall in with what he wanted, which was to be set free. This they did, and he went about the city, arousing the wonder and pity of all who knew him.

The boys quickly surrounded him, but he kept them at a distance with his staff, and begged to talk to him from afar lest he break, for as he was made of glass, he was very delicate and fragile. Boys, who are the most mischievous beings in the world, despite his pleas and shouts, would throw rags at him, and even stones, to see if he was made of glass as he said. But he screamed so and became so upset that the grownups came to scold and punish the children so they would not pelt him. One day when they had annoyed him greatly he turned on them, saying:

"What do you want of me, you knaves, tiresome as flies, dirty as bedbugs, shameless as fleas. Am I perhaps Monte Testaccio[4] of Rome for you to be throwing all these tiles and potsherds at me?"

For the sake of hearing him rail at them and upbraid them, a crowd of these young ones always followed him, and finally they came to prefer listening to him to pelting him.

---

[4] *Monte Testaccio was the dumping place for broken crockery in Rome.*

On one occasion, as he was going through the old clothes market of Salamanca, a woman who sold clothing said to him:

"Upon my soul, Master, I grieve for your misfortune, but what can I do, inasmuch as I cannot weep?"

Turning to her, he answered gravely: "Daughters of Jerusalem, do not weep for me but weep for yourselves and for your children." [5]

The clothes seller's husband understood the malice behind the words and said to him:

"Master Glass"—for this was the name Tomás had given himself—"you are more of a scoundrel than a madman."

"It matters not a whit to me," he replied, "provided I am not taken for a fool."

One day as he happened to go by the brothel and common inn, he saw many of its inmates standing at the door, and he said to them that they were baggages of Satan's army, lodged in Hell's own inn.

Someone asked him on one occasion what advice or comfort he could give a friend of his who was greatly saddened because his wife had gone off with another man. His answer was:

"Tell him to give thanks to God for letting a rival remove an enemy from his house."

"Then he is not to try to find her?" asked the other.

"He is not even to think of it," answered Glass, "for if he finds her, he will find an everlasting and true witness to his dishonor."

"If that is the case," the man went on, "what should I do to live at peace with my wife?"

"Give her what she needs, let her order everyone in the house about, but never let her rule you."

A boy said to him: "Master Glass, I would like to get away from my father, for he beats me a great deal."

To which the answer was: "Remember, child, that lashes given

---

[5] Luke, XXIII:28. *"Daughters of Jerusalem . . . weep for yourselves and for your children."* The insinuation is that the woman's husband was not the father of her children.

by parents are an honor, and those of the executioner, a disgrace."

Once as he stood at the door of a church he saw a husbandman go in, one of those who continually call attention to the fact that they are Old Christians. Behind him came one who was not in such good repute as the first, and Glass began to call out to the first: "Sunday, wait until Saturday has passed." [6]

Of schoolmasters he said they were fortunate in that their dealings were always with the angels, and that there would be no bounds to their happiness if the little angels did not turn out to be snotnoses. Someone asked him what he thought of procuresses, and he said the real ones were not those at a distance but the neighbor women.

Word of his madness and his answers and sayings spread throughout Castile, and coming to the attention of a prince or nobleman at Court, he wanted to see him, and commissioned a friend of his who was in Salamanca to send Glass to him. This gentleman, meeting Master Glass one day, said to him:

"I beg to inform you, Master Glass, that an important person at Court would like to see you, and has sent for you."

His answer was: "Your Excellency will be good enough to make my excuses, for I am not suited to a palace as I have principles and do not know how to flatter."

Nevertheless, the gentleman did send him to the Court, and to achieve his purpose he hit upon the following device: they put him in a straw pannier, of the sort used to carry glass, balancing the weight with stones, and with various glass objects stowed in the straw to make him think that it was as such that he was being transported. They reached Valladolid and entered the city by night, unpacking him in the house of the gentleman who had sent for him, who received him very warmly, saying:

"A right good welcome to you, Master Glass. What kind of a trip did you have? How is your health?"

To which he replied: "No road is bad which comes to an end,

---

[6] *The implication is that the second man was a New Christian, that is to say, of Jewish origin.*

except it be that which leads to the gallows. As for my health, it is neutral, for my pulse is at war with my brain."

The next day, seeing many falcons and other fowling birds on perches, he said that falconry was a sport suited to princes and great lords; but that they should bear in mind that the cost exceeded the pleasure by more than two thousand per cent. Hunting hares, he added, was very good sport, especially if done with borrowed hounds.

The gentleman was greatly entertained by his madness, and let him stroll about the city under the care and protection of a man who watched to see that the boys did him no harm. Within six days he was known to them and to all the Court, and at every step, in any street or on any corner, he answered all questions addressed to him. Once he was asked by a student if he was a poet, as it seemed to him that he had wits for everything. His answer was:

"So far I have been neither so foolish nor so fortunate."

"I don't understand what you mean by foolish and fortunate," said the student.

"I have not been so foolish as to become a bad poet," replied Glass, "nor so fortunate as to have the merits of a good one."

Another student asked him his opinion of poets. He answered that with regard to the art of poetry, it was very high; but of the poets themselves, very low. They asked him why he said this. He replied that of the infinite number of poets that existed, so few were good that you could count them on the fingers of one hand. And so, if there were no poets, how could he esteem them? But he said that he admired and reverenced the art of poetry, because it embraced all the other arts, making use of them all, adorning itself with all, refining and bringing out its own wonderful creations which fill the world with delight, benefit, and awe.

"I know full well," he went on, "how highly a good poet should be prized, for I recall those verses of Ovid which run:

> *Cura ducum fuerunt olim Regumque poetae:*
> *Praemiaque antiqui magna tulere chori.*

Sanctaque majestas, et erat venerabile nomen[7]
Vatibus: et largae saepe dabantur opes.

Nor can I forget the high worth of poets whom Plato called the interpreters of the gods, and of whom Ovid says:

Est Deus in nobis, agitante calescimus illo.

And also:

At sacri vates, et Divum cura vocamur.

This applies to the good poets; as for the bad ones, the rhymsters, what is there to say of them except that they are the stupidity and arrogance of the world personified?"

"It is a sight to see," he went on, "one of these poets when he gets ready to recite a sonnet to others of his own sort, the fanfare with which he goes about it saying: 'Your Excellencies will deign to listen to a little sonnet I composed last night for a certain occasion. It seems to me that, although it is of no value, it is rather pretty.' And with this he purses up his lips, raises his eyebrows, and fumbles around in his pocket, finally bringing out of a mass of dirty, dog-eared scraps of paper containing a thousand more sonnets the one he wishes to recite, and then proceeds to recite it in a honeyed, affected voice. And if his audience, out of malice or ignorance, fails to praise him, he says: 'Either Your Excellencies have not understood the sonnet, or I have not done it justice, so I think I should recite it again, and Your Excellencies should pay closer attention, for verily, verily the sonnet deserves it.' And he recites it all over again with new gestures and new pauses.

"And to hear them criticizing one another! And the yapping of the young whelps at the gray and grave mastiffs! And the back-

---

[7] *The three quotations are from Ovid's Ars amandi, and mean:*

Poets were once the concern of kings and leaders, and the choruses of old won for them large prizes; holy was the respect shown to bards and venerated their name, and great wealth was often heaped on them.

There is a god in us; he stirs and we grow warm.

And yet we speak of poets as divine, the darlings of the gods.

biting at those illustrious and gifted cultivators of the art in whom the true light of poetry shines out, and who, following it as a solace and surcease from their many and weighty occupations, reveal the divine breath of their inspiration and the loftiness of their concepts, heedless of the spite and cavilling of the ignorant, who pass judgment on matters of which they know nothing, hate what they do not understand, and would have their foolishness reverenced and their ignorance enthroned."

On another occasion they asked him why it was that most poets were poor. He answered that it was by choice, for it lay in their power to be rich, if only they knew how to turn to advantage the ever-present opportunities their ladies afforded them. For all these were fabulously wealthy, their hair being of gold, their brows of burnished silver, their eyes emeralds, their teeth ivory, their lips coral, their throats alabaster, and they wept liquid pearls. The very ground they trod, however hard and barren, instantly brought forth jazmine and roses; their breath was pure amber, musk, and civet, and all these things represented great wealth.

These, and still others, were the judgments he passed on bad poets; he always spoke well of the good ones, praising them to the skies.

One day he saw on the sidewalk of San Francisco some botchily painted figures, and remarked that good painters imitate nature, while bad ones regurgitate it. One day he made his way with all precaution, lest he break, into a bookseller's shop, and said to the owner: "This trade would be much to my liking, if it were not for one drawback."

When the bookseller asked him what this was, he answered: "The airs you put on when you buy the rights to a book, and the tricks you play on the author if he has it printed at his own expense, for instead of fifteen hundred, you print three thousand, and the author thinks it is his copies that are being sold, when you are really selling your own."

That same day six who were to be punished by flogging happened to pass through the square, and the town-crier was calling

out: "The first for robbery . . ." At this Master Glass called out to
those in front of him: "Get out of the way, brothers, he may
include one of you."

When the crier called out: "And the hind one . . ." he said:
"That must be the one who goes bail for the young lads." A boy
said to him: "Brother Glass, tomorrow they are going to flog a
procuress," to which he replied: "If you said they were going to
flog a panderer, I'd think you meant they were going to flog a
carriage."

In the crowd was one of those who bear sedan chairs, and he
asked:

"Master, have you nothing to say about us?"

"No," replied Glass, "except that each of you knows more sins
than a father confessor, but with this difference: that the confessor
knows them and keeps them to himself, while you publish them
in the taverns."

A muleteer overheard this, for all sorts of people were constantly listening to him, and said:

"Sir Retort, there is little or nothing you could say about us
for we are decent people, and necessary members of society."

Glass replied: "The honor of the master reveals that of the
servant; therefore, look on whom you serve, and you will see how
honorable you are. You serve the lowest scum on the face of the
earth. Once, before I turned to glass, I made a trip on a hired mule,
and I counted a hundred and twenty-one defects in it, all major
ones and enemies of the human race. Not a muleteer but has a
streak of the ruffian in him, a touch of a thief, and a pinch of a
cheat; if their masters (as they call those who ride their mules) are
simple-witted, they play more tricks on them than have been seen
in this city in the past twenty years; if they are foreigners, they rob
them blind; if they are students, they curse them; if members of the
clergy, they hurl blasphemies at them; if soldiers, they tremble before
them.

"The lot of you, carters, sailors, and muleteers have your own
mode of life, and a strange one it is. The carter spends most of his

life within an area of a yard and a half, for it can't be much more than that from the yoke of the mules to the seat of his cart; half the time he is singing, and the other half, cursing, or yelling 'Keep behind, there.' And if they have to lift a wheel out of a rut, they make more use of two oaths than of three mules.

"Sailors are a pagan, uncouth folk who know no other language than that of their ship, hard-working in fair weather, lazy in foul. When a tempest comes, many give orders and few obey; their God is their sea chest and mess-room; their amusement is watching the seasick passengers. Muleteers are men who have divorced themselves from sheets and have married packsaddles. They are so industrious and in such a hurry that they would sell their souls rather than lose a day's work. Their music is the clop-clop of hoofs; their sauce, hunger; their matins, getting up to feed their beasts, and their masses, going to none."

He was standing at the door of an apothecary's as he said this, and turning to the owner, he remarked:

"Yours, Sir, is a wholesome calling, if you were not such an enemy of your lamps."

"How am I an enemy of my lamps?" inquired the apothecary.

"Because," answered Glass, "whenever you run short of any oil, you supply it from the nearest lamp. And this occupation has still another drawback to it that is enough to ruin the reputation of the best doctor in the world."

When asked what this was, he answered that there were apothecaries who, rather than admit that they did not have in stock the ingredients the doctor had prescribed, substituted others which in their opinion possessed the same virtues and properties. As a result, the badly compounded medicine had the opposite effect from that which it would have had if it had been prepared as ordered.

At this point someone asked him what he thought of doctors, and he answered: "Honour the physician for the need thou hast of him: for the Most High hath created him.

For all healing is from God, and he shall receive honour of the king.

The skill of the physician shall lift up his head, and in the sight of great men he shall be praised.

The Most High hath created medicines out of the earth, and a wise man will not abhor them.[8]

"This is what Ecclesiasticus has to say about medicine and good doctors, and exactly the opposite could be said of the bad ones, for there is nobody more dangerous to the commonwealth than they. The judge can pervert or delay justice; the lawyer may, for his own benefit, defend an unjust cause; the merchant may gobble up our property; in a word, anybody with whom we must have dealings may do us a hurt; but to take our lives without fear of punishment, none of them. Only doctors can and do kill us without let or hindrance or unsheathing any sword except a prescription. And their crime is never discovered, for the ground covers it up. I remember that when I was a man of flesh and not of glass, as I now am, a patient dismissed one of those doctors such as I have just described, and called in another. Four days later the first physician happened by the shop of the apothecary who filled the other doctor's prescriptions, and asked him how his former patient was getting along, and whether the other doctor had prescribed any purge. The apothecary answered that he had there a prescription for a purge which the patient was to take the next day. He asked to see it and noticed that at the end of it the words "Sumat diluculo'[9] were written. 'All the ingredients of this purge seem good to me,' he said, 'with the exception of this *diluculo,* which contains too much moisture.' "

Because of this and other things he had to say of all professions, he was always surrounded by people who, though they did him no harm, gave him no peace. He would not, however, have been able to protect himself from the boys if his attendant had not done so for him.

Someone asked him what he should do to keep from envying

---

[8] Ecclesiasticus, XXXVIII: 1-4.
[9] *"Take upon rising."*

anyone, and he answered: "Sleep; for while you are asleep you will be the equal of the one you envy."

Another asked him what he should do to secure a commission he had been seeking for two years. And he told him: "Set out on horseback and keep an eye on the person bearing the commission, and go with him until he leave the city, and that way you will come out with what you want."

Once he chanced to pass a judge of assize who was on his way to hear a criminal case. He had a large escort, among whom there were two bailiffs. Glass inquired who he was, and when informed, he said:

"I would wager that that judge is carrying vipers in his bosom, pistols at his belt, and lightning bolts in his hands to destroy everything that falls under his jurisdiction. I recall a friend of mine who in a case that came up before him pronounced so severe a sentence that it was out of all proportion to the guilt of the defendant. When I asked him why he had administered so cruel a sentence and done such a manifest injustice, he told me that he intended to grant an appeal and thus leave the way open for the gentlemen of the Council to show their mercy, moderating his harsh sentence and imposing one proportionate to the offense. I told him it would have been better if he had done this in the first place, thus sparing them the trouble, and in this way being known as an upright and wise judge."

In the circle of people who, as has been said, were always standing about listening to him, there was an acquaintance of his wearing the habit of a lawyer, who called himself Master of Laws. Glass, knowing that he did not even hold a Bachelor's degree, said to him:

"Have a care, my friend, with that title of yours, or the Redemptorist Fathers may seize it as property that has no owner."

The friend answered: "Let us be courteous to one another, Master Glass, for you know I am a man of lofty and profound learning."

"I am well aware," answered Glass, "that you are a very Tantalus in this matter of learning, for it always eludes you on high, and you never catch up with it in its depths."

Once, standing near a tailor's shop, he saw the tailor sitting idle, and said to him:

"Master Tailor, you are surely on the road to salvation."

"What makes you say that?" asked the tailor.

"Why do I say it?" replied Glass. "Because as you have nothing to do, you have no occasion to lie." And he went on: "God help the tailor who does not lie and sew on holidays! It is a strange thing that among those of this profession hardly one can be found who sews a garment rightly, and so many who do it wrongly."

Of shoemakers he said they never, in their opinion, turned out a shoe that did not fit; if the wearer found it too tight, they told him that was the way it should be, that gentlemen of fashion always wore them tight, and that after wearing them for a couple of hours they would be as loose as sandals. If the wearer found them too loose, they told him they were better that way, in case of gout.

A sharp young fellow who worked in a provincial notary's office, plied him with questions and inquiries, and brought him news of all that went on in the city, because Master Glass held forth on everything and had an answer to everything. The clerk once said to him:

"Master Glass, last night a money changer who had been condemned to the gallows died in prison."

"He did well to hasten his death before needing the services of the executioner."

A group of Genoese were standing on the sidewalk of San Francisco, and as he went by one of them called out to him: "Come over here, Master Glass, and tell us a story."

"Not I," he answered, "or you'll hand me the bill for it in Genoa."

Once he encountered the wife of a shopkeeper out walking with her daughter who was very ugly, but all bedecked with gewgaws and pearls, and he said to the mother: "That's a good idea, paving her with stones, for it makes the walking easier."

As for pastry cooks, he said they played the game of double or nothing without running any risk, for they had raised the price of their wares from two to four, from four to eight, from eight to half a *real* with their own approval and blessing.

He had nothing but scorn for the puppet masters, saying they were mere vagabonds who treated sacred things with indecency, for in their shows they hold devoutness up to laughter. They often dumped into a sack all or most of the figures of the Old and New Testament, and then sat upon them while they ate and drank in wine-cellars and taverns. In a word, he said, it was a source of wonder to him that those vested with the authority to do so did not condemn them to perpetual silence in their shows or banish them from the kingdom.

One day as he was out walking he saw an actor dressed up as a prince, and he said as he looked at him:

"I can recall seeing this fellow appear in the theater, his face all befloured, and wearing a sheepskin coat turned inside out; nevertheless, at every step, when off the boards, he swears by his faith as a gentleman."

"Perhaps he is one," a bystander remarked, "for there are many actors who are well-born and gentlemen."

"That is as may be," answered Glass, "but what the stage least needs is persons of gentle birth. Actors, yes, who bear themselves well and are nimble-tongued. I may add that they earn their bread by gruelling work, memorizing all the time, knocking around from pillar to post like gipsies, studying how to please the public, for their well-being depends on others' pleasure. Besides, in their calling they deceive nobody, for their merchandise is always on display where all may see and judge it. The labors of the managers are unbelievable, and their trials are many, for they must earn a lot if they are not to find themselves so in debt at the end of the year that they have to declare themselves in bankruptcy. Yet, withal, they are necessary to the state, like flower gardens, shady walks, pleasant parks, and all things that afford decent diversion."

He said that in the opinion of a friend of his he who dances attendance on an actress has many mistresses in one, for she is alternately a queen, a nymph, a goddess, a scullery maid, a shepherdess, and at times he even finds himself serving a page or lackey, for all these and more roles are impersonated by an actress.

Somebody once asked him who had been the happiest man in the world. He replied: *"Nemo; for Nemo novit patrem; Nemo sine crimine vivit, Nemo sua sorte contentus; Nemo ascendit in coelum."* [10] Of fencers he said that they were masters of an art or skill which, when they needed it, they did not know how to use, and that there was something presumptuous in their trying to reduce to mathematical formulas, which are constants, the movements and angry thoughts of their adversaries.

He was particularly irked by those who dyed their beards. Once two men were quarrelling in his hearing, and one of them, a Portuguese, said to the Spaniard, grabbing his own beard, which was heavily dyed: "By this beard I wear on my face . . ." Whereupon Glass spoke up: "Careful, sir, don't say wear but dye." Another had a streaked, multicolored beard, the result of using poor dye, and Glass told him it looked like a dappled dung heap. To another whose beard was part white and part black because he had carelessly let the roots grow out, he said he should take care not to argue or quarrel with anyone for he ran the risk of being told that he lied in half his beard.

Once he told a story about a clever, intelligent young woman, who, to please her parents, agreed to marry a grizzled old gaffer. The night before the wedding he went, not down to the River Jordan, as the saying goes, but to the bottle of acid and silver nitrate with which he so transformed his beard that it went to bed white as the driven snow and arose as black as tar. When the time for the marriage ceremony came the girl demanded of her parents that

---

[10] *Nemo.* Latin for *"no one." The passages are of Biblical and classical origin, whose meaning is changed by the substitution of the word "Nemo": "Nemo knoweth the Father; Nemo lives without offending; Nemo is content with his lot; Nemo hath ascended to Heaven."*

they wed her to the husband they had presented to her, and to none other. They told her she was looking upon the very one they had presented to her and betrothed her to. She said this was not true, and brought witnesses to bear her out that the one her parents had chosen for her was an elderly, white-haired man, and as this one did not answer that description, he could not be the same one, and she would not be hoaxed. She stuck to her word, the dyed groom was much chagrined, and the marriage was called off.

Glass had the same quarrel with duennas as with those who tried to fight off time, and he never stopped talking about their affected ways, their headdresses like shrouds, their pretensions, their finickiness, and their penny-pinching. He could not bear their squeamishness, their vapors, their overnice manner of talking, with more hemmings than their coifs—in a word, their uselessness and nonsense.

"How does it happen, Master Glass, that I have heard you censure so many professions," someone once asked him, "and yet you have never said anything about notaries, when there is so much to be said?"

"Even though made of glass," he answered, "I am not so frail as to let myself be swept along by the general trend which most of the time is mistaken. It seems to me that the grammar of gossips, like the *la, la, la* of singers, are the notaries. For just as one cannot go on to the other arts except through the gate of Grammar, and just as the singer must hum before he sings, so the slanderers begin to display the viciousness of their tongues by speaking ill of the notaries and bailiffs and other ministers of justice, when the fact of the matter is that without notaries Truth would go about the world slinking through the dark, ashamed and abused. As Ecclesiasticus says: The prosperity of man is in the hand of God, and upon the person of the scribe He shall lay His honour.[11]

"The notary is a public servant, and without him the judge could not carry out his duties properly. Notaries must be freemen and not slaves, nor the sons of slaves, of legitimate birth, not bas-

---

[11] Ecclesiasticus, X:5.

tards, nor of base stock. They swear an oath of secrecy, fidelity, and that they will draw up no usurious contract; that neither friendship nor enmity, profit or loss will move them to carry out their obligations contrary to a good and Christian conscience. Now, if this calling demands so many good qualities, what grounds are there for thinking that among the more than twenty thousand notaries to be found in Spain, the devil should reap his harvest as though they were vines in his vineyard? I refuse to believe it, nor is it fair that anyone should, for, to sum it up, they are the most necessary members of a well-governed state, and if they have had too many rights, they have also done too many wrongs, and between these two extremes a happy medium could be reached which would make them mind their p's and q's."

Of constables he said that it was not to be wondered at that they had enemies in view of the fact that their occupation was either to arrest people or impound their property, or keep them under house detention and eat at their expense. He accused lawyers and solicitors of being careless and ignorant, comparing them to doctors who, whether they kill or cure, collect their fee, as do the lawyers and solicitors whether they win or lose a case.

Somebody once asked him which was the best land, and he answered: "The earliest yielding and the most fertile." The other interrupted:

"That isn't what I want to know, but which is the better place, Valladolid or Madrid."

"For the extremes, Madrid; for the intermediate, Valladolid," replied Glass.

"I don't understand you," said his interlocutor.

"In Madrid, heaven and earth; in Valladolid, the in-between floors."

Glass heard a man tell a friend that no sooner had he come to Valladolid than his wife took very sick because the soil did not agree with her.

"Better if it had swallowed her up, if she happens to be jealous."

Of musicians and foot messengers he said that their hopes and possibilities were limited, for the best the latter could hope for was to become mounted couriers, and the former, musicians to His Majesty. Of the ladies known as courtesans, he said they were more courtly than sane.

He was in church one day when they brought in an old man to be buried, a baby to be baptized, and a woman to receive the bridal veil, all at the same time. He remarked that a church is like a field of battle where the old meet their end, the young conquer, and the women triumph.

A wasp once stung him on the neck, and he was afraid to shake it off for fear he might break, but, nevertheless, he complained. Someone asked him how he could feel the sting if his body was of glass. And he replied that the wasp must be a slanderer, and that the tongues and stings of slanderers could lay low not only bodies of glass, but of bronze.

A fat friar chanced to pass near him, and one of his listeners said: "That friar is so wasted he can hardly walk."

Glass took umbrage at this, and answered: "Let no one forget what the Holy Spirit said: Touch ye not my anointed." His anger mounting, he went on to say that if they gave the matter thought they would see that of the many saints canonized during recent years and raised to the ranks of the blessed, none had been named Captain Don So-and-So, or Secretary Don What-You-May-Call-Him, or the Count, Marquess, or Duke of Such-and-Such, but Brother Diego, Brother Jacinto, Brother Raimundo, all of them friars and members of religious orders. For the communities of the religious are the Aranjuezes[12] of Heaven, whose fruits are served at God's board. He said the tongues of the malicious were like the eagle's plumage which obscures and diminishes that of all the other birds that come near it.

With regard to gamblers and gambling-house keepers he said notable things, to the effect that they are shameless cheats, for while

---

[12] *Aranjuez was one of the royal country places noted for the abundance and quality of its fruits.*

taking a share of the gains of the player who went on risking stakes, they wanted him to lose and the deck go to his adversary, so they could go on collecting their part. He praised the patience of a certain gambler who had been playing all one night and losing; although he was a man of hot temper, he did not once open his mouth, and underwent the martyrdom of a Barrabas just so his opponent would not get up from the table. He also praised the uprightness of the decent owners of gambling houses who under no circumstance would allow other games to be played in their establishment than ombre and piquet. In this way, slowly but surely, without fear of becoming known as sharpers, their takings at the end of the month were more than in places where games involving higher stakes were permitted.

In a word, the things he said were such that if it had not been for his shrieks when anyone touched or came near him, the garments he wore, the paucity of his eating, the way he drank, his refusal to sleep anywhere except under the open sky in summer, and in the hay-mows in winter, as has been said, all of which were incontrovertible proof of his madness, nobody would have thought he was not one of the sanest persons in the whole world.

This derangement of his lasted for two years or a little longer, until a monk of the order of St. Jerome, who had great gifts and skill in making the deaf hear, and even talk after a fashion, and in restoring the mad to their senses, took it upon himself, out of the kindness of his heart, to cure Glass. He treated him and cured him, restoring him to his former wits and reason. And when he saw that he was cured, he dressed him in lawyer's attire, and made him return to Court, where, giving as abundant proof of wisdom as he had formerly given of madness, he was able to practise his profession and become famous at it. He called himself Master Rueda, instead of Rodaja, returned to the Court, and no sooner had he entered the city than he was recognized by the children. But as they saw him in such different garb, they did not venture to shout at him or ask him questions; but they followed him, and said to one another:

"Isn't this that crazy Master Glass? I'll bet it is. He's recovered his wits. But he may be just as crazy when well dressed as when poorly dressed. Let's ask him something, and clear the matter up."

The Master of Laws heard all this and said nothing. He was more confused and embarrassed now than when he was mad.

The word spread from the children to the grownups, and before the Master reached Council Square, a crowd of more than two hundred persons of every sort was following him. With this escort, more numerous than that of a professor, he reached the square, where he was soon surrounded by all who were there.

Seeing the throng that had gathered about him, he lifted up his voice and said:

"Gentlemen, I am Master Glass, but not the one I used to be; now I am Master Rueda. Events and misfortunes which occur in the world with Heaven's consent deprived me of my reason which by God's mercy has been restored to me. I am a graduate in law from the University of Salamanca, where I studied in spite of poverty, and won second highest honors, from which you may infer that my abilities rather than any favor won me the degree I hold. I have come to this great sea which is the Court to take soundings and navigate as best I can. But if you stand in my way, I shall have come to navigate to my death. In God's name, do not turn your following of me into persecution, nor make it impossible for me to gain, now that I am sane, that which was mine when mad, namely, my livelihood. What you formerly asked me in public places, ask me now in my house, and you will see that the good answers I gave, so they say, on the spur of the moment, will be better if I can give thought to them."

They all listened to him, and some of them went away. He returned to his lodgings with less of an escort than when he set out.

But the next day when he went out the same thing happened. Again he pleaded with them, but to no avail. He was losing much and earning nothing. Seeing himself threatened with starvation, he made up his mind to leave the Court and return to Flanders where he hoped to use the strength of his arm, inasmuch as he could make no headway with that of his wits. And suiting his action to the thought, he said, as he turned his back on the Court: ["Oh, Court, which crowns the hopes of the audacious and blights those of the modest and upright, which fills the cup of shameless charlatans to overflowing, and starves the modest man of worth."]

With these words he departed for Flanders, where the immortal fame he had begun to win in the field of letters he finally achieved on the field of battle, in the company of his good friend [Captain Valdivia,] leaving behind him at his death the name of a wise and brave soldier.

THE GIPSY MAID

It would seem that gipsies, men and women alike, came into the world for the sole purpose of thieving. They are born of thieving parents, are reared among thieves, study to be thieves, and end up as polished and perfect thieves, in whom the impulse to steal and stealing are one and the same thing, extinguished only by death. One of this race, an old woman, a past-mistress of the art of thievery, raised a girl she said was her granddaughter, upon whom she bestowed the name of "Preciosa," and to whom she taught all her gipsy tricks, deceits, and light-fingered arts. This Preciosa turned out to be the most unique dancer to be found in all gipsydom, and the most beautiful and circumspect not only among the gipsies, but among all the beautiful and circumspect women in fame's annals. Neither sun nor wind, nor all the inclemencies of the heavens, to which gipsies are exposed more than others, could darken her face or tan her hands; and, what is even stranger, for all her rough upbringing, she seemed to have been born with finer qualities than a gipsy girl, for she was most courteous and well-spoken. Yet, withal, she was sprightly of manner, but in no wise over-bold; on the contrary, she was so virtuous that in her presence, no gipsy, matron or maid, ventured to sing lewd songs or say an unseemly word. The grandmother realized the treasure she had in such a granddaughter, and so the old eagle made up her mind to put her eaglet to the wing and teach her to live by her talons.

Preciosa proved to be a treasure house of carols, ballads, *seguidillas,* sarabands, and other types of poetry, especially ballads, which she sang with singular charm. Her crafty grandmother perceived that these airs and graces, in one so young and beautiful as her granddaughter, would be powerful attractions and means of augmenting her hoard, so she sought out and secured these materials in every way she could. There were even poets who gave them to her; for there are poets who make deals with gipsies and sell them their works, just as there are those whose customers are blind street singers for whom they invent miracles and receive a share of their earnings. Everything is to be found in the world, and this business of hunger drives wits to turn out extraordinary things.

Preciosa grew up in different regions of Castile, and when she had reached the age of fifteen her supposed grandmother brought her back to the Court and to her old camp, which is where the gipsies normally assemble, in the meadows of Saint Barbara, hoping to sell her wares in the Court, where all things are bought and sold. Preciosa made her first entry into Madrid on the day of Saint Anne, patroness and advocate of the city, with a dance in which eight gipsies took part, four old women and four girls, along with a male gipsy, a great dancer, who led them. Even though all the women went clean and well-attired, the comeliness of Preciosa's appearance was such that little by little she captivated the eyes of all who beheld her. Amidst the sound of tambourine and castanets and the steps of the dance, there rose a murmur extolling the beauty and grace of the gipsy maid, and the boys came running to see her, and the men to gaze upon her. But when they heard her sing, for it was a dance accompanied by song, that did it! Then her fame really grew, and the authorities of the celebration, by unanimous decision, awarded her the prize as the best dancer; and when they came to perform it in the Church of The Blessed Mary before the image of Saint Anne, after all had danced Preciosa took up a tambourine, to the sound of which, whirling in swift, light turns, she sang the following ballad:

> Most beautiful of trees,
> Years late in bearing fruit
> Which might have covered
> You with mourning,

And fulfill the desires
Pure of your spouse,
Doubting the hopes
Of which he was unsure;

From which delay
Was born that sorrow
Which ejected from the Temple
The most just of men.

Holy, barren land
Which finally bore
That fullness of abundance
Which nourishes the world;

Productive mint,
In which was cast the die
Which gave God the form
He assumed as man.

Mother of a daughter
To whom God chose to show
Grandeur beyond the grasp
Of human mind.

In yourself and through her,
You, Anne, are the refuge
To which our trials turn
In search of surcease.

In a sense you hold,
I do not doubt,
Pious and just sway
Over your Grandson.

Were you the chatelaine
Of the mightiest castle,

A thousand kinfolk
Would share it with you.

What a daughter, what a grandson,
What a son-in-law! At once,
Were the cause a just one,
Victory would be yours.

But being all humility,
You were the school
At which your Daughter
Learned her humble lessons.

And now at her side,
Closest placed to God,
You enjoy the greatness
I barely devise.

Preciosa's song filled all who heard her with admiration. Some cried: "God bless the girl!" Others: "What a pity the lass is a gipsy. In truth she might be the worthy daughter of some great gentleman." Others of coarser fiber said: "Wait till the wench grows and learns the tricks of the trade! A fine drag net is being woven in her to catch hearts." Another, kindlier, coarser, and more rustic, watching the grace with which she danced, called out: "Go it, girl, go it! Come, love, and tread the dust so lightly." To which she answered, without interrupting her dance: "I will tread it so lightly-oh."

When the feast of St. Anne's Eve was over, Preciosa was left a little weary, but so renowned for her beauty, her wit, her discretion, and her dancing that she was the talk of the Court. A fortnight later she returned to Madrid with three other girls, with tambourines and a new dance, all ready with ballads and gay ditties, but all of them decent, for Preciosa would not permit those who kept her company to sing bold songs, nor did she ever sing them, which many noted and esteemed her for. Never did the old woman leave her side, a veritable Argus, fearful lest someone should steal her and carry her away. They began their dance in the shade

in Toledo Street, and those who were following them quickly formed a great circle around them. While they danced the old woman went about begging from the onlookers, and *ochavos* and *cuartos* rained like hail stones on a roof, for beauty, too, has the power to arouse slumbering charity.

When the dance was ended, Preciosa said: "If you will give me four *cuartos,* I will sing you a ballad by myself which is beautiful beyond compare and tells how Our Lady, Queen Marguerite, set out for her churching in Valladolid to the church of San Llorente. I can tell you that it is deserving of fame and was composed by an outstanding poet, worthy of being the captain of a battalion."

The words were no more than spoken when most of those gathered in the circle shouted back:

"Sing it, Preciosa, here are my four *cuartos.*"

And so many *cuartos* began to rain upon her that the grandmother could hardly gather them up. Thus having reaped her harvest and gathered her vintage, Preciosa shook her tambourine, and to its merry, jingling tone, sang the following ballad:

> Off to her churching went
> The greatest queen of Europe,
> In quality and name
> A rich and admirable jewel.
>
> Like the eyes that follow her
> She draws the souls
> Of all who regard and admire
> Her devotion and her pomp.
>
> And to show that she is part
> Of Heaven throughout the orb,
> On one side the Sun of Austria,
> On the other tender Aurora she bears.
>
> Behind her follows
> A star which too early rose,

The night of the day
Which heaven and earth mourn.

And if in Heaven there are stars
Which glittering wains form,
In other wains her heaven
By gleaming stars are adorned.

Here old Saturn
His beard strokes and renews,
And though slow-footed, swift moves,
For pleasure cures the gout.

The garrulous god rides tongues
Both flattering and fond,
And Cupid in various ciphers,
By rubies and pearls adorned.

There goes angry Mars,
In the bedizened person
Of more than one gallant youth,
Amazed at his own shadow.

Beside the house of the Sun
Goes Jupiter; for nothing
Opposes good works
Done in secrecy.

The Moon goes in the cheeks
Of many a human goddess,
Chaste Venus in the beauty
Of those who this heaven form.

Wee Ganymedes appear,
Leave, return and cross
The studded ribbon
Of this miraculous sphere.

And that all may amaze,
And all surprise arouse,
Whatever meets the eye is rich,
And lavish as a dream.

Milan with fabrics choice
Makes glorious display,
The Indies with their diamonds,
The perfumes of Araby.

Beside those of mean intent,
Skulks sharp-toothed envy,
And nobility fills the heart,
Of every loyal Spaniard.

The general rejoicing
Derides wan-cheeked care,
And through streets and squares,
Runs mad with wild delight.

In a thousand blessings mute,
Silence opes its lips,
And the little ones repeat
What men's voices proclaim.

One cries: "Fruitful vine,
Flourish, climb, embrace,
And clasp your happy elm,
Years without end may it shade you,

For the greater glory yours,
For honor and good of Spain,
For refuge of the church,
And discomfit of Mahomet.

Joyous another cries:
Long live, oh white dove,
And give us as nestlings,
Eagles of double crown,

To drive from the lofty air
The furious birds of prey,
And cover with their wings
Virtues shrinking in dismay.

Another more solemn and wise,
Shrewder, and full of years,
Speaks, eyes and mouth fervent
With deep-felt joy:

This pearl you have given us,
Austrian mother of pearl,
How many plans has confounded,
How many designs cut short!

What hopes it raises high,
What soaring schemes lays low,
What fears it increases,
What promises it thwarts!

With this she reached the temple
Of the holy Phoenix who in Rome
Burned in his ashes, and from them rose,
To glory and eternal renown.

To the image of life itself,
To her who is Queen of Heaven,
Who because of her humility,
Now walks upon the stars,

To the Mother and Virgin in one,
Daughter and Bride of God,
Low bending on her knees,
Marguerite thus speaks:

What thou hast given, I give thee,
Oh, ever bounteous hand;

For where thy favor is lacking,
Misery rules the land.

My first fruits I lay before thee,
Mother and Virgin fair,
Such as they are, look on them with favor,
Receive, protect, and better them.

To thee their father I commend,
Bent like Atlas 'neath the weight
Of kingdoms and lands remote
That span the mighty globe.

The heart of the king, I know,
Rests in the hands of God,
And I know thou obtainest from Him,
What thou dost ask with pious word.

Her prayer ended, there arose
A chorus of hymns and voices,
Proclaiming that here on earth,
Heaven is to be found.

When the service was ended,
With regal pomp returned
To her orbit this fair star,
This wondrous royal sphere.

No sooner had Preciosa finished her ballad than from the illustrious audience and grave senate listening to her, many voices rose as one, saying:

"Sing it again, Preciosica; *cuartos* will fall like dirt."

More than two hundred persons were watching the dance and listening to the singing of the gipsies, and when it was at its height one of the Lieutenant Governors of the city chanced to pass that way; and seeing all those people gathered together, he asked what was going on, and was told that they were listening to the beautiful gipsy maid who was singing. The Lieutenant Governor came nearer, being curious, and listened for a time, but not to belie his gravity, he did not hear the ballad out to the end. However, as he had found the gipsy maid most comely, he sent a page of his to tell the old gipsy to come to his house that evening with the girls, for he wanted his wife, Doña Clara, to hear them. The page did as he was bid, and the old woman said they would go.

The dance and the song were finished, and as they were getting ready to leave, a page in fine livery came over to Preciosa, and giving her a folded paper, said to her:

"Preciosica, sing the ballad herein contained, for it is very good, and from time to time I shall give you others wherewith you will achieve the fame of the best balladeer in the world."

"I shall learn it with right good will," answered Preciosa; "And mark, sir, you do not fail to give me the ballads you speak of, on condition that they be seemly; and if you wish to be paid for them, let us set a price by the dozen, and a dozen sung, a dozen paid for. For to think that I am going to pay in advance is out of the question."

"Let Madame Preciosica give me enough for paper," said the page, "and I shall be content. Moreover, the ballad that does not turn out good and seemly will not enter into the account."

"I shall reserve the right to select them," answered Preciosa.

And with this they were starting up the street when from behind a window grille several gentlemen called to them. Preciosa went over to the window, which was low, and saw in a finely furnished and cool room a number of gentlemen who, some walking about, others playing different games, were passing the time.

"Do you want to give me a tip, shentlemen?" asked Preciosa, who, like all the gipsies, lisped when she talked, which is an affectation on their part, and not natural.

Hearing Preciosa's voice, and seeing her face, those who were playing left their games, and the walkers left off walking; all came over to the grille to see her, of whom they had already heard, and said:

"Come in, come in, gipsy maids; we will give you a tip here."

"It will come high," answered Preciosa, "if you pinch us."

"No, by our word as gentlemen," one of them replied, "you may come in, girl, with the assurance that nobody will touch the welt of your shoe; no, by the habit I wear on my breast."

And he laid his hand on the insignia of the Order of Calatrava.

"If you want to go in, Preciosa," said one of the three gipsy maids who was with her, "do so; as for me, I have no intention of going where there are so many men."

"Look, Cristina," answered Preciosa, "what you must be on guard against is one man and alone, and not many together; for there being many is rather a defense against the fear of being offended. Hearken, Cristina, and be sure of one thing: the woman who makes up her mind to be chaste can be so amidst an army of soldiers. True, it is well to avoid the occasion, but the private, not the public ones."

"Then let us go in, Preciosa," replied Cristina, "for you are wiser than a sage."

The old woman encouraged them and they went in. No sooner had Preciosa entered than the gentleman wearing the habit, noticing the paper she carried in her bosom, approached her and took it from her. To which Preciosa said: "Do not take it from me, sir, for it is a ballad that has just been given me, and I have not yet read it."

"Then you know how to read, child?" asked one of them.

"And write," spoke up the old woman; "for I have raised my granddaughter as though she were the daughter of a lawyer."

The gentleman unfolded the paper and saw that inside it there was a gold florin.

"Verily, Preciosa, this letter carries its own postage. Take this florin that came with the ballad."

"By my faith," answered Preciosa, "the poet has dealt with me as with a poor person. It is indeed more of a miracle for a poet to give a florin than for me to receive it. If his ballads are going to come with this supererogation, let him copy out the whole *Roman-*

cero general,[1] and send them to me one by one. I shall test them, and if they are hard I shall be soft in accepting them."

All were amazed at the gipsy maid's words, at her wit as well as the charm with which she spoke.

"Read it, sir," she said, "read it aloud; we shall see if this poet is as gifted as he is generous."

And the gentleman read after this manner:

> Gipsy maid, for your beauty
> Praises you may well receive;
> For that which you have of stone,
> The world calls you *Precious*.

> Of this truth I am sure,
> As you may prove in yourself;
> That these are never far separate:
> Aloofness and beauty.

> If as in value high
> You grow in haughtiness,
> Then woe betide the age
> Which brought you to the world.

> For a basilisk grows in you
> That slays with a single glance,
> And a power which, though gentle,
> Seems to us tyranny.

> Amidst beggars and gipsies,
> How came such beauty to be?
> How brought forth such a prize
> Manzanares' humble stream?

> For this it will achieve like fame
> To Tagus of the golden sands,

---

[1] Romancero General. *A famous collection of Spanish ballads.*

Because of Preciosa more precious
Than the rolling Ganges.

You tell fortunes,
And you always cast them bad,
Your intent and your beauty
Follow different paths.

For in the grave danger
Of looking and gazing on you,
Your intent asks pardon,
Your beauty deals death.

Enchantress you are said to be,
Like all those of your race;
But your enchantments are
Stronger and far more true;

For to carry off the spoils
Of all who gaze on you,
You, fair maid, bear
Your enchantments in your eyes.

In their power you advance,
For dancing you transport us,
You kill us with your glance
And enchant us with your song.

In a thousand ways you bewitch,
If you speak, are silent, sing, glance,
Whether you approach or withdraw
You fan the flames of love.

Over the stoutest heart
You hold sway and mastery,
My own can bear witness,
Satisfied with your rule.

Precious jewel of love,
These humble words are his
Who lives and dies for you,
Your subject lover poor.

"Poor concludes the last line," remarked Preciosa at this point; "a bad augury! Lovers should never confess themselves poor, for in the beginning, it seems to me, poverty is a great enemy of love."

"Who taught you that, girl?" one of the men asked.

"And who needs to teach it to me?" answered Preciosa. "Have I not a soul in my body? Have I not reached the age of fifteen? I am not maimed, halt, or crippled in understanding. The wits of the gipsies pursue a different course than those of other people: they are always old for their years. There was never a foolish or dull gipsy, for inasmuch as their livelihood depends on their being shrewd, astute, and lying, they keep their wits well trimmed, and let them gather no moss. You see these girls, my companions, who have not spoken a word and seem silly? Well, put your finger in their mouth and feel their wisdom teeth, and see what you find. There is not a twelve-year-old girl who does not know as much as one of five and twenty, for their teachers and tutors are the Devil and experience, which teach them more in an hour than they would otherwise learn in a year."

With these words the gipsy maid left her hearers in a state of admiring amazement, and those who were playing gave her a tip, and even those who were not. The old woman put thirty *reales* in her money box, and more gay and smiling than an Easter Sunday, she shepherded her lambs before her and left for the Lieutenant Governor's house, promising to return the next day with her flock to give pleasure to such open-handed gentlemen.

Doña Clara, the wife of the Lieutenant Governor, had already been informed that the gipsy maids were coming to her house, and she was waiting for them as one awaits spring showers, she and her handmaidens and duennas, together with those of another lady, a neighbor, who had all assembled to see Preciosa. When the gipsies entered, Preciosa shone out among the others like a torch among candles, and they all rushed over to her, some embracing her, others gazing upon her, these blessing her, those praising her. Said Doña Clara:

"Now, this is what I call golden hair! These are emerald eyes!"

The neighbor lady took her completely apart, and made a minute analysis of all her members and joints. And when she got around to a little dimple in Preciosa's chin, she said:

"Oh, what a dimple! This is a hollow into which all eyes that look upon it are going to fall."

These words were overheard by a squire of Doña Clara's who was standing by, long in years and beard, and he said:

"You call that a hollow, my lady? Well, either I know little of hollows, or that is not a hollow but a grave of quick desires. God in Heaven, this gipsy maid is so beautiful that were she made of silver or sugar she could not be better! Do you know how to tell fortunes, lass?"

"In three or four different ways," replied Preciosa.

"That, too?" said Doña Clara. "By the life of my lord the Governor, you must tell mine, girl of gold, girl of silver, girl of pearls, girl of rubies, and girl of heaven, which is the most I can say."

"Go ahead and give her the palm of your hand, cross it, and you will see the things she tells you," said the old gipsy; "she knows more than a doctor of medicine."

The Governor's lady put her hand in her pocket and found she had not a penny. She asked her handmaidens for a coin, and none of them had one, nor the neighbor either. Seeing this, Preciosa said:

"Any cross, so long as it is a cross, is good; but those of silver and gold are the best; and making the sign of the cross on the palm of the hand with a copper coin, my ladies, diminishes the good fortune, or at least mine; therefore I like to have the first cross made with a gold florin, or with a piece of eight, or, at least, of four; I am like the sextons: when there is a good offering they rejoice."

"You have a clever wit, girl, by your life," said the neighbor lady. And turning to the squire, she said to him:

"You, Señor Contreras, have you a piece of four on you? Give it to me, and as soon as my husband the doctor arrives I shall return it to you."

"I have," replied Contreras, "but I have pledged it for twenty-two *maravedis* which my supper cost me last night; give them to me, and I shall go and fetch it in the twinkling of an eye."

"Among us all we don't have a farthing," said Doña Clara, "and here you are asking for twenty-two *maravedis!* Get along with you, Contreras, you always were silly!"

One of the handmaidens, seeing the penury of the house, said to Preciosa:

"Girl, would it help out if the cross were made with a silver thimble?"

"Indeed it would," answered Preciosa, "the best crosses in the world are made with silver thimbles, provided they are many."

"I have one," replied the handmaiden; "if this is enough, here it is, on condition that you tell my fortune, too."

"So many fortunes for one thimble?" spoke up the old gipsy. "Granddaughter, hurry, it's getting dark."

Preciosa took the thimble and the hand of the Governor's lady, and began:

> Lady, beautiful lady,
> You with hands of silver,
> Loved by your husband
> Like the king of the Alpujarras;
> You are a dove without gall,
> But at times you rage
> Like a lioness of Oran,
> Or a tigress of Ocaña.
> But in the twinkling of an eye
> Your anger has melted,
> And you're soft as sugar candy,
> Or a gentle lamb.

You scold much and eat little,
Have occasional twinges of jealousy,
For the Governor is playful,
And likes to wield his wand.
While a maid, your hand was sought
By one of goodly visage;
A curse upon the meddlers
Who undo love's hopes!
If perchance you had been a nun
You would rule your convent today
Because you are the stuff
Abbesses are made of.
I would rather not say . . .
But what matters? Here it is:
You will be widowed, and once more,
Twice more you will wed.
Weep not, my lady fair;
Not always do we gipsies
Speak the gospel truth.
Weep not, fair lady; give over.
If you were to die before
Your lord and master, 'twould
Suffice to wipe out the danger
Of widowhood that threatens.
A fortune, and soon, will be yours,
Wealth in great abundance;
You will have a son in orders,
The church I cannot see.
Toledo it cannot be.
A daughter fair and white, too,
And should she take the veil,
She, too, will be a prelatess.
If your husband does not die
Within a four weeks' span,
You shall see him mayor
Of Burgos or Salamanca.
You have a mole, how lovely!
Heavens! And what a clear moon!

What a sun which there in the antipodes
Lightens dark valleys!
More than two blind men to see it
Would give more than four pennies . . .
Now is the time for laughter,
Now is the time for fun.
Be on guard against falls,
Especially falling backwards;
These may be dangerous
To ladies high-born.
There are more things to tell you,
If you await me next Friday,
You shall hear them; some are pleasant
Some forebode misfortune.

Preciosa finished her fortune-telling, and with it she aroused the desire of all the spectators to know theirs, and they all begged her to tell them. But she put them off until the coming Friday, all promising they would have silver coins with which to cross her palm. At this point the Lieutenant Governor entered, to whom they recounted the wonders of the gipsy maid. He had the girls dance a little for him, and agreed that the praises bestowed on Preciosa were just and merited. Putting his hand in his purse, he made as if to give her something, but after searching it, shaking it, and turning it upside down repeatedly, he finally brought out his hand empty and said:

"For Heaven's sake, I don't have a cent. You, Doña Clara, give Preciosa a *real,* and I will give it back to you later."

"A fine state of affairs, sir, I must say. You have come to the right place for a *real!* All of us together have not been able to scrape up a *cuarto* to cross her palm and you ask for a *real!*"

"Then give her one of your lace collars, or some trinket; the next time Preciosa comes to see us we will reward her better."

To which Doña Clara answered: "To make sure she will come back again, I am not going to give Preciosa anything now."

"On the contrary, if you give me nothing," said Preciosa, "I will never return. But I will, indeed, come back to serve such fine lords and ladies; however I will know in advance that they are not going to give me anything, and thus I will spare myself the trouble of expecting it. Accept bribes, my lord, accept bribes, and you will have money; don't institute new customs or you will die of hunger! Look, Madame, I have heard it said (and though young, I understand that it is not good advice) that one must get money by the post one occupies to pay the fines if found guilty of malfeasance, and to aspire to other positions."

"That is what rogues say and do," replied the Lieutenant Governor, "but the official who submits an honest account will not have to pay any fine, and the best recommendation for a new post is to have acquitted oneself well in that which one has held."

"You talk like a saint, my lord," answered Preciosa. "You keep on like that and we'll cut up your rags for relics."

"You know a lot, Preciosa," said the Lieutenant Governor. "Hush, and I shall find a way for Their Majesties to see you, for you are a royal morsel."

"They may want me for a jester," replied Preciosa, "and I am not suited to that, and all will be lost. If they should want me for my wise counsel, they could use me; but in many palaces the jesters fare better than the wise. I am satisfied to be a poor gipsy, and suffer the fate Heaven has in store for me."

"Come, child," said the old woman, "say no more, for you have talked a lot, and you know more than I have taught you. Don't put such a fine point on things, or they will break; talk of matters that become your years, and don't soar so high or you may fall."

"These gipsies are the Devil's own spawn," said the Lieutenant Governor.

The gipsies took their leave, and as they were going the handmaiden whose thimble had been used as silver said:

"Preciosa, tell my fortune or give me back my thimble, else I won't be able to do my sewing."

"My dear young lady," replied Preciosa, "pretend that I have told it to you, and provide yourself with another thimble; don't do any hemstitching until Friday when I shall return and tell you more fortunes and adventures than are to be found in a romance of chivalry."

They departed and joined the many peasant women who at the hour of the Angelus leave Madrid to return to their villages, and among them were those with whom the gipsies always went and travelled in safety. For the old gipsy lived in constant fear that Preciosa might be stolen from her.

It so happened that the morning of a day when they were returning to Madrid with the other gipsy girls to collect their pickings, in a little valley which lies some five hundred paces outside the entrance to the city, they saw a handsome youth richly dressed in travelling attire. The sword and dagger he wore were, as the expression goes, a flame of gold; his hat was adorned with a rich riband and plumes of many colors. The gipsies' attention was attracted to him, and they stopped to look him over from head to foot, wondering that at that time of day such a handsome youth should be in a place like that, on foot and alone. He came over to them, and addressing himself to the old woman, said:

"If, my friend, you would do me the favor of listening, you and Preciosa, here aside, to the few words I have to say, it will redound to your benefit."

"Provided we are not too far diverted from our journey, or too long delayed, be it as you wish," answered the old woman.

And calling to Preciosa, they withdrew some twenty paces from the others; and as they stood waiting, the youth said:

"Here I am, so overpowered by the wit and beauy of Preciosa, that after struggling with myself to avoid taking this extreme step, I only find myself further overpowered and less able to avoid it. I, my ladies (which name I shall always give you, if Heaven favors my desires) am a gentleman, as this insignia proves"—and drawing back his cloak he revealed on his breast one of the most prized in all Spain—; "I am the son of one whose name at the moment I do not reveal for good reasons; I am under his guardianship and protection; I am an only son, and I look forward to a goodly entail. My father

is here at Court, applying for a post; his petition is under consideration and he has almost certain hope that it will be granted. And
despite being of the position and station I have mentioned, and of
which you must now be growing aware, nevertheless I would wish
to be a great lord so as to raise to my height Preciosa's lowly estate,
making her my equal and my wife. I do not lay suit to her to deceive
her, for in the true love I feel for her there is no room for deceit of any
sort; I wish only to serve her in the manner that most pleases her;
her will is my will. In her hands my soul is as wax on which she
can impress whatever she wishes; but to keep this and treasure this,
it will not be as though pressed in wax, but sculptured in marble,
whose durability challenges the power of time. If you accept this
truth, my hope will know no discouragement; but if you do not
believe me, your doubt will keep me in a state of fear. This is my
name," and he told it to them; "I have already told you that of my
father. The house where he lives is in such-and-such a street, and
this is its description; there are people living nearby with whom you
can corroborate what I have said, and even with people who do not
live there, for my rank and name, and my father's, are not so obscure
as to be unknown in palace circles, and even in all the Court. I have
with me a hundred gold florins to give you as earnest and pledge
of what I intend to give you, for he will not withhold his fortune
who gives his soul."

While the gentleman was speaking these words, Preciosa was
watching him attentively, and undoubtedly what she heard and
what she saw did not displease her, for, turning to the old woman,
she said:

"Forgive me, grandmother, if I take leave to answer this enamored gentleman."

"Answer him as you like, granddaughter," replied the old
woman, "for I know your discretion is equal to any situation."

With this Preciosa said: "I, kind sir, though a gipsy and low and
humbly born, have a certain whimsical spirit here within me which
urges me on to great things. I am not moved by promises, nor shaken
by gifts, nor swayed by submission, nor astounded by lovers' phrases;

and although I am only fifteen years old (according to my grand-mother's reckoning, come Michaelmas I shall round them out) I am already old in thought, and grasp more than my age would promise, by my goodly wit rather than by experience. But by the one or the other, I know that amorous passions in the newly enamored are like headstrong impulses that unbridle the will, which, surmounting all obstacles, rushes heedless toward its desire, and thinking to come upon the glory of its eyes, comes upon the hell of its regret. If it achieves what it desires, desire wanes with the possession of the object of its desire, and if perchance then the eyes of the under-standing are opened, it sees fit to loathe what was formerly adored. This fear engenders in me such caution that I trust no words and doubt many deeds. I have a single jewel which I prize more than life, and that is my unsullied virginity, and I shall not exchange it for promises or gifts, because that would be to sell it, and if it can be bought, it would be of little worth. Nor shall it be taken by schemes or tricks: rather I prefer to carry it with me to the grave, and perhaps to heaven, than to run the risk of chimeras and fantasies such as dreams are made of assaulting and besmirching it. A flower is this virginity which, were it possible, ought not be offended even with the imagination. Once the rose is cut from the bush, how swiftly and easily it fades! This one touches it, that one smells it, the other plucks its petals, and finally boorish hands tear it apart. If, sir, you come only for that prize, you will not carry it off except tied with the bonds and knots of marriage; for if virginity is to bow its head, it must be only to this holy yoke, which will then not be to lose it, but to use it in happy employment that promises felicitous gains. If you wish to be my spouse, I shall be yours; but many condi-tions and investigations must precede this.

First I must know if you are who you say; then, if this proves true, you must leave the house of your parents and exchange it for our camp, and assuming the guise of a gipsy, you must study two years in our school, during which time I shall satisfy myself as to your disposition, and you as to mine; at the end of which, if you are satisfied with me and I with you, they will give me to you as your wife. But until then my relation to you will be that of sister, and your humble servant. And you should bear in mind that during this novitiate it might be that you will regain your sight, which at the moment you seem to have lost, or is at least blurred, and come to see that it would be to your advantage to flee that which you now pursue with such zeal; and your lost freedom recovered, with sincere repentance all faults are forgiven. If on these terms you wish to enlist as a soldier in our militia, the choice lies with you, and if you fall short in any of them, you shall not touch one finger of mine."

All amazed was the youth at Preciosa's discourse, and he stood bemused, his eyes on the ground, as though turning over in his mind what he should answer. In view of this Preciosa spoke again:

"This is not a matter of so little moment that in the brief space time affords us here can it or should it be settled. Return, sir, to the city and consider at leisure what best suits you; in this same place you can talk with me any feast day you like, when we are on our way to or from Madrid."

To which the young gentleman replied: "When Heaven willed that I should love you, my Preciosa, I made up my mind to do for you whatever you might decide to ask of me, although it never occurred to me that you might ask what you have. But since it is your will that mine should adjust and accommodate itself to yours, consider me from this moment a gipsy, and submit me to all the tests you like, for you will always find me the same as I now signify to you. Decide when you wish me to change my garb, which I would wish to be at once, for on pretext of going to Flanders I shall deceive my parents and secure moneys to last me for some days. It will require about a week to arrange my departure. I shall find a way to elude those who may accompany me, so I shall be able to carry out my intent. What I would ask of you (if I may already make bold to ask and request something of you) is that, if today is not the day you intend to inform yourself of my rank and that of my parents, you desist from making further trips to Madrid; for I would not wish that on one of the many opportunities that lurk there my good fortune, which costs me so dear, might be stolen from me."

"Not that, gallant sir," replied Preciosa; "know that freedom and I must go hand in hand, without lowering jealousy straitening or roiling it. Rest assured that I shall not give it such free rein that it will not be apparent to any eye that my chastity and my ease of manner match one another, and the first thing I enjoin upon you is that you must have trust in me. Mark well that lovers who begin by seeking jealousy are either foolish or overtrusting."

"You have Satan himself in your bosom, girl," said the old gipsy at this point; "you say things that would not occur even to a student of Salamanca! You know about love, you know about jealousy, you know about trust. How is this? You are driving me crazy, and I listen to you as though you were possessed of devils, talking Latin without knowing it."

"Hush, grandmother," replied Preciosa, "and know that all you hear me say is but stuff and nonsense beside the many truths I keep to myself."

Everything Preciosa was saying, and the wit she displayed, but added fuel to the fire that burned in the breast of the enamored youth. Finally they agreed that eight days hence they would meet again at that same spot, where he would come to give account of the state of his affairs, and the gipsies would have had time to inform themselves of the truth of what he had told them. He pulled out a brocade purse, which he said contained a hundred gold florins, and gave it to the old woman; but Preciosa did not want her to take it under any circumstances. Whereupon the gipsy replied:

"Hush, child; the best proof that this gentleman has given of being in love is handing over his arms in token of surrender, and giving, whatever the occasion, is always proof of a generous heart. And bear in mind that proverb which says: 'Trust in God and keep your powder dry.' Moreover, I would not have the gipsies lose because of me the reputation they have acquired over long centuries for covetousness and sharp dealing. You want me to refuse a hundred florins, Preciosa, in gold, which can be sewed in the seam of a skirt not worth two *reales,* and kept there as one who holds a right in perpetuity over the pastures of Extremadura? And if one of our children, grandchildren, or kinsmen should chance by misfortune to run afoul of the law, what greater testimony in his favor could reach the ear of judge or notary than these florins in their pockets? Three times on three different charges I have been on the point of being put astride a donkey to be flogged, and once a silver pitcher got me off, the other a necklace of pearls, and the other forty pieces of eight, which I had changed into *cuartos*, paying twenty *reales* more for the exchange. See here, my girl, we follow a dangerous calling, beset with obstacles and alarms, and there is no defense which more quickly succors us and comes to our rescue than the invincible arms of the great Philip; nothing outstrips his *plus ultra*. For a two-faced doubloon the sad visage of the crown attorney turns gay, and that of all the ministers of death, who are harpies to us poor gipsies and would rather despoil and flay us than a highwayman; never, however ragged and tattered they see us, do they believe we are poor; they say we are like the doublets of the French of Belmonte: ragged and greasy and full of doubloons."

"Please, grandmother, say no more; you are citing so many laws in favor of keeping the money that you will have exhausted all those of the emperors. Keep it, and may it bring you much pleasure; and please God you bury it in a grave where it never more sees the light of the sun, nor be there need for it to. These companions of ours must have a share of it, for they have been waiting for us a long time, and must be vexed."

"They have as much chance of seeing one of these coins," replied the old woman, "as of seeing the Turk at this moment. This good gentleman will see if he has some silver coin or some *cuartos* left, for they will be content with little."

"I have," said the youth.

And he took out of his money pouch three pieces of eight, which he distributed among the three gipsy girls, who with this were happier and more satisfied than a producer of plays who, when vying with another, sees his name written on the walls followed by: 'Victor, Victor.'

In the end they agreed, as has been said, to meet there a week later, and that when he became a gipsy the youth was to go by the name of Andrés Caballero, because there were among the gipsies those who had this surname.

Andrés (for so we shall call him henceforth) lacked the courage to embrace Preciosilla; instead, with his eyes he sent her his soul, and without it, if one may so say, he left them and entered Madrid, and they, full of contentment, did the same. Preciosa, somewhat touched (but with kindly inclination rather than love) by the gallant manner of Andrés, was longing to learn if he was who he had said. Shortly after entering Madrid, she came upon the poet of the verses and the florin; and when he saw her, he came up to her and said:

"Well met, Preciosa. Did you by happy chance read the verses I gave you the other day?"

To which Preciosa replied: "Before I answer one word, you must swear to tell me the truth by the life of the one you love best."

"That is an oath," responded the page, "which even though to comply with it were to cost me my life, I shall in no wise refuse."

"The truth I want you to tell me," said Preciosa, "is whether you are by chance a poet."

"If I were," replied the page, "it would indeed be a happy chance. But you must know, Preciosa, that very few deserve this name of poet, and so I am not a poet, but only one given to poetry; and for what I need, I shall not ask or seek the verses of others. Those which I gave you are mine, as are these I now give you; but not by reason of them am I a poet, Heaven forfend."

"Is it such a bad thing to be a poet?" asked Preciosa.

"It is not bad," said the page; "but to be just a poet I do not consider very good. Poetry must be treated like the most valuable of jewels which its owner does not wear every day, nor show to everybody, on any occasion, but only when it is fitting and justified. Poetry is a beautiful maiden, chaste, modest, wise, understanding, retiring, who keeps within the limits of the greatest discretion. She is given to solitude; fountains beguile her; meadows console her; trees soothe her; flowers rejoice her; and, in a word, she delights and instructs all those who come in contact with her."

"Even so," replied Preciosa, "I have heard said that she is exceedingly poor, and akin to a beggar."

"Quite the contrary," replied the page, "for there is not a poet who is not rich, for they all live happy with their lot, a philosophy few achieve. But, what has moved you to ask this question, Preciosa?"

"What moved me," answered Preciosa, "was the fact that as I consider all or most poets to be poor, that gold florin you gave me wrapped in your verses amazed me; but now that I know you are not a poet, but only given to poetry, it might be that you were rich, though I doubt it, because through that inclination of yours for writing verses whatever fortune you may have will trickle away, for there is not a poet, so they say, who knows how to conserve such fortune as he has, or come by that which he has not."

"Well, I am not one of those," responded the page; "I write verses and I am neither rich nor poor; and without lamenting it or discounting it, as the Genoese do when they invite a guest to dinner, I can give a florin, and even two, to whomever I like. Take, precious pearl, this second paper and this second florin it contains, without stopping to wonder whether I am a poet or not; I want you to think and believe only that he who gives you this would like to have the riches of Midas to give you."

"This paper will live for long years because it carries two souls within it: one, that of the florin, the other, that of the verses which are always full of souls and hearts. But know, Master Page, that I do not want to have so many souls in my possession, and if you do not remove one of them, I shall not accept the other: it is as a poet that I like you, and not because of your generosity, and in this way we will have an enduring friendship, for a florin may more easily be dispensed with than the confection of a ballad."

"Well, if what you want, Preciosa," answered the page, "is for me to be poor, willy-nilly, do not reject the soul which I send you in this paper, and return the florin which, once your hand has touched it, will be a holy relic to me as long as I have breath."

Preciosa removed the florin from the paper, and tucked the latter away, for she did not want to read it in the street. The page took his leave and departed in high spirits, in the belief that Preciosa had lost her heart to him, inasmuch as she had spoken to him so affably. As her purpose was to seek the house of Andrés's father, she wasted no time dancing anywhere; in a short while she was in the street where it stood—one which she knew well. When she had walked half way through it she raised her eyes to the windows with gilded grilles, by which she had been told she would know it, and at one she saw a gentleman of some fifty years, venerable of aspect and bearing, displaying the insignia of the Order of Santiago on his breast. No sooner had he seen the gipsy maid than he said:

"Come up, girls; here you will receive alms."

At the sound of his words, three other gentlemen appeared at the balcony, among them the enamored Andrés, who, when he descried Preciosa, turned pale and was on the point of losing his senses, so startled was he to see her. All the gipsies went up except the old woman, who stayed below stairs to find out from the servants if what Andrés had told them was the truth. As the girls came into the drawing room, the old gentleman was saying to the others:

"Without doubt this is the beautiful gipsy maid who is the toast of Madrid."

"It is," replied Andrés, "and without doubt she is the most beautiful creature eyes have beheld."

"That's what they say," said Preciosa who had heard all as she was coming in; "but the truth of the matter is that they are wrong by half. Pretty, I do think I am; but as beautiful as reputed, not even remotely."

"By the life of my son, Don Juanico," answered the old man, "you are even more beautiful than they say, charming gipsy."

"And which is Don Juanico, your son?" asked Preciosa.

"This youth at your side," answered the gentleman.

"Why," said Preciosa, "I thought you were swearing by some child two years old. What a Don Juanico, and what a jewel! In truth he might already be wed, and according to certain lines on his forehead three years will not elapse before he is, and to his taste, unless from now until then he goes astray or suffers a change."

"That will do," said one of the company; "what does the gipsy girl know about lines?"

At this the three girls who were with Preciosa withdrew to a corner of the room, and with heads close together began to talk in whispers. Said Cristina: "Girls, this is the gentleman who that morning gave us the three pieces of eight."

"It is, indeed," the others answered: "but we must not mention or say a word to him about it if he does not refer to it. How do we know but what he wants it kept a secret?"

While this was going on between them, Preciosa replied to the remark about the lines:

"What I see with my eyes I divine with my fingers; apart from the lines, I know that Don Juanico is ardent, impetuous and precipitate, and a great promiser of things that seem impossible; and God grant that he is not a prevaricator, which would be the worst of all. He is soon to undertake a long journey, and the roan has one notion, and he who saddles him, another; for man proposes and God disposes. He may set out for Oñez and wind up in Gamboa."

To which Don Juan responded: "Verily, little gipsy, you are right about many traits of my nature; but as for being a prevaricator, you are wide of the truth, for I pride myself on speaking it on every matter. As for the long journey, you are right, for, without a doubt, God so willing, in four or five days I shall set out for Flanders, even though you foretell that I am to change routes, and I would not like to have anything happen to me on the way that might interfere with it."

"Hush, young sir," answered Preciosa, "and commend yourself to God; everything will go well. And know that I know nothing of what I say, and it is not strange that as I talk a lot and say whatever comes into my head, I should be right about something. What I should like to do is manage to persuade you not to leave, but to calm your breast and remain with your parents to comfort their old age, for I do not look with favor on these goings and comings to Flanders, especially for lads of such tender years as yours. Wait and grow a little so you can bear the trials of war, especially as you have plenty of war here at home; all too many amorous encounters besiege your breast. Calm yourself, calm yourself, impetuous youth, and look what you are about before you wed, and give us alms for the sake of God and the gentleman you are; for verily I believe you to be well born. And if you are truthful as well, I shall cheer when all I have told you turns out to be correct."

"I have already told you, girl," answered Don Juan, the future Andrés Caballero, "that you are correct in everything except in the fear you feel that I may not be true; in this you are deceived beyond the shadow of a doubt: the word I pledge in the countryside I will fulfill in the city and wherever may be, without it being demanded of me; for no one may be held a gentleman who is tarred by the vice of lying. My father will give you alms for God and for me; for the truth is that this morning I gave all I had to certain ladies; and were they as flattering as they are beautiful, especially one of them, my satisfaction would know no bounds."

Cristina, on hearing this, with the caution she had earlier displayed, said to the others:

"Girls, may I drop dead if he doesn't say that with the three pieces of eight he gave us this morning in mind!"

"You're wrong," said one of the other two, "for he said we were ladies, and we're not; and being as truthful as he says, he wouldn't lie about that."

"A lie which harms nobody and is to the benefit and credit of the one who tells it, is not a lie to worry about. But with all this, they are giving us nothing nor asking us to dance."

At this point the old woman came upstairs and said: "Granddaughter, get through; it is late, and there is much to be done and more to be said."

"What is it, grandmother," asked Preciosa, "a boy or a girl?"

"A boy, and a fine one," answered the old woman. "Come, Preciosa, and you shall hear veritable wonders."

"Please God it does not die from birth injuries!"

"All will be well looked after," replied the old woman; "besides, so far it has been an easy delivery and the babe is a jewel."

"Has some lady given birth?" asked the father of Andrés Caballero.

"Yes, sir," answered the grandmother; "but it has been so secret a delivery that only Preciosa, myself, and one other person know about it, so we cannot tell the name."

"Nor do we want to know it," spoke up one of the guests; "but God help the one who confides her secret to your tongues and puts her honor in your hands."

"Not all of us are bad," answered Preciosa. "It may well be that there are those among us who pride themselves on being as trustworthy and true as the most presumptuous gentleman in this room. Come, grandmother, for they hold us in low esteem here. We are neither thieves nor are we asking anything of anybody."

"Do not be vexed, Preciosa," said the father; "for I believe that nothing bad can be presumed of you, at least, for your goodly countenance is your guarantor and the underwriter of your good deeds. Be so good, Preciosita, as to dance a little with your companions, for here I have a gold doubloon stamped with two faces, though neither comes up to yours, even though they are those of Their Majesties."

No sooner had the old woman heard this than she said: "Come, girls, go to work and gratify these gentlemen."

Preciosa took up the tambourine, and they all made their turns, weaving and unweaving their steps with such grace and ease that the eyes of every onlooker followed their feet, especially the eyes of Andrés, which accompanied Preciosa's feet as though their center of glory lay there. But fate so willed it that this glory was turned into a hell, for in one of her movements, Preciosa dropped the paper which the page had given her, and as it fell, the gentleman who had a low opinion of the gipsies picked it up, and opening it, said:

"Well, well. We have a little sonnet here. Stop the dance and listen to it, for to judge by the first verse, it is not at all bad."

Preciosa was upset, for she did not know its contents, and she begged them not to read it, but return it to her. But all her insistence simply spurred Andrés's desire to hear it. Finally the gentleman read it aloud, and this was what it said:

> When Preciosa takes up the tambourine,
> And the sweet sounds strike the empty air,
> Pearls they are that fall from her hands,
> Flowers they are that drop from her lips.
> One's soul is bewildered and his brain
> Turned mad by the sweet angelic acts
> Which, so pure, so chaste, so good,
> Her praise to the heavens raise high.
> She dangles from the slightest of her hairs
> A thousand swaying souls, and at her feet
> Love meekly all his arrows lays.
> Her beauteous orbs blind and give light;
> Love holds his rule because of them,
> And still greater marvels in her I suspect.

"By my troth," said the one who read the sonnet, "the poet who wrote this has a nimble wit."

"He is not a poet, sir, but a very well-favored youth and a person of great virtue."

Have a care with what you have said, Preciosa, and what you are about to say, for these are not praises of the page, but lances that pierce the heart of Andrés who is listening to them. Would you care to see this, girls? Then turn your eyes, and look upon him swooning in a chair, with a deathly sweat on his brow. Never think, maid, that Andrés loves you so lightly that the least of your unthinking acts does not wound and alarm him. Hurry to him, and whisper words in his ear that will go straight to his heart and restore him from his swoon. If not, just bring him sonnets in your praise every day, and you will see what they do to him!

All this took place as has been set forth. On hearing the sonnet Andrés was attacked by a thousand jealous fancies. He did not actually lose his senses, but turned so pale that his father said, looking at him:

"What ails you, Don Juan, that you look as though you were going to faint, so pale have you become?"

"Wait a moment," Preciosa spoke up; "just let me whisper certain words in his ear, and you will see that he will not faint." And going over to him she said, almost without moving her lips:

"A fine gipsy you'll make. How would you endure the ordeal of water if you can't stand that of paper?"

And making half a dozen crosses over his heart, she withdrew from him, whereupon Andrés took a deep breath and implied that Preciosa's words had done him good. Finally, the double-faced doubloon was handed to Preciosa, and she told her companions to get it changed and she would divide it with them. Andrés's father asked her to leave him in writing the words she had spoken to Don Juan, for he would like to know them. She said she would tell him them with right good will, and that he should know that although they seemed in jest, they had a special virtue against ills of the heart and giddiness of the head, and were as follows:

> Little head, little head,
> Keep steady, don't you slip,
> And make ready two pillars
> Of saintly patience.
> Seek
> Lovely
> Trust.
> Hearken not
> To low thoughts.
> Things you will see
> Which approach the miraculous,
> God willing,
> And mighty Saint Christopher.

"Saying half of these words, and making six crosses over the heart of the person who suffers giddiness," said Preciosa, "he will become as sound as an apple."

When the old woman heard the charm and the lie, she was

dumfounded, and Andrés more so, for he saw that it was all the invention of her quick wits. The sonnet remained behind as Preciosa did not want to ask for it for fear of upsetting Andrés again, as she knew, without having been taught, what it was to give frights, commotions, and jealous shocks to lovers.

The gipsies took their leave, and as they departed Preciosa said to Don Juan:

"Sir, any day of this week is propitious for setting out, and none is baleful; prepare to leave as soon as you can, for a fine, free, and pleasant life awaits you if you adapt yourself to it."

"That of a soldier is never so free, it seems to me," answered Don Juan, "that it does not hold more subjection than freedom; but withal I shall do as I see others do."

"You will see more than you think," replied Preciosa, "and may God accompany you in your goings and comings, as your goodly presence warrants."

These last words left Andrés in a happy frame of mind, and the gipsies departed in high spirits. They changed the doubloon, divided it up among themselves in equal parts, even though the old watch-dog always took a share and a half of what they collected, not only because of her age but because she was the compass which guided them through the ocean-sea of their dances, jests, and even lies.

The day finally arrived when one morning Andrés Caballero presented himself at the spot where he had first appeared, on a hired mule and unaccompanied by any servant. There he found Preciosa and her grandmother who, when they recognized him, received him with great pleasure. He asked them to guide him to their camp before daylight, lest he be identified if perchance anyone should be looking for him. As they were forewarned, they had been on their guard, and had come alone. Turning back, in a little while they reached their shacks. Andrés went into one of them, the largest in the camp, and immediately there came to look him over ten or twelve gipsy youths, all handsome and well-knit, whom the old woman had already told of the new companion coming to join them, without needing to enjoin secrecy upon them, for, as has already been said, they keep this with unequalled shrewdness and care. They ran their eyes over the mule, and one of them said: "We can sell this on Thursday in Toledo."

"Oh, no," said Andrés, "for there is not a hired mule that is not known to all the muleteers who travel about Spain."

"Good God, Andrés," said one of the gipsies, "even if the mule had more signs than those which will precede the Judgment Day, here we shall transform it in such a way that the mother who bore it, or the master who raised it, would not recognize it."

"Even so," replied Andrés, "this time we will do as I think and say. This mule must be killed and buried where not even its bones will be found."

"A grievous sin," said another gipsy, "to take the life of an innocent. Dismiss that idea, and let's do one thing. You take a good look at the mule so all its lineaments may be stamped on your memory, and let me take it away; then if in two hours you recognize it, you can tar and feather me like a runaway Negro."

"I will in no wise consent," said Andrés, "that the mule remain alive, however much you guarantee its transformation; I am afraid of being found unless it is underground. And if what you propose is because of the profit from selling it, I am not entering this community so penniless that I cannot pay beforehand more than the value of four mules."

"Well, if that is the wish of Andrés Caballero," said another gipsy, "then let it die through no fault on its part, and God knows I lament it, both because it is young, for it does not yet have all its teeth (which is not the case with hired mules) as well as because it must be docile, for it has no scars on its flanks, nor spur wounds."

Its death was put off until that night, and during the remainder of the day the ceremonies of Andrés's initiation as a gipsy were carried out, which were the following. One of the best shacks in the camp was cleared, and adorned with branches and rushes; Andrés was seated upon an oak stump, and a hammer and pair of tongs were put in his hand, and to the accompaniment of two guitars strummed by two gipsies, he was ordered to give two leaps in the air; then one of his arms was bared, and with a strip of new silk and a stick they gave it two gentle turns. Preciosa and many other gipsy women, young and old, were viewing all this, some with wonder, others admiringly, for so gallant was Andrés's bearing that even the men were greatly taken by him.

When the ceremonies in question had been performed, an old man took Preciosa by the hand, and leading her up to Andrés, he said:

"This girl, who is the cream and flower of beauty among all the gipsies we know in Spain, we give to you either as wife or friend; in this you may do what pleases you most, for our free and easy life is not subject to prudery or much formality. Observe her well, and see if she pleases you or if you perceive in her anything that is not to your liking, in which case select among the maidens present the one who best satisfies you, for the one you select we will give you. But you must know that once you have made your choice, you must not leave her for another, nor are you to grow tired of her, or make advances either to matron or maid. We unfailingly observe the law of friendship; no one must covet the beloved of another; we live immune to the bitter plague of jealousy. Among us, although there is much incest, there is no adultery; and when such a thing happens with a wife or a breach of faith in a mistress, we do not go to the law for punishment. We are the judges and executioners; we kill them and bury them in the hills or wastelands as if they were harmful animals. No kinsman avenges them, no father seeks retribution for their death. With this peril and danger they pursue chastity, and we live without fear, as I have told you. We hold little that is not in common except wife or mistress, for we want each to belong to the one who is her lot. Among us age as well as death may bring separation: whoever so desires may leave his old wife, if he is young, and choose another better suited to his years. With these and other laws and statutes we preserve ourselves and live happy; we are the lords of the fields, of the crops, of the forests, of the mountains, of the fountains and the rivers; the forests afford us free wood; the trees, fruit; the vines, grapes; the gardens, vegetables; the fountains, water; the rivers, fish; the preserves, game; the cliffs, shade; the valleys, coolness; the caves, shelter. For us the inclemencies of the weather are pleasant breezes; the snows, coolness; the rain, a bath; the thunder, music; the lightning, torches. Hard clods are soft feather beds to us; the tanned leather of our bodies serves us as an impenetrable armor which protects us; our swiftness is not hampered by shackles, nor turned back by chasms, nor dismayed by walls. Our stoutheartedness is not deflected by ropes, nor diminished by pillory, nor choked by water, nor tamed by the rack. We make no distinction between *yes* and *no* when it is to our advantage; we always prefer to be martyrs rather than confessors; for us the country raises pack animals, and the city, purses to be cut. Neither eagle nor other bird of prey pounces on the victim he descries more quickly than we on the opportunity that holds some profit for us; in a word, we have many skills which assure us a happy life, for in prison we sing, on the rack we are silent, by day we work, by night we steal, or to put it better, we see to it that nobody lives without giving thought to where he has laid up his treasure. The fear of losing honor does not vex us, nor the ambition to augment it keep us awake. We support no factions, nor do we arise at dawn to present petitions, or wait upon magnates, or beg favors. To us these shacks and movable camps are gilded ceilings and sumptuous palaces; for paintings and tapestries of Flanders we have those which nature has provided in these towering cliffs and snowy peaks, spreading valleys and dense woods, which are continuously before our eyes. We are rustic astrologers, for as we nearly always sleep in the open, at every hour we know the time of day or night; we see how the dawn pushes and sweeps back the stars, how she comes forth with her companion, the morning star, rejoicing the air, cooling the water, and bedewing the earth, and then after her, the sun, *gilding the heights* (as the other poet said) *and rippling the woods*. Nor do we fear the frosts when his rays fall slanting, nor being burned when they strike us perpendicularly. We turn the same countenance to the sun as to ice, to scarcity as to abundance. In a word, we are people who live by our industry and tongue, without thought for the old proverb: Church, or sea, or palace. We have what we want, for we are content with what we have. I am saying all this to you, gallant youth, so you will not be ignorant of the life you have chosen and the state you must embrace, which I have here sketched for you; there are countless other things in it which you will discover for yourself, no less worthy of consideration than those you have heard."

With this the eloquent old gipsy made an end to his discourse. The novitiate replied that he was highly pleased to have been made acquainted with such praiseworthy statutes, and that he planned to profess in that order so grounded on reason and wise precepts, and that the only thing he regretted was not having learned sooner of that gay way of life, and that from that moment he renounced the profession of gentleman-at-arms and the vainglory of his illustrious lineage, and submitted all to the yoke, or rather, the laws by which they lived, for the desire to serve them was richly rewarded by their giving him divine Preciosa, for whom he would forswear crowns and empires, and if he desired them it would be only to lay them at her feet.

To which Preciosa replied: "Even though these legislators have determined by their laws that I am yours, and as such they have given me to you, I have determined by the law of my own will, which is the strongest of all, that I accept this only on the terms we two agreed upon before you came here. You must spend two years in our company before you enjoy mine, so you may not repent of your impetuousness nor I be deceived by my hastiness. Situations alter cases; you know the terms I have laid down; if you are willing to abide by them, it may be that I will be yours, and you mine; contrariwise, the mule has not yet been killed, your attire is sound, and not a penny of your money is gone. Your absence is less than a day; what is left of it you can employ in thinking over what is to your best advantage. These gentlemen have the power to surrender my body to you, but not my soul, which is free and was born free and will remain free as long as I wish. If you decide to stay, I shall think highly of you; if you leave, I shall not misprize you, for it is my opinion that amorous ardors run wild until they are brought up by reason or disappointment; and I would not have you behave toward me like the hunter who, once he has overtaken the hare he pursues, seizes it and then leaves it to follow another that flees him. There are eyes which, bedazzled, mistake glitter for gold, but soon learn the difference between the true and the false. This my beauty which you say I have, and which you prize more than the sun and esteem more than gold—how do I know that seen close at hand you may not find it dull and but a base metal to the touch? I allow you a space of two years to explore and consider what you should choose or what it would be better for you to reject; for once you have bought the jewel, only death can relieve you of it, so it is well to take time to examine and re-examine it, and make sure of its qualities or defects; for I do not govern myself by the barbarous and insolent license employed by these my kinsmen, who leave their wives or punish them whenever they see fit. And as I shall do nothing deserving of punishment, I do not intend to take as a partner one who will cast me aside when the spirit moves him."

"You are right, oh, Preciosa," spoke up Andrés at this point; "and so, if you wish me to allay your fears and do away with your suspicions, swearing to you that I shall not depart one jot from the orders you issue me, tell me by what kind of oath you wish me to swear, or what other assurance I can give you, for you will find me ready for anything."

"The oaths and promises made by a captive to secure his freedom are seldom kept once he has it," replied Preciosa; "and the same, it seems to me, holds true of a lover who, to achieve his desire, will promise the wings of Mercury and Jupiter's thunderbolts, as a certain poet promised me, swearing by the Stygian lake. I want no oath, Master Andrés, nor do I expect promises; all I want is to leave everything to the experience of this novitiate, and I will take upon myself the task of defending myself if you should take upon yourself that of offending me."

"So be it," answered Andrés. "I should like to ask only one thing of these gentlemen, my companions, and that is not to oblige me to steal anything for at least the space of a month, for I am afraid I shall not be a successful thief if I do not receive many lessons first."

"Hush, my son," said the old man, "here we shall train you in such fashion that you will prove an eagle at the trade; and once you know it, you will take such a liking to it that it will make your mouth water. Wait till you see what sport it is to set out empty-handed in the morning, and come back to the camp at night loaded down."

"I've seen some of those empty-handed ones come back well-scourged."

"You don't catch trout without getting your feet wet," answered the old man; "everything in life involves different risks, and the acts of a thief, those of the galleys, the lash, and the gibbet. But not because a ship runs into a storm or goes down do the others give up the sea. A fine thing it would be if because wars devour men and horses, there should cease to be soldiers. Besides, he of us who receives a flogging from the law, it is as though a habit had been conferred upon him which becomes him better than a blazon on his breast, and one of the fine ones. What matters is not to wind up treading the empty air in the flower of our youth and after our first misdemeanors. As for the tickling of our backs, or slapping the water in a galley, we don't give a peanut for it. Rest now in the nest under our wings, son Andrés, and in due time we shall send you out to fly where you will never return without prey, and, as I said, you will lick your chops after each theft."

"Well, to make up for what I might be stealing during the time I am excused from it," said Andrés, "I wish to divide up two hundred gold florins among all those of the camp."

No sooner had he uttered the words than a group of gipsies rushed over to him, and raising him in their arms above their heads, they chanted: "Hurrah, hurrah for the great Andrés!"; adding, "and long live Preciosa, his beloved lady fair!"

The women did the same with Preciosa, not without the envy of Cristina and the other gipsy maidens present, for envy lodges in gipsy camps and shepherds' huts as well as in the palaces of princes, and to see a neighbor prosper who, it seems to me, has no higher merits than I, is vexatious.

After this they ate abundantly, and the promised money was divided fairly and justly; Andrés's praises were sung anew; the beauty of Preciosa was lauded to the skies. At nightfall the mule was hit in the head and buried, and with this Andrés was safe from discovery; with it they buried its jewels, that is to say, saddle, bit, and bridle, like Indians who are interred with their richest possessions.

All that he had seen and heard, and the astuteness of the gipsies, left Andrés amazed, and he determined to follow and accomplish his undertaking without assuming their customs, or, at least, avoiding doing so in every way he could, hoping through his money to exempt himself from the need to obey them in things they ordered which were unjust. The next day Andrés begged them to move their camp farther from Madrid, for he was afraid of being recognized if he stayed there. They told him they had already decided to go to the hills of Toledo, and from there go around robbing all the surrounding countryside. Accordingly, they struck camp, and gave Andrés a donkey to ride, but he refused it, preferring to go afoot, serving as groom to Preciosa who, mounted on another, was delighted to see how she had triumphed over the gallant squire; and he was no less delighted to find himself beside the one he had made mistress of his will.

Oh, mighty power whom they call the sweet god of bitterness (a title our sloth and carelessness has conferred upon him), how truly you triumph over us and how disrespectfully you deal with us! Andrés is a gentleman and a youth of fine parts, reared most of his life in the Court with all the cosseting of his rich parents, and overnight such a change has taken place in him that he has deceived his servants and friends, defrauded the hopes his parents had placed in him, forsaking the route to Flanders, where he was to have displayed his bravery and increased the honor of his name, to come and prostrate himself at the feet of a girl, and be her lackey, who although beautiful beyond compare is, after all, a gipsy. Oh, privilege of beauty, which lays low at its feet, willy nilly, the firmest will!

Four days later they had reached a village two leagues from Toledo where they pitched their camp, first giving the mayor various articles of silver as a pledge that they would steal nothing from it or its environs. This done, all the old women, and some of the girls, and the men scattered through all the villages, or at any rate, those some four of five leagues distant from that in which they had pitched their camp. Andrés went with them for his first lesson in thieving; but even though they gave him many lessons on that sally, none of them took hold; on the contrary, given his noble blood, each theft committed by his teachers wrenched his soul, and on occasion he paid out of his own purse for the pilfering his companions had committed, moved to pity by the tears of the victims. This drove the gipsies to despair, who told him that this was contrary to their statutes and ordinances which denied charity a place in their breasts, for if they felt it they would have to stop being thieves, something which in no way suited them. In view of this, Andrés then said that he preferred to do his stealing alone, unaccompanied by anyone, for he was fleet of foot if danger threatened, nor did he lack courage to face it, and he wanted the reward or punishment of his stealing to be his.

The gipsies tried to dissuade him from this intention, telling him that the occasion might arise on which he would need company, both to attack as well as to defend himself, and that a person alone could not come by much booty. But for all they said, Andrés insisted on doing his thieving single-handed, his intention being to detach himself from the gang and buy with his money something he could say he had stolen, and in this way lay as light a load as possible on his conscience. Employing this scheme, in less than a month he brought more profit to the company than four of the most renowned thieves, which pleased Preciosa not a little to see her tender lover such a fine and wily thief. But notwithstanding, she was fearful of some misfortune, for she would not have wished to see him affronted for all the treasures of Venice, holding him in high regard for the many gifts and services he had rendered her.

They spent a little more than a month in the vicinity of Toledo, where they reaped a fine harvest, and from there they made their way to Extremadura, a rich, warm land. Andrés and Preciosa held chaste, discreet, and loving colloquies, and little by little she began to fall in love with the wit and goodly behavior of her lover; and likewise his love, if it were possible for it to increase, grew, so great was the virtue, sense, and beauty of his Preciosa. Wherever they went he won the prize and wagers as the best runner and jumper; he bowled and played handball remarkably well; he threw the bar with great strength and exceptional skill; in a word, his fame soon spread throughout Extremadura, and there was not a village where the talk was not about the gallant bearing of the gipsy Andrés Caballero and his accomplishments and skills, while side by side with this fame ran that of the beauty of the Gipsy Maid; nor was there a town, village, or hamlet where they were not called in to add to the gaiety of the votive feasts or for other special celebrations. In this manner the camp was rich, prosperous, and happy, and the lovers joyous with merely beholding one another.

It so happened that, having pitched their camp among a grove of cork oaks, somewhat withdrawn from the highway, one night, about midnight, they heard their dogs barking more fiercely and longer than was their habit; some of the gipsies went out, and with them Andrés, to see whom they were barking at, and they found a man, dressed in white, trying to defend himself from the two dogs that had him pinioned by a leg. They reached him, freed him, and one of the gipsies said:

"What devils brought you here, man, at this hour and so off the road? Did you perchance come to steal? You certainly picked the right place!"

"I did not come to steal," replied the bitten man, "and I don't know if I am off or on the road, though I see clearly that I have lost my way. But tell me, sirs, is there any inn or place near by where I can spend the night and dress the wounds your dogs have caused me?"

"There is no village or inn to which we can direct you," answered Andrés; "but to dress your wounds and spend the night, you will not lack for comfort in our shelters. Come with us for, although we are gipsies, we do not seem so in our charity."

"May God show it to you," replied the man, "and lead me where you like, for the pain in this leg is considerable."

Andrés and the other charitable gipsy (for even among devils some are worse than others, and among many bad men there is usually a good one) came over to him, and between the two they led him away. The night was bright with moonlight, so they could see that the man was a youth of genteel face and bearing; he was all dressed in white linen, and slung across his shoulders and tied about his chest he wore a kind of shirt, or linen pouch. They reached Andrés's shelter or tent, and quickly kindled a light and fire; and Preciosa's grandmother, who had been notified, came to treat the wounded man. She took several of the hairs from the dogs, fried them in oil, and after washing the two bites on his left leg with wine, she put the oil with the hairs on them, and over this a little chewed fresh rosemary, bandaged them well with clean cloth, and made the sign of the cross over the wounds, saying:

"Now sleep, friend, and God willing, this will be nothing."

While the wounded man was being treated, Preciosa was standing by looking at him intently, and he at her. Andrés noticed the attention with which the young man was regarding her, but laid it to the fact that Preciosa's great beauty made her the cynosure of all eyes. Finally, after the man's wounds had been treated, they left him alone on a bed made of dry straw, and for the time being decided to ask him nothing about where he was going, or anything else.

As soon as they were a distance from him, Preciosa called Andrés aside and said to him:

"Do you remember, Andrés, that paper I dropped in your house when I was dancing with my companions and which, I think, upset you?"

"I do remember," answered Andrés; "it was a sonnet in praise of you, and not bad."

"Well, you must know, Andrés," Preciosa went on, "that the

one who composed that sonnet is this youth whom we have left there in the cabin; I am sure of this, for he spoke to me in Madrid two or three times, and even gave me a very good ballad. It seems to me he was serving as a page there; not an ordinary one, but of those in the service of some prince; and I can truly say, Andrés, that the youth is well-bred and of good parts, and remarkably decent, and I cannot think why he has come here and in such garb."

"You cannot think why, Preciosa?" answered Andrés. "For no other reason than that the same attraction which has turned me into a gipsy has made him assume the likeness of a miller and come in search of you. Ah, Preciosa, Preciosa, how clear it is becoming that you wish to pride yourself on having more than one devoted swain! If this is the case, finish me off first, and then kill this other, and do not sacrifice us together on the altar of your deceit, that is to say, your beauty."

"God help me," replied Preciosa, "how touchy you are, Andrés, and by what a frail hair hang your hopes and my reputation, since with such ease your soul has been cleft by the sharp sword of jealousy. Listen to me, Andrés, if there were scheme or deceit of any sort, would I not have known how to hold my tongue and conceal the identity of this youth? Am I, perchance, such a fool that I would give you grounds to doubt my goodness and honest intentions? Hush, Andrés, I beg of you, and tomorrow try to find out from this youth who has aroused your doubts whither he is going or what he has come for. It might be that your suspicions were unfounded, though I am not mistaken about his being the one I have said. And for your greater satisfaction, as the time has come to satisfy you, no matter what the reason or purpose this youth has come for, send him on his way at once and make him go; all our people obey you, and not one will want to shelter him here against your wishes. If this should not prove to be the case, I give you my word that I shall not leave my abode, nor let his eyes behold me, nor those of any whom you do not wish to see me. Look, Andrés, it does not distress me to see you jealous, but I should be very sorry to see you behave unwisely."

"Unless you see me out of my senses, Preciosa," replied Andrés, "any other manifestation will be slight or as nothing to make you realize how all-pervading and onerous is the bitter and heavy doubt of jealousy. Nevertheless, I shall do as you bid me, and shall learn, if possible, what it is this Master Poet-Page is after, where he is bound for, or what it is he seeks; for it may be that by some thread he carelessly looses, I shall unravel the whole skein in which I fear he hopes to ensnare me."

"Jealousy never, as far as I can see," said Preciosa, "leaves the understanding free to judge things as they are; the jealous always see things through a telescope which turns trifles great, makes dwarfs giants, and suspicions truths. For your sake and mine, Andrés, proceed in this and in everything having to do with our plans prudently and wisely; and if you so act, I know that you will award me the palm for virtue and modesty, and for truth in the highest degree."

With this she took her leave of Andrés, and he waited for the dawn to hear the wounded man's statement, his soul filled with confusion and a thousand warring fancies. He could not believe otherwise than that the page had come there drawn by the magnet of Preciosa's beauty, for the thief judges everyone to be like himself. On the other hand, the satisfaction Preciosa had given him seemed to him so convincing that it constrained him to put aside his fears and to place all his happiness in the hands of her goodness.

Day came, and he visited the bitten man. He asked him what his name was, where he was going, and how it was that he was travelling so late and so aimlessly, although first he asked him how he felt and whether the pain of the bites had disappeared. To this the youth replied that he was better and felt no pain, and would be able to resume his travels. As for his name and destination, he said only that he was called Alonso Hurtado, and that he was on his way to Our Lady of the Rock of France, on a certain errand, and that to get there as quickly as possible he was travelling by night and had come by chance upon that camp where the watch dogs had reduced him to the state in which he found himself.

Andrés did not find this explanation convincing, but highly

suspicious; once more jealousy began to raise its head, and he said to him:

"Brother, if I were a judge and you had come under my jurisdiction for some offense which made it necessary to question you as I have just done, the answer you have given me would make it necessary to put you to the torment. I do not want to know who you are, what your name is, or whither you are bound; but I would suggest that if for some reason you must lie about this trip of yours, you should do so with more verisimilitude. You say your destination is the Rock of France, yet you are leaving it to the right, a good thirty leagues behind the site of this camp; you are travelling by night to arrive more quickly, and you are off the road among forests and oak groves where there are hardly paths, let alone roads. Friend, get up and learn to lie, and be on your way. But in return for this good advice I give you, will you not tell me one truth? I think you will, for you are such a bad liar. Tell me, are you not perchance one I have often seen in the Court, somewhat between page and gentleman, who had the reputation of being a great poet, one who composed a ballad and a sonnet to a gipsy maid who in recent days was around Madrid, and was known for her singular beauty? Tell me this, for I promise you by the faith of a gipsy gentleman to keep it as secret as you feel it should be. And note well that to deny that you are the one I say would get you nowhere, for this face I see here is the one I saw in Madrid. Without doubt the fame of your knowledge made me observe you often as an unusual and remarkable man, and thus your countenance was stamped on my memory, and I have recognized you even though attired in the garb you now wear, which is different from that in which I then saw you. Be not dismayed; take courage, and never fear that you have fallen into a den of thieves, but have come to a refuge where you will be protected and kept safe from all the world. Come, now, something has occurred to me, and if it is as I imagine, you can thank your lucky stars that you have encountered me. What I imagine is that, having lost your heart to Preciosa, that beautiful gipsy maid to whom you wrote the poems, you have come here in search of her, which does not lower you in my estimation; quite the contrary. For although I am a gipsy, experience has taught me the lengths to which the mighty power of love leads one, and the changes it brings about in those who fall under its jurisdiction and sway. If this is the case, as I firmly believe it to be, the gipsy maid is here."

"Yes, she is here, for I saw her last night," said the wounded youth. With this Andrés felt as though his life were ebbing away, for it seemed to him that his worst suspicions were confirmed. "Last night I saw her," the young man repeated; "but I did not venture to tell her who I was because it did not suit my plans."

"So," said Andres, "you are the poet I spoke of."

"I am," replied the youth: "I cannot and would not deny it. It may be that where I had thought to lose myself I may recover myself, if there is faith in the forests and hospitality in the hills."

"Be assured that there is," answered Andrés, "and among us gipsies, the greatest secrecy in the world. In this confidence, sir, you can open your heart to me, for in mine you will find only what you see, without a trace of duplicity. The gipsy maid is my kinswoman, and is bound to do as I say; if you want her as your wife, I and all her kinfolk will be glad to give her to you; and if as your mistress, there will be no quibbling, provided you have money, for greed is never absent from our camps."

"I have money," answered the youth; "in the sleeves of this shirt I have girded to my body I carry four hundred gold florins."

This gave Andrés another mortal fright, for he could only think that bringing so much money was for the sole purpose of winning or buying his beloved. With a faltering tongue he went on:

"That is a goodly sum; you have only to make your purpose clear, and to the harvest! For the girl, who is not at all foolish, will see how well it befits her to be yours."

"Ah, friend," answered the youth, "you must know that the motive that has made me change my garb is not love, as you say, nor a desire for Preciosa. Madrid has beauties who can and do steal away the heart and conquer the soul as well and better than the most beautiful gipsies, although I admit that the beauty of your kinswoman exceeds all those I have seen. What has brought me to this state, afoot and the prey of dogs, is not love but my misfortune."

With these words which the young man uttered, Andrés's flagging spirits revived, as he saw that things were taking a different turn from what he had been imagining. Eager to emerge from his confusion, Andrés reassured him of the confidence with which he could reveal his troubles, and so the young man went on:

"I was in Madrid, in the house of a man of title, whom I served not as a master but as a kinsman. This gentleman had an only son, his heir, who, both because of our kinship as well as because we were of the same age and rank, treated me with familiarity and great friendship. It so happened that the young gentleman fell in love with a high-born maiden, whom he would gladly have chosen as his wife, had it not been that, like a dutiful son, his will was subject to that of his parents, who hoped to wed him to one of still higher rank. Nevertheless, he served her unseen by all eyes, which, with tongues as well, might publish his desires; mine alone were witness of his endeavors. One night, which misfortune must have appointed for the case I shall now relate, as the two of us were going down the street and past the door of this lady, we saw beside it two men, of goodly appearance; my kinsman wished to see who they were, and he had no sooner started toward them than they quickly laid hand to sword and buckler, and made for us. We did the same, and attacked them with similar arms. The encounter was brief, as the lives of our two adversaries did not last long, for in two thrusts, directed by the jealousy of my kinsman and the defense I lent him, they lost their lives—a strange case, and rarely seen. Thus triumphant in a thing we would not have wished, we returned home and, secretly gathering together all the money we could come by, we went to the monastery of St. Jerome to await the day when the occurrence would come to light and conjectures would begin about the slayers. We learned that there was no clue pointing to us, and the prudent monks advised us to return home so our absence would not cause or arouse suspicion against us. And just as we had decided to take their counsel, we were informed that the magistrates of the Court had put the parents of the maiden and the maiden herself under arrest, and that among the servants whom they cross-questioned, a maid of the lady had told how my kinsman patrolled the street of her lady day and night. With this clue they had gone to look for us, and not finding us, but instead clear proof of our flight, it was held in all the Court that we were the slayers of those two gentlemen, for gentlemen they were, and of high rank. Finally, at the advice of my kinsman the Count, and the monks, after remaining hidden in the monastery for a fortnight, my comrade, dressed in monk's habit, set out on the road to Aragon, planning to cross over to Italy, and thence to Flanders until it was seen how the matter would be settled. I wanted to divide and separate our fortunes, so our fate would not take the same course; choosing a different route, and dressed as a friar's servant, I set out on foot with a monk who left me at Talavera. From there I journeyed alone, avoiding the highway, until last night I came to this oak grove where you have seen what happened to me. And if I asked how to get to the Rock of France, it was to give some answer to what I was asked, for the truth of the matter is that I have no notion where the Rock of France lies, except that I know that it is beyond Salamanca."

"So it is," replied Andrés, "and you have already left it to the right, nearly twenty leagues from here; so you can see what a straight road you would be travelling if you were going there."

"The one I plan to travel," answered the youth, "is that to Seville. There I have a Genoese gentleman, a great friend of my relative the Count, who is in the habit of sending large shipments of silver to Genoa, and my plan is for him to make a place for me among those who transport it, as one of them, and by this stratagem I can get safely as far as Cartagena, and thence to Italy, for two galleys will soon be arriving to ship this silver. There, my friend, you have my history. Now you see that it is the child of pure misfortune rather than blighted love. But if these gipsy gentlemen would be willing to take me in their company as far as Seville, if they plan to go there, I would pay them well; for I have a feeling that I would travel safer in their company, and not beset with fear as I am."

"They will take you," answered Andrés, "and if not with our camp, as I do not know yet if we are going to Andalusia, you could go with another which we will be encountering in two days; and if you give them something of what you carry, you can overcome other even greater difficulties."

Leaving him, Andrés went to inform the rest of the gipsies of what the young man had told him, and what he wanted, together with his offer of good pay and reward. All were agreed that he should remain in the camp; Preciosa alone was against it, and her grandmother said that she could not go to Seville, or its environs, because years before she had played a joke on a cap-maker by the name of Triguillos, who was well-known there, whom she had induced to climb into a vat of water up to his neck, naked, with a crown of cypress on his head, waiting for the stroke of midnight to emerge from the vat and dig for a rich treasure which she had made him believe was buried in a certain corner of his house. She said that when the good cap-maker heard matins rung, not to miss his opportunity, he hurried so fast to get out of the vat that he knocked it and himself over on the ground, and the fall and the broken shards had cut him, the water gushed out, and he was left swimming in it and shouting that he was drowning. His wife and the neighbors came with candles and found him going through the motions of swimming, puffing and crawling along on his belly, flailing about with arms and legs, and screaming: "Help, help, I am drowning!" He was so terrified that he truly believed he was drowning. They took hold of him, and saved him from that danger; he recovered his senses, and told them the joke the gipsy had played on him; yet, nevertheless, he dug a fathom deep at the spot she had indicated, in spite of the fact that everybody told him it was a lie of hers. And if a neighbor had not interfered, because he had already reached the foundations of his house, he would have brought both houses tumbling down with his digging. The story spread throughout the city, and even the children pointed to him and told about his credulity and her lie.

The old woman told this, which was her excuse for not going

to Seville. The gipsies, who already knew from Andrés Caballero that the youth was carrying a large sum of money, gladly accepted him in their company, and offered to protect and hide him for as long as he liked, and they decided to change their route, turning left, and enter La Mancha and the kingdom of Murcia. They called the young man and informed him what they planned to do for him; he thanked them, and gave them a hundred gold florins to divide up among themselves. With this gift they became softer than sables; only Preciosa was not too happy over the stay of Don Sancho, as the youth said he was called. But the gipsies changed his name to Clemente, and so he was known thenceforward. Andrés, too, was somewhat put out, and not too pleased at Clemente's remaining, for it seemed to him that he had forsaken his earlier plan too easily. But Clemente, as though he had read his thoughts, said that he was happy to be going to the kingdom of Murcia, because it was close to Cartagena where, if the galleys called, as he thought they must, he could easily pass over to Italy. In the end, to keep him in closer view, and to watch his acts and observe his thoughts, Andrés decided that Clemente should be his comrade, and Clemente looked upon this friendship as a great mark of favor toward him. They were always together, spending freely, scattering florins, running, jumping, dancing, and throwing the bar better than any of the gipsies, and they were more than a little loved by the gipsy women, and highly respected by the men.

And so they left Extremadura and entered La Mancha, and little by little went making their way to the kingdom of Murcia. In all the villages and hamlets through which they passed they were challenged to games of handball, fencing, running, jumping, throwing the bar, and other exercises of strength, skill, and agility, and from all of them Andrés and Clemente emerged victorious, as had been said of Andrés alone. And during all this time, which was more than a month and a half, Clemente never had the opportunity, nor did he seek it, to talk with Preciosa, until one day, when she and Andrés were together, he came over to them because they called to him, and Preciosa said:

"From the moment you came to our camp I recognized you, Clemente, and there came to my mind the verses you gave me in Madrid. But I did not want to say anything, as I did not know what your intention was in coming to our camp. When I learned of your misfortune, I was deeply distressed, and my heart put up its defenses, for it was alarmed, thinking that just as there were Don Juans in this world who transformed themselves into Andreses, so there might be Don Sanchos who took other names. I am speaking to you in this manner because Andrés has told me that he has informed you of who he is, and of the reason for which he has become a gipsy." It was true that Andrés had told him all his story in order to share his thoughts with him. "And do not think that recognizing you was of no small profit to you, for thanks to me and what I said about you, your acceptance and admission to our company was made easier, and may God permit that with us you find all the good your heart desires. I want you to repay this good wish of mine by not reproaching Andrés for the lowliness of his intention, nor point out to him how ill it becomes him to continue in this state; for although I imagine that his will is the prisoner of mine, yet I should regret to see him give evidence, however light, of any repentance."

To which Clemente replied: "Do not think, unique Preciosa, that Don Juan revealed to me who he was out of any frivolity. First I recognized him, and first his eyes revealed his purpose; first I told him who I was, and first I guessed the imprisonment of his will, to which you refer; and he, giving me the credit it was fitting that he should, confided his secret to my secrecy, and he can bear witness that I praised his decision and the employment he had chosen; for I am not, oh Preciosa, so dim of wit that I cannot discern the scope of beauty's powers, and yours, which outstrips the farthest reaches of beauty, is sufficient excuse for the gravest errors, if those committed for such cogent reasons can be called error. I thank you, madam, for what you said in my favor, and I hope to repay you with my wish that these amorous entanglements may have a happy ending, and that you may enjoy your Andrés, and Andrés his Preciosa, with the approval and blessing of his parents; and that from such a handsome couple we may behold in the world the most beautiful new offspring that well-disposed nature can form. This is what I wish, Preciosa, and this is what I shall always say to your Andrés, and nothing that could swerve him from his well-directed thoughts."

So warmly did Clemente express the foregoing thoughts that Andrés wondered whether he had spoken them as a lover, or a person holding himself in check; for the foul disease of jealousy is of so sensitive and subtle a nature that it fastens upon the motes of the sun, and anything which touches the object of his passion vexes and devours the lover. But, for all this, his jealousy was not confirmed, thanks more to Preciosa's kindness than to his own happiness, for lovers always feel themselves unhappy as long as they do not possess what they desire. In a word, Andrés and Clemente were comrades and great friends, all due to Clemente's honorable intentions and the modesty and prudence of Preciosa, who never gave Andrés any grounds to be jealous of her.

Clemente had a touch of the poet, as he had demonstrated in the verses he gave Preciosa, and Andrés had his own pretensions, and both of them were fond of music. It so happened that while they were camped in a valley four leagues from Murcia, one night, to pass the time, the two of them seated themselves, Andrés at the foot of a cork oak, Clemente beside an ilex, each with a guitar, and invited by the silence of the night, they began to sing these stanzas, Andrés leading off and Clemente answering:

ANDRÉS

Behold, Clemente, the starry veil
With which this frosty night
Vies with the day,
Starring the heaven with bright lights.
And in this resemblance,
If your divine wit reads clear,
That countenance can be seen
Where beauty so great resides.

CLEMENTE

Where beauty so great resides,
And where the precious
Modesty so cherished
Goes hand in hand with goodness,
All in one being found,
Which no human tongue can praise
Without recurring to the divine,
The great, the rare, the solemn, the strange.

ANDRÉS

The great, the rare, the solemn, the strange.
A style never before employed,
Raising to heaven
Thy sweet name, unmatched
In this world, oh gipsy maid,
Arousing amaze, awe and wonder,
Which I would cause Fame
To carry to the eighth sphere.

CLEMENTE

To carry to the eighth sphere
Would be right and just,
Giving the heavens pleasure
When the sound of her name was heard;
And on earth 'twould produce
Wherever the sweet name resounds,
Music for the ears,
Peace for the soul, glory for the senses.

ANDRÉS

Peace for the soul, glory for the senses
Is felt whene'er sings
The siren who enchants
And lulls the most alert;

So is my Preciosa,
Whose smallest grace is her beauty,
My sweet delight,
Crown of grace, honor of wit.

CLEMENTE

Crown of grace, honor of wit,
Art thou, beautiful gipsy,
Cool of the morn,
Gentle zephyr in ardent summer;
Ray with which blind love
Turns iciest breasts to fire,
Force which so acts
That it gently kills and satisfies.

Free man and captive gave no sign of finishing, had there not arisen at their backs the voice of Preciosa who had been listening to theirs. Amazed to hear her, and without stirring, lending her their closest attention, they listened to her. She (improvising or singing verses which had been composed for her, I cannot say) with marvellous grace, as though in answer to them, sang the following verses:

In this amorous enterprise
In which love has me engaged,
I hold it greater happiness
To be chaste than beautiful.

The lowliest plant,
If it aspires to rise,
By favor or by nature
Reaches to the skies.

In this my lowly copper,
Enamelled with chastity,
No good desire is lacking
No wealth not superfluous.

It gives my heart no grief
Not to be loved or esteemed;
For I myself shall fashion
My good fortune and luck;

Let me do my part,
With goodness my guiding star,
And let heaven do and decide
What it then thinks best.

Let me see if beauty
Has such privilege
That, raising me so high,
I aspire to greater heights.

If 'tis true that souls are equal,
That of a peasant may
Equal through its worth
Those of royal rank.

As for mine, I feel
That it lifts me to highest rank,
For majesty and love
Occupy different seats.

With this Preciosa brought her song to an end, and Andrés and Clemente rose to receive her. The three enjoyed a pleasant colloquy, and Preciosa's conversation revealed her discretion, her purity, and her shrewdness in such a degree that Clemente found Andrés's behavior justified, which he had not thought up to then, attributing to his youth rather than his judgment his bold determination.

That morning camp was broken, and they went to take up quarters in a village in the jurisdiction of Murcia, three leagues from the city, where a misfortune befell Andrés which almost cost him his life. What happened was that after having given certain goblets and trinkets of silver as security to the village, as was their custom, Preciosa and her grandmother, and Cristina with two other girls, and Clemente and Andrés, took lodging in the inn of a wealthy widow, who had a daughter of some seventeen or eighteen years, more forward than beautiful, whose name was Juana Carducha. Having seen the gipsies dancing, the devil took possession of her, and she fell so wildly in love with Andrés that she made up her mind to tell him so and take him as her husband, even if all her kin objected. And she sought the opportunity to make her thoughts known to him, and found it in a barnlot where Andrés had gone to get two donkeys. She came up to him quickly, so as not to be seen, and she said:

"Andrés," (for she already knew his name) "I am unmarried and rich; my mother has no child but me, and this inn is hers and, in addition, she has many vineyards and two other houses. You have found favor in my eyes; if you wish me for your wife, I am yours; answer me quickly, and if you are wise, you stay here and you will see the life we lead."

Andrés was amazed at the girl's resolution, and with the speed she had requested he answered her:

"Fair maiden, I am already bespoken to be wed, and we gipsies marry only gipsies; may God keep you for the kindness you have wished to do me, of which I am not worthy."

Juana Carducha was not two fingers short of dropping dead at the withering answer, to which she would have replied if she had not seen several of the gipsy girls coming into the barnlot. She left abashed and crestfallen, and would have avenged herself had it been possible. Andrés sensibly decided to put distance between them, and avoid that snare the devil was laying for him; he could clearly read in Carducha's eyes that no matrimonial bonds were needed for her to throw herself at his head, and he had no desire to see himself on foot and alone in such a skirmish. Therefore he requested all the gipsies to leave the village that very night. They, who always obeyed him, immediately prepared, and collecting their pledges that afternoon, they left.

Juana Carducha, who felt that half her soul was leaving her

with Andrés's departure, and seeing that there was not time to seek the fulfillment of her desires, she decided to oblige him to remain by force, if not by choice. So, with the shrewdness, skill, and secrecy which her evil desires taught her, she hid among Andrés's belongings which she knew for his, some valuable corals, two lockets of silver, and others of her trinkets; and no sooner had the gipsies left the inn than she began to shout that they were making off with her jewels. At her outcry the officers of the law came, and all the villagers. The gipsies halted and they all swore that they were carrying no stolen property, and that they were willing to open all the sacks and stores of their camp. This disturbed the old gipsy woman not a little, for she feared the scrutiny might reveal Preciosa's trinkets and Andrés's attire, which she had put away with great care and secrecy. But that minx of a Carducha took care of that quickly, for after they had examined the second bundle, she said to ask which was that of the gipsy who danced so well, for she had seen him go into her room twice, and possibly he had stolen them. Andrés understood that she was referring to him, and laughingly answered:

"Fair maiden, this is my dressing room and this is my donkey: if you should find in the one or on the other what you are missing, I shall repay you with interest, in addition to accepting the punishment the law provides for thieves."

The ministers of the law immediately began to unload the donkey, and quickly found the stolen articles. Andrés was so amazed and dumfounded by this that he stood like a statue, as though made of stone, and voiceless.

"Were not my suspicions well-founded?", spoke up Juana Carducha. "See what an innocent face this great thief puts on."

The mayor, who was at hand, began to vomit forth insults against Andrés and all the gipsies, calling them notorious thieves and highwaymen. Not a word did Andrés reply to all this, perplexed and wondering, without hitting upon the girl's treachery. At this a swaggering soldier, a nephew of the mayor's, who had appeared, said:

"Take a look at the state this gipsy rogue is in, rotten with stealing. I'd be willing to bet he'll make all sorts of excuses and deny the theft, even though he has been caught red-handed. The whole lot of you ought to be sent to the galleys! How much better it would be for this rogue to be in one, serving His Majesty, insteading of going around from village to village dancing, and stealing in inns and on the heath. By my faith as a soldier, I feel like giving him a blow that will lay him at my feet."

And saying this, without further ado, he raised his hand and landed him such a blow that he brought him out of his bemusement and recalled to him the fact that he was not Andrés Caballero, but Don Juan and a gentleman; whereupon, throwing himself upon the soldier with great speed and greater anger, he snatched the latter's sword from its sheath, and ran him through, leaving him dead upon the ground.

Now began the screaming of the villagers, the lamentation of the old mayor, the swooning of Preciosa, the dismay of Andrés at seeing her in a faint, and the rushing to arms to fall upon the killer. The confusion grew, the shouting rose, and Andrés, in his concern for Preciosa, neglected his own defense; and fate so willed it that Clemente was not present at the disastrous event, having already set out from the village with the baggage. Finally, so many fell upon Andrés that they took him prisoner and bound him with two heavy chains. The mayor would have been in favor of hanging him immediately if it had been in his power. But as the village was under the jurisdiction of Murcia, it was necessary to send him there. They did not move him until the next day, and during the one he spent there Andrés underwent great abuse and sufferings at the hands of the mayor, his subordinates, and all the villagers. The mayor arrested as many of the remaining gipsies as he could, although most of them ran away, including Clemente who was afraid of being taken and his identity discovered. At last, with the indictment and a great caravan of gipsies, the mayor and his constables, together with a number of armed men, entered Murcia. In the throng were Preciosa and the unfortunate Andrés, loaded down with chains, astride a mule, handcuffed and wearing an iron collar. All Murcia turned out to see the prisoners, for the news had been received of the death of the soldier. But on that day Preciosa's beauty shone forth so that no one who looked at her did not bless her, and the news of her beauty came to the ears of the Corregidor's wife who, out of curiosity to see her, made her husband order that the gipsy maid was not to be put in the jail where all the others were lodged. Andrés was confined to a narrow dungeon where the darkness and the lack of Preciosa's light so afflicted him that he firmly believed he would never emerge from there except to go to his grave. They brought Preciosa, accompanied by her grandmother, to the Corregidor's wife so she could see her, and as soon as she laid eyes on her she said: "They rightly praised your beauty." And approaching her, she embraced her tenderly, and feasting her eyes upon her, asked the grandmother how old the girl was.

"Fifteen years," answered the old woman, "give or take two months."

"That would have been the age of my poor Costanza! Oh, friends, how this girl has opened the wounds of my unhappiness!" said the lady.

With this Preciosa took the Corregidor's wife's hands, and kissing them again and again, she bathed them in tears as she said:

"My lady, the gipsy who is a prisoner is not at fault, for he was unduly provoked; he was called a thief, which he is not; he was struck a blow in the face on which is written the quality of his nature. For the sake of God and because of who you are, my lady, let him receive the justice due him, and let not the Corregidor make haste to visit on him the punishment with which the laws menace him. And if my beauty has found any favor in your eyes, for its sake bestow the same on the prisoner, for my life will end with his. He is to be my husband, but just and honest obstacles have prevented us from celebrating our marriage as yet. If money were needed to win his pardon, our entire belongings will be sold at public auction, and even more will be given than is asked for. My lady, if you are acquainted with love and at some time have felt it, and you now feel it for your husband, take pity on me, for I tenderly and chastely love mine."

During all the time she was saying this, she never released the lady's hands, nor took her eyes from her, the while shedding bitter and piteous tears. For her part, the Corregidor's wife kept Preciosa's hands clasped in hers, gazing on her no less attentively, and with no fewer tears. At this moment the Corregidor entered, and finding his wife and Preciosa so woebegone and so linked together, he stood there, astonished by the tears and by the girl's beauty. He asked the reason for so much grief, and Preciosa's reply was to release the lady's hands, and throw herself at his feet, saying:

"Pity, my lord, pity! If my husband dies, I am dead. He is not at fault; but if he were, let me take his punishment upon myself. And if this is not possible, at least delay the trial until means for his aid can be sought and secured; it may well be that to him who did not sin through malice Heaven will send the gift of grace."

The amazement of the Corregidor grew as he listened to the gipsy maid's plea, and but for his reluctance to give signs of weakness, he would have joined his tears to theirs. While this was taking place, the old gipsy woman was turning over in her mind many, great, and various things, and after long reflection and thought, she said:

"My lord and lady, await me a little while, for I shall see that these tears are turned to laughter, though it cost me my life."

And she hurriedly left the room, leaving the others perplexed at her words. In the interval of her absence, Preciosa's tears never ceased, nor her supplication that the trial of her betrothed be delayed, her intention being to inform his father so he could come and take a hand in the matter. When the old gipsy returned she had a small coffer under her arm, and she requested the Corregidor and his wife to step into a room with her, as she had great things to tell them in private. The Corregidor, thinking that she wished to show him certain stolen goods of the gipsies to incline him in favor of the prisoner, immediately withdrew with her and his wife into an antechamber, where the old woman, falling to her knees before the two of them, said:

"If the joyful news I am about to give you, my lord and lady, does not merit the reward of forgiveness for a great sin I have committed, here I am ready to receive the punishment you wish to mete out to me; but before I confess, I would like you to tell me first whether you recognize these jewels."

And taking the small coffer which contained those belonging to Preciosa, she placed it in the hands of the Corregidor who, opening it, saw those childish trinkets, but had no notion of what they signified. His wife, too, looked at them, but neither did she identify them. All she said was: "These are the trinkets of some small child."

"That is the truth," answered the gipsy, "and the identity of the child is set forth in this folded paper."

The Corregidor quickly opened it, and read what it said: "The girl's name was Doña Constanza de Azevedo y de Meneses; her mother, Doña Guiomar de Meneses, and her father, Don Fernando de Azevedo, knight of the Order of Calatrava. I stole her away on Assumption Day, at eight in the morning, of the year 1595. The child was wearing the ornaments contained in this coffer."

The Corregidor's wife had no sooner heard the contents of the paper than she recognized the trinkets, lifted them to her lips, kissed them over and over again, and then fainted away. The Corregidor hurried to attend her, before asking the gipsy about his daughter; and when she had revived, she said:

"Good woman, angel rather than gipsy, where is the owner, I mean the child to whom these trinkets belonged?"

"Where, lady?" responded the gipsy. "You have her here in your house. That gipsy maid who brought tears to your eyes is the owner of them, and without a doubt your daughter, for I stole her from your house in Madrid on the day and the hour set forth in this paper!"

On hearing this the bewildered lady kicked off her sandals and ran all breathless to the room where she had left Preciosa, and found her surrounded by her handmaidens and servants, still weeping; she rushed up to her, and without saying a word, swiftly unfastened her bodice, and looked to see if she had under her left breast a little mark, like a white mole, a birthmark, and she found that with time it had grown larger. Then, with the same haste, she unshod her, and baring a foot of snow and marble, as though turned on a lathe, she found there what she was looking for, which was that the two last toes on the right foot were joined together by a ligament of flesh which, when she was a child, they had never wanted to cut, not to make her suffer. The breast, the toes, the ornaments, the day of the kidnapping, the gipsy's confession, and the surprise and delight the parents had felt on first seeing her, confirmed beyond a doubt in the lady's soul that Preciosa was her daughter. Whereupon, clasping her in her arms, she led her to where the Corregidor and the old gipsy were.

Preciosa did not know what to think, for she had no idea why all those examinations of her had been made, and, above all, why she found herself caught up in the arms of the Corregidor's lady, who was giving her one kiss after another. Doña Guiomar, on coming before her husband with her precious burden, transferred it to his arms, saying as she did so:

"Receive, sir, your daughter Costanza, for this is she, beyond question. In no wise doubt it, sir, for I have seen the joined toes and the birthmark on her breast, and, besides, my soul has been telling it to me ever since my eyes caught sight of her."

"I do not doubt it," answered the Corregidor, holding Preciosa in his arms; "for I have undergone the same effects as you; besides, with all these proofs together, how could it be otherwise except it were a miracle?"

The entire household was in a state of wonder, each asking the other what was happening, and they were all wide of the mark; for who could have imagined that the gipsy maid was the daughter of their masters?

The Corregidor instructed his wife, his daughter, and the old gipsy that the matter was to be kept secret until he divulged it; and at the same time he told the old woman that he forgave her the injury she had done in stealing away his soul, and that in recompense for having returned it she deserved great reward. The only thing he regretted, he went on, was that, knowing Preciosa's rank, she should have betrothed her to a gipsy who was, in addition, a thief and a murderer.

"Ah," spoke up Preciosa, "my lord, he is neither a gipsy nor a thief, even though he has slain a man. But he did it to one who had offended his honor, and he could not help showing who he was, and killing him."

"What do you mean he is not a gipsy, my daughter?" asked Doña Guiomar.

Whereupon the old gipsy briefly recounted the story of Andrés Caballero, how he was the son of Don Francisco de Carcamo, knight of the Order of Santiago, and that his name was Don Juan de Carcamo, and he belonged to the same Order, and she had his garments which he had taken off when he put on those of a gipsy. She also told them that the arrangement between Preciosa and Don Juan was that he was to spend two years with them before deciding whether they should wed or not. She extolled the chastity of both, and Don Juan's fine qualities.

All this was as amazing to the Corregidor and his lady as the discovery of their daughter, and he sent the old woman to fetch him Don Juan's garments. This she did, and returned with another gipsy who was carrying them.

In the interval of her going and coming, Preciosa's parents asked her a thousand questions, to all of which she replied with such discretion and winsomeness that even if they had not known her to be their daughter, they would have lost their hearts to her. They asked her if she felt a fondness for Don Juan. She replied that she felt no more than that which came from the gratitude she had toward one who had been willing to lower himself to the station of a gipsy for her sake; but that this gratitude would not go beyond whatever her parents desired.

"Hush, Preciosa, my child," said her father, "for I want you to keep this name of Preciosa in memory of your loss and return, I as your father will see to it that you make a marriage which is consonant with your rank."

Preciosa sighed as she heard this, and her mother who was wise, understood that she sighed because of her love for Don Juan, and she said to her husband:

"Sir, Don Juan de Carcamo being of the station he is, and loving our daughter so much, it would not be a bad idea for us to give her to him as his wife."

"She has only come back to us today," he replied, "and you already want us to lose her? Let us enjoy her for a time; for once she is married, she will no longer be ours but her husband's."

"You are right, husband," she replied; "but order Don Juan brought forth from the dungeon where he must be."

"He must be," said Preciosa, "for a thief, murderer, and, above all, a gipsy, will not have been given better accommodation."

"I am going to see him and listen to his confession," replied the Corregidor, "and once more I enjoin upon you, my lady, that no one is to know anything of this until I so decide."

And embracing Preciosa, he went at once to the prison. He entered the dungeon where Don Juan was confined, and allowed no one to accompany him. He found him with both feet in stocks, and still wearing the iron collar. The room was dark, but he ordered a transom opened, through which a dim light entered; and when he could see him, he said:

"How now, my fine fellow? If only I had all the gipsies in Spain fastened up like this, to get rid of them all in one day, as Nero wanted to do with Rome, at one fell swoop! Know, sly thief, that I am the Corregidor of this city, and I am here to learn, as man to man, if it is true that a young gipsy maid who came with you is your wife."

Hearing this, Andrés imagined that the Corregidor must have fallen in love with Preciosa, for jealousy is a body of so subtle a composition that it enters other bodies without breaking, displacing, or dividing them. But notwithstanding, he replied:

"If she has told you that I am her husband, it is full true; if she has said I am not, she has also spoken the truth, for it is not possible for Preciosa to tell a lie."

"So truthful is she?" answered the Corregidor. "That is no small merit in a gipsy. Know then, lad, that she has said you are her betrothed, but that you have not yet pledged your vows. She has learned that, in keeping with your crime, you must die for it, and she has begged me that before your death I wed her to you, because she aspires to the honor of being the widow of so great a thief as you."

"Then do, my Lord Corregidor, as she requests; and if I am wed to her, I will leave contented for the other life, provided I depart this one with the name of being hers."

"You must love her dearly," said the Corregidor.

"So much," replied the prisoner, "that if I could put it into words it would be nothing. Truly, my Lord Corregidor, my trial is ended. I killed the one who would have deprived me of my honor; I adore this gipsy maid; I will die happy if I die in her grace, and I know that God's grace will not fail us, for we have both kept chastely and to the letter what we promised each other."

"Then tonight I shall send for you," said the Corregidor, "and you and Preciosita shall be wed in my house, and at noon tomorrow you will be on the gallows; in this way I shall have complied with the demands of justice and your desires."

Andrés thanked him, and the Corregidor returned to his house and informed his wife of what had taken place with Don Juan, and of other things he intended to do. During the time he was absent, Preciosa had told her mother the history of her life, and how she had always believed herself to be a gipsy and the granddaughter of the old woman; but that she had always held herself higher than being a gipsy warranted.

Her mother asked her to tell her truly if she really loved Don Juan de Carcamo. Preciosa, blushing and with her eyes on the ground, answered that because she had believed herself to be a gipsy, and that she would improve her fortune by marrying a habited knight of so high rank as Don Juan de Carcamo, and because she had seen by experience his worthy nature and upright behavior, she had at times looked upon him with kindly eyes; but, as she had already said, she had no other wish than their desires.

Night came, and at about ten o'clock they brought Andrés forth from prison, having removed his handcuffs and iron collar, but not the heavy chain that girded his whole body from the feet up. In this manner he arrived without being seen by anyone except those who conducted him to the Corregidor's house, and with silence and secrecy they led him to a room where he was left alone. After a time a priest entered and told him to make confession, for the next day he was to die. To which Andrés replied:

"Right gladly will I make my confession, but how is it that they are not marrying me first? And if I am to be wed, it is a very poor marriage bed that awaits me."

Doña Guiomar, who was aware of all that was taking place, told her husband that the frights being given Don Juan were excessive, and that he should temper them because they might cost him his life. This seemed good advice to the Corregidor, and so he went into the room to inform the priest who was hearing Andrés's confession, that first he was to marry the gipsy to Preciosa, the gipsy maid, and afterwards he could make his confession and commend himself to God with all his heart, for He often makes His mercy to fall in the season when hope is most withered.

And so Andrés came out into the room where there were only Doña Guiomar, the Corregidor, Preciosa, and two servants of the house. When Preciosa saw Don Juan bound and fettered with that heavy chain, pale of visage, and his eyes giving evidence of the tears he had shed, her heart fell, and she grasped the arm of her mother who was standing beside her. Doña Guiomar, clasping her to herself, said:

"Be of good cheer, child; for all you see will work out to your satisfaction and good."

Preciosa, who knew nothing of what was going on, could find no consolation; the old gipsy woman was perturbed, and the bystanders agape to see how the matter was going to turn out. The Corregidor said:

"Your Reverence, this gipsy lad and maid are those Your Reverence is to wed."

"I cannot do this unless the conditions required in such cases are not first complied with. Where were the banns published? Where is the authorization of my superior to perform this marriage?"

"That has been an oversight on my part," replied the Corregidor, "but I shall see that the Bishop gives it to you."

"Well, until I see it," replied the priest, "these people will have to excuse me."

"The priest has behaved as he should," remarked the Corregidor, "and it might be that this is the hand of providence so that Andrés's punishment may be delayed; for, truly, he is to wed Preciosa, and first the banns must be published, whereby there will be a gain of time which often gives a sweet solution to many bitter difficulties. And with all this, I should like to ask Andrés whether, if fortune should so guide his affairs, and free of these frights and shocks he should find himself Preciosa's husband, he would consider himself happy being either Andrés Caballero or Don Juan de Carcamo."

As soon as Andrés heard himself called by his rightful name, he said: "Inasmuch as Preciosa has not wished to remain within the bounds of silence, and has revealed who I am, even though this good fortune should turn me into the monarch of the world, I prize her so that she is the limit of my desires; nor would I ask further favor than that of salvation."

"For this goodly courage you have shown, Señor Don Juan de Carcamo, in due time I shall make Preciosa your legitimate consort, and I now give and entrust her to you in fee, as the richest jewel of my life, and of my soul. And hold her as you say, because in her I give you Doña Costanza de Meneses, my only daughter, who just as she is your peer in love, is in no wise your inferior in rank."

Dumfounded was Andrés at the affection shown him, and in brief words Doña Guiomar related to him the loss of their daughter, her recovery, with the indubitable proofs which the old gipsy had given of her theft. With this Don Juan was even more amazed and astonished, but joyful beyond words. He embraced his parents-in-law, called them his parents and masters, and kissed the hands of Preciosa, who with tears sought his.

The secret came out, the news of the happening spread with the going forth of the servants who had been present. When this reached the ears of the mayor, uncle of the dead soldier, he saw the paths of his revenge blocked, for the rigors of justice would have no place in dealing with the Corregidor's son-in-law.

Don Juan put on his travelling attire, which the old gipsy brought him. Prison and iron chains were transformed into freedom and chains of gold; the sadness of the imprisoned gipsies, to happiness, for the next day they were released on bail. The uncle of the dead man received the promise of two thousand ducats in return for withdrawing his complaint and forgiving Don Juan. The latter, mindful of his comrade Clemente, sent for him, but he could not be found nor traced until four days later definite word came that he had embarked in one of the Genoese galleys in the port of Cartagena, and had sailed.

The Corregidor informed Don Juan that he knew for a fact that his father, Don Francisco de Carcamo, had been appointed Corregidor of that city, and that it would be well to await him so that with his consent and blessing the marriage could be carried out. Don Juan said he would not depart one whit from what he ordered; but that, before everything else, he must be betrothed to Preciosa. The Archbishop gave permission for the betrothal to be announced with a single bann. The city held a great celebration (for the Corregidor was well-liked) with fireworks, bullfights, and jousts on the engagement day. The old gipsy woman stayed on in the family, for nothing could induce her to leave her granddaughter Preciosa.

The news of what had happened and the betrothal of the gipsy maid reached the Court; Don Francisco de Carcamo learned that his son was the gipsy lad, and Preciosa the gipsy maid he had seen, whose beauty excused in his eyes the recklessness of his son (whom he had looked upon as lost inasmuch as he knew he had not gone to Flanders), and the more so as he saw how fortunate he was to have married the daughter of such a great man, and as wealthy a one, as Don Fernando de Azevedo. He hastened his departure the sooner to see his children, and within twenty days he was in Murcia. With his arrival the festivities were renewed, the wedding was held, tales were exchanged, and the poets of the city, where there are several very good ones, took it upon themselves to commemorate the strange case, together with the peerless beauty of the gipsy maid. The famous Master Pozo wrote in such fashion that the fame of Preciosa will endure in his verses as long as the ages.

I neglected to tell how the enamored daughter of the innkeeper, Juana Carducha, revealed to the authorities that her account of Andrés, the gipsy's, theft was untrue. She confessed her love and her fault, which received no punishment, for in the new-found joy of the wedded pair vengeance was buried and mercy resurrected.

RINCONETE AND CORTADILLO

One of those hot days of summer two lads chanced to find themselves in the Molinillo Inn, which stands on the outskirts of the famed plains of Alcudia on the way from Castile to Andalusia. Their age might have been around fourteen or fifteen; neither was over seventeen. Both had a pleasing air, though they were ragged, rent, and dishevelled. Cape, they had none; their breeches were of sail-cloth, and their hose, of flesh; to be sure, their shoes made up for everything, for the rope-soled sandals of the one had seen much going and coming, and those of the other, more "holey" than righteous, were soleless, and more like hobbles than shoes. The one wore a green hunting cap, the other, a flat-crowned, broad-brimmed hat without a band. Over his back and girt around his chest, one carried a chamois-colored, beeswax-dressed shirt, stuffed into one sleeve; the other carried nothing, not even a knapsack, although in his bosom could be seen a big lump which afterwards proved to be one of those Flemish collars, stiffened with grease, so worn that its threads resembled drawn work. Wrapped in it for safe-keeping was a deck of cards that were oval in shape, for use had worn down the corners, and to make them last longer they had been trimmed to that shape. Both the lads were sunbrowned, their nails dark-bordered, and their hands not too clean. One carried a single-edged sword, the other a yellow-handled knife, of the kind called cow stabbers.

The two lads had come out to pass the afternoon heat under an eave that overhung the window, and seating themselves across from each other, the one who seemed the older said to the younger:

"From what land is Your Excellency, and whither are you bound?"

"My land, Sir Knight, I know not," answered his interlocutor, "nor where I am going, either."

"Well, the truth of the matter," answered the old lad, "is that Your Excellency does not seem to be from Heaven, nor is this any place in which to settle; therefore you needs must be going on."

"Right you are," answered the younger; "but what I said was the truth. My land is not mine, for all I have there is a father who does not consider me a son, and a step-mother who treats me like a step-child; I go where chance may take me, and I shall call a halt where I find someone to give me what I need to get through this miserable life."

"Has Your Excellency any trade?" asked the older.

To which the younger replied: "Only to run like a hare, bound like a deer, and handle scissors very deftly."

"All that is very good, useful, and profitable, for some sacristan will give Your Excellency the collection on All Soul's Day in return for your cutting him paper flowers for the Tomb on Maundy Thursday."

"That is not my style of cutting," replied the younger. "My father, by the mercy of God, is a tailor and hosier, and he taught me to cut gaiters which, as Your Excellency well knows, are half hose with galoshes, better known by the name of leggings, and I came to cut them so well that in truth I could pass examination as a master, were it not that my ill fortune has hidden my light under a bushel."

"All that and more happens to good people," answered the older, "and I have ever heard it said that the best talents go begging; but Your Excellency is still of an age to mend your luck. But if I am not mistaken, and the eye does not lie, Your Excellency has other secret skills which you do not choose to reveal."

"So I do," replied the younger, "but they are not for public display, as Your Excellency has so rightly remarked."

To which the older answered: "I may tell you that you can go far and not find so close-mouthed a lad as I; and to encourage

Your Excellency to unbosom yourself and feel at ease with me, I shall take the first step and tell you about myself, for I cannot but think there is some secret design in fate's having brought us together here, and I feel that we shall be, from this moment until our dying day, true friends. I, genteel sir, am from Fuenfrida, a village well-known and famous by reason of the illustrious travellers who are always passing through it. My name is Pedro del Rincón; my father is a man of position, for he is an agent of the Holy Crusade, that is to say, a pardoner or seller of papal indulgences. Sometimes I worked at the trade with him, and I learned it so well that I could hold my own with the best in the business when it comes to dispensing bulls. But one day I developed a greater fondness for the money from the bulls than for the bulls themselves, whereupon I clasped a bag of it to my bosom, and bag and I landed in Madrid, where with the opportunities which that city daily offers, in no time I had disembowelled the bag, and left it more wrinkled than a newly-wed's handkerchief. The caretaker of the money came after me; I was taken into custody; I was given short shrift, though when those gentlemen saw my tender years, they were satisfied with tying me to the whipping post and tickling my back for a while and banning me from the capital for four years. I bore it patiently, hunched up my shoulders, suffered my turn at the whipping post, and left with such haste to fulfill my exile that I did not stop for horses. I took such of my belongings as seemed most valuable, among them these cards"—and with this he brought out those already mentioned which he was carrying in his starched collar—"with which I have earned my living playing twenty-one in the inns and taverns between Madrid and here. And even though, as Your Excellency can see, they are filthy and worn, they have a marvellous power if you know how to use them, for any way you cut them, the top card is always an ace; and if you know anything about this game you can see what an advantage it is to know that the first card you will draw will be an ace, which can count either as one point or eleven, and with this advantage, since what you are aiming for is twenty-one, your money stays at home. Aside from this, I learned from the cook of a certain ambassador various tricks at lamb-skin, or lansquenet, also known as *andaboba*; so, if you are a master at cutting leggings, so am I at the science of Vilhan.[1] With this I am safe against dying of hunger, for even if I stop at a farm there is always someone there ready to while away the time with a hand or two, as we can soon prove. Let's spread the net and see if we don't snare some bird among these mule-drivers stopping here. What I mean to say is let's us two start a game of twenty-one, as though we were playing in earnest, and if anyone wants to make a third, he will be the first to be parted from his money."

"With my blessing," answered the other, "and I am much obliged to you for having given me an account of your life, whereby you are entitled to know mine which, putting it briefly, is as follows. I was born in that pious village which lies between Salamanca and Medina del Campo. My father is a tailor; he taught me his trade and, gifted as I was, I went from cloth cutting to purse cutting. I was tired of the humdrum village existence and my step-mother's harsh treatment of me, so I left the village and went to Toledo to follow my calling there. I performed wonders in that city, for there was never a medallion dangling from a headdress nor a purse so well hidden that my fingers did not find or my scissors snip, even though Argus's eyes were watching over it. And in the four months I spent in that city I was never caught off guard, nor chased by constables, nor given away by an informer. True, there was a week when a stool pigeon working with us and at the same time with the officers of the law gave a report on my skill to the mayor who, attracted by my good qualities, wanted to meet me. But being the humble person I am, I do not enjoy having dealings with personages of such rank, and so I left the city with such dispatch that I had no time to provide myself with a mount, monies or even a wagon."

"That's of no matter," said Rincón; "and now that we know each other, there is no call for all these pretenses and high-and-mighty airs. Let's come out and confess that we don't have a penny to bless ourselves with, nor even a pair of shoes."

[1] *Vilhan or Bilhan was the legendary inventor of playing cards.*

"So be it," answered Diego Cortado, which was the name of the younger. "And inasmuch as our friendship, as Your Excellency, Master Rincón, has said, is to be for life, let us initiate it with honored and praiseworthy ceremonies."

Getting to his feet, Diego Cortado embraced Rincón, the latter in turn clasping him closely and affectionately, whereupon the two of them began a game of twenty-one with the aforementioned cards, free of dust and chaff, but not of grease and slipperiness. After a few hands Cortado could turn up an ace as well as Rincón, his teacher.

At this point a mule driver came to the door for a breath of fresh air, and asked if he could take a hand. They welcomed him warmly, and before half an hour had gone by they had won twelve *reales* and twenty-two *maravedís* from him, which was like giving him twelve spear thrusts and twenty-two thousand sorrows. Thinking that because they were only boys, they would not be able to stand up to him, he tried to take his money from them. But the one setting hand to his sword, and the other to his yellow-handled knife, gave him such a bad time that if his comrades had not come out, things would have gone hard with him.

Just then there chanced to come along the road a group of horsemen on their way to make their afternoon halt at the Alcalde Inn, half a league farther on. Seeing the fight between the mule driver and the boys, they separated them, and told the lads that if Seville was their destination, to come along with them.

"That is where we are bound for," said Rincón, "and we will serve Your Excellencies in whatever you may command."

Without further delay they rushed out in front of the mules and went off with the travellers, leaving the mule driver despoiled and furious. The inn mistress was amazed at the young rogues' good manners, for unbeknown to them, she had overheard their conversation. When she told the mule driver that she had heard them say that the cards were crooked, he tore his beard and wanted to set out after them to the other inn in order to get his money back, because he said it was a great indignity and offense to his standing

for two boys to have tricked a man like him.) His comrades held
held him back, advising him not to go, if for no other reason than
not to proclaim his lack of shrewdness and his credulity. Finally
their arguments prevailed upon him to stay where he was, though
they did not console him.

Meanwhile, Cortado and Rincón attended the travellers so zeal-
ously that for most of the trip they let them ride behind them, and
even though this gave them an opportunity to investigate the contents of the luggage of their temporary masters, for the time being
they passed it up, not to lose the chance that had been afforded
them to make the trip to Seville where they were longing to go.
But, in spite of this, as they came into the city at vespers through
the Customs Gate for baggage inspection and payment of duty,
Cortado could not restrain himself from slitting the valise or satchel
one of the party, a Frenchman, carried on the crupper of his saddle.
With his bone-handled knife he dealt it so long and deep a wound
that its contents were plainly visible, and he deftly removed two
good shirts, a sun dial, and a small memorandum book. None too
pleased with their spoils when they examined them, the boys assumed that inasmuch as the Frenchman had kept that satchel by his
side, he would not have filled it with things of such slight value as
those they had removed. They thought of having another try, but
decided not to, thinking that he might have missed what was gone
and taken good care of what was left.

Before the theft was discovered they took their leave of those
who until then had been their benefactors, and the next day they
sold the shirts at the second-hand market outside the Arenal gate,
getting twenty *reales* for them. When this transaction was completed, they set out to see the city. They were lost in wonder at the
size and splendor of its cathedral, and the great crowd of people
along the river, for it was the season for loading the fleet. There
were six galleys anchored off shore, the sight of which made them
sigh and even fear the day when their offenses might condemn
them to spend the rest of their lives aboard them. They also saw
many porters moving about carrying baskets; they asked one of them

what kind of work he was doing, if it was hard, and what he earned. The lad they questioned was an Asturian, and he told them the work was easy, there was no tax to pay, and that there were days when he earned five or six *reales,* on which he could eat, drink, and make merry like a king, without need to find himself a master to whom he would have to give security, and that he could eat whenever he felt like it, for meals were served at any hour even in the lowliest tavern in the city.

The two friends were well impressed by the Asturian's account, nor did the work displease them, for it seemed to them that it fitted them like a glove, enabling them to ply their own trade in secrecy and safety because of the opportunities it offered to enter houses everywhere. They decided to provide themselves with the necessary equipment at once, inasmuch as they had to stand no examination. They asked the Asturian what they should buy, and he told them they would each need small bags, new or clean, for bread, and three palm-leaf baskets, two large and one small, to carry meat, fish and fruit. He took them to where they were on sale, and with the money from the booty they had taken from the Frenchman, they bought everything they needed, and within a couple of hours they were skilled at their new trade, to judge from the way they used their baskets and carried their bags. Their guide informed them as to where they should go: to the meat market and San Salvador Square in the mornings; on fish days to the Fish Market and the Costanilla; every afternoon to the river, and on Thursday to the Fair.

They learned this lesson by heart, and early the next morning they took their place in San Salvador Square. No sooner had they arrived than they were surrounded by others plying the same trade, who could see that they were newcomers by the brightness of their bags and baskets. They asked them a thousand questions, all of which they answered with circumspection and restraint. While this was taking place a student and a soldier came over, and attracted by the cleanliness of the baskets of the two novices, the one who looked like a student summoned Cortado, and the soldier, Rincón.

"May it be in the name of God," both said.

"May this be a good augury for my trade," said Rincón, "with Your Excellency giving me my initiation, Sir."

"The initiation will not be a bad one for I am in funds and I am in love, and today I am giving a banquet for some friends of my lady."

"Well, you load me up as much as you like, Your Excellency, for I have the will and the strength to carry off this whole market place, and, if necessary, even to help with the cooking with right good will."

The soldier was pleased with the lad's witty remarks, and told him that if he wished to work as a servant, he would get him out of that lowly calling. To which Rincón replied that, as that was the first day he had worked at it, he did not want to give it up so soon, until he had at least seen its good and its bad side. But if he did not find it to his liking, he gave him his word he would enter his service in preference to that of a canon.

The soldier laughed, loaded him up well, and then showed him his lady's house so he would know it in the future and there would be no need, when he sent him again, to accompany him. Rincón promised to behave loyally and courteously; the soldier gave him three *cuartos,* and in a twinkling he was back in the square so as to miss no opportunity. The Asturian had instructed them to this effect, and also that when they were carrying small fish, as for example, dace, or sardines, or plaice, they might filch a few and act as tasters, sparing themselves the expense of a meal. But this had to be done with great care and foresight so as not to lose their good reputation, which was what mattered most in that calling.

For all he returned so quickly, Rincón found Cortado back at his post. Cortado came over to him and asked how he had made out. Rincón opened his hand and showed him the three *cuartos.* Cortado put his in his bosom and pulled out a purse which had once been amber-scented; it was well plumped-out.

"This, and two *cuartos,* is the payment His Reverence the student gave me. But you'd better take it, Rincón, just in case something might happen."

He had no sooner slipped it to him when, lo and behold the student appeared, sweating profusely and looking like a death's head. When he saw Cortado he asked him if he had happened to see a purse—and he gave him the description—containing fifteen gold florins, three pieces of two *reales,* and a sum of *maravedís* in *cuartos* and *ochavos,* which he was missing. He asked him if he had relieved him of his purse while they were marketing. To which, with amazing hypocrisy, not turning a hair or showing the least sign of guilt, Cortado answered:

"All I can say about that purse is that it cannot be lost unless Your Excellency was remiss in its safe-guarding."

"That's just what has happened, sinner that I am," answered the student. "I certainly must have been remiss, for it has been stolen from me."

"That is what I think," said Cortado; "but there's a cure for everything in this world except death. And the first and most important thing Your Excellency should employ is patience, bearing in mind that God made us out of dust, and tomorrow will be another day, and who lives by the sword shall perish by the sword. Who knows but what, some day, the very one who lifted your purse will repent and return it to you newly perfumed."

"I could do without the perfuming," answered the student.

Cortado went on: "Moreover, there are letters of excommunication, and banns, and diligence, which is the mother of good fortune. Though, to tell you the truth, I'm glad I was not the lifter of the purse, for if Your Reverence is in holy orders it would seem to me that I had committed some great incest or sacrilege."

"And what a sacrilege," groaned the student. "For although I am not a priest, but the sacristan of certain nuns, the money in that purse was the quarterly payment of a chaplaincy which a friend of mine, a priest, sent me to collect for him, and it is hallowed and sacred money."

"That is the thief's problem," spoke up Rincón at this juncture. "I wouldn't want to be in his shoes. There is a judgment day coming when everything will be known, and then we'll see what's what, and who the rascal was who dared to snatch, steal, and make off with the quarterly payment of the chaplaincy. What, pray, is the annual income, Sir Sacristan?"

"Go ask the whore who bore me! Am I in a frame of mind to talk about the income?" retorted the sacristan with more anger than was becoming. "If you know anything, tell me; and if not, God be with you; I am going to have the town crier publish it."

"That does not seem to me a bad idea," said Cortado; "but be sure you do not err in the description of the purse nor the exact amount it held, for if you do by as much as a farthing, you'll never lay eyes on it again, and that is my prophecy."

"Have no fear about that," answered the sacristan, "for it is more fixed in my memory than the sound of the bells. I shall not err by one tittle."

With this he took from his pocket a lace-trimmed handkerchief to wipe his face which was dripping sweat like a still, and no sooner had Cortado seen it than he marked it for his own. When the sacristan left Cortado followed him, overtook him on the cathedral steps where, calling him aside, he began to spout such a spate of nonsense about the theft of the purse and the possibility of its recovery, holding out hope but never finishing a sentence he began, that the poor sacristan listened to him in utter bewilderment, unable to make head or tail of what he was saying, though he asked him to repeat his words several times. Cortado looked him straight in the face without ever taking his eyes off his, and the sacristan did the same, bemused with his words. This gave Cortado the opportunity he needed to carry out his scheme, and delicately removing the handkerchief from the man's pocket, he took his leave of him, telling him that he should try to meet him in the afternoon in the same place, for he had his suspicions that a boy following the same trade, who was about his own size and somewhat light-fingered, had taken the purse. He was going to make it his business to find out, whether it took a few days or many.

This comforted the sacristan a little and he took his leave of

Cortado, who rejoined Rincón. The latter had been watching all that went on from a distance. A little way off there was another basket-carrier, who had seen all that had happened, and Cortado's handing over of the handkerchief to Rincón. Sauntering up to them, he said:

"Tell me, my gallants, are you members of the light-fingered gentry?"

"Gallant sir," replied Rincón, "we do not understand what you are talking about."

"You don't catch on, Sir Sharpers?" answered the other.

"We don't catch on," answered Cortado. "If you have anything else on your mind, out with it; if not, go with God."

"So you don't understand!" said the lad. "Well then, I'll spell it out for you. What I mean, gentlemen, is are Your Excellencies thieves? Though I don't know why I ask, for I know you are. But tell me, how is it you have not yet gone to Señor Monipodio's customhouse?"

"Do thieves in this part of the country have to pay duty?" inquired Rincón.

"If they don't pay duty," answered the lad, "at least they have to register with Señor Monipodio, who is their father, mentor, and protector. I would therefore advise you to come with me to do him fealty. Otherwise, if you venture to commit a theft without his approval, it will cost you dear."

"I thought," said Cortado, "that stealing was a free enterprise on which neither tax nor duty was levied, and that if payment was required, it was in a lump sum, with neck or back going security. But if this is as you say, and each country has its customs, let us observe those which prevail here, which being the most important in the world, must have the wisest of all. So let Your Excellency lead us to this gentleman you mention, for I already suspect, from what I have heard, that he is a person of standing, generous and skilled in the trade."

"Is he important, skilled and a master hand!", replied the lad. "So much so that in the four years he has been our overseer and father, only four of us have wound up with a hempen collar, some thirty have made the acquaintance of the lash, and sixty-two are on the high seas."

"By my troth, sir," said Rincón, "I no more understand what you are saying than I can fly."

"Let us be going and I will explain it on the way," answered the lad, "along with other things you should know as you know your own name."

He proceeded to explain the meaning of other terms from the thieves' cant, known as *germanía*. And his discourse was lengthy, for they had a goodly distance to go. On the way Rincón inquired of his guide:

"Is Your Excellency perchance a thief?"

"That I am," the other answered, "at the service of God and good folk, though not one of the more advanced, for I am still in the first year of my novitiate."

"This is the first time I've ever heard that there are thieves in the world to serve God and good folk," remarked Cortado.

"Sir," answered the lad, "that is too deep for me; all I know is that each can praise God in his own fashion, especially in view of the order Monipodio has given all his godchildren."

"Beyond question it must be good and holy if it makes thieves serve God," said Rincón.

"So good and holy is it," replied the lad, "that I doubt it could be improved upon as far as our calling is concerned. He has given orders that out of our takings we give a tithe or alms for oil for a lamp that burns to a highly venerated image in this city, and verily we have seen wondrous results from this good deed. A few days ago they gave the *ansia* to a *cuatrero* who had lifted a pair of *roznos*; and for all he was nothing but skin and bones and had malaria, he bore it without singing as though it were nothing at all. We of the trade attribute this to his piety, for his own strength would not have seen him through the executioner's first *desconcierto*. As I know you are going to ask me the meaning of some of the words I have used, I shall apply the remedy before I take sick, and explain them to you before you ask. Know, then, that *cuartrero* means horse thief; *roznos* are asses, begging your pardon; *ansia* is torment; first *desconcierto* means the first turn of the rope applied by the executioner. But we go even farther: we say our rosary over the days of the entire week, and there are many of us who do not steal on Fridays, nor have intercourse with any woman named María on Saturdays."

"That all seems excellent to me," answered Cortado; "but tell me, Your Excellency, is any other form of restitution or penance prescribed beyond those you have mentioned?"

"As far as restitution goes, that is out of the question," answered the lad. "It would be impossible because of the many shares into which the loot is divided, each of the ministers and contracting parties getting his cut. Therefore, the original thief can restore nothing, especially as there is no one to urge this upon us as we never make confession; and if there are letters of excommunication against us, we never learn of them for we never go to church when they are read out, except on days of jubilee, when we are sure of good pickings because of the great crowds that gather then."

"And doing no more than this, you gentlemen think you are leading a good and pious life?" asked Cortadillo.

"And what is there bad about it?" answered the lad. "Isn't it worse to be a heretic, or a renegade, or kill your father and mother, or be a solomite?"

"What Your Excellency must mean is a sodomite," said Rincón.

"That's what I said."

"They're all bad," answered Cortado. "But inasmuch as fate has brought us into this fraternity, Your Excellency will kindly lead on, for I am dying to meet this Señor Monipodio, of whom I have heard such praise."

"Your desires will soon be satisfied," said the lad, "for his house is already in sight. You gentlemen stay here at the door while I go in and find out if he can receive you, this being his hour for holding audience."

"So be it," answered Rincón.

Taking a few steps forward, the lad entered a house that not only was not prepossessing, but frankly sinister in appearance, and the other two stood waiting at the door. He quickly came back and beckoned them in, and told them to wait in a little brick-paved courtyard which was so clean and scrubbed that it shone as with carmine. To one side stood a three-legged bench, and to the other a water jar with a broken lip, on top of which was a little pitcher in the same sorry state. To the other side was a bulrush mat, in the middle of which stood a flower pot (or, as they call them in Seville, a *maceta*) of sweet basil.

The boys looked over the furnishings of the house while they waited for Señor Monipodio to come down. And as he took his time, Rincón made bold to enter a low-ceilinged room, one of the two which opened on to the courtyard, and there he saw two fencing foils and two cork shields hanging from four nails, as well as a big chest without a lid or cover of any sort, and three other bulrush mats spread on the floor. On the opposite wall there was one of those cheap prints of Our Lady, and beneath this hung a palm leaf basket and, set in the wall, a white basin, which led him to the conclusion that the basket was used as a poor box and the basin for holy water, as proved to be the case.

While he was making this reconaissance, two youths about twenty years old, dressed like students, came into the house, and not long afterwards, two porters and a blind man. Without saying a word they began to stroll about the courtyard. Before long they were joined by two old men, dressed in baize and wearing glasses, which gave them a grave air that commanded respect. Each carried a rosary with clinking beads in his hand. These were followed by an old woman with billowing skirts; without speaking a word she went into the room and after taking holy water, knelt with great piety before the image of Our Lady. After a goodly interval, during which she kissed the floor three times and raised her arms and eyes to heaven an equal number, she arose, put her contribution into the basket, and came out to the courtyard where the others were. In short, in a little while there were gathered there as many as fourteen persons of differing attire and station. Among the last to arrive were two dashing young blades, sporting long mustaches, wide-brimmed hats, Flemish collars, colored hose, out-sized swords, pistols in place of daggers, and with a buckler at their belts. On entering they cast a sidewise glance at Rincón and Cortado, as if surprised by their presence there. Coming over to them, they asked if they were members of the brotherhood. Rincón answered that they were, and at the service of Their Excellencies.

At this very moment Señor Monipodio came down, as desired as he was welcomed by that upright gathering. He looked to be about forty-five or forty-six, and was tall, dark of complexion, with eyebrows that met, and a heavy black beard. His eyes were deep-set. He was wearing a shirt whose opening at the throat revealed a thicket, so overgrown was his chest with hair. He wore a baize cape that covered him almost to his feet, which were thrust into soft slippers. His legs were covered to the ankles with wide linen breeches, and his hat was of the sort favored by rogues—broad-brimmed and bell-crowned. From a shoulder strap that crossed his chest and back hung a short broadsword resembling the Moorish variety; his hands were short, hairy, thick-fingered, with splayed nails. His legs were not visible, but his feet were uncommonly large, broad, and bunioned. In a word, he was the most uncouth and monstrous barbarian in the world. With him came Rincón and Cortado's guide, who, taking them by the hand, presented them to Monipodio, saying:

"Here, my lord Monipodio, you have the two fine lads I told you about. Put them through their paces, and Your Excellency will see if they are not worthy to enter our group."

"That I will do right gladly," replied Monipodio.

I forgot to say that as Monipodio came down all those who were awaiting him immediately made him a low, deep bow, with the exception of the two swashbucklers who, with a devil-may-care air, raised their hats and then resumed their stroll along one side of the courtyard, while Monipodio walked along the other, asking the newcomers about their trade, their home, and their parents.

To this Rincón answered: "Our trade you know from our being here; where we come from or our parents seems to me of little importance, for it is not a question of presenting credentials for admission to some honorable order."

"Right you are, my son," answered Monipodio, "and it is very shrewd of you to keep the matters you mention to yourself; if luck were to prove adverse, it would not be well to have an entry on the court records, signed and sealed by a notary, to the effect that So-and-so, son of So-and-so, residing in such and such a place, was this day hanged or flogged, or something along those lines which, if nothing more, falls unpleasantly on the ears of the good. So, I repeat, it is the part of wisdom to conceal one's place of origin, one's parents, even to change one's name, although among us nothing needs to be kept secret, and for the time being all I want to know is your names."

Rincón gave his, and Cortado likewise.

"Henceforth," Monipodio went on, "it is my wish and will that you, Rincón, be called Rinconete, and you, Cortado, Cortadillo, which are names that fit your age and our regulations like a glove. These regulations also demand that we know the names of the parents of our members, for it is our custom to have certain masses said for the souls of our deceased and our benefactors, deriving the fee for the masses from our pickings. And these masses, thus said and paid for, are held to be of great help to the aforesaid souls in their expiation.

"Included among our benefactors is the lawyer who defends us, the constable who gives us warning, the executioner who handles us mercifully, the person who when one of us goes fleeing down the street, with the crowd shouting after him: 'Stop thief! Stop thief!' steps between him and the pack to say: 'Let the poor devil go; he's unlucky enough as it is. It's his affair. His sins will find him out!' Benefactresses, too, are the women who with the sweat of their brow come to our aid, both in prison or the galleys. And our fathers and mothers who brought us into the world, and the court clerk who, if he is of a mind to, can make of a crime a misdemeanor, and give a misdemeanor a light penalty. For all these I have enumerated our fraternity each year celebrates their anniversary with such pomp and solemnity as lie within our means."

"Certainly," said Rinconete (now confirmed with this name), "this is an accomplishment worthy of the exalted and profound talent we have heard that Your Excellency possesses. But our parents are still alive; if we should have news of their passing, we shall at once inform this blessed and auspicious brotherhood, so their souls may benefit by this suffrage or anniversary mass of which Your Excellency speaks, carried out with the customary pomp and solemnity."

"So it shall be done, or my name is not Monipodio." Then turning to the guide he asked: "Tell me, Ganchuelo, have the lookouts been posted?"

"That they have," replied the guide, known as Ganchuelo. "Three sentries have been put on the alert, and there is no fear of our being taken by surprise."

"Coming back, then, to our subject," said Monipodio, "I should like to know, my sons, where your capabilities lie so I can assign you tasks according to your tastes and skills."

"As for me," replied Rinconete, "I know a thing or two about cards; I can always come up with a buried ace; I can recognize a marked card; I play a good game of ombre, four- or eight-handed; I take a back seat for nobody when it comes to shuffling or dealing off the bottom of the deck. I am completely at home in the dark, and am as good a man at drawing a straight as any veteran of Naples, and I can skin the shrewdest customer easier than I could lend him two reales."

"That's a beginning," answered Monipodio, "but it's all old stuff, which any amateur knows, and can be used only on those who don't know when to quit; but with time we'll make something of you; with these rudiments and half a dozen lessons, I trust in God that you will turn out a first-class apprentice, and perhaps even a master at the trade."

"It will be for the greater good of Your Excellency and the members of this fraternity," replied Rinconete.

"And what about you, Cortadillo, what are your claims?" inquired Monipodio.

"As for me," answered Cortadillo, "I know the trick they call 'two gets you five,' and I can clean out a pocket with speed and skill."

"Is that all?" asked Monipodio.

"Unfortunately, that's all."

"Don't take it to heart, son," said Monipodio; "you have put into a harbor where you will not founder, and a school from which you will not depart without learning all it is fitting for you to know. And in the matter of stout-heartedness, how goes it with you, boys?"

"How should it go except very well?" answered Rinconete. "We have the heart to undertake anything having to do with our calling and its practice."

"All well and good," answered Monipodio; "but I should like you to have it when the going gets rough, too, and to suffer half a dozen *ansias* without letting out a peep."

"We already know, Señor Monipodio," spoke up Cortadillo, "what *ansias* are, and we are up to anything; we are not so ignorant that we don't know that the throat pays for the tongue's wagging, and it is no small mercy of Heaven that the brave man, to give him no other name, has the choice between life or death on his own tongue. As though the word *No* had more syllables than *Yes!*"

"That's enough," Monipodio cut him short; "that argument alone persuades, convinces, obliges, and compels me to name you members in full standing, and to omit the year of apprenticeship."

"I am of the same opinion," remarked one of the swashbucklers. And with one voice all present, who had been listening to the conversation, approved the decision, requesting Monipodio to grant the newcomers all the privileges of their brotherhood immediately, because their affable bearing and bright conversation warranted it. He answered that, in accordance with their wishes, he forthwith granted and bestowed upon the youths the privileges in question, and advised them to hold them in due esteem, for they exempted them from the payment of the established tax of one half of their first theft; from the performance of any menial tasks for the whole year, that is to say, running errands to the jail for any older member or to his house, on behalf of their customers; allowed them to get drunk and eat their fill without first securing the permission of their prefect; share in the pickings of their elder brothers as though they were one of them, and other advantages which they regarded as high favor, and for which all gave thanks in courteous words.

While this was going on a boy came running in, all out of breath, and said: "The constable in charge of vagrants is coming to this house, but he doesn't have his gang with him."

"Let nobody get excited," said Monipodio, "for he is a friend and never comes to do us harm. Calm yourselves; I'll go and talk with him."

They all settled down, after their first uneasiness, and Monipodio went to the door, where he remained for some time talking with the constable. When he returned he asked: "Whose turn was it at San Salvador Square today?"

"Mine," answered the guide.

"Then how is it," asked Monipodio, "that I have not been informed about an amber purse which disappeared with fifteen gold florins, two double *reales*, and some odd *cuartos?*"

"It's a fact," said the guide, "that such a purse disappeared; but I did not take it, nor have I any idea who did."

"Don't try any tricks with me," answered Monipodio. "That purse has to show up, for the constable is making inquiries about it, and he is a friend of ours who over the year does us a thousand favors."

The lad swore once more that he knew nothing about it. Monipodio's gorge began to rise, and his eyes seemed to shoot sparks as he said:

"Let no one try to play fast and loose with the slightest rule of our order, for it will cost him his life. The purse must be handed over, and if it is being concealed to avoid the payment due, I shall give him his full share and make up the balance out of my own pocket, for, come what may, the constable must be satisfied."

Again the lad swore and began to curse, saying that he had not taken the purse nor laid eyes upon it, which only added fuel to the flames of Monipodio's ire. The whole company began to grow incensed at seeing their statutes and covenants thus flouted.

In view of all this dissension and confusion, Rinconete decided it would be well to temper them and soothe his superior officer who was bursting with indignation. So, after a word with his friend Cortadillo, he produced the sacristan's purse and said:

"Let this matter rest, gentlemen; here is the purse, not a penny short of the constable's count, which my comrade Cortadillo lifted today, and in addition here is a handkerchief he took from the same owner."

With this Cortadillo produced the handkerchief and held it out. Whereupon Monipodio said:

"Cortadillo the Good (for by this title and sobriquet he is to be known henceforth) may keep the handkerchief, for which I shall make good. And the purse will be handed over to the constable, for it belongs to a sacristan who is his kinsman, and it is well to abide by the adage that says: 'It is not too much to give a leg to the one who gave you a whole fowl.' This good constable overlooks more things in one day than we can repay in a hundred."

To a man, all present approved the gentlemanly behavior of the new initiates, and the decision and opinion of their superior officer, who stepped out to return the purse to the constable. Cortadillo received the title of "the Good" as though he were Don Alonso Pérez de Guzmán, "the Good," who tossed over the walls at Tarifa his own knife, with which his only son's throat was cut.

When Monipodio came back there entered with him two girls, their faces and lips painted, their bosoms whitened, and wearing half-length serge shawls. So brazen and shameless were they that as soon as Rinconete and Cortadillo laid eyes on them they judged them to be from a house of ill fame, and they were completely right. Directly they came in they went over with open arms, the one to Chiquiznaque and the other to Maniferro, as the two swashbucklers were called. Maniferro's name came from the fact that he had an iron hand to replace the one he had been sentenced to have cut off. The two bullies embraced them joyfully, and asked if they had brought along anything to wet their whistles.

"Would we forget that, my artful one?" answered the one who was called Gananciosa. "Your page Silbatillo will soon be along with a basket filled with what God has been pleased to provide."

And so it was, for a moment later a boy came in with a hamper covered with a sheet.

All rejoiced over Silbato's arrival, and Monipodio quickly ordered one of the rush mats spread in the middle of the courtyard, and told them all to sit down around it, and after a little snack they would discuss business. To this the old woman who had been praying to the image spoke up:

"Monipodio, my son, I am not in a festive mood, for I have had a giddiness of the head for the past two days that is driving me crazy; besides, before noon I must go to make my devotion and light my candles to Our Lady of the Waters and the Blessed Crucifix of St. Augustine, which I would not miss come snow or blizzard. The reason I am here is that last night the Renegade and the Centipede brought to my house a clothes basket somewhat larger than this one, full of household linens, and, God help me, they were still wet and sudsy, as the poor fellows had not had time to wring them out; they were sweating so that it would break your heart to see them come panting, and the sweat pouring off them; like a pair of angels they were. They told me they were following a drover who had just weighed some sheep at the slaughterhouse to see if they could relieve him of a huge catskin purse he was carrying. They did not empty the basket or count the linen, trusting to the uprightness of my conscience; and as I hope God will grant my righteous wishes and free us all from the arm of the law, I have not touched the basket and it is just as it came to me."

"Your word is not in doubt, Mother," replied Monipodio. "Leave the basket as it is, and I will come around when it gets dark and tot up its contents, and give each his share, truly and exactly, as I am in the habit of doing."

"Be it as you say, son," answered the old woman. "And as it is getting late, give me a swallow, if you can spare it, to comfort this poor stomach that is always so faint."

"Indeed you shall have it," spoke up Escalanta, as Gananciosa's companion was called. And uncovering the basket, a wine skin came to light which must have held two arrobas of wine, and a cork jar which could easily take some two liters. Escalanta filled it up and handed it to the devout old woman who, taking it in both hands and blowing off a little of the foam, said:

"You have poured me a lot, daughter Escalanta; but God will give strength for everything." And raising it to her lips, she drained the bowl without stopping for breath, and said when she had finished: "It's from Guadalcanal, and it's still got a taste of lime to it. May God comfort you, daughter, as you have comforted me; though I am afraid it may not set well on an empty stomach, for I've had no breakfast."

"It won't do you any harm, Mother," said Monipodio, "for it is well aged."

"May the Virgin make it so," replied the old woman, and went on: "Girls, look and see if you happen to have a *cuarto* for the candles I have promised, for in my haste and eagerness to bring the news of the basket, I came off without my purse."

Gananciosa said, "I've got one, Señora Pipota" (for so the old woman was called); "here you are: two *cuartos*. With one of them please buy a candle for me for St. Michael, and if there's enough for two, light the other to St. Blaise, who are my patron saints. I would like to get one for Saint Lucy,[2] who is also the object of my devotion because of my sore eyes, but I've got no more change. Some other day I'll do my duty by all of them."

"You will do yourself a good turn, daughter, and see that you are not penny-pinching about it; for it is very important for a person to carry his own candles before him while he's still alive, and not wait for his heirs or executors to do it."

"Well said, Mother Pipota," spoke up Escalanta. And putting her hand in her pocket, she gave her another *cuarto*, and asked her to place two other small candles before the saints she believed most useful and grateful. With this Pipota took her leave, saying to them:

---

[2] *St. Lucy, the patron saint of those suffering from infirmities of the eyes.*

"Enjoy yourselves, my children, while there is still time, for old age will come, and then you will weep for youth's wasted opportunities, as I do. Commend me to God in your prayers, and I shall do the same for myself and for you that He may watch over and preserve us in this hazardous calling we have chosen, without perils of the law."

With this she went on her way. After she had left, they all seated themselves around the mat, and Gananciosa spread out the sheet as a tablecloth. The first thing she took from the basket was a big bunch of radishes, and some two dozen oranges and lemons, after which came a big earthenware casserole full of slices of fried codfish. Half an Edam cheese followed, and a pot of olives, a dish of shrimps, quantities of crabs garnished with thirst-provoking capers and peppers, and three snow-white loaves of Gandul bread.

Some fourteen shared the meal, and not one of them but pulled out his yellow-handled knife, with the exception of Rinconete, who made use of his short sword. To the two old baize-attired men and the guide fell the task of serving the wine in the cork jar. But just as they were beginning on the oranges, a hammering at the door threw them into a state of alarm. Monipodio ordered them all to keep calm, while he went into the adjoining room; taking down a shield, and with his hand on his sword, he approached the door, calling out in a deep, frightening tone of voice: "Who's there?"

"It's me, Señor Monipodio, nobody, just Tagarete, the lookout this morning. I've come to tell you that Juliana Moonface is on her way here, her hair all atumble, and she is crying as though something terrible had happened to her."

As he was saying this, the woman he spoke of arrived, sobbing, and as soon as Monipodio heard her, he opened the door and ordered Tagarete to go back to his post, and the next time he had anything to report not to make such a to-do and hubbub about it, which the lookout promised he would do. In came Moonface, a wench of the same stripe and calling as the others. Her hair hung dishevelled, and her face was covered with bruises. As she entered the courtyard, she fainted away. Gananciosa and Escalanta rushed to her aid, and unfastening her bodice, they found her breast all black and blue as if from a beating. They threw water in her face, and as soon as she had recovered her senses, she began to scream:

"God's and the King's justice on that rogue of a thief, on that coward of a shop-lifter, on that lousy rascal whom I have saved from the gallows more times than he has hairs in his beard. Poor wretch that I am! Just see on whom I have lost and squandered my youth and the best years of my life—on a heartless villain, a dyed-in-the-wool criminal!"

"Calm yourself, Moonface," Monipodio interrupted her. "I am here to see that you receive justice. Tell us what has happened to you, and rest assured that it will take you longer to tell it than me to avenge you. Have you had trouble with your protector? If that is the case, and you want to pay him back, you have only to spit it out."

"Him a protector?" answered Juliana. "May I be protected in hell if I ever have anything to do with that lion among sheep, that sheep among men! Catch me eating at the same table or sharing a bed with him again! I'd rather jackals devoured this flesh of mine. Look at the state he's left me in!"

And pulling her skirts up to her knees, or a little above, she displayed the bruises she had suffered.

"This is what the ingrate of that Repolido did to me—me that's done more for him than the mother who bore him! And you know why he did it? Not because I gave him any cause for it, God knows. The reason was that he was gambling and losing, and he sent his runner Cabrillas to ask me for thirty *reales*. I sent him only twenty-four, and may the work and trouble it took me to earn them weigh in Heaven against my sins. In payment for this courtesy and kindness he, thinking I was holding back part of what he had imagined and figured I had, this morning he took me out to the country, behind the King's garden, and there, among the olive trees, he stripped me; and with his belt, not even removing the buckles—may I see him in handcuffs and irons!—he gave me such a beating that he nearly killed me. These welts you see witness the truth of my story."

Again she began to scream, again she began to demand justice, again Monipodio and all the ruffians present promised her it would be done.

Gananciosa took it upon herself to comfort her, assuring her that she would gladly give one of her most valued jewels if her man had done the same by her.

"For I want you to know, Sister Moonface," she said, "in case you don't, that you punish what you love; and when these rascals cuff and beat and kick us, it's then that they adore us. Come now, tell me the truth: after Repolido had beaten and mauled you, didn't he caress you?"

"One caress?" said the tearful girl. "A hundred thousand, and he would have given a finger of his right hand for me to go to his lodgings with him. It seems to me I could almost see the tears come to his eyes after he had whipped me so hard."

"Never doubt it," answered Gananciosa, "and he would probably weep with sorrow to see what he did to you. For these men, in such cases, have no sooner committed the fault than they regret it. You just wait and see, sister, if he doesn't come looking for you before we leave here to ask you to forgive him for what happened, meeker than a lamb."

"I tell you," Monipodio spoke up, "that that sneaking coward will not set foot inside this house until he has done open penance for the crime he has committed. To think of his daring to lay a hand on Moonface's countenance or body, a girl who in cleanliness and earning ability can compete with Gananciosa here herself, than which there is no higher praise!"

"Ah, me," Juliana spoke up at this point, "don't revile that devil so, Señor Monipodio. Bad as he is, I love him from the bottom of my heart, and the things my friend Gananciosa has said on his behalf have restored my soul to my body. I feel like going out and finding him."

"Not if you take my advice, you won't," answered Gananciosa, "because it would go to his head, and he'll lay it on to you as though you were a punching bag. Relax, sister, and before long you will see him here as repentant as I have said. If he doesn't come, we'll write him a screed in verse that will churn up his bile."

"That's a good idea," said Moonface, "for I have a thousand and one things to tell him."

"I'll be the scribe, if need be," said Monipodio; "and although I am no poet, still, if I put my mind to it, I can turn out two thousand verses before you can say scat; and even if they have their shortcomings, I've got a friend, a barber and a great poet, who can round them out whenever we ask him. But now let's finish the lunch we have begun, and later everything will be attended to."

Juliana was pleased to obey her chief, and they all went back to their *gaudeamus,* and in no time they had reached the bottom of the basket and the dregs of the wine skin. The old men drank *sine fine;* the young men, deeply, the ladies did themselves well. The old men asked to be excused; Monipodio granted their request, enjoining upon them that they keep him informed of anything that might be useful or necessary to the good of the brotherhood. They answered that they always bore this in mind, and left. Rinconete, who was curious by nature, after first requesting permission and authorization, asked Monipodio what was the function of those two graybeards, so solemn and respectable, in the fraternity. Monipodio answered that in thieves' cant they were known as *abispones*—watchers—and that what they did was to go about the city all day long, spying out the houses where a burglary could be effected at night, and following those who drew money from the Clearing House or the Treasury to see where it was taken and even where it was put. Once they had discovered this, they estimated the thickness of the walls of the house in question, and marked the best spot to cut *guzpataros* (which are holes) to enter it. In short, he said, they were as useful as any member of the brotherhood, if not more so, and that of all arrived at through their industry, they received a fifth, just as does His Majesty of any treasure. And, in addition, they were very honest and upright, of exemplary life and repute, God-fearing and devout, who attended mass daily with singular devotion . . .

"And some of them, especially those two who are just leaving, are so undemanding that they are satisfied with much less than our rules provide. Two others who are porters work at times as furniture movers, and know the entrances and exits to all the houses in the city, and where we can find good pickings and where not."

"That all seems excellent to me," said Rinconete, "and I should like to prove useful to this excellent fraternity."

"Heaven ever smiles upon worthy desires," answered Monipodio.

As they were talking, there came a knock at the door. Monipodio went to ask who it was.

"Open up, Señor Monipodio," a voice answered, "it is Repolido."

When Moonface heard the voice she lifted up hers: "Don't let him in, Señor Monipodio, don't open the door to that mariner of Tarpeya, to that tiger of Ocaña." [3]

Notwithstanding, Monipodio opened the door, and as soon as Moonface saw Repolido come in, she jumped up and ran into the room where the bucklers hung, and slamming the door behind her, began to shout from within:

"Get that devil out of my sight, that hangman of innocents, that hunter of tame doves."

Maniferro and Chiquiznaque held back Repolido who was determined to force his way into the room where Moonface was; but as they would not let him, he called out: "That's enough, crosspatch; quiet down, as you hope to get married!"

"Me married, you rascal!," screamed Moonface. "Listen to what he's thought up! Wouldn't you like it if I stepped out with you, but I would prefer a rattling skeleton to you!"

"You silly girl," answered Repolido, "let's make an end of this, for it's getting late. And don't you get all puffed up because you see me talking so meekly and coaxing you. As sure as there's a God in heaven, if my anger goes to my head, the relapse is going to be worse than the sickness. Let's both of us eat humble pie and not feed the devil."

---

[3] *Tarpeya . . . Ocaña. Malapropisms of Moonface. The first is the garbled version of the first line of an old ballad: "Mira, Nero, de Tarpeya." Tiger of Ocaña (a Spanish village) for tiger of Hyrcania.*

"I'd be willing to give him a fine dinner," said Moonface, "if he would carry you off where I'd never set eyes on you again."

"What did I tell you?" said Repolido. "By God, I am losing my patience, Lady Slut, and if I do, there's no knowing what will happen."

At this point Monipodio spoke up: "There'll be no quarrels in my presence. Moonface will come out, not because of your threats, but for my sake, and everything will be done as it should. Lovers' quarrels bring the greatest pleasure when they are made up. Come, Juliana; come, child; come, Moonface; come on out and I'll make Repolido get down on his knees and ask your pardon."

"If he does that," said Escalanta, "we will all be on his side, and beg Juliana to come out."

"If that is a surrender that is taken as a humiliation," said Repolido, "not the whole Swiss army can force me to it; but if it is to please Moonface, not only will I get down on my knees, but I will drive a nail into my forehead to show my devotion to her."

Chiquiznaque and Maniferro burst out laughing, which so enraged Repolido, who thought they were making fun of him, that he was almost beside himself.

"If anyone laughs, or even thinks of laughing, at anything Moonface or I have said or may say about each other, I am here to say he is a liar and will be a liar every time he laughs or thinks of laughing."

The lowering look that passed between Chiquiznaque and Maniferro was a warning to Monipodio that there was going to be serious trouble unless he took a hand in the matter. So, stepping between them, he said:

"That will do, gentlemen; let there be an end to these insults; swallow them, and since they are less than waist high, nobody need think they are meant for him."

"We are quite sure such threats are not meant for us," answered Chiquiznaque; "for if it entered our minds that they were, the tambourine is in the hands of those who know how to play it."

"We have a tambourine of our own, Sir Chiquiznaque," Repolido replied, "and if the occasion arises, we, too, can make the bells ring. What I have said stands: whoever thinks this is a laughing matter, lies; and if anyone thinks differently, let him step outside, and with a sword shortened by a handsbreadth I'll prove it."

With this he made as if to go out of the house. Moonface had been listening, and when she saw that he was leaving in a huff, she came out saying:

"Stop him, don't let him go, or he'll pull one of his tricks. Can't you see that he's fighting mad, and he's a Judas Mackerel[4] when he's aroused. Come back here, you great bully, you light of my eyes!"

And closing in on him, she grabbed him by the cape, and with Monipodio's help stopped him. Chiquiznaque and Maniferro could not decide whether to take offense or not, and they stood waiting to see what Repolido was going to do. Finally, at Moonface's and Monipodio's entreaties, he turned to them, saying:

"Friends should never offend or make fun of each other, and above all, when they see that they are causing a friend annoyance."

"There is no friend here," replied Maniferro, "who wants to offend or make fun of another; therefore, since we are all friends, let's shake hands all around."

"You gentlemen have spoken like true friends," spoke Monipodio, "and as such give one another your hands."

So they did at once, and Escalanta took off one of her clogs and began to beat the sole as though it were a tambourine. Gananciosa grabbed a new palm-leaf broom that happened to be there, and running her fingers across it she brought forth a sound which, though rough and muted, harmonized with that of the clog. Monipodio broke a plate in two, and nimbly clicking the pieces between his fingers supplied the accompaniment to the clog and broom.

Rinconete and Cortadillo were amazed at the new use to which the broom was put, for they had never seen this before. Seeing their surprise, Maniferro said:

---

[4] *Judas Mackerel for Judas Maccabeus.*

"So you are surprised at the broom? Well, no wonder, for there's no quicker, easier, or cheaper way of making music in the world. Just the other day I heard a student say that neither Negrofeo, who brought Arauz up from hell, nor Marion[5] who climbed on a dolphin and came out of the sea as though riding a hired mule, nor that other great musician who built a city with a hundred gates and the same number of posterns, ever invented a better kind of music, so easy to learn, so simple to play, without frets, keys, or strings, and that never needs tuning. I'd even be willing to bet that it was invented by a gallant of this city who prided himself on being Hector himself when it came to music."

"It wouldn't surprise me one bit," answered Rinconete; "but let's listen to our musicians, for Gananciosa has just cleared her throat, which means she's getting ready to sing."

So it was, for Monipodio had asked her to sing some of the popular *seguidillas*. But the one who first broke into song was Escalanta, who, in a thin, reedy voice, began:

> For a lad of Seville, ruddy as a Fleming
> Is not my heart burned to a coal?

Gananciosa took it up:

> For an olive-skinned laddie boy
> What girl would not lose her head?

And then Monipodio, clicking his pieces of broken plate faster and faster:

> Two lovers quarrel and then make up,
> The hotter the anger, the sweeter the peace.

Moonface, not wanting her happiness to be mute, took off a clog, too, and got into the act, saying:

> Stop, angry one, beat me no more,
> If you'd stop to think, you're thrashing yourself.

---

[5] *Negro feo* for *Orpheus; Arauz* for *Eurydice; Marion* for *Arion.*

"Just sing," growled Repolido, "and stop raking up what's over and done with. Let bygones be bygones, and make a fresh start, and that's all there is to it."

It began to look as though the singing would go on for a while, but just then there came a hurried knock at the door, and Monipodio went over to see who was there. It was the lookout to tell him that the Chief Magistrate was coming down the street, preceded by Tordillo and Cernicalo, a couple of neutral constables. When those within heard this news they all became so excited that Moonface and Escalanta grabbed each other's shoe, Gananciosa dropped the broom, Monipodio his clappers, and all the music turned to apprehensive silence. Chiquiznaque had nothing to say, Repolido was struck dumb, Maniferro aghast, and all of them, some going one way, some another, disappeared, running up to the terraces and roofs to make their escape by way of them to the other street.

No surprise report of harquebus, nor sudden clap of thunder, ever sowed such panic in a flock of carefree pigeons as did the news of the arrival of the Chief Magistrate in that gathering of good people. The two novitiates, Rinconete and Cortadillo, did not know what to do with themselves, so they stayed where they were, waiting to see what the outcome of that gale would be. The outcome of it was that the lookout returned to say that the Magistrate had gone past the house without any sign or indication of the slightest suspicion.

While he was informing Monipodio of this, a young gentleman came to the door dressed, as the saying goes, up to the nines. Monipodio invited him in, and sent for Chiquiznaque, Maniferro, and Repolido, giving orders that none of the others were to come down. As Rinconete and Cortadillo had remained in the courtyard, they could hear the entire conversation that took place between Monipodio and the new arrival, who wanted to know why the commission he had given him had been so badly executed. Monipodio answered that he did not yet know just what had been done; but that the workman to whom the job had been entrusted was there, and would give a good accounting of himself. Just then Chiquiznaque came in, and Monipodio asked him if he had carried out the assignment of the fourteen stitch slash.

"Which one was that?" asked Chiquiznaque. "Was it that cross-roads merchant?"

"That's the one," answered the gentleman.

"Well, what happened," said Chiquiznaque, "was that I waited for him last night at the door of his house, and he arrived before evening prayers. I came close to him, measured his face with my eye, and saw that it was so small that a fourteen stitch slash would never fit on it; and seeing that I could not keep my promise and do as my destructions bid . . ."

"Instructions, Your Excellency, not destructions."

"That's what I meant to say," answered Chiquiznaque. "As I was saying, seeing that the meanness of that face would not hold the number of stitches agreed upon, so my trip would not have been for nothing, I gave the slash to a lackey of his, and you can be sure it was larger than specified."

"I would rather," said the gentleman, "that the master had received a seven-stitcher than the servant a fourteen. The truth of the matter is that you have not carried out our agreement; but no matter. The thirty ducats I paid on account will not make me richer or poorer. I kiss Your Excellencies' hands."

With this he took off his hat and turned to leave; but Monipodio laid hold of him by his tweed cape, saying to him:

"Just a minute. You keep your word, for we have kept ours faithfully and well. There's still twenty ducats due, and you're not leaving here without paying them, or leaving security for the amount."

"But does Your Excellency call that keeping your word," retorted the gentleman, "slashing the servant instead of the master?"

"You don't have much of a head for figures," said Chiquiznaque. "Don't you remember the proverb: 'Love Beltran, love his dog'"?

"And what bearing does this proverb have on this case?" asked the gentleman.

"Isn't it the same as saying: Hate Beltran, hate his dog? Beltran is the merchant you hate; his lackey is the dog, so by striking at the dog, you get at Beltran, and the debt is settled, the commission carried out. So what you have to do is pay up without haggling."

"I completely agree," said Monipodio, "and you took the words out of my mouth, friend Chiquiznaque. So, young sir, don't start splitting hairs with your servants and friends, but take my advice and pay up for services rendered. And if you would like us to give the master another, of whatever size his face will take, consider him already under treatment."

"In that case," answered the blade, "I will be glad to pay the full price for both."

"Have no more doubt of that than that you are a Christian," said Monipodio. "Chiquiznaque will do such a perfect job that it will seem he was born with the cut."

"Then with this assurance and promise," answered the gentleman, "take this chain as security for the twenty ducats still owing, and for the forty I am to pay for the cut to come. It's worth a thousand *reales* by weight, and it may be that you will keep it, for I have in mind other fourteen-stitch cuts that will be needed before long."

With this he removed from around his neck a fine linked chain and handed it over to Monipodio who saw at once by the color and the weight that it had not come from any alchemist. He accepted it gladly and politely, for he was very well-mannered. The job was left in Chiquiznaque's hands, who promised that it would be carried out that very night.

The gentleman departed well satisfied, and Monipodio called out to the absent and frightened brothers. They came down, and standing in the midst of the gathering, Monipodio took out a notebook he carried in the hood of his cape and handed it to Rinconete to read aloud, for he did not know how to read. Rinconete opened it, and on the first page found this entry:

LIST OF SLASHES TO BE GIVEN THIS WEEK

First: the merchant at the crossroads. Price fifty florins. Received on account, thirty. Executor: Chiquiznaque.

"I think that's the only one, son," said Monipodio. "Go on to where it says: LIST OF THRASHINGS."

Rinconete turned to the next page which was headed: LIST OF THRASHINGS. Below was written: To the inn-keeper of Alfalfa Square, twelve whacks, of the heaviest, at a florin apiece. Received on account, eight florins. Time limit, six days. Executor: Maniferro.

"You might as well rub that out," said Maniferro, "because I'm going to polish that off tonight."

"Any more, son?" asked Monipodio.

"Yes, there's one more," replied Rinconete, "which says: To the hunchback tailor nicknamed Silguero, six heavy whacks at the request of the lady who left her necklace with him. Executor: Shorty."

"I am amazed," said Monipodio, "that this job is still outstanding. It must be that Shorty is sick, for it's two days past the time limit and he hasn't touched it."

"I ran into him yesterday," said Maniferro, "and he told me that as the hunchback was away sick, he had not been able to carry out his duties."

"That must be the case," said Monipodio, "for I have such a high regard for Shorty's abilities that if something like this had not come up, he would have finished it off in style. Anything more, lad?"

"Nothing, sir," answered Rinconete.

"Then go on to where it says: LIST OF COMMON OFFENSES." Rinconete turned the pages to the entry:

LIST OF COMMON OFFENSES, SUCH AS
BOTTLE BLOWS,
JUNIPER OIL SMEARINGS, NAILING
UP OF SAMBENITOS
AND HORNS, CHARIVARIS, THREATENED
SLASHINGS, CIRCULATION OF LIBELS, ETC.

"What does it say after that?" asked Monipodio.

"It says," answered Rinconete, "smearing juniper oil on the walls . . ."

"Don't bother reading the location of the house. I know where it is," interrupted Monipodio, "for I am the *tu autem* and executor of this trifling matter, and four florins out of the eight due have already been paid on account."

"Right you are," said Rinconete; "all that is written here, and further down it says: Nailing of horns."

"That's not to be read out either," said Monipodio, "neither the house nor its location; the offense is enough without making it known to everyone, for that would be a great weight on the conscience. At any rate, I would rather nail up a hundred horns and an equal number of *sambenitos,* provided I am paid for my work, than mention it to anyone, even my own mother."

"The executor of this is Nosey."

"That's already done and paid for," said Monipodio. "Look and see if there's anything more, for if I remember rightly there should be a scare for twenty florins, half in advance, our whole brotherhood the executor, and with this whole month in which to do it. It shall be carried out to the letter, and it will be one of the best things that has happened in this city in many a day. Give me the book, lad, for I know that's all there is. I also know that business is bad, but better times will come, and we'll have more to do than we can take care of. For not a leaf stirs without God's will, and we're not going to make people avenge themselves against their wishes. Besides, everyone tends to be brave when his own interests are at stake, and people don't want to pay somebody else to do a job they can carry out with their own hands."

"That's a fact," commented Repolido. "But give us your orders, Señor Monipodio, and tell us what we are to do, for it's getting late and the day is warming up rapidly."

"What must be done," answered Monipodio, "is for all of you to go to your posts, and there are to be no changes until Sunday, when we'll all gather in this same place, and all our takings will be divided up, without cheating anybody. Rinconete the Good and Cortadillo will have as their territory until Sunday from the Torre de Oro outside the city limits to the postern gate of the Alcázar. There they can play their games, and I have seen others not half so skillful come back every day with over twenty *reales* in change, not to mention the silver, working with a single deck that was shy four cards. Ganchoso will show you how to get there; and even if you spread over to San Sebastián and San Telmo, it doesn't matter, even though it is elementary justice that no one trespass on another's territory."

The two lads kissed his hand in gratitude for his kind treatment of them, and promised to perform their duties well and faithfully, with industry and caution.

Monipodio then brought out of the hood of his cape a folded paper containing a list of the names of all the members, and he told Rinconete to add his and Cortadillo's to it. But as there was no inkwell, he gave him the paper telling him to stop at the first apothecary's and write: "Rinconete and Cortadillo, members; novitate, none. Rinconete, card-sharper; Cortadillo, sneak thief," and the day, month, and year, omitting parents and place of origin.

While he was giving these instructions, one of the old men came in and said:

"I have come to tell Your Excellencies that I just this minute ran into Wolf Cub of Malaga on the Cathedral steps, and he tells me he has become so good at his trade that he could pluck Satan himself at cards alone; and he asked me to say that if he has not come at once to register and pay his respects as usual, it is because he is so tired; but that he will be here on Sunday without fail."

"I always had a feeling," said Monipodio, "that Wolf Cub was going to be a master at his trade, for he has the best and most gifted hands anyone could ask for. To be a good worker at a trade, good tools to ply it are as necessary as the talent for learning it."

"I also," went on the old man, "ran into the Jew in an inn on Tintores Street, dressed up in priest's garb. He took lodgings there because he had had word that two who had returned from Peru were living there, and he wanted to see if he could start a game with them, even if the stakes were small, for later they might become much higher. He, too, said he would be at the meeting on Sunday and give an account of himself."

"That Jew, too," said Monipodio, "is a first-class thief, and very shrewd. It's days since I've seen him, and that is wrong of him. If he doesn't mend his ways, I swear I'll strip him of his tonsure. That thief no more has holy orders than a Turk, nor does he know any more Latin than my mother. What else is new?"

"Nothing more, at least as far as I know," said the old man.

"Well and good, then," said Monipodio. "You gentlemen take this little something"—dividing forty *reales* among them—"and everybody be here on Sunday when everything will be done as usual."

All thanked him again; Repolido and Moonface embraced each other, as did Escalanta and Maniferro and Gananciosa and Chiquiznaque, arranging to meet that night, after the day's work was done, at Pipota's house. Monipodio said he would come, too, to take note of the contents of the clothes-basket, and that afterwards he had to go to attend to that matter of the juniper oil daubing. He embraced Rinconete and Cortadillo, and after giving them his blessing, sent them on their way, warning them never to have a fixed lodging or domicile, for that was in the best interests of all. Ganchoso went with them to show them their territory, reminding them to be sure and come on Sunday, for it was his belief that Monipodio planned to give them a formal lecture on matters having to do with their calling. With this he departed, and the two friends were left turning over in their minds the things they had seen.

Although nothing but a boy, Rinconete had a good head on his shoulders, and was decent by nature. As he had helped his father in the sale of indulgences, he talked well, and it amused him greatly when he thought of the words he had heard Monipodio and the other members of his guild use, such as *por modo de naufragio* for *per modum sufragii,* or *stupendous* for *stipend.* As when Moonface said of Repolido that he was a *mariner of Tarpeya* and a *tiger of Ocaña* instead of Hyrcania, and a hundred and one similar slips, or worse. What especially amused him was when she said that the sufferings she had undergone to earn her twenty-four *reales* should be applied by heaven as a discount on her sins. Above all, he was amazed at their confidence and trust that they would go to heaven, provided they were faithful in their devotions, in spite of all their thefts, murders, and other offenses against God. And he laughed when he thought of old Pipota who left the stolen clothes-basket in her house, and went to light candles to the saints, thinking thus to go straight to heaven. Nor was he less struck by the obedience and respect all of them showed toward Monipodio, that uncouth, unscrupulous barbarian. He recalled what he had read in the note-book, and the activities in which all were engaged. And, finally, he marvelled at the free and easy methods of the law in that famous city of Seville, where people so harmful and of such perverse inclinations carried on their activities almost openly, and he made up his mind to advise his comrade that they should not linger in that vicious and evil life, so insecure, so dissolute, so immoral. But, nevertheless, being young and inexperienced, he continued in it for several months more, during which time many things happened to him which would be too lengthy to relate here. So we must leave for some other occasion the account of his life and adventures, as well as those of his mentor Monipodio, and other things which took place among the members of that infamous academy, all of which are food for thought and might serve as an example and warning to those who peruse them

THE JEALOUS HIDALGO

Not many years ago an hidalgo of a village in Extremadura, the son of well-born parents, left home and, like that other Prodigal,[1] he wandered—throughout different parts of Spain, Italy, and Flanders, squandering his years as well as his patrimony. After long travels (his parents now being deceased and his estate dissipated), he finally came to the great city of Seville, where he found ample opportunity to fritter away the little he had left. Finding himself so short of money, and almost friendless, he had recourse to the remedy employed by many other wastrels who take refuge in that city, that is to say, to embark for the Indies, the shelter of the hopeless of Spain, the sanctuary of the lawless, the asylum of cutthroats, the cloak and cover of cardsharpers, the decoy of many, and the remedy of few. In short, arriving just as a fleet was making ready to set sail for Terra Firma, after coming to terms with its admiral, he assembled his gear, including a sleeping mat of rushes, and went aboard in Cadiz, taking his leave of Spain. The fleet weighed anchor, and amidst general rejoicing unfurled its sails to the wind, which blew gentle and favorable. In a few hours they had lost sight of land, and the spreading plains of the great father of waters, the Ocean-Sea, opened out before them.

Our passenger was in a pensive frame of mind, turning over in his memory the many and varied dangers he had undergone in his years of wandering, and how poorly he had managed the whole course of his life. After casting up accounts with himself, he firmly resolved to mend his ways and to take better care of such wealth as God might choose to bestow on him, and to proceed with greater caution than heretofore in his dealings with women. The fleet lay

[1] *The allusion is to the prodigal son in the Bible.*

as though becalmed while this storm was going on inside Felipo de Carrizales, as the subject of our story was called. The winds began to freshen, scudding the ships along so smartly that nobody could keep his footing. Carrizales, therefore, had to forgo his musings and give himself over to the cares involved in his voyage. It proved so fair that they reached the port of Cartagena without let or hindrance. And to conclude with everything that does not bear upon our purpose, I would say that Felipo's age, when he crossed over to the Indies, was around forty-eight, and during the twenty years he spent there, thanks to his industry and diligence, his accumulated wealth was valued at more than a hundred and fifty thousand pesos.

When, then, he found himself rich and prosperous, moved by that natural desire all have to return to their native land, and disregarding fine opportunities that were offered him, he left Peru, where he had amassed such a fortune, and converting it all into ingots of gold and silver, properly registered to avoid customs difficulties, he returned to Spain. He landed at Sanlucar, and reached Seville laden with years and wealth. He passed his riches through without problems; then he looked up his friends, and found them all dead. He thought of setting out for his old home, although he had already learned that death had left him no relative. So that, if when he set out for the Indies, poor and needy, his many thoughts tugged at him, giving him no rest on the billowy sea, now, safely ashore, they still warred with him although for a different reason. If then he had been unable to rest because he was poor, now he could not sleep because he was rich; for wealth, to one unaccustomed to it, or who does not know how to employ it, is as vexing a burden as unremitting poverty. Money brings cares, as does the lack of it; but whereas the latter state can be remedied by the acquisition of a moderate amount, the former grows by what it feeds on.

Carrizales gazed upon his ingots, not because he was a miser, for his years as a soldier had taught him to be open-handed, but wondering what to do with them, because storing them away was unprofitable and keeping them beside him was an invitation to the greedy and a bait for thieves. The desire for worrisome business

ventures had died in him, and it seemed to him that for the years
that remained to him he had more than enough money. He wanted
to spend the rest of his life in his native land and, putting his fortune
out at interest, live out his old age in peace and quiet, giving to God
what he owed Him, inasmuch as he had given more than enough
to the world. On the other hand, he took into account the fact that
his native region was very poor, and people there very needy, and
that if he went there to live he would be the target of the importu-
nities the poor make upon a rich neighbor, especially when there is no
one else to whom they can turn in their difficulties. What he wanted
was someone to whom to leave his worldly goods when his end came,
and with this in mind, he took stock of his abilities, and it seemed
to him that he could still carry the burden of marriage. But no
sooner had this idea occurred to him than he was assaulted by a
fear that rent and unravelled it like mist in the wind. For he was
by nature the most jealous man in the world, even though unmarried, and the mere thought of entering into wedlock aroused
his jealous instincts, and suspicions began to harass him and prey
on his imagination with such vigor and vehemence that he decided
then and there not to marry.

Having decided this, but not what he would do with the rest of
his life, fate so willed it that one day as he was walking down a
street, he raised his eyes and saw at a window a girl about thirteen
or fourteen years old, to judge by her appearance, so winsome of
face and so fair, that, unable to resist her charms, old Carrizales
succumbed, and laid the autumn of his years at the feet of the
spring of Leonora, as the beautiful maiden was called. Without
further ado he began a lengthy discourse with himself, saying:

"This girl is beautiful, and to judge by the appearance of this
house, she is not rich. Her tender years are a guarantee against my
suspicions. I shall wed her, shut her up, and mold her to my ways,
and thus she will conform completely to my teachings. I am not so
old that I cannot hope to have sons to inherit me. It is of no matter
whether she has a dowry or not, for heaven has given me enough
for both, and the rich need not look to marriage for wealth but for

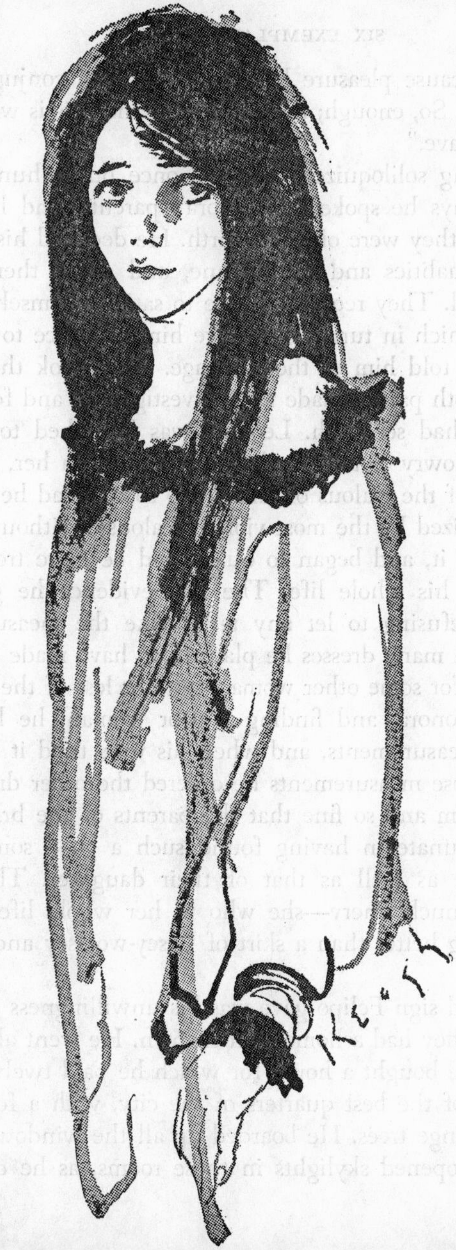

satisfaction, because pleasure lengthens life, and conjugal disaffections shorten it. So, enough; the die is cast, and this is what Heaven means me to have."

And having soliloquized thus not once but a hundred times, after several days he spoke to Leonora's parents, and learned that although poor, they were of noble birth. He declared his intentions, his personal qualities and his fortune, and asked them for their daughter's hand. They requested time to satisfy themselves of what he had said, which in turn would give him a chance to corroborate what they had told him of their lineage. They took their leave of one another, both parties made their investigation, and found things to be as each had set forth. Leonora was betrothed to Carrizales, who settled a dowry of twenty thousand ducats on her, so inflamed was the heart of the jealous old man. No sooner had he said "I do" than he was seized by the most violent jealousy, without the slightest grounds for it, and began to quake and be more troubled than ever before in his whole life. The first evidence he gave of his jealousy was refusing to let any tailor take the measurements of his wife for the many dresses he planned to have made for her. He looked around for some other woman more or less of the same build and size as Leonora, and finding a poor woman, he had a dress made to her measurements, and when his wife tried it on, it fitted her, and by those measurements he ordered the other dresses made, so many of them and so fine that the parents of the bride counted themselves fortunate in having found such a good son-in-law, for their own sake as well as that of their daughter. The girl was amazed at so much finery—she who in her whole life had never owned anything better than a skirt of linsey-woolsey and a kirtle of taffeta.

The second sign Felipo gave was his unwillingness to bed with his wife until they had a home of their own. He went about it after this manner: he bought a house for which he paid twelve thousand ducats in one of the best quarters of the city, with a fountain and a garden of orange trees. He boarded up all the windows facing on the street and opened skylights in those rooms, as he did with all the others in the house. At the street door, known in Seville as *casa-puerta*, he built a stable for a mule, and above it a hayloft and quarters for the stableman, an old castrated Negro. He raised the coping of the roof so high that anyone entering the house had to look straight up to the sky without being able to see anything else. He built a turnstile, opening from the front door to the inner court. He bought rich furnishings to adorn the house so that the hangings, the furniture, the rich canopies proclaimed the owner a fine gentleman. He also bought four white female slaves, whom he branded on the face, and two Negro women straight from Africa. He arranged with a caterer to buy and bring in food, with the condition that he was not to sleep in the house nor enter beyond the turnstile, through which he would deliver what he brought. This done, he invested part of his fortune in mortgages on various and well-situated properties, put another part in the bank, and kept some of it on hand for whatever might arise. He also had a master key made for the entire house, and put under lock everything bought in quantity and at certain seasons for the year's use. When all was thus prepared and arranged, he went to the home of his father-in-law and asked for his wife, whom they handed over with many tears, for it seemed to them that she was being taken to her grave.

Young Leonora as yet had no knowledge of what had happened to her, and joining her tears to those of her parents, she asked them for their blessing, and bidding them farewell, her hand in her husband's, and accompanied by his slaves and maid-servants, she came to her home. As soon as they had crossed the threshold, Carrizales delivered them a sermon, ordering them to keep watch over Leonora and under no circumstances to allow anyone to go beyond the second door, not even the black eunuch. And the person whom he especially charged with the care and vigilance of Leonora was a most circumspect and solemn duenna whom he had engaged as a governess, so to speak, for Leonora and to supervise everything that was carried out in the household, and to give orders to the slaves and to two maidens of the same age as Leonora whom he had also engaged so she would have persons of her own age with whom to amuse herself. He promised them that he would treat them so well that they would not find their isolation irksome, and that on all feast days, without omitting a single one, they should go to hear mass, but so early in the morning that the light of day would hardly have an opportunity to see them. The servants and the slaves promised him that they would do all he bid without complaint, promptly and cheerfully, and his bride, shrugging her shoulders, bowed her head, and said she had no other will than that of her husband and master to whom she was ever obedient.

Having taken all these measures and now installed in his house, the good hidalgo began to enjoy to the best of his ability the fruits of marriage which to Leonora, who had no experience of others, proved neither pleasant nor unpleasant. She spent her days with her duenna, maids, and slaves who, to pass the time more agreeably, indulged their fondness for sweets, and hardly a day went by that they did not prepare a thousand dishes with honey and sugar. They had all of this they needed, thanks to the abundance which reigned in the house, and their master was only too happy to give them all they wanted, for it seemed to him that in this way he kept them busy and contented, without occasion to think of their confinement. Leonora did the same as her servants, and amused herself with the same things as they; in her ingenuousness she even played with dolls, and indulged in other childish pastimes which showed her innocence and her tender years. All this delighted her jealous husband, for it seemed to him that he had chosen the best life he could ever have imagined, and that in no wise could human slyness or malice perturb his peace of mind. Thus, he missed no opportunity to shower his wife with gifts and to urge her to ask for anything she fancied, for whatever she wanted was hers for the asking.

The days she went to mass which, as has been said, was at daybreak, her parents came and talked with their daughter in church before her husband, who gave them so many presents that even though they felt sorry for their daughter because of the confined life she led, their pity was tempered by the generosity of their liberal son-in-law.

Carrizales arose early and awaited the arrival of the caterer for whom, the night before, he had left a note in the turnstile telling him what he was to bring the next day. After the caterer had gone, Carrizales left the house, usually on foot, after locking both doors, the street and the inner one, leaving the Negro between the two. He went to attend to his business affairs, which were not burdensome, and was soon back. Locking himself in the house he amused himself with pampering his wife and caressing the servants, all of whom liked him because he was unassuming, pleasant, and, above all, generous with them. A year of novitiate went by in this manner, and they took their vows in that life, determined to endure it until the end of their days; and this might have been the case had not the wily perturber of mankind interfered, as you shall now hear.

Let him who holds himself to be the wisest and wariest of men say what more precautions old Felipo could have taken for his security. He would not even have a male animal in the house. No tom-cat ever pursued its mice, nor was a dog's barking ever heard there. By day he took thought, by night he did not sleep. He was the patrol and sentry of his house, the Argus[2] of what he cherished; no man ever passed the door of the inner court. His dealings with his friends took place in the street. The figures in the draperies which adorned his rooms were all women, flowers, woodland scenes. The entire house reeked of chastity, reserve, modesty; even the stories which the servants told, gathered about the fireplace, in the long winter nights when he was present, were free of all hint of lewdness. In Leonora's eyes the old man's silver hairs seemed of pure gold, for a maiden's first love leaves an imprint on her soul like a seal on wax. Her husband's exaggerated vigilance seemed to her wise care; she thought and believed that what happened to her was common to all newly wed wives. Her thoughts never went beyond the walls of her house, nor did her wishes desire aught but her husband's pleasure. Only on the days when she went to mass

---

[2] *Argus in Greek mythology was known as the all-seeing because of his countless eyes. Set by the goddess Hera to watch over her husband Jove, he was slain by Hermes, and Hera transferred his eyes to the tail of the peacock.*

did she behold the streets, and as this was so early in the morning it was only on the way back from church that there was light enough to see them. Never was there a convent so safeguarded, nor nuns so cloistered, nor golden apples so watched over.[3] Yet, for all this, it was impossible to forestall or avoid the calamity he most feared, or, at any rate, to believe it had happened.

There exists in Seville a species of idle, good-for-nothing wastrel, young men about town, the sons of residents of the various parishes—the wealthiest of them. They are worthless, presumptuous, well-spoken. Of all this and of their mode of attire and behavior, their nature and the rules they observe toward each other, there would be much to say, but out of respect it shall be omitted. One of these gallants, a bachelor, to whom the name of "arrow" is given (the newly married are called "blanket-warmers") chanced to observe watchful Carrizales's house, and seeing that it was always closed, he was taken by a desire to know who lived there. He pursued his investigations with such tenacity that he found out everything about it that he wanted to know. He learned about the old man's jealousy, the beauty of his wife, and the care with which he guarded her, all of which aroused in him the desire to see whether by force or industry such an embattled fortress could be stormed. He discussed the matter with two unmarried friends of his and one of the "blanket-warmers," and they decided to see if they could put the idea into action, for there is never a lack of advisers and helpers for such enterprises.

They considered ways to attempt such a difficult undertaking, and after talking it over at length they agreed on the following plan. Loaysa, as the young blade was called, would give out that he was leaving the city for a few days to remove himself from his friends' sight; and so he did. He then dressed himself in clean linen breeches and shirt, but over them he put on garments so patched and torn that there was not a beggar in the city who went about so ragged. He trimmed his beard a little, covered one eye with a patch, band-

---

[3] *The allusion is to one of the twelve labors of Hercules which was to steal the golden apples of the Hesperides guarded by an ever-watchful dragon.*

aged one leg, and hobbling along on crutches, he turned himself into a poor cripple, more convincing than any real one.

In this guise he stationed himself every night at the hour of the Angelus at the door of Carrizales's house, which was already locked up with the Negro Luis shut in between the two doors. Settling himself there, Loaysa took up a guitar, somewhat greasy and lacking several strings, and as he had certain musical gifts, he began to strum gay, merry airs, altering his voice so as not to be recognized. He then went on with ballads of Moors and Moorish maidens, singing them in a rollicking manner with such grace that all who came through the street stopped to hear him, and there was always a swarm of urchins about listening. Luis the Negro, with his ear to the keyhole, was entranced by the music, and would have given his right arm to be able to open the door and listen to his full satisfaction, for Negroes have a great fondness for music. And when Loaysa wanted those who were listening to leave him, he stopped singing, put up his guitar, and taking his crutches, moved off.

Four or five times he serenaded the Negro (for he was doing it for his sole benefit), thinking to himself that the breach in that stronghold could and would be through the Negro. Nor did he err in his thought, for one night when he arrived at the door as was his custom, and began to tune his guitar, sensing that the Negro was on the alert, he said to him in a low voice through the crack of the door:

"Luis, would it be possible for you to give me a little water, for I am parched with thirst and can't sing."

"No," answered the Negro, "for I do not have the key to this door and there is no hole through which I can give it to you."

"Who has the key?", asked Loaysa.

"My master," replied the Negro, "and he is the most jealous man in the world. If he knew that I was here now talking to someone, it would be as much as my life is worth. But who are you that is asking me for water?"

"I am a poor cripple, lame in one leg," answered Loaysa, "and I earn my living begging alms of kindly souls in the name of God.

I also teach a few colored people and other poor folk to play the guitar, and there are three Negroes, who are slaves of three of the best families, whom I have taught to play with such art that they can sing and play in any dance or tavern, and they have paid me very well."

"I would pay you much better," said Luis, "if I had a chance to take lessons; but that is impossible because my master, when he goes out in the morning, locks the street door, and does the same when he returns, leaving me walled up between two doors."

"I swear to you, Luis," answered Loaysa (who had already found out the Negro's name), "if you could find some way that I could come in on certain nights and give you lessons, in less than two weeks I would have you so proficient with the guitar that you could play with the best of them on any street corner. For I may tell you that I have great skill in teaching, and besides I have heard it said that you have fine ability, and from what I hear and can judge from your voice, which is treble in tone, you must sing very well."

"I don't sing badly," replied the Negro, "but what good does it do me, for the only song I know is the one about the star of Venus and one called "By a green meadow"; and the other one they sing which goes:

> To the bars of a window
> My trembling hand clasped . . .

"All those are as nothing," said Loaysa, "compared with what I can teach you. I know all those about the Moor Abindarraez,[4] and his lady Jarifa, and all those sung about the life of the great Sufi Tomumbeyo,[5] as well as sarabandes in the sacred mode, which leave the Portuguese themselves amazed. And I teach these in such a manner and with such ease that even if you do not exert yourself,

---

[4] *Abindarraez, the last of the Abencerrajes, one of the noble Moorish families of Granada, whose love of the beautiful Jarifa was sung in ballads and told in the novel* The Last of the Abencerrajes.
[5] *A general of Alexandria, famous for his manly beauty and his courage.*

before you have eaten three or four measures of salt, you will find yourself the complete master of any kind of guitar."

The Negro sighed and asked: "But what good does all this do me, if I don't know how to let you into the house?"

"That's easily fixed," said Loaysa. "You manage to get hold of your master's keys, and I will give you a piece of wax, and you press them into it so that the wards are stamped in the wax. Because of the liking I have taken to you, I will ask a locksmith who is a friend of mine to cut the keys, and in that way I can come in at night, and teach you better than Prester John[6] of the Indies. For it seems to me a great pity that a voice like yours should be lost for want of the support of a guitar. I may tell you, brother Luis, that the best voice in the world loses in worth when it is not accompanied by some instrument, whether guitar, lute, organ, or harp. But the instrument that best suits your voice is the guitar, as it is the handiest and cheapest of all."

"All that seems good to me," answered the Negro, "but impossible, for the keys never come into my possession, as my master never lets them out of his hand during the day, and at night they sleep under his pillow."

"Well, you'll have to think of something, Luis," said Loaysa, "if you want to become an accomplished musician; of course, if you don't, there is no need for me to tire myself further giving you advice."

"Do I want to!" answered Luis. "I want to so much that there is nothing I would not do, if only it were possible, for the sake of becoming a musician."

"If that's the case," answered Loaysa, "I will give you, under the door, if you scrape away some of the dirt from the step, a pair of pliers and a hammer, and at night you can remove the nails of the lock easily, and then with the same tools we can put the plate back on so no one will notice that it has been loosened. Once I am inside with you in your hayloft, or wherever it is you sleep, I will

---

[6] *Prester John, a fabulous medieval Christian monarch of the East.*

so quickly do what I have to do that you will see even more than I have promised you, to my own credit and your greater competence. As for our provisions, have no care; I will bring supplies enough for both of us for more than a week, for I have pupils and friends who will not let me suffer want."

"As for food," answered the Negro, "there is nothing to fear, for with the rations my master gives me, and the left-overs I get from the women, there would be enough for two more of us. Give me the hammer and pliers you speak of; I will make a hole here by this step through which they can be passed, and then I will cover and seal it over with clay. Even if I have to do some pounding to get the plate off, my master sleeps so far from this door that it will be a miracle or our bad luck if he hears it."

"Then let's get busy," said Loaysa. "Within two days, Luis, you will have all you need to put our virtuous plan in action. And take care not to eat phlegmy things, for they are not good for your voice; on the contrary, they are harmful to it."

"Nothing makes me as hoarse as wine," answered the Negro; "but I wouldn't give it up for all the voices in the world."

"Don't even think such a thing," said Loaysa, "nor would God permit it. Drink, son, drink and may it agree with you. Wine drunk with measure never did anyone any harm."

"I drink it with measure," answered the Negro. "I have here a jug that holds exactly two quarts. The slaves fill it for me without my master's knowing, and the caterer, on the quiet, brings me a little skin that also holds exactly two quarts, which makes up for what the jug lacks."

"May my life be as good as yours seems to me," answered Loaysa. "A dry throat can neither growl nor sing."

"Go with God," said the Negro. "But see that you do not fail to come here and sing every night until you bring me what you need to get in, for my fingers are itching to get at the guitar."

"Of course I will come," answered Loaysa, "and with new tunes."

"That's what I want," said Luis; "and now sing me something

so I can sleep sweetly. As for payment, rest assured that I will pay you better than if I were rich."

"That is of no importance to me," said Loaysa; "you can pay me according as I teach you. Now listen to this ditty, and when I am once in the house, you will see wonders."

"So be it," answered the Negro.

After this long conversation Loaysa sang a lively ballad, leaving the Negro so happy and pleased that he could not wait for the hour to come to open the door.

As soon as Loaysa left, more quickly than would have seemed possible with his crutches, he sped away to give his counsellors news of his good beginning, which seemed an omen of a good end. He found them and told them of the arrangements he had made with the Negro, and the next day they found tools of the sort that would cut through any nail as though it were made of wood.

The "arrow" did not fail to return to sing for the Negro, nor did the Negro fail to make the hole through which his teacher could pass what he was to give him, taking care to cover it up so that, unless one suspected something, the hole would never be noticed. The second night Loaysa gave him the tools, and Luis tried out their strength, and almost without effort, he had the nails severed and the plate of the lock in his hands. He opened the door and drew inside his Orpheus[7] and teacher, and when he saw him with the two crutches and in rags, and his legs all bandaged, he was amazed. Loaysa was not wearing the patch over his eye, as it was not necessary, and as soon as he was inside he embraced his good pupil and kissed his cheek, and put a plump wineskin in his hands, and a box of preserves and other sweetmeats, of which he carried a well-stocked bag. Then throwing aside his crutches, as though he had no infirmity, he began to caper about, to Luis's great surprise. Loaysa said to him:

"Know, brother Luis, that my lameness and pitiable state come

---

[7] Orpheus, in Greek mythology the son of Apollo and one of the Muses. He is represented as so marvelous a musician that the wild beasts came to hear him.

not from illness, but from my ingenuity, whereby I earn my bread begging in God's name. Thanks to it and my music, I lead the best life in the world. And those who are not ingenious and shrewd-witted die of hunger; all this you will learn in the course of our friendship."

"That's as may be," answered the Negro; "but let's hurry and put this plate back in place so no one will see that it has been moved."

"Gladly," said Loaysa. And taking nails from his knapsack, he put the lock back just as it was before, to the Negro's great relief. Then he went up to the Negro's loft, and stowed his things away as best he could. Luis lighted a wax candle, and Loaysa produced his guitar, and strumming it soft and low, the poor Negro was so carried away by the music that he was beside himself. After he had played for a while, Loaysa brought out refreshments again which he gave to his pupil and, even with the sweets, he drank so deeply from the wineskin that this left him even more transported than the music. Then he put the guitar in Luis's hands, and as the poor Negro's brain was floating in wine, he could not hit a fret. But in spite of this Loaysa made him believe that he already had learned at least two tunes, and the strange thing was that the Negro believed it, and all night long he did nothing but strum the untuned guitar on which some of the strings were missing.

They slept the little of the night that was left, and about six o'clock in the morning Carrizales came down and opened the inner door as well as that giving on the street, and waited for the caterer, who arrived shortly; and after putting the supplies through the turnstile, he left. Carrizales called the Negro to come down and get the barley for the mule and his own rations, and after giving them to him, the old man departed, locking both doors without noticing what had been done to the street door, which pleased teacher and pupil mightily.

No sooner had the master left the house than the Negro seized the guitar and began to play it with such vim that all the serving women heard him, and asked through the turnstile:

"What is this, Luis? Since when do you own a guitar, or who gave it to you?"

"Who gave it to me?" answered Luis. "The best musician in the world and one who in less than six days is going to teach me six thousand tunes."

"And where is this musician?" asked the duenna.

"Not far from here," the Negro replied, "and if it wasn't for shame and fear of my master, perhaps I would show him to you and by my faith it would make you happy to see him."

"And where would he be that we could see him?" inquired the duenna. "For no man ever came into this house but our master."

"That will do," said the Negro. "I don't want to tell you any more until you see what I have learned and he has taught me in the short space I have said."

"In truth," said the duenna, "if it is not some devil, I don't know who could make a musician out of you so quickly."

"Go along with you," said the Negro, "some day you will hear and see him."

"That's not possible," said one of the maids, "for there are no windows that open on the street to see or hear anybody."

"Never mind," said the Negro, "there is a remedy for everything except death, and especially if you can or will keep your mouths shut."

"And how we will keep them shut, brother Luis!" said one of the slaves. "We'll keep as quiet as though we were mutes, for I tell you, friend, I am dying to hear a good voice, and since they shut us up in these walls, we haven't even heard the song of a bird."

Loaysa was listening to these conversations with great satisfaction, for it seemed to him that everything was moving toward the accomplishment of his design, and that good fortune was leading him by the hand. The maids finally went off after the Negro had promised them that when they least expected it he would summon them to hear a fine voice. Fearful lest his master should return and find him talking to them, he turned his back and went off to his quarters and cloister. He would have liked to take a lesson, but he was afraid to play during the day for fear his master might hear him. The latter returned shortly, and locking the doors in the customary manner, he retired into the house. And when Luis received his dinner that day through the turnstile, he told the Negro woman who brought it to him that after the master was asleep that night, they should all come to the turnstile without fail to hear the voice he had promised them. To be sure, before he said this he had earnestly begged his teacher to have the kindness to sing and play that night at the turnstile so he could keep his word to the maids that they would hear an exceptional voice, assuring him that he would be regaled to his heart's desire by them. The teacher allowed himself to be coaxed a little before acceding, but in the end agreed to do as his good pupil asked, just to please him, without any other motive. The Negro embraced him, and kissed him on the cheek to show his happiness over the promised favor, and that day he served Loaysa as good a meal as he could have eaten in his own house, or perhaps better, for there might have been less abundance in his home.

Night came, and at about midnight there was a whispering at the turnstile. Luis understood at once that it was the caravan that had arrived. Calling to his teacher, they came down from the loft with the guitar well strung and better tuned. Luis asked who and how many there were listening. They replied that all of them with the exception of their lady, who was in bed with her husband, which was a disappointment for Loaysa. Nevertheless, he decided to launch his plan and satisfy his pupil; and gently plucking the guitar he brought forth such tones that the Negro and the flock of women listening to him were lost in admiration. And how shall I describe their feelings when they heard him play "It grieves my heart" and wind up with the devil-possessed sarabande, which at that time was new in Spain. Not a one, however old, but tripped a measure, nor a young one who did not disjoint herself, all muffled in silence, with sentinels and spies on the alert to warn them if the old man woke up. Loaysa also sang them *seguidillas,* which raised the pleasure of his listeners to its peak, and they besought the Negro to tell them who that marvellous musician was. The Negro explained that he was a poor beggar, the best-looking and most gallant to be found among all the needy of Seville. They begged him to fix it so they could see him, and not to let him leave the house for a fortnight, and they would treat him like a king and give him whatever he wanted. They asked how he had found a way to let him in the house. To this he answered never a word, but to their other questions he said that if they wanted to see him they should make a little hole in the turnstile and then cover it over with wax, and, as for keeping him in the house, he would do what he could.

Loaysa, too, spoke to them, putting himself at their service, with such fine-spoken words that they could tell that these did not come from the wits of a poor beggar. They besought him to come to the same spot the next night, and they would manage to have their mistress come to hear him, in spite of the fact that her husband was such a light sleeper, which came not from his years, but from his jealousy. To this Loaysa answered that if they would like to listen to him without fear of the old man, he would give them a powder to put in his wine which would make him sleep sounder and longer than usual.

"Sweet Jesus," said one of the maids, "if that were true, what good luck would have come through these doors without our knowing or deserving it! That would not be a powder of sleep for him, but a powder of life for us and for my poor lady Leonora, his wife, whom he does not let out of his sight for a second. Dear sir, bring that powder and may God give you all you wish for. Go, bring it quickly, and I myself will mix it with the wine and serve it. Would to God the old man might sleep three days and three nights, which would be that many in which we could rejoice."

"I will bring it," said Loaysa, "and it is such that it does no harm to the person who takes it beyond inducing a heavy sleep."

All of them urged him to bring it as quickly as he could, and they agreed to bore a hole in the turnstile with an auger and to bring their mistress so she could see and hear him. With this they took their leave. Even though dawn was approaching, the Negro wanted to take a lesson, and Loaysa gave it to him, telliing him that of all his pupils, none had a better ear. And the poor Negro did not know and never learned how to play a scale!

Loaysa's loyal friends came by night to listen at the street door to see if their friend had anything to tell them, or needed anything. By a signal they had agreed on, Loaysa knew they were there, and through the hole under the threshold he told them briefly how well his plans were working out, and asked them to be sure and find him some soporific to give to Carrizales, for he had heard that there were certain powders which produced that effect. They told him they had a friend who was a doctor who would give them the best he knew, if there was such a thing. And encouraging him to pursue his enterprise, and promising to return the next night with all precaution, they hurried away.

With night the flock of doves came to the decoy of the guitar, among them the guileless Leonora, fearful and trembling lest her husband awaken. Overpowered by this fear, she had not wanted to come, but her servants, especially the duenna, had told her so much about the charm of the music and the gallant presence of the poor musician (whom, without having laid eyes on him, she praised to the skies, lauding him above Absalom[8] and Orpheus) that the poor young lady, convinced and persuaded by them, was induced to do a thing that had never entered her thoughts. The first thing they did was to bore a hole in the turnstile so they could see the musician, who was no longer wearing his beggar's attire but was dressed in full yellow taffeta breeches, sailor fashion, and a doublet of the same trimmed with gold braid, a satin cap to match, and a wide starched lace ruff, all of which he had brought in his knapsack, foreseeing that the occasion might arise when it would be desirable to change clothing.

He was young, agreeable, and good looking, and as for such a long time the women had seen nobody but their old master, it

---

[8] Absalom, son of King David. There is probably a confusion here, for it was David who was known as a musician.

seemed to them that they were gazing upon an angel. They took turns at looking through the hole, and so they could see him better, the Negro moved the candle up and down his person. After all had viewed him, including the black girls, Loaysa took the guitar, and sang so beautifully that night that he left them utterly astounded and captivated, from the old woman to the youngest of the girls, and they all begged Luis to think up some way that his teacher could come inside so they could see and hear him closer at hand and not through that peep hole, and without the fear that their master might surprise them and catch them red-handed, which would not happen if they had him hidden inside.

This their mistress violently opposed, saying they were not to do such a thing, or permit such entry, for she would regret it from the bottom of her soul. From where they were they could see and hear him safely and without danger to their honor.

"What honor?" asked the duenna. "The King has enough for us all. Let your ladyship stay locked up with your Methuselah, and let us amuse ourselves as best we can. Besides, this gentleman looks so honorable that he will ask nothing more of us than we desire."

"My ladies," Loaysa spoke up, "I came here with the sole intention of serving you heart and soul, distressed by your unheard-of confinement and the opportunities of which you are deprived by this cloistered life. I am a man, by the life of my father, so mild, so gentle, and so affable, that I will do nothing but what you order me. If one of you ladies were to say: 'Master, sit here, Master, go there, lie down here, go over there' I would do it like the most domesticated and trained dog who jumps at the mention of the King of France's name."

"If that is the case," said Leonora in her artlessness, "what means can be taken so the Music Master could come in here?"

"Well," said Loaysa, "if Your Ladyships will endeavor to get a wax impression of the key of this middle door, by tomorrow night I can have a duplicate made which we can use."

"If you get a duplicate of that key," said one of the maids, "you'll have those of the whole house, for that is a master key."

"There's no harm in that," answered Loaysa.

"That's a fact," said Leonora; "but this gentleman must first swear that he will do nothing else when he is here inside than sing and play when told to do so, and that he will stay shut up and quiet wherever we put him."

"I swear," said Loaysa.

"That oath is worthless," said Leonora. "You must swear by your father's life, and by the cross, and kiss it so we can all see."

"I swear by my father's life," said Loaysa, "and by this sign of the cross which I kiss with my impure mouth."

And forming a cross with his two fingers, he kissed it three times. When he had done this, another of the maids said:

"See here, sir, you must not forget that matter of the powders, which is the secret of everything."

With this they made an end to the conversation that night, all very happy with the arrangement. And fortune, which was guiding Loaysa's affairs from good to better, brought along his friends at that hour, which was two o'clock after midnight. Giving the signal agreed upon, which was tooting a penny whistle, Loaysa spoke to them, and told them how well his negotiations were progressing. He asked them if they had brought the powders, or some other thing, as he had asked them to do, to put Carrizales to sleep; and he also told them about the master key. They answered that the powders, or a salve, would be ready the following night, and its virtues were such that if rubbed on the wrists and temples it would bring on a deep sleep from which one would not awake for two days unless the places where it had been rubbed were washed with vinegar, and that he should give them the wax impression of the key which they would also have made without any trouble. After this they went their way, and Loaysa and his pupil slept for the few remaining hours of the night, Loaysa looking forward eagerly to the following one to see if the promise of the key would be carried out. And even though time seems slow-moving and lazy to those who wait upon it, the fact is that it runs as quickly as thought itself, and the desired end arrives, for time never stops nor rests.

So the night and the hour to gather at the turnstile came, and all the maid-servants of the house, young and old, black and white, made their appearance, for they were all longing to see the music master inside their seraglio. The only one who did not come was Leonora, and when Loaysa asked about her, they answered that she was in bed with her husband who had locked the door of their chamber and had put the key under the pillow. They added that their lady had told them that when the old man fell asleep, she would see if she could get hold of the master key and take an impression of it on wax, which she had at hand already softened, and that in a little while they would go and get it out through a cat hole.

Loaysa was amazed at the precautions the old man employed, but not because of this did his desire flag. At that very moment he heard the sound of the penny whistle, and going over to the accustomed spot, he found his friends there, who gave him a little jar of ointment having the properties already described. Loaysa took it and told them to wait a little while and he would give them the pattern of the key. He returned to the turnstile and told the duenna, who was the one most eager for him to come in, that she should take the ointment to the Lady Leonora, explaining to her the property it had, and that she should manage to anoint her husband with it so carefully that he did not feel it, and she would see wonders. The duenna did as he bade her, and when she came to the cat hole, she found Leonora waiting there, stretched out full length with her face at the hole. The duenna stretched herself out in the same manner, and putting her mouth to her mistress's ear, in a low voice she told her she was bringing her the ointment and how she was to use it. Leonora took the ointment, and told the duenna that it was impossible for her to get the key from her husband, for he had not put it under the pillow, as was his custom, but between the two mattresses at about the middle of his body. However, she was to tell the music master that if the salve worked as he said, she would be able to get hold of the key whenever they wanted it and in this way it would not be necessary to make a wax impression. She bade her go at once and tell him, and then to come back and see how the ointment was working, for she was going to apply it to her husband immediately.

The duenna went down to inform Master Loaysa of all this, and he dismissed his friends who were waiting for the key. Trembling and noiselessly, hardly daring to breathe, Leonora managed to rub the salve on the wrists of her jealous husband, as well as in his nostrils, and when she touched them, it seemed to her that he moved, and she almost died of fright. However, as best she could she rubbed the salve on all the places she had been instructed, and it was as though she were embalming him for the tomb.

It did not take the drugged ointment long to give manifest signs of its powers, for almost at once the old man began to snore so loudly that it could be heard in the street, which was music to the ears of his wife, more harmonious than that of the teacher of her Negro. Still unable to believe what she was seeing, she went over to him and shook him a little, and then more, and then a little more to see if he would wake up. And finally she was so emboldened that she rolled him from side to side without his awakening. When she saw this, she went to the cat hole, and in a voice not so low as at first called to the duenna who was waiting there, and said:

"Congratulate me, sister; Carrizales is sleeping like the dead."

"Then what are you waiting for, my lady? Go get the key, for the music master has been awaiting you for over an hour."

"Just a moment, sister, I am going for it," answered Leonora.

And going back to the bed, she put her hand between the mattresses, and took out the key without the old man's being aware of it. Once she had it in her hands, she began to leap for joy, and without a moment's delay opened the door and handed the key to the duenna who received it with great delight. Leonora ordered her to open the door to the music master and bring him into the hall, for she was afraid to leave the room for fear of what might happen. But, above all, she was to make him repeat the oath he had sworn not to do anything but what they told him to, and if he was unwilling to ratify this, she was under no circumstance to let him in.

"It shall be done as you say," said the duenna. "By my faith, he shall not come in if he does not first swear once and again and kiss the cross six times."

"Don't set a limit on him," said Leonora, "let him kiss it as many times as he wants to, but see that he swears by the life of his father and mother and all that he loves best, because in that way we will be safe and will get our fill of hearing him sing and play, for, by my soul, he does both with great delicacy. Come, don't waste time, let us not chatter the night away."

The duenna picked up her skirts, and with lightning speed was at the turnstile where all the household was waiting for her. When she showed them the key she had in her hand, they were so delighted that they raised her in their arms, like a newly appointed professor, saying: "Long may she live!" And it made them still happier when she told them there was no need to have a new key cut, for from the way the anointed old man was sleeping, they could use the house key as often as they liked.

"Come then, friend," said one of the maids, "open up the door and let this gentleman in, for he's been waiting a long time, and we'll give ourselves such a feast of music as never before."

"Wait a bit," answered the duenna. "We must get him to repeat his oath of the other night."

"He is so good," said one of the slaves, "that he won't care how many oaths he takes."

Whereupon the duenna opened the door half way, and called to Loaysa, who had been listening to all that was said through the hole in the turnstile. When he reached the door he would have rushed in, but the duenna, putting her hand against his breast, said:

"You must know, my good sir, that by God and my conscience all those within the doors of this house are virgins like the mothers who bore us, with the exception of my lady; and even though I look as if I were forty years old, though I lack two and a half months for thirty, the same is true of me, God help me. And if I look older than my years, it is because disappointments, sufferings and tribulations add a naught to one's age, and sometimes two, depending on their effects. This being the case, as it is, it would not be fitting that in exchange for two or three or four songs all the virginity encompassed within this house should be lost; for even this Negro girl called Guiomar is a maiden. Therefore, my fine gentleman, before Your Lordship enters into our kingdom you must take a solemn oath that you will do no more than we order; and if it seems to you that this is asking too much, just stop and think how much more is at stake. If Your Lordship's intentions are good, you will have little objection to taking the oath, for a good payer does not mind giving security."

"How well Mistress Marialonso has spoken," said one of the maids, "like the wise and knowing person she is. If the gentleman is not willing to take this oath, he should not come in."

At this point Guiomar the Negro girl spoke up in her broken Spanish: "Me think even he no swear, let him come in with devil and all; him here, everything forgotten."

Loaysa listened with great serenity to Mistress Marialonso's harangue, and with an air of solemnity and circumspection answered:

"Rest assured, sisters of mine and companions, that my intention was never other than to give you pleasure and satisfaction to the limits of my powers. Therefore I am in no way averse to taking this oath you ask. But I wish you would trust my word a little, for being the sort of person I am, it is as good as my bond. And I should like you to bear in mind that a coarse cloak may hide something quite different, and a poor cape often covers a good drinker. But so you may all be assured of my good intentions, I am willing to take my oath as a Catholic and righteous man; so I swear by the holy powers, and their inviolate strength, and by the entrances and exits to the holy Mount of Lebanon, and by all that is mentioned in the foreword to the true history of Charlemagne, with the death of the giant Fierabras, not to exceed or overstep the oath I have taken and the orders of the least of these ladies, under penalty that if I were to do or wish to do otherwise, from now to then and from then to now this is to be considered null and void and worthless."

When Loaysa had reached this point in his oath, one of the maids, who had been listening to him with the closest attention, cried out in a loud voice:

"That is an oath that would melt a stone. A murrain on me if I want him to swear any more, for with what you have already sworn you could go down the gorge of Cabra!"

And taking him by the breeches, she pulled him inside, and all the others gathered round him. One of them quickly ran to carry the news to her mistress who was standing guard over her husband's slumber, and when the messenger told her that the musician had come in, first she rejoiced and then she became disturbed, asking if he had taken the oath. The maid told her he had, and with the newest form of oath she had ever heard in her whole life.

"Well, if he has sworn," said Leonora, "then he is in our power. Oh, how wise I was to make him swear!"

As she said this the whole crew arrived with the music master in their midst, Luis the Negro, and Guiomar lighting their way with candles. When Loaysa saw Leonora, he made as if to throw himself at her feet and kiss her hands. She, silently and by signs, made him arise, and all stood mute, not venturing to speak for fear their master might hear them. Seeing this, Loaysa told them that they could talk aloud for the salve with which their master had been anointed was of such nature that, aside from not taking his life, it made a man like dead.

"I do believe it," said Leonora, "for otherwise he would have awakened twenty times, for his many infirmities make him a light sleeper. But since I rubbed the salve on him he has been snoring like an animal."

"In that case," said the duenna, "let's go into that front room where we can listen to this gentleman sing and enjoy ourselves a little."

"Let's go," said Leonora, "but, Guiomar, you stay here on guard, and let us know if Carrizales wakes up."

"Me Negro girl stay," wailed Guiomar, "white women go. God forgive them all!"

The Negro girl remained behind, and the others went to the drawing-room where there was a rich dais. There they all sat down with the music master in the middle. Taking a candle in her hand, Marialonso began to look the rogue of a musician over from head to foot. "Look at his top-knot, so pretty and so curly," said one of the maids. "What white teeth!" "Not a peeled pine-nut that is whiter or prettier," said another. "Oh, what big bright eyes! And bless my soul if they are not green; you'd think they were emeralds," another added. This one praised his mouth, the other his feet, and between them all they made an anatomical fricassee of him. Leonora alone said nothing, but sat with her eyes fixed on him, and little by little she found him better fashioned than her husband. At this point the duenna took the guitar which the Negro was holding, and put it in Loaysa's hands, asking him to play and sing a song that was very popular in Seville at the time, and that went like this:

> Mother, oh my mother,
> Guards you set o'er me.

Loaysa satisfied her request. All the women got up and whirled through the measures of the dance. The duenna knew the words, and she sang them with more spirit than voice.

> Mother, oh my mother,
> Guards you set o'er me,
> But if I guard not myself
> Yours are all in vain.

> They say it has been written,
> And rightly so, indeed,
> That it is on abstinence
> That appetite feeds.
> Love that is locked in,
> Grows with might and main,
> So better far it is

To cast away the chain,
For if I guard not myself,
Yours are all in vain.

If the inclination
Does not guard itself,
There's no guard will do it,
Fear, or rank, or station.
Through death it will break
Till it wins the bliss,
And make no mistake,
For if I guard not myself
Yours are all in vain.

The one inclined to love
Is like unto the moth
Which heedlessly pursues
The candle's mortal flame.
Though hedged in with guards
Many though they be,
Ready and prepared
To carry out your aim,
If I guard not myself
Yours are all in vain.

Of such a nature
Is the power of love,
That the fairest one
It turns to a chimera,
Her breast turns to wax,
Her desire to fire,
Her hands to wool,
Her feet to felt,
So if I guard not myself
Yours are all in vain.

The circle of girls, led by the duenna, had just finished their song and dance when Guiomar, the sentinel, rushed in, shaking from head to foot as though in a fit, and with a hoarse, low voice said:

"Master awake, lady, lady, master awake, getting up, coming."

Whoever has seen a carefree flock of pigeons in a field, eating what other hands have sown, rise in terror at the furious report of a gun, forgetful of their feeding ground and flying in confusion and bewilderment through the air, can imagine what happened to the flock and circle of dancers, aghast and terrified by the unexpected news Guiomar had brought. Each was thinking how to excuse herself, and all of them of their salvation, one running here, the other there, hiding in the attic and in the corners of the house, abandoning the music master who, laying aside his song and guitar, all dismayed, was at a loss to know what to do. Leonora wrung her beautiful hands, Marialonso beat herself in the face—but gently; in a word all was confusion, terror, fear. But the duenna, who was the most astute and cool-headed, ordered Loaysa to go into her room while she and her lady remained in the drawing-room, and she would think up some excuse to give the master if he found them there. Loaysa quickly hid himself away, and the duenna listened carefully to see if her master was coming. But as she heard nothing, she took heart and little by little, step by step, she stealthily approached the room where he was sleeping. Hearing him snoring as before, and having made sure he was asleep, she picked up her skirts and went running to bring her mistress the good news, at which she rejoiced greatly.

The shrewd duenna did not wish to lose the opportunity fate had given her to enjoy, before any of the others, the charms she imagined the music master to possess, and so, telling Leonora to wait in the drawing-room while she went to call him, she left her there and went in where he was, as chagrined as he was thoughtful, awaiting word of what the anointed old man was doing. He cursed the worthlessness of the salve and berated his friends for their credulity and himself for not having the foresight to try it out on somebody else before using it on Carrizales. Just then the duenna came in and assured him that the old man was sleeping like a log.

He gave a sigh of relief and stood listening to the many and loving words Marialonso was saying to him, from which he deduced what was in her mind, and decided to use her as bait to fish her mistress. And while the two were conversing, the rest of the servants, who were hidden in different parts of the house, one here, the other there, came back to see if it was true that their master had awakened. Finding all in silence, they went into the drawing room where they had left their mistress, from whom they learned that he was still asleep. When they inquired about the music master and the duenna, she told them where they were, and all of them, with the same silence with which they had slipped back, stationed themselves outside the door to listen to what was going on.

The Negro girl Guiomar was in the group, but not Luis. As soon as he had heard that his master was awake, he ran to his loft to hide, clasping his guitar to his breast; covering himself with the blanket of his humble bed, he lay sweating with fear. Yet notwithstanding, every now and then he softly plucked a string of the guitar, such was his passion for music—may the devil take him! The maids overheard the wooing words of the old harridan, and each of them called her everything she could lay her tongue to; not one employed the word "old" without joining to it the epithet and adjective of "witch," "whiskery," "hag," and others which out of decency we shall omit. But funniest of all were the expressions employed by Guiomar the Negro girl, who, being Portuguese and talking broken Spanish, cursed her with hilarious effect. The outcome of the conversation between the music master and the duenna was that he agreed to comply with her desires on condition that she would first turn her mistress over to him to do as he liked with her.

It cost the duenna no small struggle to accede to what the music master asked; but in return for the satisfaction of the desire that had already taken possession of her soul and her body and the marrow of her bones, she promised anything he wanted. Leaving him she went to talk with her mistress, and when she saw all the maids gathered around her door, she told them to go to their rooms, and another night they would have the chance to enjoy the musician with less or no alarm, for that night the excitement had spoiled things.

They all understood that what the old woman wanted was to be left alone; however, they had no choice but to obey her, for she had authority over them all. They departed, and she went into the drawing-room to persuade Leonora to yield to Loaysa's wishes, with such a long and well-knit argument that it seemed as though she had been preparing it for days. She praised his manners, his courage, his charm, and his many graces; she described how much more pleasurable the embraces of a young lover would be than those of her old husband, telling her the secret and the duration of the delight, along with many other things in the same vein which the devil put into her mouth, with glowing words, as vivid as they were efficacious, and which would have moved not only the tender and candid heart of simple trusting Leonora, but that of a marble statue. Oh duennas, born and bred to wreck a thousand modest and good intentions! Oh, those long and impressive veils, chosen to lend dignity to the drawing-rooms and parlors of ladies of rank! How they contravene the purposes of their almost obligatory calling! In short, the duenna said so many things, and so convincingly, that Leonora yielded, Leonora was led astray, Leonora was lost, making a mock of all the precautions of wise Carrizales who was sleeping the sleep of the death of his honor.

Marialonso took her lady, whose eyes were swimming in tears, by the hand, and almost by force led her to where Loaysa was. Giving them her blessing with a devil-like titter, she closed the door after her, leaving them alone. She lay down to take a nap in the parlor, or, more exactly, to await the pleasure of her turn, but as she had lost so much sleep during the preceding nights, she fell sound asleep.

It would have been fitting at this juncture to ask Carrizales, if we did not know that he was sleeping, what all his precautions, his wariness, his warnings, his exhortations, the high walls of his house, had availed him; the fact that no one bearing the name of a man had ever entered, not even in spirit; the narrow turnstile, the thick walls, the lightless windows, the confinement; the fine dowry he had settled upon Leonora, the gifts he showered upon her, the kindly treatment of his servants and slaves, sparing nothing he thought they might need or want. But as we have said, there was no point in asking him, for he was sleeping more than he should; and if he had been able to hear, and by chance answer, he would have been unable to give any better answer than to shrug his shoulders and raise his eyebrows, and say: "All this came to naught as the result, so I believe, of the evil designs of a worthless, depraved youth and the maliciousness of a treacherous duenna, together with the inexperience of an entreated and persuaded young girl." God save us all from such enemies against whom the shield of prudence offers no protection nor the sword of precaution.

Nevertheless, Leonora's virtue was such that, at the moment when she had most need of it, it held firm against the villainous powers of her astute deceiver, for they were unable to vanquish her. He wore himself out for nothing, she was triumphant, and the two of them fell asleep. At this point Heaven decreed that, despite the ointment, Carrizales should awake. As was his habit, he felt all over the bed, and not finding his beloved wife there, he leaped out, terrified and dismayed, with more speed and strength than might have been expected in one of his years. When he found that his wife was not in the room, that the door was unlocked, and the key had disappeared from under the mattress, he was on the point of losing his mind. But then, collecting himself a little, he went into the hall, and walking on tiptoe, not to be overheard, he came to the drawing-room where the duenna was sleeping, and seeing her alone, without Leonora, he went to her room. Opening the door without making a sound he saw what he would have wished never to see; he saw what he would have preferred to be sightless rather than see: he saw Leonora in Loaysa's arms, sleeping as though they rather than the jealous old man were under the effects of the ointment.

Carrizales's heart seemed to stop beating at the bitter sight; his voice stuck in his throat, his arms fell helpless at his side, and he stood there like a marble statue; and even though anger produced its natural effects, reviving his fainting spirit, his suffering was so great that he could hardly breathe. Despite all this, he would have wreaked the vengeance that great affront demanded if he had had a weapon at hand. He made up his mind to seek a dagger in his room and return to cleanse the blot on his honor with the blood of his two enemies, and even with that of his entire household. Having taken this honorable and imperative decision he returned to his room, with the same precaution and silence with which he had come, but his grief and distress so clutched at his heart that he fell fainting on his bed without being able to do a thing.

Came the dawn and found the young adulterers clasped in the net of each other's arms. Marialonso awoke and would have gone to claim what it seemed to her was her due; but seeing that it was late, she decided to leave it for the following night. Leonora was in dismay at seeing how far advanced the day was, and cursed her carelessness and that of the vile duenna. With timorous steps the two of them made their way to the room where her husband was, praying under their breath that they might find him still snoring. When they saw him silent on the bed, thinking the ointment was still working, they embraced one another joyfully. Leonora went over to her husband, and taking him by the arm, shook him from side to side to see if he would wake up without the need to wash him with vinegar, which they had been told was necessary to arouse him. With the movement Carrizales came out of his swoon, and giving a deep sigh, said in a faint, piteous voice:

"Ah me, poor wretch that I am, to what a sorry pass my fortune has brought me."

Leonora could not make out clearly what her husband was saying; but when she saw that he was awake and talking, surprised that the effect of the ointment had not lasted as long as it was supposed to, she came over to him, and putting her face against his, and clasping him to her, she said:

"What ails you, my lord, for it seems to me you are complaining."

Hearing the voice of his sweet enemy, the unfortunate old man slowly opened his eyes, and like one bemused and spellbound, he fixed them on her, and remained gazing at her for a long time, after which he said:

"Be good enough, my lady, to send for your parents at once in my name; for I have a strange sensation in my heart which makes it difficult for me to breathe, and I am afraid the end of my life is at hand, and I would like to see them before I die."

Leonora undoubtedly believed that what her husband was saying to her was true, but she thought it was the strength of the ointment that had put him in that state. Telling him she would do as he asked, she sent the Negro to go and call her parents immediately, and putting her arms around her husband, she fondled him as she never had before, asking him what it was he felt, with such tender and loving words as though he were the thing she loved best in the whole world. He looked at her with sad delight, feeling as though every word or caress of hers was a lance that ran his soul through.

The duenna had already told the household and Loaysa about the illness of her master, impressing upon them that it must be something serious for he had neglected to order the street doors locked when the Negro left to summon the lady's parents, which was in itself a surprising thing, for neither of them had ever entered that house since their daughter's marriage. All of them went about silent and perplexed, none hitting upon the cause of their master's indisposition. From time to time he sighed so deep and painfully that it seemed as though each sigh were tearing out his soul. Leonora wept to see him in that state, and he laughed like one who was out of his mind as he considered how false her tears were. At this point Leonora's parents arrived, and when they found the door to the street and that of the courtyard open, and the house buried in silence, they were amazed and not a little disturbed. They went to the room of their son-in-law and found him, as has been said, with his eyes fixed on his wife, her hands in his, and the two of them weeping profusely, she, because she saw the tears her husband shed, he, to see how feigned hers were.

As soon as her parents came in, Carrizales spoke and said:

"Your Excellencies will please sit down here, and everyone else is to leave the room except Mistress Marialonso."

They did as he said, and when the five of them were alone, without waiting for anyone else to speak, he said in a quiet voice, drying his eyes:

"I am sure, my lord and lady parents, that it will not be necessary to bring forward witnesses for you to believe the truth of what I am about to tell you. You will recall, for it is not likely that you have forgotten, with how much love and goodly intention one year, one month, five days, and nine hours ago, you gave me your daughter as my lawful wife. You also know how generously I dowered her, the dowry being such that more than three of her same station could have wed on it and been considered rich. You will also recall the care I took in dressing her and adorning her with everything she fancied and I judged suitable for her. You have seen, too, how, in keeping with my nature, and fearing the ill which, beyond a doubt, is going to end my days, and with the experience my long life had given me of the many and strange things that happen in the world, I wished to guard with the greatest care I could this jewel which I had selected and you gave to me. I raised the walls of this house, did away with the view of the windows on the street, doubled the locks of the doors, put in a turnstile, as though it were a convent. I banned from it forever all that had the name or likeness of a man; I gave her maids and slaves to do her bidding; I never denied them or her whatever they asked of me; I made her my equal; I shared my most secret thoughts with her; I made her mistress of my fortune. All this was done, in a word, so I might be assured of enjoying without fear what had cost me so dear, and to avoid her giving rise to any jealous thought entering my mind. But as human diligence cannot forestall the punishment which divine will chooses to lay upon those who do not place in it all their desires and hopes, it is not to be wondered at that I was defrauded in mine, and that with my own hand I manufactured the poison which is doing away with my life. But as I see the state of wonder you are all in, hanging on my words, I shall conclude this long preamble and tell you in a word what it is impossible to say in a thousand. What I have to say, sir and ladies, is that all I said and did concluded this morning when I found this one (pointing to his wife) who came into the world to destroy my peace of mind and my life, in the arms of a handsome youth who at this moment is hidden away in the chamber of this foul duenna."

As Carrizales uttered these final words, Leonora's heart seemed to stop beating, and she fell across her husband's knees in a faint. Marialonso turned the color of a sheet, and such a lump rose in the throats of Leonora's father and mother that they could not utter a word. Carrizales went on:

"The vengeance I plan to take for this affront is not that which is ordinarily employed; for just as I exaggerated in what I did, I wish my revenge to be of the same nature, wreaking it upon myself, as the person most responsible for this crime. For I should have stopped to think how ill-matched were this girl's fifteen years with my near fourscore. Like the silkworm, I myself fabricated the house in which I shall die, and I do not blame you, misguided child"—and saying this, he leaned over and kissed the senseless cheek of Leonora—"I do not blame you, I repeat; for the counsels of sly old women and the wooing of enamored youths can easily defeat and triumph over the slight wits that go with tender years. But, so that everyone may see the quality of the devotion and trust with which I loved you, in this last moment of my life I wish to prove it in such a way that it will live on in the world as an example, if not of kindness, at least of a foolish fondness never before seen or heard of. Therefore I would have a notary brought in at once to write my will anew, in which I shall double Leonora's dowry, and ask her, when my days are over, which will be very soon, to agree to marry that youth whom the gray hairs of this mistreated old man never offended. And thus she will see that if while I was alive I had no thought but of what might please her, I do the same in death; and I want her to have her pleasure with him whom she must love so much. The rest of my fortune

I shall leave for pious ends, and to you, my lord and lady, enough so you may live honorably for the rest of your lives. Let the notary come quickly, for my suffering is so great that it is untying the knot of my life apace."

With these words he sank into a deep swoon and fell down at Leonora's side, their faces resting against each other. It was a strange and terrible sight for the parents as they looked at their loved daughter and their dear son-in-law. The wretched duenna did not wait to hear the recriminations she expected from the parents of her lady, but left the room and went to inform Loaysa of all that had occurred, advising him to leave the house instantly, and that she would let him know through the Negro whatever happened, for there were no longer doors or keys to impede it. Loaysa was amazed at the news she gave him and taking her advice, he put on again his beggar's garb and went to tell his friends of the strange and unheard-of outcome of his suit.

Meanwhile, Leonora and Carrizales still being in a faint, Leonora's father sent for a notary who was a friend of his, and who arrived when the daughter and son-in-law had regained their senses. Carrizales dictated his will in the terms that have been stated, making no reference to Leonora's misstep, but asking and urging her to marry, if he should die, the youth he had mentioned to her in secret. When Leonora heard this, she threw herself at her husband's feet, and with her heart fluttering in her breast like a bird, she said:

"Live many years, my husband and my heart's beloved; and even though you have no reason to believe anything I tell you, I want you to know that I have offended you only in thought."

And as she began to excuse herself and to tell the truth of what had happened, her tongue became dumb and she fainted again. The suffering old man embraced her, senseless as she was; her parents embraced her, and they all wept so bitterly that it was impossible for the notary who was writing the will not to share in their grief. The will provided for all the servants of the house, gave the slaves and the Negro Luis their freedom, and to the perfidious Marialonso he left nothing but the wages due her. However, the wound he had suffered was so great that on the seventh day they bore him to his grave.

Leonora was left a rich and griefstricken widow. And when Loaysa was expecting that she would comply with the dictates of her husband's will, of which he had been informed, instead of this a week later she took her vows as a nun in one of the most closely cloistered convents of the city. He, thus flouted and in a pique, departed for the Indies. Leonora's parents were left very sad, though they found consolation in the legacy they had been left in their son-in-law's will. The maids were similarly consoled, and the slaves with their freedom. The wicked duenna was left poor and bereft of all her evil hopes.

And I was left with the desire to reach the end of this episode, an example and mirror of how little trust can be put in keys, turnstiles, and walls when the will is left free; and how much less can be put in innocent, tender years if there are duennas in their nun-black attire and long white coifs around to whisper things in guileless ears. The one thing I do not know is why Leonora did not make more of an effort to excuse herself and convince her jealous husband how guiltless she had been in that whole affair. But confusion tied her tongue, and the rapidity of her husband's death gave her no opportunity to exonerate herself.

THE ILLUSTRIOUS KITCHEN MAID

In Burgos, that illustrious and renowned city, there lived, not too many years ago, two wealthy gentlemen of rank. One of them was called Don Diego de Carriazo, the other, Don Juan de Avendaño. Don Diego had a son he named after himself, and Don Juan had one he baptized Tomás. These two young gentlemen, who are to be the heroes of this story, we shall call for the sake of brevity simply by their family names, Carriazo and Avendaño. Carriazo was about thirteen or a little over, when, seized by a roguish impulse—and without any harsh treatment on the part of his parents having a share in it, but just following his pleasure and whim—he cut loose, as the young say, from his parents' home. He wandered out into the big world, so satisfied with his life of freedom that despite the discomforts and hardships involved, he never missed the abundance he enjoyed in his home, nor did the long walks or the cold bother him, nor the heat molest him. As far as he was concerned, all the seasons of the year were springtime—sweet and mild. He slept in hay stacks as though they were feather beds; he stretched out in the straw loft of an inn as though he were lying between linen sheets. In a word, he passed his vagrancy tests with such flying colors that he might have given lessons in the subject to the renowned Alfarache.[1]

In the three years he was absent from his home, he learned to play knuckle-bones in Madrid, cards in the taverns of Toledo, and basset on the battlements of Seville. In spite of the fact that the poverty and hardships that went with this way of life were foreign to Carriazo, he bore himself like a prince in it. A mile off, in a

---

[1] *The reference is to Guzman de Alfarache, the "hero" of Mateo Aleman's famous picaresque novel.*

thousand different ways, he gave evidence of his gentle birth, for he was generous and liberal with his comrades. He rarely visited the shrines of Bacchus, and although he drank wine, it was in such limited amounts that he was never in the ranks of those lamentable creatures who, after a drop too much, become so flushed that their faces look as though bedaubed with vermillion and ochre. In short, Carriazo proved himself a virtuous rogue, clean, well-bred, and more than commonly wise. He passed from class to class in the school of roguery until he received his Master's degree in the tuna fisheries of Zahara, which is the *non plus ultra* of roguery.

Oh, all you kitchen scullions, dirty, fat, and shiny, all you false beggars, sham cripples, pickpockets of Zocodover Square[2] and of Madrid, eagle-eyed blind reciters of prayers, errand boys of Seville, hangers-on of the underworld, and the innumerable mob included under the denomination of rogue! Lower your mainsails, reef in your top: you have no right to call yourselves rogues if you have not taken two courses at the tuna fishing academy! There, there is where work and sloth go hand in hand. There you will find clean dirtiness, sleek obesity, ever-ready hunger, abundant satiety, bold-faced vice, continual gaming, a fight a minute, killings over points of honor, indecent remarks at every step, dancing as though at a wedding, songs sung as though printed, ballads with a refrain, and verse of the lewdest. Over here one is singing, there, arguing; farther on, fighting or gaming, and stealing everywhere. Liberty reigns there, and work has its reward. Many fathers of high rank go to look for their sons there, or have them fetched from there. And they are as loath to depart that life as though they were on their way to the gallows.

But all this sweetness I have described has a touch of bitterness, for no one can sleep soundly without the fear that at any minute he may be transported from Zahara to Barbary.[3] For this reason they take refuge at night in coastal watch towers, and there they post

---

[2] Zocodover, *a famous square of Toledo.*

[3] Barbary. *The northern coast of Africa, which was infested with pirates who often kidnapped persons and held them for ransom.*

sentinels and look-outs, putting their trust in the eyes of these so they can close their own. It has, however, happened on occasion that sentinels and look-outs, rogues, captains, boats and nets, and all the gallimaufry gathered there have lain down in Spain and arisen in Tetuan. But not because of this fear did our Carriazo refrain from spending three summers there to have a good time. His last summer luck smiled so kindly on him that he won almost seven hundred *reales* at cards, with which he decided to buy himself new clothes and return to Burgos and his mother's eyes, which had shed many tears over him. He took leave of his friends, of which he had many and good; he promised them that he would join them again the following summer if sickness or death did not prevent; he left half of his soul with them, and all his hopes he committed to those arid sands which seemed to him cooler and greener than the Elysian fields. And as he was used to travelling afoot, he took to the road, and on his two hemp sandals made his way from Zahara to Valladolid, gaily singing as he went along the song "Three ducks, mother." He spent a fortnight in the latter city waiting for the color of his face to change back from bronze to fair, and to give himself an overhauling and divest himself of the earmarks of the rogue and become the facsimile of a gentleman. All this he did with ease, thanks to the five hundred *reales* he had when he reached Valladolid; and of this he even put aside a hundred to hire a mule and a lad, thus appearing before his parents happy and in style. They received him with great joy, and all their friends and relatives came to congratulate them on the safe return of Don Diego de Carriazo, their son. It should be pointed out that on his travels Don Diego changed his name from Carriazo to Urdiales, and by this name he was called by those who did not know his rightful one.

Among those who came to visit the newly returned youth were Don Juan de Avendaño and his son Don Tomás, with whom Carriazo renewed and confirmed the bonds of friendship, for they were of an age and neighbors. Carriazo told his parents and everyone a thousand wonderful and elaborate lies about the things that had happened to him in the three years he had been away; but not once

did he allude, even in passing, to the tuna fisheries, though his thoughts were ever on them, especially as the time approached when he had promised his friends he would be coming back. He found no pleasure in hunting, with which his father kept him busy, nor did the many, decent, and pleasant entertainments which the city afforded solace him. Every pastime wearied him, and to the finest that were offered him he preferred those he had known in the tuna fisheries.

His friend Avendaño, seeing that he was often sad and full of thought, on the strength of their friendship took the liberty of asking him the reason for this, and offered to cure it if he could, and if necessary, with his very life blood. Not to give affront to the deep friendship they had for each other, Carriazo decided not to keep it from him; so he gave him a full description of life in the fisheries, and told him how all his sadness and melancholy came from his longing to return to it. So vividly did he paint it that when Avendaño had heard him through, he praised rather than scoffed at his taste. In short, the result of the conversation was that Carriazo so swayed Avendaño's inclination that he made up his mind to go with him and enjoy a summer of that delightful life he had described. Nothing could have pleased Carriazo more, for he felt that he had won a valuable ally to second him in his low leanings. They immediately laid their plans to get together all the money they could, and the best method they hit upon was this: in two months Avendaño was to go to Salamanca, where for three years he had been studying the Greek and Latin languages for his pleasure and where his father wanted him to continue and enroll in the faculty of his choice; with the money the father would give him for this they would have enough for their purpose.

At the same time Carriazo informed his own father that he would like to go with Avendaño to study in Salamanca. His father heartily agreed, and after talking the matter over with the elder Avendaño, they decided to arrange for them to live together in Salamanca in the style that befitted sons of theirs. The day of departure came; their fathers provided them with money, and sent along with them a tutor to govern them, a man distinguished for his kindness rather than his shrewdness. The fathers gave their sons instructions as to their conduct and how they should comport themselves to grow in virtue and learning, which is the benefit every student should aspire to receive from his labors and vigils, especially the well-born. The lads listened to them with a humble and obedient air; the mothers wept; and after receiving the blessing of all, they set out on their own mules with two family servants, in addition to the tutor who had let his beard grow to lend authority to his position.

When they reached Valladolid, they told the tutor that they would like to spend two days in that city to see it because they had never been there before. The tutor scolded them roundly, telling them that persons like themselves, hastening to begin their studies, ought not to waste an hour—much less two days—on such childish pastimes, and that it would be a load on his conscience if he let them stay there even for a minute. They were to continue their journey immediately, or they would find out what was what.

This was the extent of the shrewdness of the tutor—or steward (whichever we prefer to call him). The young fellows, who by this time had gathered in their harvest, for they had already relieved their tutor of the four hundred gold florins he was carrying, pleaded with him to allow them just that one day, during which they wanted to see the Argales fountain, whose waters were beginning to be piped into the city through large, broad aqueducts. So, though against his will, he gave them permission. His plan was to avoid the expense of lodging there, spend the night instead in Valdeastillas, and then cover the eighteen leagues between Valdeastillas and Salamanca in two days, rather than travel the twenty-two leagues from Valladolid. But as man proposes and God disposes, everything turned out exactly contrary to his desires.

The lads, mounted on their fine mules, with one of the servants, set out to see the Argales fountain, famous for its antiquity and its waters, despite the rivalry of the Caño Dorado and the noble Priora, not to mention that of Leganitos and the proud Castellana, beside which the Corpa and the Pizarra of La Mancha must hold their peace. They reached Argales, and when the servant thought Avendaño was looking in his saddle bags for something to drink out of, he saw him take out a sealed letter, telling him he was to return to the city at once and deliver it to his tutor, and when he had done so, to wait for them at the Campo Gate. The servant obediently took the letter, returned to the city, and they set off in the opposite direction, sleeping that night in Mojados; two days later they were in Madrid. Before another four had elapsed, they sold the mules in the public market, and for one they received six florins on account, and for the other the full price in gold. They dressed themselves in peasant garb, with short loose jackets, wide breeches and hose of brown cloth. The next morning an old clothes dealer bought the clothing they had been wearing, and by night they looked so different that their own mothers would not have recognized them. Light of luggage, in the manner Avendaño liked and was familiar with, they started for Toledo on foot and without swords, for the old clothes dealer, although he did not traffic in these, had bought them, too.

Now let us leave them on their way, for they go content and gay, and see what the tutor did when he opened the letter which the servant brought him and found its contents to be as follows:

"We beg of Your Excellency, Master Pedro Alonso, to be patient and return to Burgos, where you will tell our parents that we, their sons, after due deliberation, having considered how much more fitting for gentlemen are arms than letters, have made up our minds to exchange Salamanca for Brussels, and Spain for Flanders. We are taking the four hundred florins, and we plan to sell the mules. Our praiseworthy intention and the long road ahead of us are sufficient justification for our misconduct, although nobody will adjudge it so except a coward. We are leaving immediately; our return will be at the pleasure of God. May He keep Your Excellency as He is able and these your humble pupils desire. At Argales fountain, on the point of setting out for Flanders. Carriazo and Avendaño."

Dumfounded was Pedro Alonso as he read the epistle, and turning quickly to his valise, he found that its emptiness bore out the truth of the letter's contents. At once, on the mule that had been left him, he set out for Burgos to inform his masters of the turn of events so they might take measures and hit upon some means of overtaking their sons. But of these matters the author of this narrative says nothing, for just as he left Pedro Alonso mounted on his mule, he resumed the account of what happened to Avendaño and Carriazo upon their entry into Illescas, stating that at the gate of the city they met two muleteers, Andalusians, to judge by their appearance, dressed in broad linen breeches, slashed linen doublets, chamois jackets, wearing curved daggers and swords without a sword belt. Apparently one was coming from Seville, and the other was going there. The latter said to the first:

"If it were not that I have to catch up with my masters, I would stay a while longer to ask you a thousand and one things I want to know. I am amazed at what you have told me about the Count hanging Alonso Genís and Ribera without being willing to grant them an appeal."

"God save us," answered the one from Seville, "the Count laid a trap for them, claimed jurisdiction over them, alleging that they were soldiers, and took unfair advantage of them, without the high court being able to get them out of his clutches. I can tell you, friend, that he's got the very Devil in him, that Count of Puñonrostro, and he plays the devil with us. For ten leagues around, Seville has been swept clean of rogues, and not a thief sets foot in its vicinity. They all fear him like fire, though it is said that he will soon give up the post of Military Governor, for he does not have the patience to be continually locking horns with the gentlemen of the high court."

"Long life to those gentlemen," said the one on his way to Seville. "They are the fathers of the wretched and the refuge of the afflicted. How many poor devils are eating dirt only because of the ire of some all-powerful judge, or some magistrate who is either badly informed or prejudiced! Many eyes see more than two, and the venom of injustice does not poison many hearts as quickly as one."

"It's a preacher you've become," said the one from Seville, "and at the rate you're going, you won't be finished soon, and I can't wait. Tonight don't go to the place where you usually lodge, but to the Inn of The Sevillian, for you will see there the most beautiful kitchen maid that anyone ever laid eyes upon. Marinilla of the Tejada Inn is dirt by comparison. I won't say any more except that gossip has it that the son of the Corregidor is head over heels in love with her. One of those masters of mine up ahead swears that when he goes back to Andalusia he's going to spend two months in Toledo at that very inn just to feast his eyes on her. I already gave her a little pinch for a keepsake and got a clout on the head in return. She is as hard as marble, as unsociable as a mountain shepherdess, and as prickly as a nettle; but she has a face of glory, and the look of a fine harvest. In one cheek she has the sun, and in the other the moon; one is of roses, the other of pinks, and on both there are lilies and jasmine, too. All I can say to you is go and look for yourself, and you will see that what I have said is as nothing to what I could have said of her beauty. I would gladly give my team of gray mules as a dowry if they would give her to me for my wife, but I know they won't. She is a jewel for some archpriest, or count. Once more I say, you will see for yourself. And now goodbye, for I am leaving."

With this the two muleteers took their leave of one another, and the two friends who had overheard their talk and conversation fell silent with wonder, especially Avendaño, in whom the muleteer's mere account of the kitchen maid's beauty had aroused a burning desire to see her. The same thing had happened to Carriazo, but not to such a degree that he did not prefer to get to his tuna fisheries rather than stop to see the pyramids of Egypt or any of the other seven wonders of the world, or all of them put together.

Repeating the words of the muleteers, and mimicking and mocking the manner and gestures with which they had said them, they amused themselves on the road to Toledo. Once in the city, with Carriazo, who had already been there before, acting as guide, they descended the Sangre de Cristo slope and came to the Inn of The Sevillian, but they did not venture to seek lodgings there as they were not fittingly attired. By this time it was dark, and although Carriazo kept insisting to Avendaño that they must find lodgings somewhere else, it was impossible to drag him away from the door of the inn where he stood waiting in the hope that the illustrious kitchen maid might show herself. Night was closing in and the kitchen maid did not come out. Carriazo was beside himself, but Avendaño would not move. Finally, on the pretext that he wanted to inquire about some gentlemen from Burgos who were going to Seville, he went into the courtyard of the inn. He had no more than done so when from a room that opened on to the courtyard, he saw a girl who looked to be fifteen, or thereabouts, dressed in the attire of a peasant, come out with a lighted candle in her hand.

Avendaño paid no attention to the girl's attire, gazing only at her face, and it seemed to him like those in the paintings of angels. He was struck speechless by her beauty, and could think of nothing to say, so bemused and carried away was he. The girl, seeing him standing there, said:

"What do you want, brother? Are you perchance the servant of one of the guests of the house?"

"I am nobody's servant but yours," answered Avendaño, all confused and embarrassed.

At these words the girl said to him: "Get along with you, brother; we who serve have no need of servants." And calling to her master, she said: "Sir, come and see what this young man wants."

Her master came out and asked him what he wanted. Avendaño replied that he was looking for certain gentlemen of Burgos who were on their way to Seville, one of whom was his master, who had sent him ahead by way of Alcalá de Henares to attend to some business, and had told him to go on to Toledo and wait for him at the Inn of The Sevillian, where he would break his journey; furthermore, he expected him to arrive that night, or the next day at the latest. He gave his lie such a color of truth that the innkeeper swallowed it, and said to him:

"Then remain here in the inn, my friend, and wait until your master arrives."

"Many thanks, Sir Host," answered Avendaño, "and will you please have a room made ready for me and a companion who is travelling with me, and is waiting outside. We have money and will pay you as well as the next one."

"Right gladly," answered the innkeeper, and turning to the girl, he said:

"Costancica, tell Argüello to give these young gentlemen the corner room, and to put clean sheets on the bed."

"Yes, sir," answered Costanza, as the maid was called.

With a curtsey to her master she disappeared from sight, and her absence was to Avendaño like the sun setting upon a wayfarer and dark, gloomy night descending. However, he went out to inform Carriazo of what he had seen and the arrangements he had made. Carriazo recognized by a thousand signs that his friend had been struck down by the plague of love, but he decided to say nothing about it for the time being until he could see for himself whether the cause which gave rise to the praises and hyperboles which raised Costanza's beauty to the very skies justified his state.

They entered the inn, and Argüello, a woman about forty-five who was in charge of the beds and rooms, led them to one which was neither for gentlemen nor servants, but for persons midway between the two. They asked for supper, and Argüello informed them that they did not serve meals at the inn, although they did cook and prepare what the lodgers brought in; but that there were taverns and taprooms nearby where they could order whatever they wanted for supper without reservations. They took her advice and went into a nearby taproom where Carriazo ate what he was served, and Avendaño what he carried with him, namely, thoughts and fancies.

Carriazo was amazed at Avendaño's lack of appetite. In order to learn what was going on in his friend's mind, he said to him as they were returning to the inn:

"I think we ought to get up early tomorrow so as to reach Orgaz before the sun gets too high."

"I do not favor that idea," answered Avendaño, "for before we leave this city I want to see all its famous sights, such as the Sagrario chapel, Juanelo's engine,[4] the Vistillas de San Agustín, the King's Garden, and the Vega."

"Very good," replied Carriazo, "two days will be enough for that."

"I may tell you that I intend to take my time about it, for we are not hurrying to Rome seeking an appointment of some sort."

"Ho, ho," replied Carriazo. "Unless I am very much mistaken, my friend, you are more inclined to remain in Toledo than to continue the pilgrimage we have set out on."

"That is a fact," answered Avendaño, "and I may add that it would be as impossible for me to forgo the sight of this maid's face as it is to enter heaven without good works."

"That is high praise," said Carriazo, "and a decision worthy of a heart as noble as yours! It well befits one Don Tomás de Avendaño, the son of Don Juan de Avendaño, a gentleman, well-to-do, young, well-endowed, to lose his head over a kitchen maid at the Inn of The Sevillian!"

"It seems the same to me," answered Avendaño, "that a certain Don Diego de Carriazo, son of a father of that same name, knight of the Order of Alcántara, heir-apparent to the same, no less favored in body than in mind, should have fallen in love—and with whom, do you think? With Queen Guinevere? Oh, no, not at all, but with the tuna fishery of Zahara, which is uglier, so I have heard, than the temptations of St. Anthony."

"Hoist by my own petard," replied Carriazo. "You've paid me back in kind. Let this be the end of our controversy, and let us be off to sleep. Tomorrow will be another day, and may it bring success."

"Look, Carriazo, you haven't seen Costanza yet. When you do, you have my permission to insult or reprimand me as much as you like."

"I can see what the outcome of this is going to be," said Carriazo.

---

[4] *A Moorish engine for raising water from the Tagus river which was repaired by Juanelo Turriano of Cremona.*

"What?" asked Avendaño.

"That I will go on to my tuna fishery and you will stay with your scullery maid."

"I won't be that lucky," said Avendaño.

"Nor I so foolish that by following your bad choice I miss my good one."

Chatting in this fashion, they came to the inn, and went on with their conversation for half the night. When they had been sleeping hardly an hour, or so it seemed to them, they were awakened by the sound of oboes in the street. They sat up in bed listening, and Carriazo said:

"I'll bet it's day already, and some kind of a festival is going to be held at the monastery of Our Lady of Carmen which is near here, and that's why they're playing the oboes."

"It's not that," replied Avendaño, "because we have not been asleep long enough for it to be day yet."

As they were talking there came a knock at the door of their room, and when they asked who it was a voice answered:

"Young men, if you want to hear a fine serenade, get up and look out of the window in that front room; there is nobody in it."

The two got up and when they opened the door there was no one there, nor did they know who had called them. But as they heard the sound of a harp, they decided a serenade was going on, and so, just as they were, in their nightshirts, they went into the front room where three or four other guests were already at the windows. They found themselves a place, and in a few moments, to the accompaniment of the harp and a guitar, they heard a beautiful voice sing this sonnet, which remained graven in Avendaño's memory:

> Rare lowly being who raises
> Beauty to such towering heights
> Wherein nature outdid herself,
> Giving a foretaste of Heaven,
> Whether you speak or laugh or sing,
> Now gentle, now stern of mien

(Mark of your gentilesse)
You bewitch the powers of the soul.
That the peerless beauty you hold
May be known as it should,
And the virtue which is your pride:
Leave off serving, and be served
By all whose hands and brows
Gleam with sceptres and crowns.

Nobody needed to tell the two lads that the serenade was in honor of Costanza, for the sonnet had made it patent. Its effect on Avendaño was such that he would have been willing, for the sake of not hearing it, to have been born deaf and continue so all the days of his life which, from that moment, turned as bitter as only one whose heart is pierced by the sharp lance of jealousy can know. And the worst of it was that he did not know of whom he could or should be jealous. But his doubts were quickly dispelled by one of those standing at the window, who said:

"Did you ever hear of such a fool as that son of the Corregidor, going about serenading a scullery wench! To be sure, she is one of the most beautiful girls I have ever seen, and I've seen many; but that is no excuse for seeking her favors so openly."

Another of those around the window added: "I've heard it said on good authority that she pays him as much heed as though he were a nobody. I'll bet at this moment she is slumbering soundly behind her mistress's bed, where they say she sleeps, without giving a thought to serenades or songs."

"That is a fact," answered the other, "for she is the most proper maid anyone has ever heard of; and it is remarkable that being in this busy inn, with strange people coming and going every day and having to be in and out of the bedrooms, nobody has ever heard of her committing the slightest impropriety."

These remarks gave Avendaño new life and strength to listen to the many other songs the musicians sang to the sound of different instruments, all directed to Costanza who, as the guest had said, was sound asleep. With the coming of day, the musicians departed, signalling their farewell with the oboes. Avendaño and Carriazo returned to their room, where the one who could slept until the morning; then the two of them arose, both longing to see Costanza. But whereas the desire of the one was born of curiosity, the other was that of a lover. However, Costanza satisfied them both as she came out of her master's room, so beautiful that it seemed to both of them that all the praises lavished on her by the mule driver fell short of reality. She wore a skirt and bodice of green flannel, trimmed with the same material. The bodice was cut low, but the guimpe was high and pleated at the throat, with a heading of embroidered black silk, like a necklace of jet stars upon a column of alabaster, than which her throat was no less white. About her waist she wore a cord of St. Francis, and from a ribbon hanging at her right side, a great bunch of keys. She did not wear clogs, but double-soled red shoes, with hose which were not visible, except at the sides, and were red, too. Her hair was plaited with strands of white gimp, and the braid was so long that it hung below her waist. Its color was lighter than chestnut, almost blonde, and it looked so clean, so smoothly combed, that none other, even if of threads of gold, could vie with it. Two little pendants of glass, resembling pearls, hung from her ears; her hair served her as coif and headdress.

As she came out of the room she crossed herself, and with quiet devotion make a deep genuflection before an image of Our Lady which was hanging on one of the walls of the courtyard. As she raised her eyes she saw the two youths gazing upon her, and no sooner had she noticed them than she went back to the room from which she had come, calling out to Argüello to get up.

Now we must tell what impression Costanza's beauty made on Carriazo, inasmuch as we have already told its effect on Avendaño when he saw her for the first time. I can only say that she seemed as beautiful to him as to his comrade, but she aroused his love far less—so much less, that he would have wished not to spend another night at the inn, but to set out at once for the tuna fisheries. At this moment, in response to Costanza's call, Argüello came out in the hall, with two other girls, said to be from Galicia, who were also

servants in the inn. The reason for so many was the number of
people who stopped at the Inn of The Sevillian, which is one of the
best and most frequented in all Toledo. The guests' servants came
asking for barley for their mounts; the innkeeper came out to give it
to them, cursing his maids because of whom his hostler—who used
to portion it out with care and honesty, not wasting a single grain—
had left. Avendaño when he heard this, said:

"Don't worry, Sir innkeeper; give me the account book, and during the days I stay here I shall take such good care in apportioning the
barley and straw that is ordered that you will never miss the hostler
you say has left."

"I shall be truly grateful to you, my lad," answered the innkeeper, "for I cannot look after this as I have many other things to
attend to outside. Come with me, and I will give you the ledger,
and don't forget that these mule drivers are the very devil, and they
will steal a measure of barley from under your nose with no more
qualms than if it were straw."

Avendaño went down to the courtyard, took over the book, and
began to distribute measures of feed with ease and despatch, and
to enter them with such accuracy that the innkeeper, who was watching him, was so pleased he said:

"Would to God your master never got here and you were willing to stay on at the inn. Believe me, you'd never regret it. The fellow who left came to my inn some eight months ago, ragged and
gaunt, and when he went off he had two fine suits of clothes and
was as fat as a beaver. Because you should know, son, that in this
house there are many perquisites in addition to the wages."

"If I were to stay," answered Avendaño, "the emoluments would
not matter much to me; I'd be satisfied with whatever I got for the
sake of being in this city which they tell me is the finest in Spain."

"At any rate," said the host, "it is one of the finest and richest.
But we've got another problem now, and that is finding someone to
go to the river and fetch water, for the other lad who, with a fine ass
I have, used to keep the water jars full to overflowing and the house
like a lake, has left, too. One of the reasons the mule drivers like

to bring their masters to my inn is because of the abundant supply of water they always find here. They don't have to take their animals to the river for there is water for them right here in big tubs."

Carriazo had been listening to all the conversation, and, seeing that Avendaño was already fixed up with a job at the inn, he didn't want to be left out; moreover, he thought how pleased Avendaño would be if he kept him company. Turning to the innkeeper, he said: "Bring on your ass, Sir Host; for I will know how to cinch it and load it as well as my comrade knows how to keep your ledger."

"Yes, indeed," said Avendaño, "my comrade Lope Asturiano will haul you water like a prince, and I vouch for him."

Argüello, who was listening to all they were saying from the hall, spoke up when she heard Avendaño say that he would vouch for his comrade.

"May I ask, my fine sir, who is going to vouch for you? For it seems to me that you are more in need of a guarantor than to offer a guarantee."

"Hold your tongue, Argüello," said the host, "and don't stick your nose into what is not your business. I'll vouch for both of them, and none of you is to start bickering with the lads of the house. It's because of you women that they all leave."

"So these lads are staying here?" asked another of the maids. "By the sign of the Cross, I wouldn't trust them with the wine-skin if I were travelling with them."

"That's enough of your coarse remarks," said the host; "now go about your business and let the lads alone, or I'll take a stick to you."

"Indeed!" answered the maid. "What fine jewels they are! The fact is, master, that you have never found me so forward either with the lads of the inn or those outside it as to hold me in such low esteem. They are scoundrels who leave when the notion takes them, not because of anything we do to them. A fine lot they are, I must say, who need no excuse to steal off like thieves without saying a word."

"What a talker you are, sister," answered the innkeeper. "Now hold your tongue and get to your work."

While this was going on, Carriazo had already saddled the ass, and leaping astride it, he set out for the river, leaving Avendaño greatly pleased at his gallant decision.

So now we have Avendaño converted into a hostler, going by the name of Tomás Pedro, and Carriazo, alias Lope Asturiano, changed into a water boy, metamorphoses that oustrip those of the big-nosed poet.[5] Argüello had no more than heard that the two were staying on at the inn than she set her sights on Asturiano and marked him for her own, making up her mind to flirt with him so that, even though he was of a shy, retiring nature, he would become as soft as a glove. The finicky Gallega had the same plans about Avendaño, and as the two were close friends, by reason of their association and talk, and because they slept together, they confessed to one another their amorous resolve, and that very night made up their minds to begin the conquest of their dispassionate lovers. But the first thing they decided was that they would have to ask them not to be jealous of anything they saw them do with their persons, for it is hard for maids to regale those of the household unless they make friends of those outside the house. "Hush, brothers," they said, as though they had them in their presence and were already their amours or paramours, "hush, and cover up your eyes, and let the one who knows how play the tambourine, and the one who understands it guide the dance, and there will not be a pair of canons in this whole city more pampered than you two by us, who are your good friends."

While Gallega and Argüello were maundering on in this fashion, our good Lope Asturiano was on his way to the river, down the Carmen slope, his thoughts on the tuna fisheries, and the sudden change in his plans. Whether because of this, or Fate's designs, at a narrow pass in the road he encountered a water-carrier coming up with a load of water. As Lope was going down hill, and his ass was spirited and frisky because it had been standing idle, it gave the tired bony animal it met such a greeting that it knocked it to the

---

[5] *The reference is to the Latin poet Ovid, author of the* Metamorphoses. *He was nicknamed Naso—Big Nosed—because of the size of his nose.*

ground, breaking the jars and spilling the water. The veteran water-carrier, indignant and wrathful, attacked the new recruit, and as the latter was mounted, before he could alight and defend himself, he managed to land a dozen blows which were not at all to Asturiano's liking. When he finally got off his ass he was so enraged that he rushed upon his enemy, grabbed him by the neck with both hands and flung him to the ground. His head hit a stone which laid it open, and there was such an outpouring of blood that Lope thought he had killed him.

When the many other water-carriers coming along saw their comrade in such straits, they rushed at Lope and holding him fast, began to shout: "Police, police! This water-carrier has killed a man!"

And with these outcries and accusations they fell upon Lope with fists and sticks. Some of them went to the aid of the man on the ground and found that he had his head split, and was on the verge of death. The shouts ran from mouth to mouth all the way up the slope, and in Carmen Square came to the ears of a bailiff who, with two constables, rushed to the site of the quarrel as quickly as though they had wings on their feet, just as the wounded man had been laid across his ass, and that of Lope seized. Lope was encircled by more than twenty water-carriers who held him fast and were belaboring him in such a way that his life was in more danger than that of the wounded man, seeing how the fists and cudgels of the avengers of an injury to one of their own rained upon him.

When the bailiff arrived he pushed the men back, handed Asturiano over to the constables, and leading his ass, with the wounded man across his own, brought them to the jail with such an escort of people, and all the boys who were running along, that it was hard to pass through the streets. The noise of the crowd brought Tomás Pedro and his master to the door of the inn to see what was the cause of the uproar, and their eyes lighted upon Lope between two constables, his face and mouth covered with blood. The innkeeper quickly looked about for his ass, and saw it in the hands of a third constable who had joined the others. He inquired the reason for those seizures and was told the facts of the case. He was much concerned about his ass, fearing he might lose it or that the costs of recovering it might be more than it was worth. Tomás Pedro followed his comrade, but he could not get close enough to say a word to him, with so many people around him and the close guard the constables and bailiff kept over him. He did not leave him until he had seen him jailed, in a dungeon, with two pairs of fetters, and the wounded man in the infirmary, where he remained while the wound was dressed, and he saw that it was very serious, as the surgeon said. The bailiff impounded the two asses, as well as five pieces of eight the constables had taken from Lope.

Tomás, dejected and deeply distressed, returned to the inn where he found his new master no less downcast than himself. He informed him of what had been done with his comrade, of the dangerous state of the wounded man, and the whereabouts of the ass. And he went on to say that to the present misfortune there had been added another no less vexing, which was that a close friend of his master's had met him on the way and told him that his master, who was in a great hurry, to save two leagues had gone from Madrid by the Azeca ferry, and would spend that night in Orgaz. He had given the friend twelve florins for Tomás, with instructions to proceed to Seville, where he would wait for him.

"But this is not possible," Tomás went on, "for how can I leave my friend and companion in jail, and in such danger? My master will have to excuse me for the time being; and as he is so kind and upright, he will overlook any fault of mine toward him in exchange for not being guilty of one toward my comrade. Your Excellency will do me the favor of accepting this money and attending to this affair; and while this is being used, I will write to my master, telling him what has happened, and I am sure he will send me money enough to get us out of any danger."

The innkeeper's eyes opened as wide as saucers in his delight at seeing that in part the loss of his ass would be made good. He took the money, and spoke encouragingly to Tomás, telling him that he had acquaintances of importance in Toledo who had great influence in legal circles, especially a nun who was a relative of the chief magistrate and could wrap him around her little finger, and a laundress of the convent of that same nun had a daughter who was an intimate friend of the sister of a friar who was on close terms with the confessor of the aforesaid nun, and this laundress washed for the inn . . .

"And if she asks her daughter, as there is no doubt she will, to talk with the sister of the friar, and she with her brother, and he with the confessor, and the confessor with the nun, and the nun is willing to send a note (which will be no problem) to the chief magistrate, entreating him to take a hand in the affair, we can be sure of a favorable outcome. All this, of course, provided the water-carrier does not die, and provided we have grease for the palms of all the ministers of justice, for unless they are well greased they squeal louder than an ox cart."

Tomás was heartened by the offers of help his master had made, and amused by the many and roundabout ways in which he arrived at it. And although he realized that in all this he showed more slyness than candor, nevertheless he appreciated his good intention, and handed the money over to him, promising that there would be much more where this came from, for he had complete confidence in his master, as he had already said.

When Argüello saw her new lover led away, she hurried to the jail to take him food, but they would not let her see him, which sent her away cross and indignant, but unswerving in her good intention. In short, within a fortnight the wounded man was out of danger, and in another week the surgeon declared him cured. By this time Tomás had made the pretense that he had received fifty florins from Seville, and taking them out of his pocket, he handed them over to the innkeeper with letters and the feigned seal of his master. As mine host had not the slightest interest in ascertaining the truth about the correspondence, he took the money which, being in gold coins, pleased him greatly.

In consideration of six florins the wounded man withdrew his charges; ten more paid Lope's fine, and the costs and the impounding of the ass. Lope was released from jail, but he did not wish to rejoin his comrade, giving as his excuse that during the time he had been in jail Argüello had visited him and had made amorous overtures to him, which so annoyed and outraged him that he would let himself be hanged before he would reciprocate the desires of such a slut. What he was going to do, inasmuch as Tomás was bent upon carrying out his plan, was to buy himself an ass and follow the trade of water-carrier as long as they were in Toledo, and in this way he would not be taken up or jailed as a vagrant. With a single load of water he could wander about the city all day long, looking at the silly girls.

"Pretty girls, you should say, and they also have the reputation of being the most circumspect women of Spain, and their beauty and their circumspection go hand in hand. If you don't believe me, look at Costancica, the leavings of whose beauty would embellish not only the belles of this city, but of the whole world."

"Gently, friend Tomás," answered Lope, "let us go slowly in this matter of the praises of Mistress Kitchen Maid, unless you want me to think you are not only crazy, but a heretic, too."

"Kitchen maid you call Costanza, brother Lope?" answered Tomás. "May God forgive you and open your eyes to your mistake."

"Isn't she a kitchen maid?" retorted Asturiano.

"I have yet to see her wash her first dish."

"What does it matter if you haven't seen her wash her first dish, if you have seen her wash the second, and the hundredth?"

"I tell you, brother," answered Tomás, "that she does no dishwashing, nor does she occupy herself with anything but her needlework and looking after the silverware here in the inn, of which there is much."

"Then tell me," said Lope, "why is she known all over the city as the illustrious kitchen maid if she does no dishwashing? It must be that as she washes silver, and not dishes, they call her illustrious. But, leaving this aside, tell me, Tomás, how do your hopes stand?"

"Hopeless," replied Tomás. "All these days you have been in jail I have not been able to say a word to her, and to the many praises the guests address to her, her only answer is to lower her eyes and not open her lips. Her modesty and reserve are such that they arouse as much admiration as her beauty. What tries my patience is knowing that the son of the Corregidor, who is a lively lad and somewhat overbold, is mad about her, and woos her with music. Hardly a night goes by that he does not serenade her, and so openly that they name her in the songs, and praise her and extol her. But she does not hear them, nor from night until morning does she leave the room of her mistress, the shield which keeps the sharp arrows of jealousy from piercing my heart."

"Well, how do you plan to overcome the impossible obstacles in the way of your conquest of this Portia, this Minerva, this new Penelope, who in the guise of a maiden, and a kitchen wench, has won your heart and made you craven and weak?"

"Make all the fun you like of me, friend Lope; all I can say is that I am in love with the most beautiful face Nature could have shaped, and the most incomparable virtue that exists in the world today. Costanza is her name, not Portia, Minerva or Penelope; she serves in an inn, that I cannot deny; but what can I do if it seems to me that the hidden hand of fate inclines me, and my own choice eloquently moves me, to adore her? See here, my friend," Tomás went on, "I don't know how to explain to you the manner in which love exalts the lowly person of this kitchen maid, as you call her, in my eyes, and raises her so high that seeing it, I do not see it, and knowing it, I do not recognize it. It is impossible for me, even if I try, to take thought of the lowliness of her station, if you can call it that, because instantly her beauty, her grace, her repose, her virtue, her modesty erase this idea from my mind, and lead me to believe that beneath that rustic exterior there must be concealed some lode of great treasure and value. And, finally, whatever the reason, I love her dearly, and not with that vulgar love with which I have loved others, but with a love so pure that it asks nothing more than to serve her, and aspires to her love in return, repaying me with chaste affection the debt due my own chaste inclination."

At this point Asturiano, giving a great shout, burst forth:

"Oh, Platonic love! Oh, illustrious kitchen wench! Oh, what

happy times are these in which we see beauty awaken love without malice, virtue kindle a flame that does not burn, grace please without inciting, and low estate endowed with power and strength to be raised upon the wheel of so-called Fortune! Oh, my poor tuna fish, which will have to spend this year without a visit from this your devoted admirer! But the coming one I shall make it up in such a fashion that the captains of the most prized fisheries will have no complaint of me."

"I see, Asturiano, how openly you mock me," said Tomás. "What you can do is to take yourself off to your fisheries, and I shall pursue my chase, and you will find me here on your return. If you want to take with you your share of the money, I shall give it to you forthwith; so go in peace, and let each follow the path along which his destiny leads him."

"I thought you were smarter than that," said Lope. "Can't you see that I'm only joking? But as I see that you are in earnest, I shall truly help you in everything you wish. I ask only one thing of you in return for all that I intend to do for you, and that is not to put me in situations where Argüello can make up to me or seek my favors, for I would prefer to forgo your friendship rather than run the risk of having hers. By God, friend, she talks more than a court reporter, and her breath reeks of wine a mile off. All her upper teeth are false, and it looks to me as though her hair was a wig. And to cover up and hide these shortcomings, since she revealed her foul designs to me she has been daubing her face with white lead, and she plasters it on so thick that it looks like a ship's painted prow."

"That is all true," answered Tomás; "the Galician wench who torments me is not that bad. What you can do is to make this your last night at the inn, and tomorrow you buy the ass you talk about and look for lodgings somewhere else. In that way you can escape the ambushes of Argüello, while I suffer those of the Galician and the fatal ones of my Costanza's beauty."

The friends agreed on this and went to the inn where Asturiano was received with great show of affection by Argüello. That night there was a dance at the door of the inn in which many of

the mule drivers staying at the inn and others nearby participated.
Asturiano played the guitar; the women present were the two Galician wenches, Argüello, and three other maids of the inn. Many
came wearing masks, more drawn by the hope of seeing Costanza
than by the dance; but she did not appear nor come out to see it,
thus leaving many hopes blighted. Lope played the guitar so mar-
vellously that they said he made it talk. The girls, especially
Argüello, asked him to sing them a ballad. He answered that if they
would dance as it was done in the theater, he would sing, and so
they would make no mistake, they were to follow everything he
said as he sang, and not depart from it.

Among the mule drivers there were good dancers, and among
the girls as well. Lope cleared his throat and spat twice, while he
thought about what he would say. And as he had a quick, easy,
natural wit, and a great gift for improvising, he began to sing:

> Step forward, beautiful Argüello,
> Maid once, and no more,
> And making a deep curtsey,
> Take two steps back.
> Take her by the hand,
> You called Barrabás,
> Mule driver of Andalusia,
> High priest of roguery.
> Of the two Galician maids
> Who live at this inn,
> Let the fat-faced one step forward,
> Leaving her apron behind.
> Hold her tight, Torote,
> And then the four together,
> All hands round and a swing,
> Begin a *contrapas*.

As Asturiano called the steps, they all obeyed to the letter, but
when he said they were to begin the *contrapas*, Barrabás, which was
the nickname by which the mule driver was known, interrupted:
"Brother musician, watch what you are saying, and don't call

anyone poorly dressed, for there's nobody here in rags,[6] and we all dress the best we can."

The innkeeper, hearing him display his ignorance, said to him:

"My lad, *contrapas* is a foreign dance, and has nothing to do with rags."

"Then why," replied the driver, "make it so fancy? Let him play sarabandes, chaconnes, and folias such as we know, and let her rip; there are people here who can tread all the measures."

Without a word, Asturiano went on with his song:

> Then enter all the nymphs
> And the sprites who share their sport,
> For the chaconne is a dance
> More ample than the sea.

> Ready with the castanets,
> Bend down and rub your hands
> Well in this sand,
> Or dirt of the dung heap.

> Well done, all of you,
> I have no fault to find,
> Cross yourselves, and give the devil
> Two figs from your fig tree.

> Spit on the foul fiend,
> So we may have our sport,
> For from the chaconne
> He is never far apart.

> I change the tune, Argüello divine,
> More beautiful than a hospital;
> For you are my new muse,
> Look with favor on me.

---

[6] *This is a somewhat far-fetched play on the French name of a dance, the* contrapas, *and the Spanish* "con trapas"—*in rags—which the mule driver took it to mean.*

Then heigh-ho the chaconne,
That makes life so jolly.

The exercise it gives
Prospers the health,
Shaking dull sloth
From all our limbs.

Laughter swells the breast
Of dancer and player,
Of onlooker and listener
Of music and dance.

Feet scatter quicksilver,
The body liquefies,
And slippers lose their soles,
To the owner's delight.

Spirits and nimbleness
Revive in the old,
And the young grow blither,
As loudly they sing:

Then heigh-ho the chaconne
That makes life so jolly.

Time and again
Has this fine lady,
Arm in arm with the gay sarabande,
The *pésame*, the *perra mora*,[7]

Tried to slip through the cracks
Of nunneries devout,
To trouble the chaste peace
That dwells within its walls.

How often it has been rebuked,
By the very ones who adore it,
Because the lewd think it evil,
And a fool may so regard it.

Then heigh-ho the chaconne
That makes life so jolly.

This dusky Indian wench,
Who, so rumor assures,
Is guilty of sacrilege greater
Than any Aroba thought of;

She to whom pays tribute
The crowd of kitchen wenches,
As does the throng of pages,
And the army of lackeys,

Says, swears, and holds as true,
That for all the proud airs
Of the haughty *zambapalo*,[7]
She is the cream of the crop.

Then heigh-ho the chaconne
That makes life so jolly.

All the while Lope was singing, the crowd of mule drivers and kitchen maids, twelve in all, were turning themselves inside out in the dance. As Lope was preparing to sing other tunes of more weight, substance, and claim to attention, one of the many masked spectators said, without removing his domino:

"Hold your tongue, drunkard. Hold your tongue, toper, wine-skin, hand-me-down poet, musicaster."

He was followed by others heaping so many insults and evil

---

[7] *These are all names of dances which have disappeared, at least under these names.*

looks upon him that Lope judged it the part of discretion to keep quiet. But the mule drivers took such umbrage that if it had not been for mine host, who managed to calm them with his sensible words, it would have turned into a free-for-all. Even so, fists would have entered into play if at that moment an officer of the law had not shown up and ordered them all to bed.

No sooner had they left than to the ears of all those in the neighborhood who were still awake there came the voice of a man who, sitting on a stone in front of the Inn of The Sevillian, sang in tone so melodious and captivating that it filled them with wonder and they could not choose but listen until the end. But the one who was most attentive was Tomás Pedro, inasmuch as it was he who was most directly affected. For him it was not only a matter of hearing the music, but catching the words, for these to him were not songs, but letters of excommunication which rowelled his soul. What the musician was singing was the following ballad:

> Where are you, unseen of eye,
> Sphere of beauty,
> Radiant human orb,
> Fashioned by hand divine?
>
> Empyrean realm, where love
> Has its residence,
> First cause which bears
> All delight in its wake;
>
> Crystalline spot where
> Waters transparent, pure,
> Both cool the flames of love
> And feed and fan them;
>
> Bright new firmament
> In which two conjoined stars,
> Without aid of borrowed light,
> Illumine earth and sky.

Joy which bars the way
To the murky sadness
Of the father whose belly
Entombs his own sons;

Humility which will have none
Of the praise lavished upon
Great Jove, who is moved
By her benignity so lavish.

Invisible and subtle net
Which confines in prison harsh
The adulterous warrior,
Victor in all battles;

Fourth heaven and second sun
Which obscures the first,
When by chance it shows itself:
To see it is chance and delight;

Grave ambassador, who speaks
With such rare wisdom
That it convinces without words,
Far more than if it tried;

Of the second heaven you have
Only its beauty,
And of the first only
The glow of the moon.

To this sphere, Costanza,
Mean fortune has assigned you
A place, which unworthy of you,
Your happiness beclouds.

Forge your own fortune,
Consenting to alter
Your aloofness to kindness,
Your shyness to gentleness.

With this, lady, willst see
How envious of your fortune
Will grow those proud of lineage,
Those great because of beauty.

And if you would shorten the road
Here in me you have
The richest and purest devotion
Love ever put in a heart.

The final verses and two brickbats which came flying through the air were all one. If instead of landing at his feet they had found their mark on the musician's head, they would easily have driven out of his mind once and for all both music and poetry. The poor fellow was amazed, and he started up the slope with such speed that a greyhound could not have overtaken him. Unhappy state that of musicians, bats, and owls, always exposed to downpours and abuse of this sort! All those who had been listening to the voice of the victim of the stoning approved of what had happened to him, but none so much as Tomás Pedro who, though he admired the singing and the composition, would have preferred that the object of all this serenading were some other and not Costanza, although none of it ever reached her ears.

Barrabás, the mule driver, who, too, had been listening to the music, did not share this opinion, for when he saw the singer take to his heels, he said:

"Be off with you, simpleton, false troubadour, may fleas devour your eyes. Who the devil taught you to sing to a kitchen wench about spheres and heavens, and all this business of wheels of fortune? Why didn't you tell her, a black curse on you and all who liked your lay, that she is as straight as a stalk of asparagus, white as milk, soft as down, chaste as a novitiate monk, skittish and wild as a hired mule, and harder than a piece of plaster? If you had told her that, she would have understood and liked it; but to call her ambassador, and net, and first cause, and highness and lowness is more to the understanding of a student of theology than of a kitchen maid. Truly there are poets in this world who write lays which the devil himself could not understand. Me, at any rate, though I am Barrabás, I cannot figure out what this musician is driving at, so just imagine Costancica! But she knows better; there she is in her bed laughing at Prester John himself. But this musician is not one of those sent by the Corregidor's son, for he has several, and once in a while you can understand them; but this one—confound him, he puts me in a bad humor!"

Barrabás's hearers were greatly amused, and his criticism and judgments seemed to them very shrewd.

With this they all went off to their beds, and things had no more than quieted down when Lope heard a soft tap at the door of his room. "Who's there?" he asked, and a low voice replied:

"It's Argüello and Gallega; open up, we're dying of cold."

"Why, we're in the middle of the summer," answered Lope.

"Stop making jokes, Lope," answered Gallega; "get up and open the door. We're all dressed up like archduchesses."

"Archduchesses, at this hour of the night?" replied Lope. "I don't believe it; I think you must be witches or great strumpets. Be off with you at once; if you don't, by the Lord Harry, I swear that if I get up I'll turn your backsides the color of a poppy with the buckle of my belt."

Taken aback by this cutting answer, so different from what they had expected, fearful of Lope's fury and defrauded of their hopes and their designs thwarted, they slunk away, sad and disappointed, to their beds. But before turning from the door Argüello said, with her mouth to the keyhole:

"Honey was not made for the ass's mouth."

And with this, as though she had voiced some profound

thought and taken fair vengeance, she returned, as we have said, to her lonely bed.

When he heard them go, Lope said to Tomás Pedro, who was awake: "Look, Tomás, set me to fighting two giants, or if when the moment comes to help you I have to crack the jaws of half a dozen, or a dozen lions, I will do it as easily as I quaff a cup of wine. But don't make it necessary for me to measure my strength with Argüello, for that I will not do even if I am shot full of arrows. See what maids of Denmark fate offered us tonight! Well, morning will soon be here, and tomorrow is another day."

"As I told you, friend," answered Tomás, "you do as you like. Either continue with your pilgrimage, or buy an ass and become a water-carrier, as you had decided."

"I will be a water-carrier," answered Lope. "Let's see if we can get a little sleep before it gets light, for this head of mine feels as big as a bucket, and I'm not in a mood for talking now."

They went to sleep, and morning came. They got up, and Tomás went to distribute the barley, and Lope to the horse-market, which was near by, to buy a serviceable ass.

It so happened that Tomás, giving his thoughts free rein in the solitude of the quiet afternoons, had composed some love poems and had written them down in the same book in which he entered the sales of barley, planning to copy them out later, and then tear up or erase those pages. But before he could do this, having stepped outside and left the book on the barley bin, his master picked it up to look over the accounts, and found the verses which, after he had read them, left him perplexed and startled. He took them to his wife, but before reading them to her, he called Costanza, and with great insistence, backed up by threats, demanded to know if Tomás Pedro, the new stable boy, had ever made advances to her, or been overbold in his speech, or given evidence of tender feelings toward her. Costanza swore that his first word to her, on that or any other subject, was yet to be spoken, and that never, not even with his eyes, had he given indication of harboring any improper thought. Her master and mistress believed her, accustomed as they were to her telling the truth about whatever they asked her. They told her to leave the room, and the innkeeper said to his wife:

"I don't know what to think about this. You should know, madam, that Tomás has written here in the feed ledger several poems which make me suspect that he is in love with Costancica."

"Let's see them," answered his wife, "and I'll tell you if there is anything in them."

"That's an excellent idea," answered her husband; "as you are a poet, you'll discover their meaning right away."

"I am not a poet, but, as you know, I have a good head on my shoulders, and I can recite the four prayers in Latin."

"You'd do better to recite them in the common tongue, for your uncle the priest has already told you that you make a thousand blunders when you pray in Latin, and what you say is no prayer at all."

"That arrow came out of his niece's quiver. It makes her green with envy to see me take up my Book of Hours in Latin and go through it like a knife through butter."

"Have it your own way," replied her husband. "Now listen, for these are the verses:

> Who finds the happiness of love?
>   Who holds his peace.
> What conquers its severity?
>   Constancy.
> What attains its joy?
>   Persistence.
> Thus, well might I
> Win victory's palm
> If in this endeavor my soul
> Is silent, constant, and persistent.
> On what does love feed?
>   Favor.
> And with what does its fury wane?
>   Offense.

Does it not thrive on disdain?
    It fades.
Truly in this is seen
That my love will immortal be,
For the cause of my distress,
Neither offends nor disdains.

What awaits him who despairs?
    Total death.
Then what death cures the ill?
    Death by half.
Then, 'twould be well to die?
    Better to suffer.
For as the saying goes,
And take this truth to heart,
After the wild tempest,
Comes the calm.

Will I reveal my passion?
When the time comes.
And what if it doesn't?
But it will.
Meanwhile death may come.
Let but so wax
Your faith and high hope,
That once Costanza grows aware
Your tears she will turn to smiles.

"Is there any more?" asked the hostess.

"No," replied her husband. "But what do you think of these verses?"

"The first thing to do is to find out if Tomás wrote them."

"There is no doubt about that, for the handwriting in the ledger and that of the poems is the same, and cannot be denied."

"See here, husband," said the hostess, "from what I can see, although the verses refer to Costancica, from which we might think they were written to her, not on that account should we affirm this to be the truth as though we had seen him writing them. Anyway, there are other Costanzas in the world besides ours. But even supposing they were written to her, he says nothing in them to offend her honor, nor does he ask anything that matters. Let us be on guard, and put the girl on her guard. If he is really in love with her, never doubt that he will write more verses and try to give them to her."

"Wouldn't it be best," said her husband, "to get rid of him and in that way our worries would be over?"

"That is for you to decide; but the fact is that, according to you, the lad does his work so well that it would be a shame to dismiss him for such a trifling reason."

"All right," said the innkeeper, "we'll be on the alert, as you suggest, and time will tell us what we should do."

Having reached this decision, he put the book where he had found it. When Tomás returned, looking anxiously for his book, to spare himself further fright, he copied out his verses, tore up the sheets of the ledger, and decided to risk revealing his feelings to Costanza at the first opportunity that presented itself. But as her modesty and aloofness were never laid aside, she gave nobody occasion to look at her, much less engage her in conversation. And as there were so many people and so many eyes in the inn most of the time, the difficulties of communicating with her were multiplied, to the despair of the poor lover.

But it so happened that one day Costanza appeared with a scarf tied about her cheeks, and when someone asked her why she was wearing it, she said she had a bad toothache. Tomás, whose desires had sharpened his wits, in a flash had what seemed to him a brilliant idea, and he said:

"Mistress Costanza, I shall give you a prayer in writing, and if you say it twice your pain will disappear as if by magic."

"That would be good," answered Costanza, "and I will say it, for I know how to read."

"But I will give it to you on one condition," Tomás went on, "and that is that you show it to nobody; for I set great store by it, and it would not be good for it to become misprized because many know it."

"I promise you, Tomás," replied Costanza, "that I will not give it to anybody, so let me have it at once, for the pain is making me suffer a great deal."

"I shall copy it out from memory, and give it to you very soon."

These were the first words Costanza and Tomás had exchanged in all the time he had been at the inn which was now some twenty-four days. He went off, wrote out the prayer, and was able to give it to Costanza without anyone seeing him, and with great satisfaction, and even greater devotion, she went into a room by herself, and unfolding the paper saw that it read as follows:

"Lady of my soul: I am a gentleman from Burgos; if I outlive my father, I shall inherit an entail carrying an income of six thousand ducats. The fame of your beauty, which has spread for leagues around, led me to leave my home, change my attire, and in the guise you see me, come to work for your master. If you would consent to be mine, in the manner that best befits your virtue, decide what proofs you demand of me to inform yourself of the truth of what I have said. And once you have so informed yourself, if it is your pleasure, I will be your spouse, and will hold myself the most fortunate being in the world. All I ask, for the time being, is for you not to make public thoughts as pure and devoted as are mine, for if your master learns of them and does not believe them, he will condemn me to banishment from your presence, which will be the same as sentencing me to death. Allow me, lady, to see you until you believe me, bearing in mind that he does not deserve the cruel punishment of not seeing you whose only crime has been to adore you. You can answer me with your eyes, when none of those who are always watching you can see, for your eyes are such that if angry, they slay; if compassionate, they restore to life."

All the time Costanza was away reading the paper, Tomás's heart was throbbing, fearing and hoping, fearing the sentence of his death, hoping for the restoration of his life. When Costanza finally emerged, so beautiful, even though her face was muffled, that if it were possible for any circumstance to enhance her beauty, one might say that the surprise at having seen in the paper Tomás had given her something so different from what she had expected, had heightened her beauty. She came out with the paper torn to bits in her hand, and said to Tomás, whose knees were quaking so he could hardly stand up:

"Brother Tomás, this prayer of yours seems more like witch-craft or a ruse than a holy prayer, and so I do not care to put faith in it or use it. For that reason I have torn it up so someone more easily taken in than I shall not see it. Learn other easier prayers, for it is impossible for this to be of any profit to you."

And with this she went into her mistress's room. Tomás was left dumfounded, but somewhat consoled in view of the fact that his secret desire remained locked in Costanza's breast. It seemed to him that as she had said nothing abut the matter to her master, he was not in danger of being sent away. It also seemed to him that in this first step he had taken to achieve his ambition he had over-come a mountain of obstacles, and that in important and uncertain enterprises, the greatest difficulty lies in the beginning.

While this was taking place at the inn Lope Asturiano was looking for an ass at the market where they were sold; and although he found many, none of them satisfied him. A gipsy was doing his best to sell him one whose agility was due more to the quicksilver that had been poured into its ears than to its own fleetfootedness. But what was pleasing in its gait was offset by its body, which was very small and neither of the size nor cut that Lope wanted. What he was looking for was one that was big enough to carry him as well as the water jars, whether full or empty. At this point a lad came up to him and whispered in his ear:

"Young sir, if you are looking for a good animal for the trade of water-carrier, I have an ass close by, in a meadow, than which you'll find none stouter or better in the whole city. And I'd advise you not to buy one from the gipsies, for although they may seem sound and strong, they are all doctored up and ailing. If you'd like to buy the kind you need, come with me and hold your tongue."

Lope, believing what he said, told him to take him and show him the ass he praised so highly. The two went off, side by side, till they came to the King's Garden where in the shade of a water wheel a number of water-carriers were resting while their asses grazed in a pasture nearby. The seller pointed out the ass he was offering for sale, and it delighted Lope, and all those gathered about praised the ass as being strong, willing, and a good eater. They agreed on the price, and without further inquiries or information, the water-carriers acting as agents and go-betweens, Lope bought the ass, and all the appurtenances of the trade, for sixteen ducats. He paid the full amount in gold crowns. Everyone congratulated him on his purchase, on his taking up the trade, and assured him that he had bought the luckiest kind of an ass, for its master had earned in less than a year, without stinting or overworking himself, in addition to his keep and that of the ass, enough for two suits of clothes, besides the sixteen ducats with which he planned to return to his native town where a marriage had been arranged for him with a distant relative.

In addition to the intermediaries in the sale of the ass, there were four other water-carriers who were playing cards, stretched out on the ground, using their capes as a card table. Asturiano stopped to watch them, and observed that they were playing, not like water-carriers, but like archdeacons, for each of them had a pile of a hundred *reales* in copper and silver. One hand was dealt on which they staked everything, and the winner took all. Two of those who had sat in were cleaned out, and they got up, whereupon the seller of the ass said that if there were a fourth he would play, but that he did not like a three-handed game. Asturiano, who was as soft as sugar and, as the Italians say, never needed to be coaxed, said he would make up the fourth. They sat down, things went along briskly, and as he preferred to stake money rather than time, in a little while Lope had lost the six florins he had, and not having a penny left, he said that if they were agreeable, he would play the ass. They accepted the offer, and he bet a quarter of the ass, saying he wanted to play it by quarters. Things went so badly with him that in four straight deals he had lost the four quarters of the ass and the very one who had sold it to him had won it back. As he was getting up to take back his property, Lope pointed out to him that he had staked only the four quarters of the ass, but that the tail was his, and they must give it to him and then they were welcome to the ass.

His demand for the tail aroused great hilarity, and there were some with a smattering of the law who were of the opinion that his demand was unjustified, saying that when a sheep or any other kind of animal was sold, the tail was included, for it was of necessity a part of one of the hind quarters. To this Lope replied that the sheep of Barbary normally had five quarters, the fifth being the tail, and when the sheep in question were butchered, the tail brought the same price as any of the quarters. As for the tail being considered a part of an animal that was sold live and not slaughtered, that he granted; but his was not sold but bet, and it had never been his intention to play the tail, and it must be handed over to him at once with all appended and appertaining thereto, which was from the base of the brain, with the whole spinal column, where it had its origin and from which it descended, to the very last hairs.

"Supposing it is as you say," said one of them, "and that they give it to you as you request, then you can sit down beside what's left of the ass."

"So be it!", answered Lope. "Give me my tail, otherwise, so help me God, nobody is going to take my ass, not if all the water-carriers in the world come for it. And don't think that because there are so many of you here you can play tricks on me, for I am a man who knows how to go up to another man and sink two hands-breadth of dagger into his guts, without his knowing from whom, or how, or whence it came. Besides, I don't want to be paid the value of the tail, so much for so much, but I want the actual tail, cut from the ass, as I have said."

The winner and the rest of the water-carriers did not think it would be prudent to try to settle the question by force, because

they estimated that Lope's mettle was such that he would not permit it. With the training he had acquired in the tuna fisheries,
where every sort of bluff and bullying is practised, and the most
incredible oaths and boasts employed, he then and there tossed
aside his hat, pulled out a dagger he was wearing under his cape,
and took up a stance that aroused fear and respect in all that watery
company. Finally, one of them, who seemed more prudent and
sensible, got them to agree to play a hand of cards with the tail
staked against a quarter of the ass. They willingly agreed, Lope
won the hand, the other was piqued, staked another quarter, and in
three hands he found himself assless. He then wanted to play
money; Lope did not want to, but they all insisted so much that he
finally had to agree. He won the honeymoon money, and the other
was left without a cent. This caused him such anguish that he threw
himself to the ground and began to beat his head against the hard
earth. Lope, who was well-bred, generous, and compassionate, raised
him up and returned all the money he had won from him, as well
as the sixteen ducats for the ass, and he even divided up what he
had left among the bystanders, leaving them amazed at his liberality.
If this had happened in the days of Tamburlane, they would have
raised him to king of the water-carriers.

With a great escort Lope returned to the city, where he told
Tomás what had happened, and Tomás in turn informed him of
the favorable progress of his affairs. Not a tavern, a taphouse, or
gathering of rogues that did not hear about the wagering for the
ass, the trick of the tail, and Lope's bravery and generosity. But as
the foul beast of the populace is, for the most part, evil, evil-minded,
and evil-tongued, it took little account of good Lope's generosity,
valor, and quick-wittedness, remembering only the episode of the
tail. As a result, he had not been about his water carrying more
than two days when he saw he was being pointed out by many,
saying: "That is the water-carrier of the tail." The boys, those little
pitchers with big ears, learned about it, and as soon as Lope appeared at the entrance to any street, they followed at his heels
shouting, one here, one there: "Asturiano, give us the tail, Asturiano,

give us the tail!" Lope, beset on all sides by this shouting and jeering, decided to keep quiet, thinking that this insolence would drown in his immutable silence. But he was wrong. The quieter he was, the more the boys yelled. Whereupon he decided to see what anger would do, and getting off the ass, he chased them with a stick, which was like setting a light to a powder train, or trying to cut off the heads of a hydra, because for every one he cut off, that is to say, for every boy he whacked, that very same instant not seven, but seven hundred sprang up, demanding the tail with more vehemence and insistence. Finally he decided to withdraw to an inn where he had taken lodgings after leaving his comrade, fleeing from Argüello, and remain there until the influence of that ill-starred planet had passed and the boys had forgotten about that tail they so wickedly demanded.

For six days he did not leave his inn except at night, when he went to see Tomás and find out how his affairs were progressing. The latter informed him that after giving the paper to Costanza he had never been able to address a single word to her, and it seemed to him that she was even more reserved than usual, for once when he was on the point of saying something to her, she had said to him, even before he could approach her: "Tomás, I feel fine, so I have no need of your words or your prayers. Be happy that I am not denouncing you to the Inquisition, and don't weary yourself." But she had said all this without anger in her eyes or any other gesture that might indicate the least severity. Lope told him about the way the boys had tormented him, asking for the tail, because he had demanded that of his ass to settle accounts with his adversary. Tomás advised him not to go out of his house, at least, not riding the ass, and that if he did, he should choose lonely and remote streets. And if this was not enough, to give up the trade of water-carrier, and this would put an end to such an indecent demand. Lope asked if Gallega had bothered him any more. Tomás said no, but that she went on trying to woo him with gifts and tidbits she filched in the kitchen from the guests. After this Lope went back to his inn, determined not to leave it for another six days, at least not with the ass.

It must have been about eleven that night when suddenly and unexpectedly there appeared at the inn many officers of the law, and following them, the Corregidor. Mine host was upset, as were many of the guests, for just as when a comet appears it arouses forebodings of misfortune and calamities, so the law, when suddenly and in mass it enters a house, frightens and dismays the most innocent conscience. The Corregidor went into a parlor and sent for the host, who came in fear and trepidation to find out what he wanted. The Corregidor asked him with great solemnity:

"Are you the keeper of this inn?"

"Yes, sir, and your humble servant."

The Corregidor ordered all those present to withdraw from the room and leave him alone with the innkeeper. When this had been done, and the two were alone, the Corregidor said to him:

"Host, what serving people have you in this inn?"

"Sir, I have two Galician maids, a housekeeper, and a stable boy."

"Is that all?"

"That is all, sir."

"Then, tell me, host," the Corregidor went on, "where is a girl they say works here, who is so beautiful that she is known throughout the city as The Illustrious Kitchen Maid, and it has even reached my ears that my son Don Periquito is in love with her, and not a night goes by that he does not serenade her?"

"Sir," answered the host, "it is true that the girl called The Illustrious Kitchen Maid is in this house; but she is neither my servant nor not my servant."

"Host, I do not understand what you mean by 'she is neither my servant nor not my servant.'"

"It's just as I have said," answered the innkeeper, "and with Your Excellency's permission, I will tell you all about it, something I have never breathed to anyone else."

"First I would like to see the maid before hearing anything more about her; ask her to come here."

The innkeeper opened the door and called out: "Wife, tell Costanza to come in here."

When the hostess heard the Corregidor ask for Costanza, she became upset and began to wring her hands, saying: "Woe is me! The Corregidor wants to see Costanza, and alone! Something terrible must have happened. That girl's beauty drives men crazy."

Hearing her, Costanza said: "Mistress, do not be upset. I will go and see what it is the Corregidor wants, and if anything untoward has happened, you may rest assured that it is not my fault."

And without waiting for them to call her a second time, she took a silver candlestick with a lighted candle and went into the Corregidor's presence more shyly than timorously.

As soon as the Corregidor saw her, he ordered the host to close the door of the room. When this had been done, he got to his feet, and taking the candlestick from Costanza's hand, he brought the light close to her face, and looked her over from head to foot. As Costanza was startled, a deep flush had come over her face, and she stood there, so beautiful and so modest, that it seemed to the Corregidor that he was gazing on the beauty of an angel that had come down to earth. After regarding her well, he said:

"Host, this is not a jewel intended for the lowly setting of an inn. I can see at a glance that my son Periquito is wise from the way he has employed his thoughts. I may say, damsel, that not only can you and should you be called illustrious, but most illustrious, but these titles should not be linked to the name of kitchen maid, but to that of duchess."

"She is not a kitchen maid, sir," said the host; "all she does is to keep the keys of the silver, of which, God be praised, I have a fair amount, on which the distinguished guests who come to this inn are served."

"Nevertheless, I repeat, host," said the Corregidor, "it is neither decent nor fitting that this maiden should be in an inn. Is she perchance a relative of yours?"

"She is neither my relative nor my servant. And if Your Excellency would like to know who she is, when she is not present, Your

Excellency will hear something which, in addition to pleasing, will amaze you."

"I would indeed like it," said the Corregidor. "Costanza, you may go, and you may expect from me what you might expect from your own father, for your great modesty and beauty put all who see them under the obligation of holding themselves at your service."

Costanza answered never a word. With great dignity she dropped the Corregidor a deep curtsey, and left the room. She found her mistress breathless with eagerness to know what it was the Corregidor wanted of her. She told her everything that had taken place, and that her master was about to tell him certain things—she knew not what—that he did not want her to hear. The hostess was not easy in her mind, and she did nothing but pray until the Corregidor had left and she saw her husband free.

While the innkeeper was closeted with the Corregidor, he said to him: "Sir, by my reckoning it is fifteen years, one month and four days today since a lady arrived at this inn in pilgrim attire, travelling in a litter, accompanied by four mounted servants, with two ladies-in-waiting and a maid following in a carriage. She also brought two mules richly caparisoned carrying a fine bed and kitchen utensils. In short, the appurtenances were of finest quality, and the pilgrim was clearly a lady of rank. Even though she looked about forty, or perhaps a little more, she was still very beautiful. She was sick and pale, and so exhausted that she ordered her bed prepared at once, which was set up in this very room by her servants. They asked me who was the physician of most repute in this city. I told them Doctor de la Fuente. He was sent for and came at once. They discussed her illness in private, and as a result of this consultation, he ordered her bed placed elsewhere so she would have complete quiet. They moved her at once to another room upstairs where she could have the comfort the doctor recommended. None of the men servants entered their mistress's room, only the two ladies-in-waiting and her personal maid. My wife and I asked the servants who the lady was, her name, whence she came and where she was going, if she was maid, wife, or widow, and why she was wearing a pilgrim's habit. To all our questions, which we asked a number of times, all they would say was that she was a lady of great rank and wealth from Old Castile, and that she was a widow, without any children to inherit her wealth. As she had been suffering from dropsy for several months, she had vowed to make a pilgrimage to the shrine of Our Lady of Guadalupe, and for that reason she was dressed as a pilgrim. As for her name, they had orders to call her only "The Lady Pilgrim." This was all we learned at the time. But after three days, during which the pilgrim remained at the inn because she was ill, one of her ladies-in-waiting came to my wife and me to say the lady wanted to see us. We went to find out what she wished, and after the door was closed, in the presence of her women and almost with tears in her eyes, she said these words, as I recall them: 'Good people, heaven is my witness that through no fault of mine I find myself in the dire plight I shall now explain to you. I am with child, and so close to my time that labor pains are upon me. None of the men servants who have accompanied me know of my trouble or my misfortune. I have neither been able nor have I wished to hide it from my women. To flee the malicious eyes of my native province, and so this hour would not come upon me there, I took a vow to visit Our Lady of Guadalupe. It must have been Her will that my labor should come upon me in your house. It is now in your power to help and succor me, with the secrecy due one who has placed her honor in your hands. The payment for your kindness, for so I wish to call it, if it does not correspond to the great good I hope for, will at least suffice to give proof of my great gratitude. Let these two hundred gold ducats in this purse be an earnest of my intention.' And taking from beneath her pillow a gold and green knitted purse, she placed it in the hands of my wife who, like the foolish soul she is, and without thinking what she was doing, so amazed and fascinated was she by the pilgrim's words, took the purse without uttering a word of thanks or fitting politeness. I recall that I told the lady nothing of the sort was necessary; that we were not people whose motive for performing an act of kindness when the occasion arose was self-interest rather than charity. She went on to say: 'What you must do, friends, is to decide at once where to take the child I bear, and think up a lie to tell the person to whom you entrust it. For the time being it will have to be someone in the city, and afterwards I want it taken to a village. What is to be done later, if God sees fit to bring me safely through my labor and let me fulfill my vow, you will know when I return from Guadalupe, for by then I shall have had time to think and decide what is best. I have no need of a midwife, nor do I want one, for from other more honorable deliveries I have had, I feel sure that the help of these women of mine will see me through my difficulties, and spare me another witness to my misfortune.'

"At this point the unhappy pilgrim fell silent and broke into a flood of tears which were, in part, assuaged by the many and kind words of my wife who, by this time, had come to her senses. I went out at once to seek a place to take the child she should bear, at whatever time it came into the world, and between twelve and one that same night, when everyone in the inn was asleep, the good lady brought forth a girl child, the most beautiful my eyes had ever beheld, who is this very one Your Excellency has just seen. Neither did the mother complain during the delivery, nor the daughter cry at birth; in all there was marvellous repose and quiet, as befitted the secrecy of that strange case. The lady remained in bed six days longer, and during this time the doctor came to see her. But never once did she tell the reason of her illness, nor did she take the medicines he prescribed for her. Her only intention was to deceive the men servants with the visits of the doctor. She told me all this herself when she was out of danger, and a week afterwards she got up with the same swelling, or one that feigned that which she had rid herself of.

"She went on her pilgrimage, and twenty days later she returned, now almost recovered, for little by little she did away with the artifice by which after her delivery she simulated dropsy. When she returned the child had already been put to nurse in a village two leagues from here at my orders, giving out that she was my niece. She was baptized with the name of Costanza, which was as the mother had requested, who, happy with what I had done, gave me when she left a gold chain I still have, from which she removed six links which, she said, the person who came for the child would bring. She also cut a sheet of white parchment in curves and waves, as when you join your hands and write something on the fingers which can be deciphered when the fingers are joined together, but when the hands are separated the message is divided, because the letters are separated, but when the fingers are brought together again, they meet and match so they can be clearly read. What I mean is that one half of the parchment is the soul of the other, and when fitted together they can be read, and when separated, it is not possible, except by guessing at the other half. Nearly the whole chain was left with me, and I have it all, and am still waiting for the countersign, although she told me that within two years she would send for her daughter, charging me to raise her, not as befitted her rank, but in the manner that a peasant girl is brought up. She charged me, too, that if for any reason it was not possible for her to send for her soon, I was not to tell her the circumstances of her birth even after she reached the age of understanding. She begged me to forgive her for not telling me her name or who she was; this she reserved for another more important occasion. In short, giving me four hundred more gold ducats, and embracing my wife with tender tears, she departed, leaving us amazed by her wisdom, courage, beauty and modesty. Costanza remained in the village two years, and then I brought her here with me, and I have always dressed her in the attire of a peasant, as her mother ordered me. Fifteen years, one month and four days I have been waiting for the person who is to come for her, and the long delay has destroyed my hope of this coming. If they do not come for her during this present year, I have made up my mind to adopt her as my daughter and leave her all I possess, which amounts to more than six thousand ducats, God be praised.

"It now remains for me, Sir Corregidor, to describe to you, if it is possible to find words for it, the goodness and virtues of

Costancica. First and most important of all, she is profoundly devoted to Our Lady. She confesses and takes communion every month; she knows how to read and write; there is no better lace maker in Toledo; she sings like an angel when she is working at her lace; in decorum she has no equal. As for her beauty, you have seen it for yourself. Don Pedro, Your Excellency's son, has never once spoken to her, although it is true that from time to time he sends her a serenade which she never listens to. Many gentlemen, some of them titled, have lodged in this inn, and have delayed their journey for days for no other reason than to feast their eyes on her beauty. But I know for a fact that not one of them can truthfully say that she has ever given him a chance to say one or more words to her. There, sir, you have the true history of The Illustrious Kitchen Maid, who is never in the kitchen, and I have not departed one jot from the truth."

The host said no more, and the Corregidor was silent for a long time before answering, so amazed was he at the incident the innkeeper had related. Finally he told him to let him see the chain and the parchment. The host went and brought them, and he saw that they were as he had described them. The chain was made up of intricately carved links, and on the parchment there were written, one below the other in the space to be fitted into the missing half, these letters: T I I T E R E I N. He saw that to understand their meaning it would be necessary to match them to those on the other piece of the parchment. It seemed to him a clever device of recognition, and he judged that the pilgrim who had left that chain with the innkeeper must be a very rich lady. Having made up his mind to remove that beautiful girl from the inn as soon as he had made arrangements with a convent to receive her, for the moment he was content to take with him only the parchment, charging the innkeeper that if by chance Costanza was sent for, he was to notify him of who it was that was seeking her before showing him the chain that had been left with him. He then departed, as amazed by the tale and circumstances as by the beauty of The Illustrious Kitchen Maid.

All during the time the innkeeper was with the Corregidor, and with Costanza when they sent for her, Tomás was beside himself, his mind assailed by a multitude of thoughts, not one of which pleased him. But when he saw the Corregidor leave and that Costanza was staying, his spirit took breath and his fainting pulse revived. He did not venture to ask the innkeeper what the Corregidor had wanted, nor did mine host say anything about what had taken place except to his wife, with which she calmed down, giving thanks to God for having delivered them from such a great fright.

The next day, around one o'clock, there arrived at the inn two elderly gentlemen of dignified appearance, attended by four mounted men. After first inquiring of one of the boys who was following them if that was the Inn of The Sevillian, when he told them that it was, they all went in. The four men alighted, and went to help the two gentlemen dismount, by which it was apparent that they were their masters. Costanza came out with her customary good breeding to see the new guests, and no sooner had one of the old men laid eyes upon her than he said to the other:

"I think, Don Juan, we have found the object of our search."

Tomás, who had come out to take charge of the horses, immediately recognized the two servants of his father, and then his own father and Carriazo's, who were the two gentlemen the others deferred to. And although he was surprised to see them, he concluded that they had set out to look for him and Carriazo in the tuna fisheries, having been informed by someone that they would find them there and not in Flanders. But he was ashamed to let them see him in that guise, and so, risking everything, he put his hand up to his face and passed in front of them, to look for Costanza. Kind fate so willed it that he found her alone, and quickly, with stammering tongue, fearing that she might not give him a chance to speak to her, he said:

"Costanza, one of those old gentlemen who has just arrived is my father, the one you will hear called Don Juan de Avendaño. Inquire of his servants if he has not a son named Don Tomás de Avendaño. I am that son. In this way you can discover and make sure that I have told you the truth about my rank, and that I am truthful in all I have offered you. And now, farewell, for I do not intend to return to this inn until they have left."

Costanza answered never a word, nor did he wait for her reply, but went out again, covering his face as before, and hurried to tell Carriazo that their fathers were at the inn. The landlord shouted for Tomás to come and feed the horses, but as he did not appear, he looked after them himself. One of the two elderly men called aside one of the Galician maids, and asked her what was the name of that beautiful girl he had seen, and whether she was the daughter or relative of the innkeeper or his wife. The girl answered:

"The maid's name is Costanza. She is not a relative of either the landlord or his wife, nor do I know who she is. All I can say is that I wish the devil would fly away with her. I don't know what there is about her, but she doesn't give the rest of us girls here in the house a chance. We've got our good points just like anybody else. Not a guest comes but the first thing he asks is who is that beautiful girl, or says: 'How pretty; isn't she sweet; not bad at all; she outshines the best of them; may I never see anything worse.' And of us they don't even say: 'What have you got there— women, or devils, or what are they?' "

"Then, according to that," answered the gentleman, "she must let herself be petted and flirt with the guests."

"Oh, yes," answered the girl, "you just try and hold her foot while she's shod! A fine chance of that! Good Lord, sir, if she would only let them look at her, she could be rolling in money. She's pricklier than a hedgehog; she's a mill of Hail Marys; she embroiders and prays all day. When the time comes for her to work miracles, I'd like to have part of what's taken in. My mistress says she wears a hair shirt next to her skin. How do you like that!"

The gentleman was delighted with the girl's remarks, and without stopping to have his spurs removed, he called the innkeeper, and taking him aside to one of the rooms, he said:

"Mine host, I have come to recover a pledge of mine you have had in your keeping for some years; to redeem it I bring you a thousand gold florins, these links of a chain, and this parchment."

And with this he produced the token of the links of the chain. The innkeeper immediately recognized the parchment, and pleased beyond words by the offer of the thousand florins, he rejoined:

"Sir, the pledge you wish to redeem is in this house; but not the chain nor the parchment with which to corroborate the truth of the matter to which I believe Your Excellency refers. So I would ask you to be patient, and I shall be back quickly."

He flew to inform the Corregidor of what had happened, and tell him how two gentlemen had come to his inn looking for Costanza. The Corregidor had just finished his dinner, and in his eagerness to learn the end of the story, he called for his horse and hastened to the inn, bringing with him the parchment. The moment he laid eyes on the gentlemen, he came forward with open arms to embrace one of them, saying:

"Of all things! Welcome, Don Juan de Avendaño, my cousin and master!"

The gentleman in question threw his arms around him, saying: "This is indeed a welcome, my good cousin, for here I behold you and in the state of health I would have wished. Cousin, embrace this gentleman, who is Don Diego de Carriazo, a great gentleman and friend of mine."

"I am already acquainted with Don Diego," answered the Corregidor, "and I am his very humble servant."

After they had embraced one another with great courtesy and affection, they went into a room with the landlord, who by now had the chain.

"His Excellency, the Corregidor, already knows the purpose of your visit, Don Diego de Carriazo. If Your Excellency will bring forth the links that are missing from this chain, and the Corregidor will produce the piece of parchment he has in his possession, we can make the test I have been waiting to do for so long."

"This being the case," replied Don Diego, "there will be no need to explain again to His Honor the Corregidor the reason for our presence, for he can see that it is in accord with what you have told him."

"He has told me something, but there is still much I do not know. Here is the parchment."

Don Diego produced the other piece, and when they were put together, the letters of the part the innkeeper had which, as has been said, were: T I I T E R E I N, matched those on the other half: H S S H T U S G, and all together read: T H I S I S T H E T R U E   S I G N. The pieces of the chain were compared and found to be identical.

"That is settled," said the Corregidor. "Now what remains to be learned, if it is possible, is who were the parents of this beautiful pledge."

"I am the father," replied Don Diego. "The mother is no longer living. Let it suffice to say that she was of such rank that I might have been her servant. And although her name must be concealed, neither her reputation nor she should suffer for what might seem a misstep or common fault. Know, then, that the mother of this pledge, when bereft of the great gentleman who was her husband, went to reside in a village which was her fief, and there lived an irreproachable, retired life with her servants and vassals. Fate so willed it that one day, as I was hunting in the outskirts of her village, I decided to pay her a visit. It was the siesta hour when I arrived at her castle, for so her great house might be termed. I left my horse with a servant of mine, went up, without encountering anyone, to her very chamber where she was lying asleep on a black divan. She was extremely beautiful, and the silence, the solitude, the occasion aroused in me a desire more bold than decent, and without stopping to voice my thoughts, I closed the door after me, and going over to her, awoke her, and holding her tightly, I said: 'My lady, make no outcry, for your screams would only publish your dishonor; nobody has seen me enter this room, for my luck, which could not be better since it allows me to possess you, has weighed down the eyes of your servitors with sleep, and should they come in response to your cries, they can only take my life, and that will be in your very arms, nor will my death restore your lost reputation.' In short, I took her against all her will and by main force. She, wearied, exhausted, and dismayed, either could not or would not speak a word to me, and I, leaving her as though stupefied and bewildered, departed as I had entered, and went to the village of a friend of mine, which was some two leagues distant. The lady moved from that village to another, and without my ever seeing her again, or seeking her, two years went by when I heard that she was dead. About twenty days ago her steward sent for me with great urgency, telling me by letter that it was a matter that affected my happiness and my honor. I went to see what he wanted of me, without a thought of what he was to tell me entering my mind. I found him at death's door, and to save time he informed me as briefly as possible that when his mistress was dying she told him what had happened to her with me, and that as a result of that ravishment she had been got with child, and that to conceal her state she had gone on a pilgrimage to Our Lady of Guadalupe, and had given birth to a daughter in this inn, and the child had received the name of Costanza. He gave me the tokens by which to find her, which were those you have seen, the chain and the parchment, as well as thirty thousand gold florins, which his mistress had left as her daughter's dowry. He also told me that the reason he had not given them to me as soon as his mistress died, nor told me what she had confided to him in trust and secrecy, was out of pure covetousness, to keep the money for himself. But that as he was about to give an accounting to God, to lighten his conscience he was giving me the money and telling me where and how I could find my daughter. I took the money and the tokens, told all this to Don Juan de Avendaño, and we set out for this city."

Don Diego had just reached this point in his story when loud cries were heard at the street door, saying:

"Tell Tomás Pedro, the stable boy, that they have arrested his friend Asturiano, and that he is to go to the jail where he is waiting for him."

The Corregidor, when he heard the words "jail" and "arrest," called out that they should bring in the prisoner and the constable in whose custody he was. The constable was informed that the Corregidor, who was there, had ordered him to come in with the prisoner, and so he did.

Asturiano came in bleeding at the mouth, in a very sorry state, and in the firm grip of the constable. As soon as he entered the room he recognized his father and Avendaño's. Greatly disconcerted, to conceal his identity, he kept his face covered with a handkerchief as though stanching the blood. The Corregidor asked what the lad had done, and the constable replied that he was a water-carrier called Asturiano, to whom the street urchins were in the habit of shouting: "Give us the tail, Asturiano, give us the tail." Then briefly he explained why they kept asking him for the tail, at which they all laughed heartily. He went on to say that as he was coming off the Alcántara Bridge, the boys had pestered him so, that he got off his ass and running after them, caught one, whom he had beaten within an inch of his life. When they tried to arrest him, he had resisted, and that was the reason for the deplorable state he was in.

The Corregidor ordered Asturiano to uncover his face, which he stubbornly refused to do, until the constable went over and took the handkerchief from him, whereupon his father recognized him, and said in great indignation:

"Don Diego, my son, what is the meaning of this? What are those clothes you are wearing? You haven't yet forgot your rogue ways?"

Carriazo knelt down at his father's feet, who with tears in his eyes, held him in his arms for a long time. Don Juan de Avendaño, knowing that Don Diego had travelled with Don Tomás, his son, inquired after him, and was told that Don Tomás de Avendaño was the stable boy at that inn. At this the amazement of all gathered there knew no bounds, and the Corregidor ordered the innkeeper to bring him in.

"I don't think he is around," answered the landlord, "but I will see if I can find him." And he left to look for him.

Don Diego de Carriazo asked what was the meaning of these

transformations, and what had induced them to become, the one a water-carrier, the other an inn stable boy. To which young Carriazo replied that he could not answer those questions so publicly, but that he would tell him when they were by themselves.

Tomás Pedro was hidden in his room from which he could see, without being seen, what his father and Carriazo's were doing. He was disconcerted by the arrival of the Corregidor and the hubbub going on in the house. Someone told the innkeeper where he was hidden; he went up for him, and willy-nilly, made him come down. Even so he would not have made his appearance if the Corregidor himself had not come out to the courtyard, and called him by name, saying:

"Come on down, kinsman; there are no lions or bears here who are going to eat you."

Tomás came down, and with lowered eyes and great humility, knelt before his father, who embraced him joyfully, like the father of the Prodigal Son when he recovered what he had given up for lost.

While all this was happening the Corregidor's carriage arrived so they could return in it, for the great occasion did not permit of going on horseback. He called for Costanza, and taking her by the hand, led her to her father, saying:

"Receive this jewel, Don Diego, and esteem it as the richest your heart could desire. And you, beautiful maid, kiss your father's hand, and give thanks to God who by this happy circumstance has altered, uplifted, and improved the lowliness of your condition."

Costanza, who neither knew nor could imagine what had happened, all confused and trembling, could think of nothing to do but kneel before her father, and taking his hands, she began to kiss them tenderly, bedewing them with copious tears that fell from her beautiful eyes.

Meanwhile, the Corregidor had persuaded his cousin Don Juan that they should all come home with him. Despite Don Juan's demurral, he would not take no for an answer, and so they all mounted in the carriage. But when the Corregidor told Costanza to enter, too, her heart fell, and she and the mistress of the inn threw their arms around one another, and set up such a bitter lament that it was heartbreaking to listen to. The mistress said:

"What now, my darling daughter, you are going and leaving me? How have you the heart to leave this mother who has reared you so lovingly?"

Costanza wept and answered her with equally tender words. Whereupon the Corregidor, touched by their grief, ordered the hostess to get into the carriage, too, and not be separated from her daughter, for that was how she looked upon her, until Costanza left Toledo. So the inn mistress and all the rest got into the carriage and went to the house of the Corregidor, where they were warmly welcomed by his wife, who was a great lady. They ate sumptuously, and after dinner Carriazo told his father that for love of Costanza Don Tomás had gone to work at the inn, and he was so deeply enamored of her that even if he had not learned of how high rank she was, being Don Diego's daughter, he would have taken her for his wife, kitchen maid as she was. Afterward the wife of the Corregidor dressed Costanza in the clothing of a daughter she had who was the same age and size as Costanza, and if she was beautiful attired as a peasant, in court dress she looked like an angel. It became her so well that it was evident that she had been born to be a lady and nothing was too good for her.

But amidst so many who were happy, there was one who was sad, and this was Don Pedro, the son of the Corregidor, whose first thought was that Costanza was not for him, and he was right. For the Corregidor, Don Diego de Carriazo, and Don Juan de Avendaño agreed among them that Don Tomás should marry Costanza, whose father would bestow upon her the thirty thousand florins her mother had left her; the water-carrier, Don Diego de Carriazo, should marry the daughter of the Corregidor, and Don Pedro, the Corregidor's son, would wed a daughter of Don Juan de Avendaño, and his father would secure a dispensation because of their kinship.

In this way all were happy, gay, and satisfied, and the news of the marriages and of the good fortune of the illustrious kitchen maid spread throughout the city, and a multitude of people came to see Costanza in her new attire, which became her as has been said. They saw the stable boy Tomás Pedro metamorphosed into Don Tomás de Avendaño, and they observed what a gallant youth Lope Asturiano was, once he had changed his clothes, and had given up the ass and the water jars. But for all this, even as he went through the streets in his finery, some urchin would call out asking for the tail!

They tarried a month in Toledo, after which Don Diego Carriazo and his wife, his father and Costanza, with her husband, Don Tomás, and the Corregidor's son, who wanted to meet his cousin and future bride, returned to Burgos. Mine host was the richer by a thousand florins, and the many jewels Costanza gave to her mistress, which was the name by which she always called the one who had raised her.

The story of the illustrious kitchen maid afforded the poets of the golden Tagus occasion to give full rein to their pens in extolling and celebrating the peerless beauty of Costanza, who still lives in the company of her good stable boy, as does Carriazo, with three sons who do not take after their father or know that such things as tuna fisheries exist. Today they are all studying in Salamanca, and their father, whenever he happens to see some water-carrier's ass, recalls the one he had in Toledo, and is fearful lest, when least expected, in some comedy, the cry: "Give us the tail, Asturiano, give us the tail!" will again crop up.